THE LORE OF WIND DRIVERS

SLAVES OF THE BIJOU

SECOND EDITION

A HOOK-A-BOOK NOVEL BY

J.T. STADD

The Beauty of
Storytelling & Imagination

Acknowledgements

To those of you, past and present, who stayed in my face and refused to back down to keep me from losing sight of my goal, I thank you.

To those of you who embellished my silly ideas and tirelessly read my scripts and stories, the boy who failed high school English…

To those of you who sat with me for hours in bookstores and coffee shops while working to fulfill your own dreams, because you knew that in turn it would help me fulfill mine…

To those of you who called me a coward, countless times for trying to give up, and pushed me instead to keep going, constantly harassing me with, 'when will your book be finished?'…

I thank you all from the depths of my heart. Each word is for you, and without any of you, none of this would be possible.

CHAPTER ONE

If you'd told me that in three days I'd intentionally plunge into an abysmal hole at the heart of a planet, I'd have laughed in your face. Yet there I was perched on that ledge, dizzy, nauseated, staring into a pit that wouldn't cease, a simple boy with no clue what I'd begun. Zephyr. Wind driver. Words with no meaning before that time. However, I'd embarked on a journey of unbelievable proportions, and to think it all nearly crashed and burned, all because of Mom.

"No," she exclaimed, her voice laced with disbelief. "Absolutely not! It's final. I can't believe you even had the nerve to ask!" she yelled and stormed off to her room.

Abandoned and frustrated, I stood there with an empty crumbled paper as her door slammed in my face and on my dreams. Of all times! It was the one favor I'd trade any other to embrace, willing to hear 'no' for the rest of my life if it meant 'yes' that once. The disappointment. The embarrassment my friends would never let go of! Funny thing was, though annoyed and irritated to no end, a part of me *deep* inside turned to mush. I leaned into the thin door, hearing her muffled cries through the pillow burying her face.

I was tormented as I headed to my room with my conscience torn in two, then plopped on my squeaky mattress and stared at the empty consent form. Her absent signature meant living a dream or suffocating in a fantasy. However, a thought crossed my mind. Yeah, that thought. I shouldn't. She'd kill me. But I couldn't resist thinking it. Every kid did at some point in life, right? So why not? I'd cowardly practiced it before but never had the balls to make it happen. Teacher's notes and homework assignments, all with a big fat "F" scribbled on the top page. "Make sure your mother signs this," teachers frequently nagged.

But this was different. My heart pounded as I sat up in bed with my rebellious side nudging me to act. I slid a black pen and blank paper from my top drawer, warmed my fingers and scribbled that god awful 'S' Mom jotted with such ease.

Five times. Ten times. I was ready, and out it went.

CHAPTER TWO

To say I lost sleep would've been an understatement. I tossed and turned all evening with fired up nerves, believing the night had punished me with extended hours of darkness.

I was an average teen and by no means an angel, having delved into my fair share of mischief. What teen hadn't? Still, something about that wayward decision weighed heavier than most. More was at stake, especially Mom's sanity. She'd been through the gutter those years, but even so if not that moment, when else would I get my turn? Never had I felt so strong about anything in life, but for unfeigned reasons, that I did. Only problem? I overslept! The endless toss and turns had robbed me of sleep, cozying me in the late hour of my supposed departure. I knew it the moment I believed my twin bed felt like heaven.

I slapped the blaring alarm and sprung from my comforter, grabbed my head to catch my bearings, then blazed into action. Good thing was Mom would never know, if I made it in time that was. She'd long gone to work, allotting me the lone role of morning adult. Usually, not a problem, but that day I grabbed my backpack and dumped every book, a laptop and strayed papers into a heap on the bed before lunging in the closet. Knee and elbow pads? Ready. Head lamp? Check. Gloves? Had em.

I ran to the kitchen to fill my water bottle, stepping over Growl my old westie, who never moved from the rug by the sink. With my heavy hiking boots unlaced, I snagged my helmet and leftover granola bar then stormed out the door. Wish I could've driven my motorcycle, but the dusty broken thing needed to be fixed. So, to the driving service waiting out front it was.

Something about the strong rush of air peeling my face always felt right. Either way, there was no making the field trip bus in time, they were more than halfway through the drive. So straight to our hiking spot I went, hopeful to catch them before they were too far in.

With the forbidden permission slip clenched between my teeth, I launched myself into the backseat of the car. My heart raced with excitement and fear as we sped towards our destination, a twenty-minute ride that felt like an hour. But I was determined to get there and taste the thrill of rebellion, and after what seemed a lifetime, we'd finally arrived.

CHAPTER THREE

Our tires crackled over the rock filled path next to the busted yellow school bus on the side of the road. But it was empty, so I pounded the closed door to wake the slobbering driver snoozed across the front bench.

"They already head in?" I yelled, peering at him through the dusty window.

"Yeah," he muttered annoyed, slow and groggy to open the door. "Ten minutes in, give or take," he guessed.

That was good enough for me. Ten minutes alone, I'd catch them in no time and had already strapped the light and helmet to my head. I was ready; my knee and arm pads were on, my hands snugged in each glove and the water bottle clipped to my belt. I tossed my empty backpack on his front seat and turned to bolt when he stopped me.

"Wait! Your permission slip!" he barked as if he cared, still grumpy from being startled awake.

I handed the half-crumbled, half-wet sheet that again found its way between my lips.

"Thanks," he waved me off, already slumped in his chair as I dashed off a second time.

I staggered over loose rocks and sprinted up the slope, eventually reaching the mouth of the cave, no thanks to my heavy boots. Running uphill, with added weight and humid conditions, was exhausting. Sweat already dampened my shirt, but I refused to slow down. The adventure had yet begun as I footed my way up to leveled terrain, to the twenty-foot archway waiting to swallow me whole. Jagged V-shaped rocks graced its bow like the teeth of a great white.

"The shark," I whispered respectfully, the name we'd given that entrance. "Ready or not?"

I entered with a chill wiggling up my spine, my first warning to back down before the hair on my arms frizzled north. I didn't fear the monster before me, I feared the toll that cave had taken on my family. Nonetheless, I refused to quit, siphoning strength and courage as I filled my lungs with the mountain's moist air, before dashing into the beast's belly.

The walls glistened with wet stone, with the ceiling's first trickles wetting my sleeve no more than fifty feet in. But I kept on the move, diving into darkness with daylight dwarfing behind. Then splash. My boot sunk in the soggy wet moss and squished its arctic water down my sock. The chill fumbled my foot and sent my hand straight into the same soggy mess. One dry sock, one dry glove and a definite bruise. I rotated my wrist and popped it back in place, then pushed on without a classmate in sight. They couldn't have drifted too far, and after another hundred feet across the scraggly rocks, it was *hello* darkness.

My headlamp lit up the horizon, the infinite weightless water drops dancing across the black backdrop like snowflakes on a wintry night.

"Woohoo!" I yelled at the walls.

The echo bounced back like a lone basketball dribbled in a vacant gym. But anxious to find what resided beyond that echo, I pushed on to the real challenge ahead, the back of the cavern's throat. I halted at the dead end and hunched over, face to face with a five-foot wall of trickling water. Below, left to right, sat the small nooks that branched from the main cave. That's where my map came into play, reminding me of the infamous names that marked each nook.

The Fender Bender.

The Ab Cruncher.

The Skin Scraper.

And last but not least, the Dungeon.

I crawled into the Skin Scraper then paused. Was it the Skin Scraper or the Dungeon? I remembered hearing one in class, the other being the one I hoped it would be. I could've sworn it was the Skin Scraper, but for some reason, the Dungeon rang more familiar the longer I lingered unsure.

I poked my head into the Skin Scraper and closed my eyes, calming my breath while my ears searched for echoes of laughter. But while sifting through the darkness, I heard nothing more than the mountain's blowing breath, and the symphony of trickling water that dripped and splashed at varying intervals.

"Hellooooo?" I yelled.

My echo clapped the empty distance and returned with no answer. What of the Dungeon? After repeating the effort and yielding the same result, I began to doubt my place and time. The bus driver confirmed no more than ten minutes, but had his siesta disoriented him from the time they'd gone in?

It was time to make another slightly childish decision. Which entrance would I dive in alone? My gut whispered the Dungeon and so did my heart, so I got on all fours, strengthened my resolve and never looked back. Quickly, I gained distance. The pace was smooth, the pathway spacious and I should've reached them in no time as I mindlessly scurried from one rock to the next. And then I realized, I'd been all speed and no appreciation.

Look how far I'd made it alone, how I'd summoned the courage to defy Mom. I wanted to die when I believed I'd missed that experience, and now that I was there, I'd done nothing but haste from one step to the next. I needed a breath just to soak in the moment, to linger in the feel of it and understand what I felt. I'd catch up, eventually. Thirty of them couldn't have ventured too far, and from what I remembered the trek was no more than a couple of hours.

That was enough to get me off my hands and knees, to flip on my back and shine my head lamp across the ceiling. An instant chill from the damp ground pushed through my fabric as I gazed at a thousand droplets just waiting to let go. Patiently they hung with barely any weight to give, before I extended my arm and grazed them onto my glove. The cold and wet canopy, tinted with nature's recurring shades of brown, sturdy and strong enough to carry the weight of the world above. And there where I laid beneath all that noise and chaos, was so peaceful and quiet, without a murmur stirred beyond the clamor of my breath.

It made me think of Dad and why his love of being a geologist. Why such fondness for Earth and the foundation on which it stood? He'd sit at his desk for hours, with his magnifying glass engorging the oval of his eye as he dissected every speck in a stone, mesmerized by their slew of designs, colors, shapes and sizes.

At night, he'd often catch me peeking from the crack of his door before turning to invite me in. I'd readily plop on his lap as he highlighted details I'd never have grasped alone. I never understood what he explained. Still, it was my most cherished spot, and a warm memory to comfort the chilly draft of air before a drop of water splat between my eyes. The shiver brought me back to reality, reminding me I had some catching up to do. It was time I move on.

CHAPTER FOUR

Forty-five minutes! I crawled and ate dirt for forty-five minutes with no sign of my class. My palms ached from keeping my weight off the jagged rock. The fronts of my knees managed, thank God for the kneepads, but the skin creases behind were rubbed raw from the straps.

I'd pause and stretch every ten to fifteen minutes, easing my thumb beneath the elastic bands to loosen the tension. But my eyes purged the dark ahead, waiting to see if the rest of me would cower. Up to that point it was all fun and games, but then the real challenge came.

From there out, for who knows how long, any wiggle room was not in the cards. My tunnel drastically shrunk, from a hole I could sit up and move around in, to a crawl space that forced me to mimic a worm. Three feet wide, maybe two and a half tall, just enough room to flatten to my belly.

I had no issues with claustrophobia, but doing that alone, shook me a bit. I would've done anything to have my best friend Nijal, to hear his repeated sarcasm fill the air while I naturally questioned what the hell I was doing. Where were the others? How fast were they moving and how had I not caught up? Then came the obvious, did I crawl into the wrong opening? That one I quickly shook from my head, especially if I was to have the balls to see it through.

Faced with two options, it was my one and only chance to turn back, literally. Once in, there was no room for U-turns or cowering back the opposite direction. It was all forward, and I had to decide if that's what I really wanted. Hell, no! I plopped on my butt for the last time and mindlessly gazed into the pitch-black ahead. I was halfway there, so why not make the best of it? It required the same effort to reach the other side than to turn back, right?

A deep, chilled breath gathered my nerves and kept them from sprouting loose, along with a small chug of water to wash down my fear. I wasn't sure when I'd have the chance again, to squeeze my arm down my side to unclip the bottle from my belt. Then, with a second breath, into the void I dove.

"Okay. Okay. Okay," I whispered, bolstering my push forward. "You'll be fine. You've got this. A liter of water and a granola bar—who can stop me?"

After breathing in bravery and a mouthful of dirt, I plopped on my belly and stretched my arms ahead, gripping protruding rocks to help squeeze me inside. Instantly I realized how stupid I was, but at least I had gloves, already allaying my first gash to the hand. The fabric soaked in the red stains from my knuckles, and by the time I was done, I was sure to resemble raw meat. That would be my dead giveaway and what I couldn't hide from Mom, never believing my grated skin would tell my tale.

After poking my butt in the air till it hit the ceiling, I scooted my knees up as far as they'd go then pushed with my lower half, all while pulling my upper body with strength in my arms. That was one way. The other? A foot placed on each side to push me inch by inch, inspiring a newfound respect for every inch worm on Earth.

It took forever, and I couldn't figure how Father enjoyed it alone, not while being trapped in the tunnels of my mind. Silence renewed my appreciation for sound; there wasn't any. My ears constantly searched for the slightest drip, crack or thud, anything away from my paranoid breaths. Good thing no one could hear how I sounded, each breath heavy and ragged, disturbing the tranquility of that peaceful air.

Same went for my eyes, eagerly searching beyond my headlamp to find a classmate ahead. But what use? It didn't keep me from scraping my arm, again. If not a scrape my helmet got jammed, if not my helmet, my shoelace got caught. If not the shoelace, I was taking off my glove to wipe the spattered mud from my eyes while trying not to gunk it back in my glove.

"Oh yeah! My water bottle too!" I shouted.

It jammed just as I'd settled the other chain of events, but I carried on groaning as the darkness pressed in. The air became cooler. The mud more frigid to touch as my gloves drank the ground's moisture with an unquenchable thirst. But after pushing through a grueling twenty-minute belly crawl, I prayed my eyes deceived me as to what lied ahead, or that perhaps it was just a trick of the light. But it wasn't. My body-hugging slither space of a hole was completely blocked by fallen rubble.

CHAPTER FIVE

My breath caught in my throat as I considered my next move. "Come on! Are you kidding me?" my frustration echoed against the impenetrable walls.

My eyes hadn't misled me, and my buried attempt to yell rendered even less comfort. Why me? A cruel joke? Had I truly crawled into an irreversible place? I wiggled backwards, my heart sputtering as I became gridlocked by my water bottle wedged against the wall. I instantly thrashed with panic from the feeling of being stuck, then thrusted forward as my breaths thickened.

Jordan. Relax. Don't panic. I wasn't sure if I'd spoken aloud or if my thoughts were simply that brash in that silence. I paused for an inhale of fresh air and ideas. "You'll be out in no time," I pep talked myself, assuring I heard the words to keep grounded before my second attempt against the mound ahead.

I heaved my palms with all the weight I could, shifting a handful of rocks forward. 'Yes!' I thought, finding the space to shimmy my arm down my side. It was snug, but my arm scraped back and forth between my hip and the wall.

'Okay, here we go. You got this Jordan,' I thought, boosting confidence to shove off the jitters that rushed to eat me alive. Most rocks ahead were the size of baseballs. So, I'd grab one and scrape it down my side, gently toss it to my foot, then kick it back as far as it rolled. One after another tumbled behind, giving me the courage to even sing out loud.

"London Bridge is falling down, falling down, falling down. London Bridge is falling down, my fair lady," I chanted.

Why that song? At first, I hadn't a clue why *it* popped in my head, but then it clicked. It was comforting to sing of a sturdy, fortified structure having crumbled to its knees. I echoed the lyrics a hundred times, snagged a rock, kicked it, then repeated. I'd found my groove, so I thought, until the buildup behind became harder to kick. Before long, nothing moved in either direction.

"Something's gotta give!" I yelled, disrupting the rhythm of my once merry tune.

Claustrophobia became real in ways I'd never imagined. Sandwiched from head to toe, the earth seemed to descend. I swear it crushed me on all sides, tightened along my back to press me in my grave. I couldn't move. My mind played tricks on me, then my lungs tightened as hyperventilation set in. Panic grabbed my neck like a giant's hand. I stuffed my glove across my nose and mouth to stiffen the flow of oxygen as my throat swelled like a balloon. I was spiraling out of control, losing hope when a shimmer on my left pierced the corner of my eye.

I lost sight of whatever it was, frantic to catch it when my light snagged it again. My heartbeat tempered the moment I found it, slowing my breaths to a normal pace. I was determined not to lose it a second time, hardening my eyes on its place as I slowly descended my cheek against the cold grit of my hand. I never reached, just stared, memorizing where it sat as its amber glow calmed the roiling thoughts in my head. Finally, the cramming walls seemed to retreat.

Only a few stones sat between it and I, and after finding calm I jostled to my distraction. I was just within reach when my helmet jammed, so I ditched it and my left elbow pad to distend my arm, mashing my cheek against the rock pile ahead as I stretched every tendon through a gutter of daggers. I nearly had my prize, straining and skimming it with the tip of my glove, then my stretch gave out.

My arm was jelly. I pulled it back through the gauntlet, tasting wet earth as I bit the mud slung glove to tug it free. Yuck! Nevertheless, round two. I nestled closer and lunged again, with the taste of blood layering my tongue from my cheek in the stone. The cavern of knives had their way again, puncturing my fingertips to the pit of my arm. But just a little more and I nipped the stone's edge with my nail, clawing and clipping till it wormed within my grasp. Bingo! I had it!

I rolled it back through the cutthroat lair and exacerbated each gash a fourth time over. Trickles of blood seeped over the gutter's edge, coloring the clay surface with droplets of red. My arm was shredded, and I only found relief by pressing against the cold wet ground. My cheek kept numb from the stone in my jaw, but even still, my plight eased. For the moment, none of it outmatched the fascination in my hand, and I couldn't help but wonder 'what on Earth had I found?'

Centuries of crud was caked to its surface and hid the true jewel stuck inside. It was a mere speck in the grand cavern, barely the size of a baby mango, but its presence was undeniable. Like a hidden treasure waiting to be discovered amidst the hard earth, the parts I could reach were tantalizing to touch. But beneath its visible surface, something even more precious waited to be unearthed, a mystery begging to be solved within its golden-brown hue.

Quickly, I grabbed a jagged rock to chisel off its hardened edges. They crumbled with ease, leaving a smooth, icy marble touch to greet my fingers. Then the notion hit me to turn off my light, the only smart thing I did that day, when the stone within countered with a soft glow of amber. And beneath that glow, suspended in its heart? A thousand glittering flecks, glistening as if I stargazed the universe above. I wasn't sure if I'd hallucinated. Thought I was, lying beneath the earth in pitch black with a constellation blazing in my hand? Whatever I held leapt my morale. I flicked on my light and shoved the stone in my pocket, then pushed on singing my merry tune.

"London bridge is falling down," I sang with ambition, while my mind burned through a squillion questions.

What was it and how did it get there? Where was it from? Father never mentioned anything of its kind, and I couldn't recall anything of its likes in his office. Had it been lost? Had it emerged from the depths of Earth's crust, and would I find another if I continued to dig? I wondered how I of all people stumbled upon something so rare during a trek of sheer recklessness.

The thought of it fueled my dig, but it wasn't long before my spirits burst like an overtaxed balloon. My helmet bottlenecked, again, and that time I was stuck, for real. I furiously kicked, pushed and shoved with neither heap budging, then the old familiar tremors of panic crept back in.

"No!" I screamed.

My heart pummeled the murky ground, shoving my back against the ceiling with every beat. Was I atop the ground or was the ground atop me? I was desperate. Each inhale grew heavier to draw in and even harder to expel, forcing me to shout with panic.

"Help!" I screamed again and again, till the dry earth caked my throat.

Who did I yell for? Who would heed? Who would hear my panicked screams of desperation echoing through that secluded clammy air? I must've yelled a thousand times, rattling the flesh in my throat till a compulsion of coughs replaced my words. I couldn't choke, not there, so I stopped to breathe as desperation lugged me down a rabbit hole.

"I give up," I cried, as the thought of been buried alive set in.

Of all my troubles, I foolishly thought how Mom would kill me! Not only had I disobeyed and believed I'd get away with it, but now, buried alive?! My mother's scourge should've been the least of my worries, but somehow it weighed heavy regardless. We'd suffered enough of the same before, giving reason to doubt I'd ever find her forgiveness.

As a last desperate hope I attempted to make the dreaded call, using my 'clean' hand to pull my phone from my pocket. Reluctant, yet hopeful, I opened my phone.

"Come on, come on, come on," I pled the earth around.

But just as I'd figured, that hope for a signal ran blank on my screen. I growled in frustration as reality slapped my face, and it was time to admit, I was trapped.

CHAPTER SIX

Despite the miserable ups and downs, I never gave up thrashing and kicking, squirming and wiggling to set myself free. Two hours felt like days with no progression. My soles cramped. My palms throbbed and begged me to stop, so I paused to rest my aching bones, realizing the moist ground was a rising concern. Given all the other exigencies, I hadn't paid much attention to how wet I'd become or how low my body temperature had dropped. And having worked up a sweat wouldn't make it any better.

Mud coated the gashes along my arm, about the only positive thing that worked in my favor. I ditched my gloves to release the cold trapped to my hands and jammed them beneath my armpits for warmth. With my knees cuddled to my chest, with barely enough room to fold, I ran through my checklist of being stuck in a cave.

Lights off. No need to waste batteries. So I stuffed my elbow pad beneath my neck like a pillow then abolished my only means of sight. Next? Eyes closed. In that level of darkness, with zero illumination, you'd burn your retinas searching for a glimmer you'd never find. So with my eyes closed in the lone cold dark, in came my imagination with the warmest thoughts.

"Hot beef stew. Yummy!" I yelled deliriously. "I'll have a grande hot mocha please. No, make it a venti!"

Only a couple of hours and my mind scattered like confetti in the wind. I was sure it was past noon from the last I'd seen my phone, with time dragging like the rest of me. So I kept myself from peeking, hoping my classmates would notice my absence, or the lazy bus driver would realize I wasn't there.

The thought of it pulled me from my skin, but just as that bug of loneliness started to nibble, that amber hue from before lit up the folds of my pocket. The stone! I yanked it loose for a second glare, holding it to my chest like a warm light. It had no warmth to give, but I couldn't help but wonder from where came its light?

I had no plans and nothing to give, so I simply lied there stuck in its glow, mesmerized for who knows how long by what I held. But the longer I stared, the more my curiosity grew, and the more my anxiety began to subside. My mind calmed, my eyes drooped, and I slowly drifted into a daydream.

CHAPTER SEVEN

Somehow, I was back outdoors. My eyelids wouldn't budge, but an agreeable summer breeze swept across my skin. My hands were still filled with gritty sand, but it was warm and dry, opposite of the cold, damp soil I'd muscled through in the cave.

And water? Not the echoing trickles that splashed from the ceiling. A tranquil 'whoosh' sang to my ears like waves caressing a shore.

I fought my eyes open and plunged from darkness to sheer blinding light. Slowly, I blinked my surroundings alive, wondering if I dreamed or if I'd died and awoken in that next place. How had I gone from a cave beneath the earth to lying on a shore I'd only seen in brochures, with a sky that only existed in paintings? The water was too blue, the sand too soft and too white to be real.

Leery, I sat up on guard and let my eyes explore, realizing I enjoyed the sedative waves alone. A bird or two chirped in the distance, but no bark of animals, no chatter, no honking horns or bustle of city streets. I sat alone at the center of nowhere, perched between a majestic ocean and a layer of groomed jungle that had to be a dream!

I bore the same clothes from the cave, but cleaner, while my arms held a separate surprise. They'd healed. Not a scratch left its signature from that canyon of daggers. I scrunched the sand to convince myself it wasn't real, then poured it from one hand to the next. The touch of it became addictive. Soft and white, powdery like flour with an iridescence of colorful specks melding throughout its grains. It couldn't be real, so I stood to prove otherwise.

The moment I did I lost balance, further disbanding that uncertainty of a dream. Dreams weren't like this. They're different, so uncanny and overly cushioned. This was odd, anomalous, and I couldn't figure why till I noticed the air. Neither its gravity nor its breeze burdened my stance, so I glided my palm through the open to find out why. Then a wave rippled from the pass of my hand as if I'd dipped and swirled it through a pond. It spilled between my fingers and pushed against my palm, the same as when speeding down the highway with your hand out the window.

"What on Earth?" I questioned myself.

Not believing what I'd just witnessed I mimicked the gesture, cupping air as if scooping a palm full of water. Again it rippled, behaving as if water and air had somehow become one. With the third try I forced it from my palm as if I'd tossed a stone through the air, then aimed the shore and did it again, as if aiming a pitch at a catcher's glove. The sand skirted from my pathway!

"No freaking way!" I yelled, baffled, excited and unable to stop.

I had to try again, cupping my hand then flinging it at the ocean as if tossing a stone at its face. Thunk! The water splashed as if a rock had smacked through. What was happening? Where was I? My mind toyed with me. I even thought to awaken myself back in the cave and save what was left of me from expiring. But then again, why? If that were my end, why not loiter in that make believe to pass the time? I'd exhausted my options anyway. There was nothing I could do but shiver in the cold, gloomy air, while I somehow felt warm in that place. The thought of that dark hole sent a chill through my pores before I abated it and focused back where I stood!

"Oh, God, please let this be the best dream I've ever had while I'm dying," I prayed.

To dig my feet in the shore was like a child's first day on a beach. The sun's warmth sat in the sand, radiating back towards me and seeping into my soles. The deeper I plunged, was like sinking into a pot of warm honey, slowly sinking me deeper into its sugary embrace. Each step felt like unearthing hidden treasures, as if the sand had been waiting for me to reveal its secrets. What a feeling, only rivaled by my next breath of air!

I inhaled long, deep breaths of it, each intake enabling me as if life begged me to relish its taste. It was the combination of citrus blossoms, freshly cut grass, and a hint of sea salt, all mingled with a subtle undertone of warmth and promise. It was the fragrance of a perfect summer day, intoxicating and alluring.

Nothing hurt. Nothing taxed me or felt too daunting as my mind and spirit roamed the free air. But then it hit me like a sixth sense, two eyes from within the trees dragging across my skin like the pointy edge of a toothpick. I whipped towards the forest and caught two stunning flowers bouncing more than the rest. Someone had been there. Someone was watching, but somehow I wasn't afraid.

"Hello?" I yelled, boldly hustling that direction.

Then whoever was there suddenly dashed away. I lunged in pursuit, failing against someone like a feather on their feet. Large leaves and plants slapped me as I whisked by, obscuring me from where I was or which direction I ran. Still, I kept chasing with glimpses of long dark hair, but no way of catching sight to whom it belonged.

"Hellooo. Wait up!" I hollered.

I gained on her and nearly had her in sight, then the ground opened from beneath my feet. Down I plunged, twenty feet smack into its deck. Wham, so I thought, believing I'd hit bottom before realizing there was never a wham. True I'd fallen, but just before the wallop came a cushion of air, rushing between the dirt and my sprawled fingers as it had on the shore.

Slowly, I descended and closed the six-inch gap, finding myself alone in some dumb person's trap that had me debating whether to wake up before the dream turned sour. Would I be taken, eaten alive? It's what my friend Nijal would say after watching one too many movies, but what stopped me was the realization that I had control. I was lucid dreaming, maneuvering my every step! So, couldn't I have simply leapt from that stupid pit? I raised both arms above my head as if a red cape blew behind, but feeling like an idiot I took the hard route instead. A twenty-foot climb.

On that climb I realized the hole wasn't for me. The protruding roots provided too easy an escape, and my ascent was much easier than any attempt in the gym. I was fairly athletic and above average at sports, but I'd never made a rope climb with such a breeze. I was up in seconds, back at the surface and came face to face with a girl of pure beauty.

Her startled gasp stopped my thought, and if I only knew then in whose eyes I glared. The girl who'd unknowingly alter my life, who'd swell my soul with more love than I knew to give. She was the one who'd fuel my ambition and help me soar beyond any obstacle. The one who'd push me to achieve greatness beyond measure. If only I knew then.

Instead, mere attraction awakened my senses that day in ways it never had before. My fingers, mind and muscles all ceased to exist as her visage struck me to a paralyzing halt. I lost focus, my strength and lastly my grip as the root vine tore across my palms. Back in the ground's mouth I went. Then wham!

For some reason, there was a wham that time and the ground left its mark to prove it so. But at the bottom of that twenty-foot drop, I again doubted it a dream. The root stings on my palms burned like hot iron. My hips and shoulders squawked real pain when the ground sent its thud up my back.

Somehow, I rolled away the agony, completely ignoring the aching throb as a blanket of dark hair spilled over the edge. Her hands covered her mouth with guilty blame, while I again stared from below with the pain forgotten. 'Stop gawking, Jordan,' I reminded myself while stumbling to my feet. It wasn't like me to gawk and stare, but with her my eyes simply refused to listen!

I stood and brushed the dirt from my pants, strangely dispelling the ache in my bones before slowly gesturing my way back to the roots. I eased back up so as not to spook her again. I'd advance and she'd step back, until our eyes nearly fell on level plain. That time, I kept my grip.

"Hi," I muttered, half in and half out of the pit.

She said nothing, but her concern eased into a smile before she turned to rush away.

"No, wait!" I yelled, "Come back, please. I'm not a threat, I could use your help."

She stopped and kept her distance with her back towards me, hushed, waiting, pretending to be absent while the fringes of her hair danced in the breeze.

"I'm Jordan. I'm coming up now, but please don't run. Don't be scared," I pled.

Cautious, I climbed into the open while her back kept against me, easing to my knees with a safe distance between us.

"I'm Jordan," I affirmed, "a little lost, and with no clue where I am or how I got here."

Eventually, she turned my way, barring me from caring to look anywhere else. Her feet were adorned with simple leather sandals, and with her long, slender legs that propelled her through the forest, I couldn't help but notice why she'd moved so quickly and gracefully. The animal skin that loosely wrapped her thighs accentuated her subtle curves, and a delicate chain of jewels shimmered around her midriff like a sparkling necklace, adding a touch of glamour to her otherwise wild appearance.

Her fair skin was unblemished, untouched by the harsh elements around. Despite being amid the wilderness, she bore no visible weapons and gave off an aura of confidence and fearlessness. Suddenly, I became aware I was again staring in awe, scolding myself a second time as I yanked my eyes to hers.

I didn't want to give the wrong impression, then found her eyeing me the same. And while she picked me a part like a ball of cotton, her trinkets invited me for a second look. The leather strap on her neck dangled a sky-blue crystal, plunged just above her bosom. It was my favorite color, amongst the other jewels that wrapped her waist, entwined her wrists and those laced through her hair. Her bracelet however, struck me more curious than the rest. It covered her wrist and went halfway up her forearm, with nickel sized gems gleaming every color of the spectrum.

"Hi," I mustered again as she caught me mid-stare.

I sounded like a buffoon, a buffoon still trapped in the best dream of his life.

"Are you MonTu?" she asked, her voice tinged with anxiety. My confusion became evident as she repeated once more, "Do you come from water or sky?"

"I'm not sure. I opened my eyes and there I was, lying in the sand where you found me."

I had no clue as to why at the time, but tension left her face and eased to a smile. In time, I'd learn the weight of that meaning and why my answer sparked such a gush of relief.

"Grateful arrival. I am Kaylaira," she greeted with a kiss to my cheek.

I inadvertently closed my eyes from the touch of her lips, shuddered from the tingle that flew up my spine. I prayed she didn't feel it. It wasn't my first kiss from a girl, but sure felt like it was.

"Thank you. You are absolutely divine," I sputtered.

What had I just said? I couldn't believe I spoke so boldly! Me flirting? I never flirted; I didn't know how! And to think those words managed to weave past my lips. I panicked and back stepped, but her smile spread wild as I turned as red as an apple. I shuffled for a better intro, but before I could speak, the rumbles of an earthquake trembled my head. I searched the jungle but found no tremors. The land simply roared in the folds of my imagination. I reached for Kaylaira feeling I'd fall. She reached back, but before she grabbed hold my eyes suddenly opened… my real eyes.

CHAPTER EIGHT

"Just hold still," a voice bellowed, "See if you can try and put your helmet back on. We've almost got you."

It was far from Kaylaira's sweet tone, the unfamiliar voice of some random man. Confusion swept me up, and I must have coughed a gallon of dirt before opening my eyes to trails of dust, tumbling through spurts of stirred light. It wasn't my light, but enough to find my helmet. I reached to grab it, but could barely move beyond the violent, involuntary shiver of my arm.

Cold soaked me from top to bottom, numbing my limbs from the damp rock and the absence of having moved from where I lied. The mountain size lump on my head, that I felt! The plastic of my elbow pad swelled it stiff, aching every part of my body as I shifted from *bedrock*. Delirious humor, I guess.

It took a moment to pry my quivering arm from my side, to flick my headlamp to max and learn what was real. Incoherence bit me hard! Where were the warm sands of the beach, or the green plants of the jungle that measured the width of my torso? Was *this* the dream, that the reality?

"Snap out of it, buddy. We're gonna need you awake to make it out alive," the stranger grunted.

My languor wore off as my coherence pulled together, and the bundle of rock I'd kicked behind was practically gone. It wasn't a dream. I was back to reality, being rescued? I should've felt relief, but startlingly enough, I didn't. Those five minutes away were the most elated time of my life, and a part of me wished things ended there than back in that silly hole. Besides, how had they found me so soon anyway?

"W-what time is it?" my teeth chattered.

"What time is it?" he repeated, as if my question lacked valid concern. "Nine-ish?"

"N-nine-ish? At n-night?" I asked in disbelief.

"Yeah, PM kid."

Nine?! How so, when I'd barely closed my eyes just a few minutes before? Mom was going to kill me! A slew of headlamps flashed in front of me, with the last of my rock pile being removed. I was better off asking if they'd restack it, entomb me and forget I ever existed.

"You alright? You hurt?" several bombarded me.

They called off the rescue from the other end and dragged me back to an open space. Hot chocolate! Yes! Fresh socks and gloves, loaded with thermal heat warming packets! My blood danced in my veins. They even swapped my shoes for a dry pair. With my head cleared, muscles loosened and numb bones coming to life, we coordinated my slothful crawl back to the entrance. And what a feeling it was to set eyes on that opening.

I stretched up and out into the night's cool air, feeling as if I'd been reborn again. The tension and stiffness melted away, and the open space around me seemed to expand infinitely, as if I'd been contained in a tiny box and was now released into the vastness of the world.

My spine popped like bubble wrap. Every joint in me welcomed life, then the magnitude of my rescue set in. I was shielded and wrapped with a warming blanket, my clothes stripped and replaced with fresh ones. It… felt… heavenly!

A bustling crowd had gathered at the foothill, news media, fire trucks and paramedics, with a thundering applause of cheers and whistles breaking loose the moment I emerged. The lights, the movement, the flourishing buzz of curiosity—it overwhelmed me. However, just two eyes became my concern, the two that permeated my soul from the front of the crowd… Mom's.

Ashamed and embarrassed, I stumbled toward her beneath a firefighter's arm, expecting the news team to video a slap in the face. She grabbed me instead, fumbled to her knees and held me like a crying child. My heart sank. Why put her through it? Was my need for an adventure worth her pain? I clenched her with equal gratefulness and sorrow and whispered a thousand apologies in her ear.

"I'm sorry," I added to it like a cherry on top.

My throat was too dry to say anymore, and the reason I declined a statement to the news team as an ambulance ushered me away with Mom glued to my side. A third cup of hot chocolate, or warm liquid heaven I called it, moistened my throat to finally allow words.

"How did they find me?" I began.

An explanation followed with an obsessive caress of my hand. The school was puzzled by the count of thirty-nine consent forms with only thirty-eight students present. That sparked the bus driver to then reveal my last-minute arrival after another student recognized my bag. They plucked my forged signature and contacted Mom, then immediately dispatched a search party.

"You ventured through a barricaded tunnel?" she asked.

"Barricaded?" I echoed.

"Yes, they were aware that tunnel had collapsed and was unstable. That's why it was sealed."

I assured her I'd disobeyed, but no barricade kept me from entering. Oh the look in her eyes once I revealed that truth. They momentarily widened as the pieces fell into place, as if she accepted some uncovered truth while reflecting a journey of some hidden memory. Whatever it was, she hadn't grasped it until I'd spoken those words. Either way, at that point she didn't care, and I wondered how long before the caresses would turn into nails clawing my skin.

"It's just," she started, and I knew where it was going. "You know this is how we lost your father. I understand your need to rekindle his passion, to walk in his footsteps. But how am I to go on if I lose you the same way we lost him?"

I sat in silence, with no words or amount of explanation to contest her truth. How could I have been so selfish? Hand in hand, in silent commemoration, we arrived at the local medical center.

CHAPTER NINE

"A clean bill of health," the doctor informed, after Mom and I rode the heels of a sleepless night. "You suffered mild hypothermia, but we were fortunate enough to find you in time," his lips moved, but all I heard was Kaylaira's voice. Why couldn't she be real? Why did someone so perfect only live in a dream? "You should be grateful. Not a scratch," he went on.

Not a scratch? Last I remembered, it seemed I'd lost a battle to a horde of raging cats. Nonetheless, he was right. My arms were completely clear without a cut or bruise. Or perhaps that too was another figment of my imagination?

After a final exam, and my veins pumped full of fluids, I was cleared to head home. But it wasn't till stepping through our front door that I realized my load was light. The stone!

"Promise you'll never do this again?" Mom asked, her words landing like a gentle but firm breeze against my conscience.

I nodded of course, concealing the devious plan already drawn in my head as she embraced me to her bosom then collapsed on her bed.

I meandered to mine, hiding the signs of my soon to be defiance. Then from behind closed doors, I freaked. Where I had it last, I couldn't remember. My pocket? The clothes I wore? Did they have it at the station or had it tumbled out in the cave? Maybe a first responder kept it for himself, or did I ever have it at all? My phone was broken and there was no way to call without giving away what I planned. I was told to rest, but rest was far from my mind.

"Mom?" I called back in her room. Her blankets were up to her chin. "I need some fresh air. I'm gonna head out for a bike ride."

Burnt out, after having stayed with me the entire night, she tried dissuading me, but with a little whining it would do me good, she waved her hand in conceit. I'd never pedaled so purposefully. I burst through our small-town toward the first response station, asking the same question a hundred times while pointed to the next person in line. Finally, I landed the worker with my possessions on his way out the door, ripped the plastic bag and fumbled through my belongings. No stone.

"Is this everything?" I inquired, rifling through the plastic.

"That's it," he assured.

"Are you sure? There was nothing else?" I pressed urgently.

"We stripped your clothes and placed them directly in the bag. I'm sorry, but this is all there was."

He had no reason to lie, and the more I retraced my actions the more convinced I was that I'd left it where it was found.

"Ugh!" I roared in frustration.

"Looking for something in particular? Anything I can help you with?" he asked.

"Yeah," I chuckled, "a ride to the cave?"

How desperate did I look? I expected him to pop the idea, but to my surprise, he agreed. Thankfully, he handled the burden of our drive with rescue stories pertaining to the cave, children and adults alike. The highlight? The geologist who lost his life years prior. This guy was obviously new in town with no clue who I was.

"Not sure why they don't just block the whole damn thing off," he went on.

Block the cave? Immediately I jumped in the cave's defense.

"Would you close an ocean for a swimmer's unfortunate drowning?" I returned.

I couldn't hold back. What right was there to smother one passion that held as much risk as another?

"Well, guess you've got a point. Never considered it in that light," he pointed after pummeling my words.

Better than getting pissed and dumping me halfway. I thanked him as soon as we arrived and snagged my bike from his truck, but his lips moved faster than my legs could get away.

"Just a minute," he interjected. "You aren't going back inside, are you?"

His tone conveyed a mix of concern and disbelief, but I promised having zero intention of crawling back in. That's all he wanted to hear.

"The cave is the last place I wish to be," I lied.

Somewhat content, if not a little skeptical, off he went while I staved off the urge to dart up the hill. His truck took forever to leave my sight, but once gone, I was off like a madman. I stashed my bike at the foothill in case I got stuck again. That way someone would hopefully notice another idiot had gone inside. An idiot with no head gear, no knee or arm protection and no lamp. Failure in the making.

Still, I couldn't stop the urge. A whispering breeze from within those dark walls seemed to pull me by the hand. I wasn't even close to slowing down. The stone was my obsession, Kaylaira my delirium, and in some ways, I felt out of place the longer I remained outside. Maybe it was more stupidity or delusion, but either way, I was set to test the difference and needed to improvise.

My teeth ripped my sleeves like a vicious beast, then tied them for elbow pads. Same went for my pants, wiggling my finger through miniature holes before tearing the bottoms out into kneepads. My bike had a strapped light to its frame, so with my socks and a little ingenuity it made its way around my head, fastened as if I were set for my first karate match. Then up I went, searching the incline where I'd met the crowds, already knowing the stone would be nowhere in sight.

"Stupid, stupid, stupid," I repeated, knowing what I was about to do, but still not smart enough to deter me from doing it.

I stripped the caution tape, removed the handful of rocks barricading the opening and scooted inside. That time I moved with purpose from one stone to the next, dodging the abrasive edges across the familiar ground. No phobias held me back. No fears slowed me as I mindlessly pushed between the body-hugging walls that pressed me between Earth's pulse. My concern wasn't getting wedged, it was leaving without the stone and not returning to that vivacious dream. I couldn't shake it, nor the girl it birthed in my head. It made my journey bolder, faster. I even smiled like a fool, talking and laughing to myself as if Kaylaira and I were already chatting.

As far as the stone and it's worth, or what I'd do once I'd found it? Who knew. I was a geology rookie, but smart enough to know I needed a plan. If presented to the right institution, that stone could've ended our financial woes, and I convinced myself that was the reality I was after while knowing very well it was all for a girl.

With my knees and elbows rubbed raw and my palms blistering red, again, I turned the last corner where fragments of broken rubble lined the floor. My heart started racing, my nerves shook my arms under the strain of my weight.

"Please be here, please be here!" I whispered, passing the heap that detained me the day before. But sifting through its pieces I found it bare.

"No no no!" I lamented in darkness.

My thoughts blurred, then flashed to the paramedic. Did he have it? Had he lied, or had I only dreamt the stone was real? Fortune never fell in my lap, that's the kind of person I was. So how would I, of all people, unearth a rock that lustered a universe inside? Me? Sounded silly to even think it.

I sank in the rubble in full defeat, removed the sweaty socks from my forehead and yanked the light dug in my brow. How was I so foolish to do that to Mom, and yet there I was, again? Solace gave me comfort and silence presented a solution. Maybe that's why Dad fell in love with those dark, crammed spaces. There, I could breathe. There I could hear my inner voice with my thoughts set free. Perhaps that calm is what guided me to the stone.

I froze before its glow. *It* was there. It was real, and I never took my eyes from it even for a second before I shuffled to it giggling like a five-year-old child. I plucked it from the ruins, wondering what I held and what had brought it alive before shuffling back to the entrance. Then a wave of serenity held me in place. What would happen once I stepped outdoors? Somehow, I knew everything was about to change. So why not stay and consume that moment of peace?

On my back in the silent dark, my head filled with thoughts of Dad's work and Mom's quandary with what I'd done. I felt a balance I'd never found outdoors, and after basking in that feeling for a calming hour, I returned home to soak my thoughts in the tub. I thought it would help me rest, but it didn't. I tossed and turned as if the night would never end, then realized my need to feed what I'd begun, not deprive myself of a moment like that.

"Mom?" I called, stirring her sleep from the sofa.

"I'm here," she stretched.

"Dad's office, mind if I shuffle through his old papers?" I asked, knowing she wouldn't object.

With a kiss on the forehead, she headed to bed and I to his office, ironically deemed, 'the cave.' Our home was extremely modest, but I'd venture to say his office was the biggest room in the house. A library of books swelling with knowledge towered up to the ceiling with half its shelves out of reach. And I stood six feet tall. Jewelry cases lined some of the lower halves, showcasing an exceptional rock collection with more stashed in the drawers. Everything was as he'd left it.

Dried up pens stood in the same case. A fat outdated calendar sat in the middle of his desk, marked with the last day he was there at the house. And yeah, his fake, look alike rock that my tiny hands could never pry apart. He'd twist the top with a loud pop open, teasing I'd find diamonds if only I had the strength. I never could, but those diamonds were usually ice cream money he'd occasionally leave on Fridays, knowing I wanted to hang out with my friends after school. And now, it held the little notes I wrote to him as a child.

I found his old watch and strapped it to my wrist, shocked the antique still ticked. In his world of madness, I hadn't a clue where to begin but used the step stool to start in the farthest corner of his shelf. An old notebook was stuffed heavy with old research papers. There were volumes of them, page after page of scribbled notes and presented essays. He'd made some noteworthy findings in his lifetime, but I only cared for one.

I searched that evening till my eyes burned red. Page after page I carefully turned, so as not to miss the slightest detail that could provide an answer. I went on into the early hours but came up short, 4am before I threw in the towel. I'd nearly missed another night's sleep.

I zipped the stone in a plastic bag and shoved it beneath my pillow. With the bike ride home and eyes exhausted from flipping pages, it didn't take long to doze off. But never in a million years did I believe the amazing would happen...

CHAPTER TEN

I was running, instinctively coursing a familiar path. How? I didn't know, but gargantuan plants whacked my face, with green being the only color I saw. Then a familiarity dawned… the hole! But just as I remembered the ground dropped from beneath my feet, and down I went, again. Wham!

Yep, that time, a wham.

I rolled in that very same dirt-filled, debilitating hole, hugging my shoulder from the jarring thud. 'The dream? Again?' I wondered but couldn't figure how, until a head of flowing hair peeked over the ledge. The moment I saw her she jutted away.

"Wait! Please don't leave," I yelled, leaping to my bare feet in my t-shirt and sleeping shorts?

Ignoring the why or how was the only way I'd catch her, figuring I'd learn later how a dream repeated where I'd left off. I darted up the wall faster than the day before, just as her hair whipped from my sight. But up top there she was again, pretending to have abandoned me as I emerged from the hole. Was I to follow the same as what I'd said before?

"Just please, don't go. I am so lost and could use your help," I stammered, then slowly stood. I was so beyond ecstatic to see her again that her name slipped from my mouth. "Kaylaira, right?" I asked.

Startled, she turned to me and backed away. What was different? Why had the sound of her name shuddered her with fear? She didn't know me, and I was as much a stranger as I'd been the day before.

"No, no wait, please."

"Where do you come from?" she asked, continuing to step away.

"Neither the sky nor the water. I opened my eyes and there I was, on the shore, where you found me," I fumbled. "But only this time, everything started just moments after?"

"How do you know my name?" she proceeded.

"Honestly, I don't know how, but I met you yesterday. Don't you remember?" I stuttered. Wrong answer.

"I don't believe you. This is some ploy," she threw in my face, backing away as if I sought to cause her harm.

Not the result I hoped for. And as she turned to run, I thought of one action to save me… to wake up! My eyes thrust open from jumping a mile from my bed. I panted as if I'd been held under water, then knelt by my mattress to steady my breaths. Cold water did the trick and snapped me out of my crossover daze.

"I'm losing my mind," I whispered, bathing my face in the bathroom mirror as the water gave a sense of the 'here and now.'

I was home in my room and had never left. But why the jungle? Why the hole and why so real, and the knot of pain throbbing between my shoulders where I'd whacked the ground? I tiptoed back to bed, afraid to get in as I pulled the stone from the bag beneath my pillow.

"What are you?" I whispered to it, wishing it whispered back.

Its edges flaked into the folds of my sheets, springing the idea of Father's electric polisher. Back in his office I went, carefully chiseling the sides with his old magnifying glass sharpening my view.

"You're still awake?" Mom startled me; the grinder slipped and nicked the gemstone.

"Mom, you scared me," I blurted, as her eyes roved the mess I'd made. "I'm sorry, did I wake you?" I asked, attempting to redirect her focus from what I held.

"No," she answered. "Just needed water and saw the light on. You should be sleeping? It's almost six."

"I know. I can't. Still restless, I guess. Probably just need a few days to shake it off. Figured why not polish some of Dad's old rocks."

She hugged me and kissed the top of my head, sunk in the memory of his work while oblivious to what I'd done.

"You know, it's warming to see you in here with his old things," she said. "Still, try to rest?"

Mom and I did our best. We were a good team, with no folly nor unnecessary drama, minus the cave. With a kiss to the head off she went, while I panicked and grabbed the stone. I searched it a dozen times over, praying the grinder hadn't gone through. I never found a scratch.

I intentionally nipped it a second time, but it kept unscathed, leaving me to question its durability. So I took the risk, started the grinder and grazed it hard. Nothing. I dug even harder, intent on splitting the thing in half, but not a scratch. The stone was unbreakable, and polishing became mindless at that point.

I ground off the crusty edges without a care in the world, yielding a perfect, tree sap colored stone the size of a large egg. Its insides were murky. The constellation couldn't be seen, but its outer shell refracted light as sharp as a mirror. I even pushed my tongue across its skin and found no fault in its surface. It was one of a kind, my golden egg, but what was I to do with it?

With my crumb-filled bed being the last spot I wanted to lay, I slipped on slacks and shoes then headed up front. Mom's leftover heat warmed that worn spot on the sofa where I curled beneath a blanket to ponder what was next. I figured Dad's old colleagues could help, but the longer I held the stone the more my thoughts swayed. It was my find and I wanted to keep it, no matter what price they'd put in my hand. And it was that thought that carried in my head when my eyelids gave in.

CHAPTER ELEVEN

Again, I fell. No Jurassic sized leaves smacked my face. No waves of hair dashed in the distance. Just me, dropping in the same cursed hole that greeted me each arrival. And yeah, wham!

I couldn't figure how those falls weren't the death of me as I rolled to my feet, ignoring the third shoulder jolt while trying to remember what not to say. Long strands of dark hair dangled over the edge then quickly disappeared.

"No, wait! Please," I begged, already scaling the sides. "I need your help."

'Don't say her name. Don't say her name,' I repeated in my head, pretending we'd never been acquainted. That was a chore, especially since she'd consumed my every thought since the moment we'd met. Yet there we were again, for the third time, eye to eye when I dropped to my knees with my hands in the air.

"Please, don't run. I need your help," I pled, halting her steps at the sound of my desperation. "I don't know where I am, what I'm doing, or how I got here."

"Are you MonTu?" she asked with her back still towards me. "From where do you come, the water or the sky?"

"Neither," I replied, "I simply opened my eyes and there I was - lying on the shore where you found me. "I'm Jordan, and… I have no idea what I'm doing here," I hopelessly admitted.

As she turned to face me our eyes clashed as intensely as before, a silent battle between two souls, each combing the other in search of purity. I wondered what her glower dissected. As for me, what I saw was changeless, an unconquerable virtue that burst like the sun through stubbornest of clouds. I saw the innocence children possess, through a girl who'd seen heartache and refused to let it pervade or define who she was meant to be. It was that unwavering strength that made her beauty even more radiant, pure and unscathed, beauty that a world of pain had failed to tarnish. From the inside out and beyond her skin thrived an endless reservoir of cheer, and it unnerved me to think what she'd derived from a look at me.

"You're a friend," she finally approved, her stern gaze edging into the smile from our first encounter.

I'd made it! I'd passed that horrible test as well as that defiant hole. She stepped forward, lent her hand and gently kissed both cheeks, assured she'd found me sincere.

"I'm Kaylaira."

"Kaylaira. What a name to remember," I helplessly toyed beneath my breath.

We melded as easily as nature, like autumn's changing leaves or the first blooms of spring. She gazed at me without hesitance, without reserve, as rapt with my presence as I was with hers. Or was it nothing more than my style of arrival that gave her such restfulness? But why?

"Jordan," she softly uttered; her lips sampling each syllable like a taste of wine. "No one has arrived in your manner for ages. We have our lores, but nothing any of us have witnessed to tell. Your manifestation here is … beyond delight. Grateful arrival to Elatia."

"Elatia. Another beautiful name," I said, still fixated on why her ease at my 'manner of arrival.' "What is it about my manner of arriving that brings you relief?"

Her brows crinkled and her mind shifted to a deeper thought.

"Because we're not ready for what's to come, and I was afraid you were them, the MonTu and the beginning of 'their arrival.' They manifest themselves from the water and sky, but with much more malicious pursuits. But you are not them," she sighed, her brows smoothing back to an eased expression.

"They don't sound too friendly," I presumed.

Her intense glare told me something deadly was about to happen, washing me with her wave of dread. Whatever was to come, they'd already prepared for the worst.

"No, they are not. For as long as we can remember, 'the arrivals' have only brought genocide. My parents, their parents, and so on. My mother perished as a result of the last, and because of them I was never acquainted with my pre-parents. So when I look at you Jordan and sigh relief, it's because I see hope. Please accept my gratitude for finding no evil in your nature," she smiled, "Hope."

"I'm sorry for starting the conversation in such a dark tone," I sympathized. "I didn't know. Why do they come? The MonTu?"

"Fuel," she answered, "to power their distant reigns. Our planet powers them, their fleet, their warriors, all for a term of eight cycles, and then they return."

Eight cycles? My mind spun through equations, starting with her features that conveyed an age of no more than eighteen. Was it too soon to ask? Rude in her culture? I guessed a cycle fell close to a year, making the arrival every eight? How could a planet power a space traveling militia for eight years? That's when I knew I was dreaming and sputtered a laugh of disbelief, and she quickly tuned in to my apprehension.

"Why do you laugh? Our planet is small, but one of a kind!" she defended. "A unique flow of energy surges from our core. An energy that powers, energizes, and heals."

"Must be why your air here is so funny."

"Funny? How so?" she asked.

I assumed she'd know, then cupped a draft in my palm and shoved it between her ankles as a brief demonstration. A heap of dirt puffed onto her feet, and that's when it all changed. Her jaw plunged. Her eyes ricocheted from the ground as both pupils burst like a broken gum ball machine.

"What is it?" I stepped back alarmed.

Her body went weightless and dropped her to her knees, as if she'd forsaken all the respect and manners she'd learned.

"A w-wind, a wind driver!" she gasped with her eyes still bloated. "The others! There's little time. We must inform the others!"

In one swift action she clasped my hand and pulled herself to her feet, already circled back to drag me the other direction. "Come," she implored, with her thrust nearly wrenching my shoulder from its socket.

"Wait, wait," my feet dug in, but she possessed the pull of a man. "Kaylaira, wait. Slow down. Wind what?"

I yanked back with all my strength to keep her at bay, but her spirit was wild and untamed, her pulse pounding in the grip of my hand. Physically, I couldn't stop her. It was my hesitation she saw, my fear and uncertainty that somewhat subdued her aggression as she synced with my terror filled eyes.

"How did you come to be here?" she blurted, out of breath.

I knew no other way than to tell the truth. So out went my story starting with the cave, finding the stone and how it led me to that dream on the beach. Except, I was no longer sure it was a dream. Was it? Things got weirder by the minute. I was fully aware of what was happening and had full control. Dreams are hazy and fuzzy, a constant flux leaving you tussling to get where you're going. But not this. This was tangible. There was progression, and instead of recurring, it conveniently picked up where I'd left off?

"A bijou!" she exclaimed, "You discovered a bijou. You are a wind driver! You command the zephyr at will!"

"Zephyr? Bijou? Wait, how does finding a special stone in a cave make me, a… wind driver?" I asked, not wanting to say it aloud.

"A bijou is not found, it presents itself and only one pertains to each world," she answered. "Somehow, you found the one leading to ours."

My throat tightened and I tried not to panic! It was still a cool dream, right?

"Can I give it back?" I asked, slightly distressed. "What am I to do with it?"

"No. It cannot be returned," she giggled, as if I'd made the most absurd request in the history of life's existence. "Who would? It is the highest honor."

The swell in my throat tightened. I nervously convinced myself I was still in a dream, then clung to that notion to not hyperventilate. So, dream it was and I played along. If I didn't like or want what I saw, I'd simply wake up, rid myself of the stone and never sleep again, right?

"Okay, Kaylaira," I pleaded for her reasoning ear, without a drop of her attention broken from my lips. "Please understand, I have no clue what this means. Bijou, zephyr, wind driver? I'm a commonplace teenager with an extraordinarily boring life. I learn at a school." I babbled and laughed as if she understood the word. "I may sneak a beer from time to time. I did forge Mom's signature, but that's it. That is it! That doesn't make me a rebel or a badass ready to take on some space fighting militia. I'm not that guy! I'm not whatever it is you believe me to be. I don't even think this is real. Is it?"

She met me with a blank stare. Might as well have spoken it in Chinese, or perhaps she just didn't care. I leaned back, still pulling to keep her from dragging me to the wolves when her tension lessened. Finally, she released me. Her manner softened and her gaze inhaled me with an indulgent warmth. Her stare kept me captive, trapping me in her world unable to break away.

"You're not alone, Jordan. We learn this together," she gently affirmed. "This is the first we've discovered this as well, so be at peace and know that I'll keep by your side our entire journey."

Our entire journey? A thousand people could whisper those words in that exact fashion and not one of them could overwhelm me the way she did. I was but a weightless seashell and her words were the sea. Helpless and overtaken, the trust embedded in her gaze surrendered me to her resolve, when the call of my name spooked me from beyond.

"Jordan," the familiar voice far from Kaylaira's called. "Jordan, it's late. Are you sure you're okay to stay home alone from school?"

I searched the forest, stunned to realize it was Mom's voice solely in my head. Had she invaded my dream? Her words floated from the kitchen, over to where I slept on the living room sofa. It was the most bizarre thing I'd experienced, me realizing I'd overslept for school while dwelling on another planet. However, I was far from wanting to wake up. So I excused myself from Kaylaira like a fool and tried the only sensible thing I thought of, answer back.

"Mom?" I mumbled in my groggy morning voice, still gripping that fantasy while determined not to wake. "Please, I just need sleep. I'm okay, I promise to call."

"Okay, dear. Make sure to check in."

Her kiss jumped the space and time that kept us so distant before landing on my cheek. I was baffled to feel the press of her lips against my skin but still refused to wake up. For once, being groggy finally worked in my favor. Mom knew that my morning routine was done with my eyes closed.

With Mom and school put behind me, I turned to Kaylaira, shocked and in doubt that I'd bought into her story. But when her hand extended and begged I take hold, I forgot the world and she alone was enough. As for what I was about to delve into, I had no inkling, but not a second went by where I could resist. Destined for whatever journey she pledged, I reached out and accepted her hand.

Chapter Twelve

What life would I find amongst her people? Peace? Turmoil? Perhaps some outlandish trial to gain a rite of passage? She promised none of the above and agreed to acclimatize me to their ways before my dramatic debut. If it was time spent with her then how could I lose?

She clasped my hand with no reserves as we headed back to shore, as if we were two children oblivious to the spark of arousal. Not I. Chills crawled my arm each time she brushed against me as I selfishly indulged her hand. It was bliss, blood rushing and heart pounding at the temples, while she narrated the way of their land. I should've listened. I needed to know where I was and why I was there, so back on shore I forced myself to hear her words.

"How old are you?" I asked, as we nestled in sand.

"I've survived seventeen cycles," she answered.

Would that equate to seventeen years? Was she old, young? How long was a cycle? Her looks screamed my age, but a life of breathing that air could've place her well-beyond me! Never had I wanted to be more than just a senior in school, hoping that she and I were on par.

"I've survived eighteen years, barely," I chuckled. "Up until my recent exploits in the cave. How many cycles? I'm not sure."

Tales of her land kept me on edge. I was all ears, other than the glimpses I stole from her skin that freely peaked from her clothing. Not out of self-gratification, but rather an irresistible curiosity. She was flawless, free from any blemish or bruise as if she existed outside of time, untouched by the harsh realities of illness or imperfection. She beamed like the soft aura enfolding a candlelight, and I couldn't help but wonder if she'd ever known the evils of sickness?

"When were you last ill, or didn't feel well?" I asked, drawing her blank.

"Ill? Harmful within? You refer to the re-creation?"

"Re-creation?" I misunderstood.

I expounded, but sickness was a state of being far from her knowledge, something that only happened during a time she called 'the re-creation.'

"I am one of fortune," she explained. "Few of my people experience a life as full as mine, so we taste it to the fullest, assuring everything we do is rich, plentiful, and with no scarcity. But every eighth cycle, our planet's life is bled from its veins and all you see is taken by the MonTu."

The MonTu were the culprits that descended from the sky, thus her persistence to understand my manner of arriving. It was a process they deemed as 'the transference,' an extraction of their energy and life via their planet's core. All vitality would be siphoned away, and once the MonTu rejuvenated and sought what they were after, they'd abandon her people to scavenge for crumbs.

"When you say nothing—" I started.

"Nothing," she interjected, slicing my sentence in half. "No life. No green. No food or wildlife. The forest is as barren as this sand, with the spirit of our world vanquished. The prosperity you see is merely a result of time. It eventually heals, before they return."

"Then how do you survive?" I rushed to ask.

Her eyes misted, with hatred bundled in two tear globs. "Most do not. The transference leaves few, and the time after finishes most who remain. My mother gave birth to me during an arrival. I guess I was too young to understand what really took place. I remember stockpiles of dried fruits and grain, extensive periods in darkness hidden from light. We dwell beneath the surface when they arrive, enduring bouts of starvation or the time you call, ill."

Her eyes latched to a small shell she twirled in her hand, reliving a hurtful memory as if it flickered on its crust, then a tear finally trailed down her cheek.

"Your family?" I softly edged on. She nodded, still fastened to the shell.

"At first, we ate small meals as a family, but then I remembered wondering why the men would just sit and watch. Only the mothers and children would eat. After some time, my mother joined them. They sat so weak and frail, could barely move, but always watched with a smile as we ate alone. And I, quickly becoming wrathful when my belly wasn't full," she confessed, as a second tear trailed the first. "What I'd give today to have understood. It's not the transference that kills you Jordan, it's the time that follows, the time during the re-creation."

Her tears sunk me into distress and her grief locked me in their cause. This girl I barely knew, a figment of my imagination, wrenched my heart as if her lost family were mine. My stomach churned. My mind spun with anger and wonderment. Who could be so callous, behave so heartlessly to someone so pure? What cruelty in the universe had shaped such self-seeking brutes to willingly deprive their needs for selfish gain? Outsiders so cruel to let children, families and even babies perish. For what? To power an army? And do what with that power? Why not fight back? The thought vomited from my lips.

"Why give in? Why not resist, fight back?" I urged, feeling I was a part of their fight.

"Resist?" she scoffed. "We did! Our ancestors long ago. That's when we were introduced to will-benders, enforcers sent to punish our retaliation and taught us to never try again!"

"Will-benders?"

"Yes. And as a reminder of our ancestors' uprising, a customary offering is now rendered upon each arrival. Four are chosen to serve them at the onset of their call. If our offering pleases and fulfills what they require, they gift them with honorary deaths, a sacrifice that allows the remaining to go untouched."

Death? A sacrifice they thought to be honorable? Her words set me ablaze like flames on a trail of fuel. I looked about, recapturing the most peaceful dwelling imaginable then glared back into her eyes. She had no malice and knew of no malevolence. But surely she was right. She seemed as defenseless as a baby hatchling, and any attempt to defy entities beyond the stars would sure be their endgame.

She grazed my arm to calm the ardor her tales had unchained. My fists had unknowingly tightened and my posture stood on guard. My brows even touched from aggression that not even she herself unveiled. But with the glide of her fingers, all tension bled out, sopping my rage like water on a blistering flame.

"Guess I understand your first question a little better now, from water or sky, but I still don't see where this places me," I said, unsure how a stone from a cave positioned me amongst them.

Then the first smile since the onset of her explanation broke free. "You are a wind driver," she happily uttered.

Wind drivers, their legends of ancient warriors who once roamed their lands, second only to the king himself. They ruled the skies and were masters over wind and air. Wind drivers were untouchable and the protectors of their lands.

"A swipe of their hand was said to destroy armies," she exclaimed, returning her to vigorous belief.

"So what became of them? I pursued.

"Time. They were eventually spread thin, squandered and outnumbered in swarms of battles with the MonTu," she explained. "But that was then. This is now, and you can help us!"

Until that moment, I'd forced myself to reason that their world was but a wild dream. But the longer I listened, the less I wanted to believe. My legs even sprang me up from the sand, a natural reflex to avoid facing what I was about to do. Hear any more, or open my eyes and face the unknown on the other side?

"Kaylaira, I want to believe, but this is beyond me. I'm not even sure I'm really here, with you, in this land!" I exclaimed. "And me? Of all people? You have no idea."

Before I could object further she stepped close and took my hand, her eyes piercing me like two sharp needles.

"Could you at least try?" she implored.

Could I try? How could I refuse? From that day I never found the strength to pull away from her. Her words carried a gentle charm, making me realize that she was the answer to dreams I'd yet dared to dream. I yearned to be close to her, tethered from that point forward to the sound of her voice.

"How can I try?" I asked, skeptic, yet weakening to her resolve.

"Collectively, with help from the others. We start with the village to see what they know, then piece our history together. It's the only way. I wish I alone were enough, but I'm not," she regrettably acknowledged. "Please, all I need is for you to try. Give yourself and us a chance to understand why you're suddenly here."

The real me vanished in her hands, as did my resolve, and before knowing it I'd already made up my mind.

"Okay," I faltered, "Let's find a way to stop them."

CHAPTER THIRTEEN

I was on the brink of hysteria, moments from feeling I'd collapse. Psychosis? Some degenerative neural episode I suddenly faced? What delusion had I undergone, and how long would that dream or alternate perception play out before I was declared mentally insane?

First off? Me, some expected savior of their world? My cheeks twinged at the absurdity, working themselves into a grin of denial as I gritted my teeth to choke back laughter. What would happen once she realized what I wasn't, and how far was I to go before the point of no return?

As we trekked to her village, the unearthly sounds of their forest kept my head in a spiral. Every crackle and clatter spun me in a different direction. My eyes wandered like two rolling marbles, back and forth between Kaylaira's smile and the forest's bubbling life. But her hand kept in mine, my anchor and the only reason I pushed on through that carved path of towering jungle.

Somehow, in that sea of greenery, there was peace and control, a perfect balance between order and havoc as if every plant and tree had found its rightful place on the planet. No plant rivaled another's territory, no trees lay haphazardly in a space it didn't own and no carpet of deadened foliage blanketed the ground. Nature thrived in its own wild harmony, yet simultaneously classified as a true jungle.

I often left the forest's intricacies to study her thoughts, searching for signs of deception that would warn me away. Deceit however, was not in her nature. Her eyes sparkled from the life around and her jubilant smile budded from within, fed from the peace and serenity of her land. And my presence? Nothing short of spurring her ambition to protect the place she called home.

It took me a moment to relax and immerse myself in what she saw. But I eventually found it, tracing her glee back into the forest. What a mind-boggling world it was. Soaring trees shaded us from the sun. Sprouting limbs hovered over us like hanging bridges over city highways, each teeming with a kaleidoscope of life. Winged and creepy crawlers burst with feisty colors, buzzing on and off leaves large enough to wrap a baby.

A monstrous gecko emerged the length of my arm, speckled with blue and sun-bright green. Its lightning speed scurried it up a tree, shooing a flock of fiery birds into the sky with their orange and red feathers painting the ground from takeoff. From one side to the other life dashed above, then disappeared into the thick before emerging someplace else. It was a guessing game. Which magical door would unveil what life hidden behind?

Kaylaira traipsed fearless, bold and unafraid. I was edgy and jerked my sight from one marvel to the next.

"You're safe," she assured as she caught my unease. "There's nothing here to fear."

Her timing was impeccable, but didn't keep my skin from falling from my bones as a ball of fur speared towards me faster than my eyes could follow. Off a tree branch it dove to the ground, then lunged straight at me. There was no time to see anything else, except for its flesh shredding claws before my eyelids buckled. My legs stiffened. My back locked in place. I tensed for a slash to the face when my arms filled with a ball of overflowing fur. I bit my lip to keep my terror in my mouth.

"Wonder!" Kaylaira softly rebuked it, watching me pretend I hadn't melted into a puddle of fear. Was I to run? Fight? Hold still? "Easy," she muttered with every bit of calm.

Her hand landed on my heart as if she'd heard its thump. It slowed my breathing, but my heart resumed fiercely as I cranked my head across the two-inch gap, engaging the two ginormous eyes staring back. Its claws could've grated the flesh from my bone as it bounded from my arms into hers. But it did so with such gentle care, then propped on her hip like a toddler.

To recall 'I was safe' was a challenge, but it still seemed the case at the time, even as those cavernous, murky eyes the size of silver dollars inhaled my gaze like two black holes. It had no pupils. Shades of electric blue highlighted its woolly face, enhancing the brown and burnt orange shading the tips of its white fur. But beyond its features I found something remarkable, something I'd only found in a human being… a seemingly charming expression.

Four arms protruded from its torso, each ending with two fingers and a thumb. Its face resembled a monkey's, with long, sharp ears that jutted up like a bat's, capable of hearing even the faintest of sounds from miles away. Back home if we saw it, we'd run.

"Jordan, meet Wonder," Kaylaira introduced us.

Wonder glanced me over, blinked with an inner eyelid, then reached to greet me with one of its four arms.

"It wants to formally greet me by hand?" I asked with excitement outweighing fear. "This is unreal!"

Slowly I extended my shaky hand, erupting with giddy laughter as its callous palm gripped my fingertip. My first handshake with an alien, a creature beyond basic instinct capable of intellect and delight. Wonder was in fact adorable, and it was his innocence that altered the way I perceived the forest.

"Why name him Wonder?" I asked.

"Because we have no idea from where he came. He's the only one of his kind we know of; perhaps a non-native," she said. "Some believe he was abandoned or forsaken by the MonTu during an arrival many cycles ago."

Kaylaira naturally roused its playful manner, and as she removed a nut from a hidden pouch lining her inner clothing, it gave thanks by fluxing its multi-colored tail. He cracked the shell with teeth I'd hate within any range of my fingers, then gobbled the nut like a ravaged beast. Still, their connection was strong and singular, bordering that of a mother and child while he coddled her hand as she stroked his fuzzy head.

"With those teeth, I sure hope he remembers me," I said at a second glance.

"Remember? Not a problem," she smirked, "His memory is flawless; once he sees, he never forgets, no matter the volume or complexity. Here, give me your hand," she swayed me with a morsel placed in my palm.

Wonder's sweet charm rose to the surface, and it was nearly impossible to see him as a threat. My panting faded. My heart dropped to a *slower* beat as I edged my trusting hand towards its mouth. But he saw food and I was way too slow. So fed up with my dawdling it snatched it from my hand, then munched it down before again fluttering its tail. Then with a quick embrace around Kaylaira's neck, it was off her shoulder and up a tree, vanished like the wind while I struggled finding to where he'd gone.

"Any other furry surprises waiting to greet me?" I asked with my eyes in the trees.

"Trust the forest. I promise you'll find no harm," she reassured to mellow my fears. "In fact, take a moment and I'll show you. Close your eyes, inhale the air and listen for your aria."

"My what?" I asked.

"Your aria. Listen up high to the swaying trees. To the flyer's chirps and whistles, the trills and croaks of the critters crawling the soil, then tell me what you hear," she explained.

My aria? Feeling as dumb as a rock, I closed my eyes and opened my ears, unsure what I'd find that would instill such trust.

"Do you hear it?" she asked.

At first I had no clue what to listen for, hearing nothing more than forest clatter.

"Listen closer," she insisted and grabbed my hand.

Her touch sunk me in the soil, and only then did I sense the hidden that I couldn't before. It was more than just the melodic birdsongs that rivaled a symphony, there was something more that raised a smile to my face. The deeper I listened, the stronger it became.

Each chirp and whistle began to sync with the next, weaving its way through the air with a hauntingly beautiful melody that seemed to speak to my soul alone. Lost in its melodic tune my past and present vanished. My ability to know worry or fear disappeared as I was rendered helpless in a web of peace, till my body hit the ground and jolted me awake.

"Whoa!" I spurted, barely stopping my face from eating dirt. The shock stole my breath, snapped me from a cheer I could've dwelt in for ages.

"How did it feel?" she asked, exhilarated with my initial response!

I could barely answer.

"What was that?" I asked, still unable to catch my breath. "Music? I can't explain, but it was music— incredible sounding music that came from everywhere. Every sound conformed to a tune, a lullaby. And I'm not sure how I know this, but was it just for me? My own written tune? Was I the only one to hear it? Is that what you meant— my aria?"

"Yes, the zephyr's enchanting sounds, and what the open sings, is for you alone. Each hears what it wishes," she smiled. "Try again."

Excitement nearly kept me from settling down, but with a deep breath and the caress of her hand, I closed my eyes and gnawed my way back. The chirps. The buzzes. Each sound skirted the next, and before knowing it my serenade flowed, my aria, stumbling me into a place of unspeakable harmony as the tune washed over me as it had before.

Every trouble I'd felt was tossed out the window as every grain of me struck leveled plain. Balance of thought, of self, balance of will and purpose with her world. Relaxed would be an understatement. It was the dream dreams dreamed of dreaming. Bliss and a moment of perfection, disallowing evil or negative to be evoked even if I tried. I embraced the zephyr's tune with all I had, until her finger poked my cheek.

"Jordan," she whispered.

I struggled to open my eyes, but not as I would from a dreary sleep. I hungered to remain there, to keep that state of peace and clarity for fear I'd never find it again.

"Jordan," she again whispered, her thumb gently prodding my eyelids.

I opened them, glaring up into the overhead branches with my head sunk in, grass? I pried myself from the cushion of blades, grasping to find how I'd gone from standing to sprawling on the forest floor. Kaylaira sat cross-legged before me, delighted to nourish a small range of creatures that bundled up to her hands.

"What? That's weird. I could've sworn we were standing," I said, still woozy.

"You were," she snickered, scattering the animals with a brush of crumbs. "After some time, you made yourself more comfortable here on the ground."

"Some time?" I asked. "How? I barely closed my eyes."

"Actually, it's been a small portion of our burn," she debated, pointing at the position of their sun. "But you were melding with our land and I didn't want to wake you. I wanted you to take it in. It'll make you strong."

A small portion of the day? I measured the sun and ran numbers through my head as if I'd know how to calculate the difference. But then again, why else was I nestled in grass? I wanted to care for the hours I'd lost, but at the same time I didn't, still longing to preserve that serenity.

"How do you feel?" she asked, helping me to my feet.

"Like I'm not the same Jordan anymore," I laughed, still shaking the persistent calm wanting to pull me back under. "Like I de-aged? As if years of worry are gone."

"Good. The village then? Are you ready?" she asked.

"I am."

My aria! That was the point I realized it wasn't a dream. And without a care in the world and more primed than ever, I took her hand and to the village we went.

CHAPTER FOURTEEN

I no longer feared the inquisitive critters springing onto our path, poking their hands and mouths for a handful of treats Kaylaira always seemed to have. But eventually, our tree coverage thinned and the lush foliage dispersed, where the makings of every childhood fantasy fell into view.

Wonderment sunk my lip like a torpedoed ship, then adrenaline rushed my limbs as I leveled on the edge of their village. The soaring trees were first to awe me, like standing in a cathedral of nature where each trunk towered a hundred feet high. Their branches stretched forty to fifty feet out, interlocking like two loving hands with the adjacent trees. It was a bridgeway of timber in the skies, like the towering highways in larger cities.

But their heights didn't awe me alone, it was the tops and middle trunks, each outfitted with seemingly impossible tree homes. I had a tree house once, if it's what you'd venture to call it. These however, belonged in a fairytale. There were balconies I'd die to sit upon to watch distant sunsets, or to overlook the horizon from a bird's eye view.

A child suddenly dropped from one and took my gaze with her, plummeting forty feet on a wooden plank, down a pulley system balanced with weighted stones at its end. It was clear that they'd mastered both beauty and functionality, and I couldn't help but feel admiration for what they'd accomplished.

Her ride carried her below into a wide tempered river, where every tree trunk plunged beneath its waters. I couldn't help but smile as I watched! What other way was there to feel? The tranquility even detached me from Kaylaira's hand, something I thought impossible as I plopped on the river's edge and took it all in. Next to me, elated, she watched me gobble it in like an overfilled hand of popcorn.

Children frolicked barefoot from one tree to the next, across root systems that crawled like snakes between trees. Roots were their everything, the same as the branches above, from barricading small swim holes at the base of each tree to serving as passageways. Some stalks skimmed the river's surface, others climbed high from the water's edge, begging the young to plunge from platforms into their naturally created pools.

"Look, a traveler!" an ecstatic child yelled from up high.

His voice carried through the trees and roused dozens of spirited children from their playful sports. Then I realized his finger had landed on me.

"A traveler! Yeah! From where?" they excitedly screamed, scurrying from their places to find who Kaylaira had brought in.

Some splashed from the water, others poured from their balconies like slow drips of honey. I jumped to my feet as the village converged, looking to Kaylaira as my only sense of guidance, but calm continued to define her.

"No worries, remember?" she said, gently resting her hand on my shoulder to ease my agitation.

It freed me of worry, surrendering me to the onslaught of young, drenched children rushing me like a horde of eager puppies. No restraint held them back as they welcomed me as family. The gathering mass pushed and peacefully shoved, removing small jewels from their arms and necks as they alternated presenting their tokens of appreciation.

What had I done? To what did I owe such kindness? Back home I'd need a reason. But there? Absolutely nothing. It was second nature, with no excuse needed beyond the simple welcoming of a guest. I gladly accepted their gifts and embraces, plucking strings in my heart and nearly drawing tears as I bit back the urge from their eager greeting faces.

A thin leather strap made its way around my neck, just like Kaylaira's, with a purple translucent crystal dangling on its end. Then another, bright orange. Then another before my arms were next, weighed with smaller gems on stringed bracelets shaded every color of the spectrum. Their vivacious welcome never ceased. Eventually, their weight forced me from my heels to my butt as they squatted next to me touching my skin, twirling my hair while probing my textured fabrics.

"From where do you hail? From water or sky? Are you among us now?" the questions jumbled in. "Are you MonTu? Are you here to take us from our homes?" a worrisome child asked. My heart fell apart with no answer to give.

"Calm down, children," Kaylaira insisted. "One at a time. He is a friend to us with no need to worry."

"What's your name?" a little one asked.

I was still taken back with what they knew they'd soon face, barely able to squeak my name. "I'm Jordan."

"Funny," the girl giggled.

"Oh yeah? And what's yours?" I asked.

"Naymelia."

"Naymelia. That's one of the most beautiful names I've ever heard."

A smile and rosy cheeks blushed her face, wiggling her tiny fingers into my hand as she instantly became fond of my presence.

"Uh oh, someone likes you," Kaylaira whispered.

"I don't know what to say," I stumbled. "Thank you. Thank you all for these gifts. This is unreal, and yes, you have nothing to worry about. I mean, no, no you have nothing to worry about. Kaylaira was right; I am a friend."

Everything Kaylaira had word fed me echoed in my ear, blazing the harrowing imagery of their doom through my head. Their enemy descending from the clouds. Losing their utopia of a home while the green around turned to scorched earth. The deaths of their families and planet repeated without end and all collapsed on me at once. But to see them at that moment, with the dark storm that would soon hover their home, made it impossible to believe their joy. How could they flush it from their demeanor? To what extent did the children know what would happen? Perhaps all the details were yet to be revealed?

"Come see our home!" one insisted with a yank on my hand.

The others shouted in compliance, with Kaylaira removing the gifts from my neck and arms to let them drag me to a stalk from a nearby tree. The stalk was no more than a couple feet wide and not all of us fit at once. So several rushed ahead tugging my arm, some loitered behind with Kaylaira while others raced across the adjacent roots along parallel trees.

The wood was slick and uneven. Dips and grooves could trip or leave me with a stubbed toe, not to mention the unwanted plunge in the river. With my boots providing some grip, I spread my free arm to keep balance while they charged barefoot without a thought of it.

"Here, this way!" a child insisted.

He diverted me from an entwining stairwell, up to the wooden plank they used to plummet from above.

"This way is more fun, trust me!" he exclaimed.

I hesitated, wondering if it would handle my weight when they shoved me on before I could respond. With both feet atop the plank, the rope sat in between.

"Medium!" a child yelled up.

"Gotcha!" the other yelled down, leaning his head from the balcony edge.

I'd lost track of Kaylaira, my refuge, racing to spot her in the crowd as a jolt sent me up. She seemed undisturbed and gave no reason to abandon my quest, so on I went, lifting past a beach ball sized rock suspended from the other end of the pulley. A crank system reeled me up and the rock countered my weight.

Fifteen feet, thirty, forty-five. It was a taller tree of course, with those anticipating my ascent from below shrinking like ants on a log.

The faster ones raced up ladders and pulleys of nearby trees, waiting to greet me up top. I was nearly there, within reach of the balcony when a crackle halted the reel.

I clutched the rope, my lifeline while I helplessly dangled sixty feet in the air. My heart raced between fear and exhilaration. My muscles tensed, and even the slightest breeze seemed to make me sway, heightening my sense of exposure.

"Uh oh," the child reeling me up uttered.

I barely found Kaylaira, but saw the assurance leave her face.

"Is everything okay?" she shouted.

"The pulley just—" the kid attempted to explain, silenced by a brash pop I'd rather have not heard.

The tension released, the plank let go and the air once considered a friend became my enemy. Down I plunged with my heart in my throat, screaming bloody murder while spinning head over heel. Fear suffocated the air from my lungs. All I saw was the river, waiting for me like a dead end. With less than ten feet to fall my eyes squeezed tight, envisioning my fate end with a splat over water. I thrusted my hands forward as if I'd stop, but just before the water's reach, a shove between the shoulders sprung me awake.

"No!" I belted, leaping from the cushions on my living room sofa.

"Jordan! Wake up!" Mom asserted as she shook my arm. "What's the matter with you?"

My hair was damp. The pillow cushion was drenched with sweat. Out of breath and damned in a daze, I came to grips with the squeeze of Mom's hand, and the wipe of her sleeve across my beading forehead.

"Honey, snap out of it!" she implored with a nervous chortle. "You were dreaming. Don't worry, you're still here on this raggedy sofa. You're not falling anywhere," she laughed amused.

I sat up cautious as if the river still baited me, scooting against the armrest of our couch. It felt assuring to feel it jammed against my back as she plopped in front of me with plenty of chuckles left in her belly.

"Don't you hate those? When you're just falling for no reason?" she asked.

"Yeah. Something like that," I spat out still catching my breath.

She headed to the kitchen and heated the kettle, explaining her need to come early to check on me. Thank goodness she had.

"Wait. A little early? What time is it?" I asked, wondering how long I'd spent adrift.

"It's five, honey. I only left an hour early," she answered.

"5pm? I slept the entire day?" I retorted.

I'd fallen asleep before she left for work. The sleep didn't bother me, it was believing I'd been in 'la la' land no more than a couple hours when in reality I'd been there all day. Three hours max, I guestimated, before shuffling the numbers in my head. My half cooked up calculation; an hour of real time gone for every twenty minutes of dream time. The entire day had passed!

I wiped the worry from my face as she returned with a cup of tea.

"Find anything interesting in your father's office?" she asked.

"Yeah, um, a couple of rocks," I mumbled for a laugh. "I guess I'm trying to look at things the way he did; see his work through his eyes to know if there's something I'm missing."

"Something in particular you're looking for?"

I wanted to tell her but decided to swallow that pill.

"Not sure yet," I answered.

We finished our tea and a short Mom and son talk, all with me trying not to explode. I couldn't relate what I'd experienced without sending her over the edge, not after my adventures in the cave. But I had to tell someone! Anyone! I had to tell Nijal!

Chapter Fifteen

It was time I fickle with my best friend's head and engage his twisted, fantasy filled, alternate mind of reality. Movies, video game storylines, comic books, he'd seen and read them all, and he and I had been locked at the hip since first grade. What I knew he knew. What he knew, well everyone knew. He'd start a sentence, I'd finish it. I'd dart him a look, he knew what I thought. He'd be the first to laugh the hardest and loudest, but the last to judge strongly for what I was about to tell him. I banged on the back door of 'Beans'—the café where he bussed tables after school. He knew my knock.

"Welcome to Beans!" he swung the door open and yelled. "Dude, you're a celebrity!"

"What?" I asked with no clue what he referenced.

"You looked great on the news, covered in blankets and mud. Couldn't come by, so tried calling and texting but no reply," he informed while whipping off his filthy apron.

"My phone is busted. Listen, you got a minute?" I scurried.

"Yeah, I could use a break. Why, what's up? What else you do?" he insinuated.

He already knew I was out of character, closing the back door as we plopped on two trash cans. I'd rehearsed how to tell him my goings-on but never perfected the delivery. Is there ever a right way to deliver 'I'm crazy?'

"Look. I have to tell you something," I blurted, already off the trash can and pacing. "And before you ask, no, I'm not crazy and no, I haven't been smoking any funny fumes."

"Riiiight. I'll be the judge of that. Come on, spit it out, let's hear it."

Still unsettled on how to put it, I simply pulled the stone from my pocket and handed it to him. His eyes sparked with the same curiosity, then he dropped it of course, before holding it to the sunlight with one squinted eye. 'A mosquito in amber inside?' Or had I given him a 'dinosaur egg?' He'd guess all day if I allowed it, but my patience ran empty. I cut him short and narrated every turn, from the cave to my recurring dream without a breath in between. Then I waited, out of breath and at the end of my story with just a long blank stare returned.

"Yeah, you're definitely on something strong, buddy," he laughed. His chuckles grew louder each second. "Sure you don't have any more to share? Just for experimental purposes? You know, see if I have the same dream so that way I can help you?"

"Listen, cut the crap, Nijal. I need you to stop being five for a moment and believe me," I insisted.

"Okay fine. I'll be six," he giggled.

I was nuts! Why believe I could tell anyone, him included? Nijal's a lot to handle, spilling pranks and sarcasm before his first morning piss. I'd grown immune to it, just not that day and decided to jump on my bike when he grabbed my arm.

"Okay, okay, relax. I'll be serious, but come on, dude. You know me! Do you really expect to tell me this and me not laugh?" he answered, still biting back a smirk. "I mean, really? Me?"

He had a point. Would I not have laughed in his face?

"I know, I know. Just try and amuse me. Imagine it's real and guide me through it. Pretend I'm a character in one your stupid video games," I pleaded.

He recapped what I'd told him, or at least the parts he'd heard. There was a hot girl, I possibly had powers, and yeah, there was a hot girl, leaving him to ramble on about me always being the lucky one, apparently even as I slept.

"Focus!" I asserted. "Character? Movie? Story? What would happen in one of your fantasy stories?"

He actually became serious.

"Okay, okay. First off, my games aren't stupid. Secondly, in pretend world, everything happens for a reason, always," he started. We were finally getting somewhere! "It's the evolution of good vs. evil. It's always there with nature constantly struggling to balance the two. That being said, if you met someone it's for a reason. If you have powers, it's for a reason. You don't just get powers, okay? So better learn why and better learn how to use them, 'cuz I'm sure it means you're about to get your ass kicked by something bigger and much stronger than you. Let's see what else?"

He thought long and hard, the same scrunched face from math class when trying to solve an equation. What I found provoking? I never told him of the MonTu arrival, I never told him of a bigger threat.

"Oh yes, you met the beautiful girl for a reason so—" he laughed. "No need to neglect that, my friend! I mean, might as well have a little fun while roaming in Pretendville, right?"

He went on to explain that my placement was no coincidence, so I needed to find my place and purpose. Learn my enemy. Find the key, or the box of secrets hidden in every culture's past. Possibly things they knew or may not know or simply didn't wish to tell me.

"You really want me to indulge in this?" he smirked; he was on to something, on a roll and didn't want to stop.

"Yes, please!" I prodded him on.

"Okay, okay, just, I don't wanna get into this, you know, get going and then you're like, 'Oh I'm just kidding around, man' and make me look like an idiot after I'm all warmed up," he warned.

"I won't, come on. I promise, I need this. Keep going," I confirmed. He saw it real, in my eyes at least. "Believing me or not is your choice. Just help me first."

"Okay, so um, tell me about this thing you do with the air, your powers?" he mocked me with air quotes.

"Well, so far, I've noticed I can push air," I told him.

"Push air?" he sarcastically laughed. "So can I, every time I eat a cheeseburger and fries! Does that mean I have powers on Earth?" he chuckled.

Too vague. Once his cackling settled I explained what happened on the shore, the movement of air and the feel of it in my hand. And like a loosened kinked hose, the nerd in him gushed free.

"You're an aerokinetic!" he shouted.

"An air-connect what?" I countered confused.

"No! An aero-ki-ne-tic," he uttered, distinctly pronouncing each syllable to highlight my idiocy on the subject. But at least I'd gotten him started.

"Okay, so that means?" I asked.

"Oh, you can fly dude," he insisted with confidence. "Aero kinesis is clearly the best power you could ever have, I would say."

"Flying? That's what I assumed and of course I tried, but let's just agree that it didn't happen," I complained.

"Nah, trust me. If you control the air, you can fly. You're obviously a novice and just don't know how."

"Okay, well what else?"

"What else? You mean, what else can't you do? Dude, it's air! Look how much of it you have floating around. It's everything. That's why it's such an envied ability. Let me dumb this down for you, a lot! You can push junk over or pull it toward you, compress objects or make them expand, deflect projectiles, launch them back, increase your physical attack, boost your speed, turn invisible, create shielding; oh yeah, and fly." he uttered in a single breath. "Give me by tomorrow and I swear I'll have a legit name for each of those moves. Like if you're gonna hurl something, we can be like Jordan, wind repulsion! Man, you better be glad it ain't me over there cuz I'd be king!" he yelled with his arms in the air. "Wait, let me sleep with you."

"Huh?" I jumped back.

"No, no, no," he laughed. "Not like that. Don't get your hopes up. Let me hold the rock and sleep at the same time, see if I can be your travel buddy. Share some of the love, man, especially if you want me to believe you."

Kind of made sense, and he'd just given me the perfect incentive to keep bribing him along.

"Keep helping me through this, and I'll see what I can do. Pretty sure I'll need a ride in your old beetle or a cover story for missing school, king," I sarcastically replied.

"So every time you sleep this happens?" he asked again.

"Every time so far when I have the stone. And this time I'm falling. I'm always falling," I added.

I filled him in on my previous trip-ups in the hole, along with my current plunge from the tree before Mom shook me awake.

"Dude!" he startled me as he jumped from the trash can. "Now's the perfect time!" he blurted, then saw we weren't on the same page for the first time in our lives. "Test your power. You're falling, right? So why not scare the poop from your pants during the fall? Maybe it'll force something bigger out of you, and hopefully that's the only thing you force out. Extreme emotion, that's what you need."

He rambled on and worded it with seemingly undeniable logic, but I still wouldn't bite.

"That, I'll definitely have to sleep on," I told him.

"No, you won't," he threw back, chuckling. "'cuz then it'll be too late."

Right again. With a fist bump we parted ways, leaving me to ponder his strategy during my bike ride home. Once there, I was restless from having slumbered all day, so I settled on the floor of Dad's office and scrounged for missing clues. Understand my purpose. Learn my powers, learn my enemy, find a key and understand why I was there. And yeah, extreme emotion. Did I really care to give that part a try?

I psyched myself for an intentional sixty-foot plunge the moment I'd close my eyes. I'd never been so nervous over the basic concept of falling asleep. What if Nijal was wrong? What if his plan backfired and I ended up killing myself in the dream, or worse, triggered something worst in real life?

Before storming to bed, I shuffled several books in Dad's bottom cabinet, alerted to a clink behind. Jackpot! Father wasn't much of a drinker, but occasionally celebrated new finds with a decent glass of scotch. I never discovered his stash, but having stumbled across his fortune, I too upheld his tradition that would sure help me snooze!

Like every other teen, there'd been times Nijal and I snuck shots here and there, just because, but never a staple nor a cause to abuse. This was different, and for a good purpose I reasoned.

Assuring Mom was out for the night, I anxiously knocked down a glass. Okay, maybe I chugged it. I knew it was sacrilegious to a true scotch connoisseur, especially being the good stuff, but it was too late for guilt. I was floating on cloud nine and smiled without purpose, waddling back to my room with enough sense to cozy on the floor instead of my bed. Last thing I needed was a leap out of my sheets, breaking my neck from a three-foot fall while trying to accomplish a pretend one over fifty.

I yawned and grew woozy as the scotch did its job, then with a pillow beneath my head my eyes suddenly fell. Then the remaining night took to the wind.

Chapter Sixteen

"Here, this way!" a child blared.

I was back. Like deja vu, a cluster of petite hands shoved from all over, pulling me across the roots to the small winding stairwell before nudging me towards the pulley instead. They placed my feet on the wooden plank.

"This way is much more fun, trust me!" the boy exclaimed as he had before.

What the hell was I doing? Was Nijal crazy, and I just as dumb to believe anything he'd said? I should've elbowed them from my path, taken the stairs like any smart person would, but guess I wasn't that smart! Instead, there I stood frozen like a dumb block of ice, and my time was slipping.

"Medium!" the child yelled up.

"Gotcha."

That time I knew exactly where Kaylaira stood as the medium rock flopped over to counter my weight. We locked eyes as the crank jolted up, briefly numbing me to my ascent as the pulley sent me into the sky. Her smile gave me confidence as well as the children's cheers, something I hadn't recalled on my first attempt. Still, what did they know? They had no clue what was about to happen.

Fifteen feet. Twenty-five, thirty-five. My arms and legs trembled. I clenched that rope as if I'd tear it apart but never left Kaylaira's eyes. Forty, forty-five, the point of no return where I idiotically pondered the water's depth. It couldn't have been more than four to five feet deep. Why would I think that then? If it didn't work, I was a dead man.

Crack! Pop!

"Jordan, you've got this," I whispered as the cranking stopped.

Each exhale quivered with fear. My throat was as dry as tree bark and palms shredded from gripping the rope. I'd officially turned psychotic.

"Wind repulsion. Just a push of my palms and I soar, right?" I pumped myself.

"Uh oh," the child uttered.

"Is everything okay?" Kaylaira shouted.

"The pulley just—"

Snap! The tension released and the air freed me again. My eyes pinched closed. My molars slammed tight shoving grunts between my teeth. Head over heel I spotted water, then a tree branch, then water as fear grabbed my throat. Twenty feet. Ten. Extreme emotion? Nope. Nijal was wrong! I wasn't going to make it.

CHAPTER SEVENTEEN

I was drowning, asphyxiating on my own breath as water spattered my face.

"Nooo!" I swung and fought the current.

Or was it water at all? Touch kicked in before sight as my fingers slithered across textured wood. Was I underwater, clinging to one of its roots? I couldn't discern and was still choking when my fingers found another's. But it didn't make sense. They were warm and I held to it for dear life, before realizing I was above ground.

"Relax," the serene voice whispered. "Take deep breaths."

Confusion set in. Was it Mom? Was I sprawled across my sofa, again, or being rescued by a stranger in the cave? Neither. I knew that touch. It differed from others and eased me then the same as it had before. My hectic gulps to breathe slowed. Calmly I sipped the soothing air as it rushed between my lips, coating my throat as it breezed into my lungs.

I couldn't have been under water, not while a damp bandage rested on my forehead, allowing me to trust the blurry world as I opened my eyes. My focus leapt like a ping pong ball from one side to the next, except it wasn't my vision, it was Kaylaira's crystal blue necklace swaying left to right between my eyes. What a perfect way to awaken.

"What happened?" I asked.

She was hesitant to answer. Her interest was more absorbed in what lied in the distance as we rocked side to side in a hammock. Her face was frozen with bewilderment, drawing me from her lap to see what she gazed at when a dizzying headache slapped me back down. The children were there as well, just as bemused and anticipating my awakening.

"They're a little taken back," she warned. "As am I."

Taken back? What had I done? I forced my head up and shook the spin, following her eyes from the children to the tree from where I'd plunged. But it wasn't there. It and its two neighbors tilted aside like leaning towers of Pisa. The bottom trunks sprawled open like claws, half in open air, half beneath water as if the Earth had uprooted them willingly.

"What happened?" I jumped.

"I'm not sure," she replied. "One moment you were falling, and the next an explosion of air. The trees blew back, and water went everywhere."

I hadn't noticed her soaking hair and clothes before then, nor the children's.

"The children?" I panicked, before she quickly calmed me.

"They're safe, happy in fact. You gave them the thrill ride of a lifetime. Trust me, they're grateful," she smirked. "I told you before, we may not have nor look like much, but it takes a lot more than a splash of water to keep us down."

I surveyed the damage as my headache subsided, rattled to the bone by what I'd done. The children fixated on my every move but carefully kept their distance.

"They don't fear you," she comforted me. "Just give a moment for them to take it in. Your ability is a tale we've only heard passed through the ages, never seen with our eyes."

"I'm sorry," I frantically apologized. "I could have hurt one of them. I have no clue what I'm doing and no idea why I even tried in the first place. It was a friend's stupid idea."

"Well. You should thank your friend. In some ways, it worked. It brought something out of you," she smiled. But I was still hesitant to her optimism.

"How can I fix this?" I asked.

"Fix?" she remarked, still as calm as the temperate river. "Nature will heal at its own bidding."

She pointed to the foot of one of the loosened trees. At first I saw nothing, then squinted for a better look, believing I'd fallen in a dream within a dream. I hastened to the water's edge to assure it was real, and it was. The unearthed roots bent and twisted as if bound by a spell, grappling beneath the water to heave their trunks upright.

"As I said before," Kaylaira stepped behind, "our planet holds the unique gift of an extraordinary healing, including you once you learn to use it. It's the reason the MonTu invaded and the purpose of their arrival, said to remove countless lifetimes of injury from their hardened conquests. We know little else outside of our world, but from what we understand, it is an unequivocal power no other possesses nor can replicate."

I reflected on her words, recounting the number of dives I'd taken since I'd arrived, including that one. Not a broken bone. Not a single life-threatening injury. I'd felt pain from each fall, but at some point, it simply vanished. Even as we stood there nothing ached nor bruised. I was as boundless as the hour before.

"Come," she gestured to a distant tree, "or the children will never leave you to rest."

The children bunched as one and lurked a few paces behind. Their gaze addressed me differently, as if I'd reached an elite status that swelled their sense of pride for having witnessed the 'miracle' by my hand. I was less a friend and more a champion, embedding an impression I didn't intend. It was all happening too soon. I'd done nothing yet was already held a hero.

I followed Kaylaira while still plagued with guilt, but in her world pessimism was short-lived as she led me to a prominent tree, the crown jewel of the forest. It buried me beneath its shadow. And near its peak? One of the more astounding tree homes of the forest. Raw timber stretched out like a cone from its trunk, holding the balcony's platform with a three-hundred-and-sixty-degree view on its fringes.

"This is the coolest thing ever," I uttered.

Adrenaline rushed me ahead like a child stepping into his first magical theme park. Lily pads the size of small cars staggered a footpath over water. I thought twice before crossing, but Kaylaira mindlessly dashed to the other side. My first step wobbled. My second even more, but my weight held as she gestured to cross, darting me from one lily pad to the next till I landed against the tree. She smirked mischievously.

"What's so funny?" I asked.

She shied away without a word, guiding me to my answer at the bottom of the narrow stairwell that wrapped the trunk, away from the pulley on the opposite side.

"I imagine this would be a more fitting choice to proceed. Don't you agree?" she asked, tickled with laughter as she grabbed my hand and heaved me up the stairs!

No restraint on my part. I wholeheartedly agreed and looped the seventy-foot climb, but by the time I reached the top, I was spent. Sweat bit my eyes and trickled off my nose. My thighs and calves tingled with the prick of a thousand needles. My lungs blistered as if I'd inhaled my first drag of smoke. All the while, Kaylaira barely winced as we stopped short of her home, just beneath the deck where I masked my exhaustion.

"All this is yours?"

"It is," she smiled.

"How did you ever build this?" I asked, marveling at the mastering craftsmanship from beneath the deck.

"I'd be selfish to claim the credit," she replied. "On occasion, the stronger trees survive the transference and hold to a measure of life. Once the visitors abandon us, even a single tree clinging to a breath can save the weaker. Usually, this one," she exhaled with passion and pride.

Her palm gently grazed the bark as if she felt its heartbeat. That towering pillar of wood was more than a home, it was a life giver, the reason her people and planet endured.

"All you see here has been passed down for generations, having survived numerous sieges and is the closest thing I have to family."

I was bursting to explore, given by my restless legs charging up the remaining steps as she welcomed me onto her balcony. The distant horizon took my first breath, her dwellings took my second, starting with the tree that rose through the center of her home. Ahead, next to the rising trunk? An oval, rotating door where a visionary's artistry excelled at its finest!

A fat letter 'K' sat at its center, written in bold, striking flowers that stretched above my height. They were pressed between thin sheets of papyrus that held them together, her personal touch I could tell, derived from her smile as proof of her crafty hand. I was all eyes. My heart thumped with anxious excitement as I pushed the door's edge, flipping it open like a standing coin to find any person's fantasy waiting behind.

'It could only exist in a dream,' I believed, as I circled the trunk at the center of her home. A tricolor of bamboo flooring laid its foundation where the indoors and outdoors melded without effort. My attention bounced between the two with both claiming my devotion. It was the perfect panorama view, with no walls or obstructions to barricade the splendor outdoors.

I pieced her life together beneath that ceiling of intertwining branches, starting with her lounger for two. It was fiercely lined with furs and absorbent pillows, with a short, flattened stone serving as her makeshift table. Or perhaps she'd lie in the hammock, strung between two posts on her balcony, swaying gently in the breeze as she watched the sun set over the horizon. What a place to watch her day come to its end!

She trailed my every step, pleased how taken I was with the place that told her story. Nestled at the heart of her home along the sturdy tree, stood a wooden tub. It could devour me whole, set behind a sprawl of thick vines to shield her intimate moments bathing beneath the sky. Curiously, the tub was full of water, crowned with a handful of delicate purple flowers floating softly atop its surface.

"How do you transport water up this high?" I asked.

"From a rain basin above," she pointed, "or reeling pouches from the river if up for the challenge. The water is always purified, with these."

She daintily plucked an inch worm from the tree bark bearing the same purple color, meandering back and forth when the water needed to be cleansed. Once purified, they released blossoms, the itty-bitty purple flowers that rode the surface as a sign the water was clean. Gently, it inched its way back to the bark with the same softness it had when crawling to her finger.

Just beyond, in the next room was where she slept, on a plush cushion atop a bed of bamboo. White netting dangled from above to shield her from an evening breeze. My mind drifted senselessly, imagining how amazing it would be to lie by her side, both watching the sun dip below the trees. But perhaps I'd stared too long? She caught me in mid-wonder and searched my eyes for clues. My face blushed red. Quickly I broke away and meandered to the balcony, embarrassed my thoughts had been exposed.

"Oh, look," I distracted her, as a butterfly three times the normal size landed on the railing next to me.

"A flapping beauty," she said, pretending she hadn't noticed my painted skin while hers blushed just as red.

Getting the gist of her lingo wasn't hard. Flyers I assumed were birds and blossoms were flowers. Flapping beauties? Butterflies, and this one clung to her finger the instant she stepped by my side, the same as all the wildlife had.

"You have a special way with nature. They're drawn to you, as if they know your peace," I said.

"Possibly. Or perhaps more toward the delicacies in my pouch."

"Still, this place is breathtaking," I sighed.

I leaned on my elbows and soaked in the carrot-colored haze pushing across the horizon. As much as I'd loved to have drowned in that blanket of orange, it was an innocent scare that suddenly burst that serenity from my head.

"They're here, they're here!" Naymelia yelled behind, spooking the butterfly from Kaylaira's finger.

Naymelia had snuck in, eagerly announcing an incoming group of exhausted men. I caught sight of them in the distance, my age and younger, trekking their way toward the village.

"They've returned!" she again screeched with a yank on my arm.

"My apologies. We are still working on announcing ourselves before entering," Kaylaira said, eyeing the guilty little girl who tugged my hand. "But there still seems to be a little work needed."

"So, who are they? Those arriving?" I asked, with an uncertain eye on the advancing group.

"My father," Naymelia blared.

"Her father and some of our eldest left several burns ago for preparations," Kaylaira explained.

Burns? Days.

A cheer burst from the youngsters below before she divulged anymore. They paraded the approaching group, and it didn't take long for that lively bunch of younglings to point out Kaylaira's tree, precisely where I stood. My gut became unsettled, and it was at that point I knew that 'dream' was about to change.

"Come," Kaylaira insisted as Naymelia still tugged my arm. "They will be curious to your arrival."

As if I hadn't felt enough pressure, my throat tightened, with the feeling that things were about to get worse.

Chapter Eighteen

My dream of a dream suddenly became a dreadful task as Naymelia dragged me down the looping stairs. My thoughts scattered like startled butterflies. Each loop around the trunk regrettably drew me to the same person, a boy my age if not older. Tall and imposing, he was a living statue of disdain with a body honed by labor. His presence was suffocating, and his glare bitter cold.

I wished those steps took longer to descend, but we'd somehow already made it to the foot of the tree. Worst yet, I breathed like an asthmatic. A horrible impression to give, especially when every man who walked our way boomed with unbridled energy and enthusiasm. The force of their voices filled the air like a thunderstorm, leaving little room for my presence to be heard.

"Daddy!" Naymelia screamed, pulling from my hand to leap in the very arms of the guy whose eyes stabbed cold.

"Baby girl!" he returned, dropping to a knee for a squeeze to his heart.

"Draythian," Kaylaira greeted him.

She too welcomed him with the familiar kiss to both cheeks. A brother? Cousin? Or worse, a boyfriend? He turned to Kaylaira's call, his gaze shrinking my presence as if I didn't exist. 'Who was this stranger his daughter had clung to so kindly? Who had Kaylaira welcomed into their home?'

"And our guest?" he quickly inquired, keeping to his disdain.

"A friend, sent by the bijou," she told him.

The guys behind shuffled with a disturbing stir. But before I could speak, Naymelia blurted the one thing I hoped to avoid. "Daddy, he controls the wind! I saw it!"

No! I wanted to melt into the river there on the spot. Her words shifted his demeanor, showing no signs of relief that I'd be his possible protector. Only doubt brimmed behind that perfect smile I envied, attached to his eager glare that waited to expose me as fraud. He'd chew right through me if he saw the need.

"Controls our wind? The zephyr? How astonishing," he said with the least note of amazement. "A wind driver? In our presence!" he announced with an elevated voice. "A wind driver claims to be in our presence!"

The others whispered shock amongst themselves, and it was Draythian's hesitance to accept the truth that sparked the younger ones to blare their testimonies. A million little voices shouted what Naymelia confirmed, but still intimidated, I'd yet said a word.

"Children," Kaylaira calmly uttered. They instantly quieted.

"Shocker, right?" I managed to say, unsure how to address the spreading rumors to a thousand glaring eyes. "I wouldn't believe it either. Jordan. My name is Jordan."

What a pathetic intro! I kept the nerves from quivering my hand as I stuck it out to greet him, still hiding exhaustion beneath my breath. He accepted my gesture with a generous clasp, but I couldn't help but wonder if it was intentional, crushing my hand with his iron grip as a secret test of strength he believed I'd fail. Or perhaps it was his natural strength. But I'd never know, willing to die before giving away the pain of his grasp.

"Grateful arrival to Elatia," he said, though the impression was far from feeling desired. "With a possibility as this, a gathering is in order. Allow us time to reunite with our families, then we'll reconvene at the give-and-take circle thereafter," he told Kaylaira.

Thereafter? A measly twenty minutes. The give and take circle? A place where all matters of weight were divulged. Kaylaira guided me through a path of trees beneath the darkening sky to a distinctive patch of land beyond their village. The green was eerily flawless. The circle was measured to perfection, with a wood burning fire taken from the pages of a magazine sweltering at its center. The children anxiously followed, but simultaneously halted at a designated point.

"What happened?" I asked, wondering what kept them.

"They are not allowed in the circle. We decided it for their safety, to keep them from hearing what would bring them worry or unrest. Their lives are short-lived, but we preserve their purity of youth as long as we can."

"Okay, and what exactly is about to happen? Why the give and take circle?" I nervously asked, in hopes that nothing daunting was required of me to give.

Their history was fuzzy, and with so many having lost parents at such a young age, not much was remembered or passed along. Each depended on the other's revelations to reveal the collection of their past. Those in the dark willingly took that knowledge, not for their sole advantage, but for the collective wellbeing and survival of their culture. All who entered the circle were entrusted to remain transparent, and now, that included me. Hide nothing. Relay the succession of events just as I had with her to allow the others to unravel the mystery behind my presence.

"Still yourself," she said, stroking her favorite spot on my hand. She could sense my unease with such ease. Did I give it away nakedly? Or had she already learned to read me so well? "I'm with you, I'll keep you safe just as I promised in the forest."

'She was with me,' I reminded myself as the others filed in from the trees. It was the quickest twenty minutes I'd known as we approached the fire pit, with no time to rehearse a monologue. The moment we sat, my fingers seeped into a pillow of grass I never thought possible to touch, helplessly whooshing my hands across its blades, drunken by the tingle of its soft texture as the blade tips caressed my hand.

"Grateful arrival," Draythian roared from behind.

My lawn fetish was cut in half as he and the others approached. They followed his lead to mark him as alpha, single filed and ten at most, circling counterclockwise to their place amongst the fire. From what I could tell, we were all close in age.

"Jordan. A pleasure to have you among us. I apologize if your presence made us somewhat... leery. We are accustomed to visitors of a different sort as Kaylaira may have told you," he said.

Couldn't argue with that. Still, he simmered in an arrogance I failed to see in the others.

"What he means is, we have no visitors other than those that willingly bring destruction to our world," another spoke.

"Not to mention one possessing the abilities of a wind driver," added another.

"I understand. But believe me when I say I'm just as puzzled as the rest of you as to how any of this came about."

"Then tell us your story," one stated. "This is the give and take. Give as much as you can, and we will take that lore into our knowledge. In turn, we'll give you all we know to hopefully derive a meaning."

With a deep breath, still not believing what I was about to say, I started from the beginning just as I had with Nijal, from the moment I entered the cave to my repeated awakenings on their shore. They guzzled every drop from my lips like honey, down to the moment I met Kaylaira on their coastline.

"I found him lying in the sand," she confirmed.

"What led you to the shore?" Draythian asked. She thought long and hard over a question she'd failed to answer herself.

"Honestly, I'm not sure," she said, still combing her thoughts for a reason. "Something just whispered to go. I felt I needed to be there. It's not something I had reason to ponder till now, to tell you the truth."

"The bijou, where do you keep it?" another asked.

I tapped my pocket, realizing for the first time it wasn't there. But there was no need to panic. I knew it was home safe by my side, unable to pass the crossover with me.

"Always with me. My father was a geologist, a student of meaningful rocks. So I knew your bijou was not from our world, and I'm pretty certain no one's seen anything of its kind," I explained, but my words made them squeamish. "Wait. What does it mean? Why am I here?" I asked, infected by their fear induced concern.

They shared silent glances, each awaiting the other to dispel what they surmised. But no one spoke, and all looked to Draythian's lead.

"What does he really know?" he asked Kaylaira. She reported all she'd spoken, the visitors, the planet, the role of a wind driver.

"Wind drivers were sworn protectors," someone shouted, as if my presence no longer mattered. "And he isn't aware of this role? How can this be?"

"How do we leave our fate to someone with no knowledge of how vital they are to our survival?" another roared, loosening all reservation!

"Wait. Whoa! Time out!" I intervened. How dare they speak so little of me in plain sight. "No one is leaving their fate in my hands. Just as you've said, I haven't a clue why I'm here or what I'm doing. There's some misunderstanding, an apparent mix-up and I'm not even sure this is real. You speak of lives at stake, and that's not a chance I've committed to yet."

My resentment disturbed Kaylaira, and for the first time I felt her distant.

"Jordan, please. You must. You're the only hope we have," she pled.

Her plea crushed my spirit.

"We have a chance, for once, a chance to make a stand. So why do I alone wish to make that sacrifice?" she asked the others.

"Kaylaira, always thinking you're alone. You're not alone," a resolved voice affirmed.

"And if we fail?" another threw in.

"Then good, we fail trying, no longer as slaves," another blurted in Kaylaira's defense.

Slaves? They seemed so free and at peace that I'd yet perceived them in that light. Slaves, tethered to me and a bijou. Their divisiveness was unmistakable, and I remained at odds as to where I fit as they shouted from both sides. 'How to make use of me? Could I be trusted?' Some judged me so easily with contempt, sparking a flame that awoke my anger. What did they know of me, my character or my will?

"Wait!" I shouted, stomping their turmoil. "All this back and forth on how to use me or if I can be trusted, and so far, I'm as much in the dark now as when I arrived."

What were they not telling me?

"What is it? It's your time to give," I snapped. "This is the give-and-take circle is it not? I gave, and now I'm ready to take. There's something you aren't giving, and I'd like to know what it is before you continue to bash me in my face."

Another bout of reluctant silence ensued, before a defiant voice broke free. "They arrive in three burns," he stunned me.

The tension stiffened and the silence roared, with a chill crawling my pores even by that fire. Three days? Their urgency slapped me in the face, and the reason for their bickering suddenly became clear. A mere three days marked their decline from a fulsome existence to one of annihilation, and I was bound as its focus.

"Three days?" I whispered, barely able to say it aloud.

No one faced me. All eyes set on the flames, searching for ways to erase the haunting reality when Draythian broke the eerie silence.

"So now you understand."

The scorched wood crackled through the darkness. It was so loud, yet I somehow stood over it, unsure at what point I came afoot. Just three days? I couldn't let them trust me, not with this.

"I have no clue what I'm doing," my voice shook in the open. "Some of you wish I never came, I know. I see it on your faces. Others are delighted at what you believe to be a chance at survival. But I just met you! So how can you expect me to carry the existence of your people on my shoulders? That's more than a burden anyone should carry!"

"How can you hear that most of us will die soon and yet refuse to lend a hand?" a voice spoke for the first.

Ouch. His words slapped hard, but his head was so low in thought I could barely read his expression. Who was he? He differed from the rest. And though I was stuck between a dangerous choice and a calamitous one, there was no refuting the conviction of either side. Could I stand idle? Would it not eat away my soul whether asleep or awake? How deplorable would that make me, refusing to aid in their lingering, drawn out deaths? I was doomed with either course and irate with my options, and for that reason, I abandoned the circle.

"You force me into an impossible situation," I uttered on my way out. "But from where I stand, it's not just for me to decide. Some of you don't even want me here and prefer I not help. Make up your mind first, before validating what I can or can't offer."

It was too late. The words left my mouth before I could crowd them back in as I left them to their fire. Naymelia crossed the forbidden line, downtrodden and the first to approach as I left the circle, as if I'd already revealed my disheartening answer.

"Will you not help us?" she so innocently asked.

Did she even understand what was at stake? My hardened edge crumbled like rotten wood. She was too young to know of suffering or death. But even at her fresh age, she seemed well versed with what was to come, spreading her arms in search of comfort.

"What do you need me to do?" I asked as her short arms barely met around my waist.

"Stop the bad guys from taking daddy," she answered.

Draythian. Was he one of the chosen Kaylaira spoke of, destined to befall the 'honorable' death? To look down in her powerless eyes! Her sorrow clashed on one side with the shock of three days pounding from the other. I wanted to leave, and gently moved Naymelia aside while stripping my resolve to look back at Kaylaira. It was the only way I found the strength to will myself awake.

Chapter Nineteen

Oddly enough, I never juddered awake. Sprawled on my bedroom floor, where I'd nodded off the night prior, my eyes simply opened with no excuse to keep closed. I needed a timeout without another world's existence burdening my head.

6:30am! It was the first time I ever beat my alarm before I stared at the crazed lunatic glaring back in the bathroom mirror. What had become of me? I was anxious and unsettled, nauseated with the thought of going to school. However, the thought of staying home nauseated me even more.

I waited by the front door, earlier than any time of my school career to show Mom I was good to give it a whirl. Fortunately, she dropped me off, but within fifteen minutes of stepping through the halls I knew I was doomed to torture.

"Dude you were on the news. Celebrity! What was it like alone in the dark for so long? Did you take your night light?" And my favorite, "Captain Caveman!" all in constant repeat from teachers and students alike.

If not for their pestering, my own inner voice stalked me and refused to back down. What was my plan? How many lives was I willing to sacrifice? Was I foolish enough to believe I could handle this? And ultimately, '*Was I starting to believe it was actually real?*'

At times I pondered if I were there and still dreaming, like in biology class when the lights dimmed for a film, momentarily thrusting me back into the cave. But nothing hit quite as hard as a history lesson, a quote on a printout above the chalkboard.

"*Those who deny freedom to others, deserve it not for themselves,*" Abraham Lincoln.

I'd read those words all year a thousand times without absorbing a shred of their meaning. Then, to say the least, it spiraled me into a panic. The cave. Naymelia's sadness. A world up in flames.

"Jordan, you alright?" the professor asked.

My face dripped wet and my palms were sweaty, while the students openly murmured behind.

"Yeah, just need fresh air," I assured, already out of my chair and headed for the door.

What kind of a monster would I be to deny their freedom? I had to get out! I needed to be free! A mound of dying voices had suddenly screamed in my head. Though above ground and out of the cave, I'd never felt so inhibited.

Nijal routinely liberated me from the inquisitive circling crowds, but there came a point when I was done. We escaped to the loft of an old barn on the edge of our school property, ignored the lip-locked couple sprawled on the bale of hay and headed upstairs. Other than an herbal meetup or a well-hidden make out spot, for whatever reason, no one went.

"Bro, you look like mud," Nijal laughed, taking a long-drawn puff from his burning paper. "I believe that cave messed with your head. Come on, you gotta tell me what you're really trying to pull?"

"I told you Nijal, nothing different from what I already mentioned," I gasped, struggling to stay calm.

"So I guess you're sticking by the whole traveling to another world theory?" he joked. "Did you at least make out with the hottie? I mean, you're gonna, right?"

He didn't believe me. Sarcasm coated his every word, or his herbs had already coiled through his brain.

"Listen, I can't do this alone anymore. What will it take to make you believe me?" I implored.

"Take me with you?" he answered cynically.

At first I objected, but the thought took root. It would be night if I returned, so why not take him while everyone slept? He was a great friend, and no one else could handle this as well as him. Besides, I needed help and could use some convincing I hadn't cracked at the seams.

"Deal," I threw back. He sprung from his bale of hay and stomped out his lit companion.

"Wait. What? Deal? You're actually agreeing?" he shot up in disbelief.

A second confirmation sprawled him in a dance across the straw laid floor. The wood boards creaked, and it was a wonder we didn't fall through.

"My gosh this is gonna be incredible," he formed into a tune.

I needed him to see, needed him to know it wasn't Jordan's make-believe. The biggest problem I foresaw was forcing ourselves asleep, figuring Dad's scotch was in for another ride down the hatch.

"Noooo," he objected. "Not the scotch. Listen, don't worry about the sleep part, I got you covered."

I asked how, afraid to hear what he'd schemed before he rambled about his mom's sleeping pills, admitting he'd downed a few from time to time. Whatever. At least seeing him on my side was a breath of fresh air.

"So this isn't just a cat in the tree thing, this is a save a whole 'nutha world thing? Damn, bro!" he nodded, having heard me out on everything from the village to Draythian and the pow-wow at the circle. "You're gonna do it, right? I mean, if you say it's real?"

My half-interested shrug spawned him in front of me, a little too close to my nose.

"Bro? You gotta do it! We'll do it. Why not? They tell us to live our dreams," he said, bursting with amusement as he caught his unintended humor. But in that moment of suspended laughter, a thought latched his floating mind. "Ooh!" he sprung back. "Talk to Coach Johnson."

Coach Johnson? I'd settled on Nijal being too far in the clouds, then he divulged his logic. Coach Johnson was ex-military and highly acknowledged, years he carefully avoided discussing with his measly students. Any student with the balls to inquire about it was abusively dismissed for the attempt. Not a bad thought, but how was I to go about it? He liked me, but enough to let me keep my head?

"If anyone can tell you how to hold your own, it's Coach Johnson," he assured. "You just gotta man up and hope he doesn't choke the life from you before you get an answer."

With no better solution and having squandered the rest of the day in the barn, I headed to Coach's office, each footstep dragging heavier than the last. I needed a navigator to help weather the storm, and Coach's door was always open. Johnson was old school, perched in a chair with his feet on the desk, preferring a wrestle with the newspaper over the ease of scrolling the news on his phone.

"Well well, look what the cat dragged in," he said. He didn't budge from behind his paper yet had somehow caught sight of me.

There had never been bad blood between us, just a snag the few times I refused to join his athletic teams. 'A complete waste of talent,' he'd blurt each time we'd pass in the halls, and other times he'd just shake his head with shame. He never went beyond that however, knowing my father's early death hampered any desire for extracurricular activities.

"To what do I owe this pleasure? Coming to beg to play on the team? Or still here to disappoint me?" he bluntly asked. His voice always seemed to rattle the office window; a deep resonance ruffled from his pit, toughened by endless years of shouting and commanding. "And don't think I didn't hear about your incident in the cave; just figured you'd heard enough from everybody else. Trust me, I know what it's like."

Great! Hadn't said a word and he'd already shaded my plan. I was nothing like him. He commanded. The man moved mountains with the least of words, was graced with intuition and the very substance of respectful fear.

"Thank you, sir. I appreciate that. I'm also sorry to disappoint you, yet again. This is officially a non-sports related visit," I said. His interest piqued, and for the first time he poked his head from behind his paper. "I could really use some of your military knowledge and advice?"

He leaned forward and propped his elbows on the edge of his desk. "Ah, thinking of joining the ranks?" he roared.

The word "no" was at the tip of my tongue when I figured it was too fast for another let down. Instead, I stretched the truth, a little. The more I thought on it, the more I convinced myself I *was* considering the ranks, of sorts.

"I am sir," I replied, and I couldn't have answered better. Life roused his countenance.

"Well sit on down, what can I help you with?" he thundered.

I snuck in "writing" an ethics paper that weighed decisions of right and wrong, and how it pushed me to consider joining. It was the only way I figured to ease into conversation.

"Sir, I'm fully aware it's something you don't discuss and believe me, I wouldn't ask if it weren't more important to me than you could possibly imagine."

"Shoot," he uttered, with both eyes warning to tread softly.

"Um, was there ever a time you made a questionable call? I mean, a moment you knew your very command would lead to death?" I asked. "Kids here have their infamous stories about you, but I was kind of hoping to get one firsthand, without the second-hand ad lib. No mention of reference of course."

The question triggered a memory, a deep one apparently, and I quietly watched the thought sink in then uproot what he'd vigorously worked to bury. His silence rivaled the cave and forced me to the edge of my seat, teetering between falling to the floor or standing to sneak out when his smile froze me still. Leaned farther back than his chair allowed, he lingered in whatever flashback I'd unearthed.

"It was me and eight others," he recounted, the event that tainted him forever and moved him to abandon his military career. Stuck and outnumbered, they faced two choices when forewarned of a village attack.

"We could either run with a small chance of survival or rush the enemy head on. If we ran, over a hundred men and women in that village would've lost their lives, without a doubt. If we rushed the enemy? We'd slow them down and give the others below a chance to survive, or at least the chance to decide whether to cock their weapons or flee. I believe you're smart enough to know what that meant for my men and me."

"What did you do sir?" my voice quivered.

His silent glare jabbed hard with a resounding answer, lingering us in another discomforting silence before I broke our hush. "How many did you lose?"

His glare penetrated even deeper, flicking the heart of my eye like the tip of a pin. "All of them," he whispered.

His voice gave way, the first time since I'd known the man. His answer snatched my breath and quickened the pulse along my throat.

Was I to suffer the same? Would they die? Draythian? Naymelia… Kaylaira? Guilt riddled his face. This poor soul and the burden he lugged around those school hallways. What if I were him, the lone survivor, solitary with blame after marching children to their deaths?

Never had I held someone in such high esteem as then. And while sitting there serene in thought, he saw my truth, knowing it went far beyond an ethics paper.

"You alright?" he asked, snapping me from the delirious nightmare I envisioned. "For a moment, it felt like you were the one that led those troops to their deaths. There's something else, Mr. Elatus. What is it? Why did you really come here?"

I broke a little, unhinged from his previous response having weakened my throat. He could see right through me.

"I just need to know how to defeat an army, defeat an army with a handful of people who've never fought a day in their lives," I spilled, knowing I sounded absurd. "Sorry."

I stood to leave, holding myself together before I cracked to make him question me further. Or worse, mandate I see the school therapist.

"Most of those men with me weren't as experienced in the field," he uttered, stopping my foot from passing his doorway. "But boy, you should've seen the hell they raised before going out."

"How?" I turned and asked.

"Sometimes Jordan, the strength you possess doesn't come from within, it comes from others and an unbreakable belief in what you're fighting for. There was a moment in each of those young men's minds, a connection that made them realize they weren't fighting for their lives, their lives were already gone. They were fighting to save others," he smiled. "That brings me comfort, and because of their actions that village survived."

A tear squeezed from my eye as I continued out the door.

"Hey," he stopped me, "promise you're not involved with something stupid."

"I promise, sir," I half laughed. "Thank you for your time."

I rushed from his office with my decision made, ready to fight for Elatia's dream. It was time I grasped that success sometimes comes from failure. Whether they'd have me or not, I was ready. After all, per Coach, it was the ethical thing to do.

CHAPTER TWENTY

What was Nijal thinking? I'd practically spent more nights at his house than my own, but he obviously saw that visit a little different. Candy, pretzels, soda? A spread of goodies blanketed his bedroom floor.

"Dude, it kind of feels like we're going camping or something," he admitted with a horrible fidget. "You bring the jewel of the Nile?"

Impatient, he hurried off the lights as I eased the stone from my pocket, glued to its browning glow and the galactic aura in my hand.

"This thing glows? With no batteries? You never said it glows!" he began to spazz, instantly dwarfed into an overgrown kid. From then out, he was all jitters. "Is this real? Are we really about to do this?" he blurted, back-stepping with second thoughts before I invited him to back out. "No, no, no, I'm just suddenly getting a little shaky," he giggled admittedly, air-drying the nerves from his fingers. "I mean, you're starting to make me believe this is real."

"It is, and soon I can check off convincing you I haven't lost my mind and get back to figuring out what I'm meant to do."

I unwrapped a candy bar on his futon, relatively more mine than his, and cozied in.

"So what do we do?" he asked, plopped parallel on his bed.

"I go first. I need time to handle the dozen to one team up I've strayed into. Then I bring you in," I told him.

"How?"

"Well, knocking out seems to be the hard part. Once I'm under it's like I know I'm asleep but have control. I mumbled to Mom before and should be able to do it again to give you a heads up. Just remember, do *not* fall asleep before. What takes an hour for me could be over three for you."

"Video games, bruh," he answered, already strapping a headset around his ears. "Now hurry up and get over there, so I can finally tell you you're tripping."

He chucked me the bottle of pills instructing me to take one before bedtime. That with a mouthful of pretzels, and all I remembered was a tug on my eyelids. Nijal went to high five me, but I barely managed.

"See you on the other side brotha," his last words before another's voice centered me back at the fire pit.

"They come in three days," someone blurted in Nijal's same sentence. The circle, the flawless fire and absence of bickering was the unnerving moment I'd returned to... the loom of their three-day doom. I sat there in shock the same as I had before, pretending I'd never left while trying to shake the crossover. All eyes searched the dancing flames before Draythian lopped the ghostly silence, again.

"Now you understand," he said.

I knew the conversation better than the rest, but not enough to keep quiet that time. Coach Johnson's admonition and the quote from history class, '*Those who deny freedom to others, deserve it not for themselves,*' heaved me from the circle to brood a few steps away. How was I to convey the same conviction and readiness as the man who roused tears from my eyes at school? In came an exceedingly deep breath and out went my heart.

"I don't know you, any of you, and you don't know me. I have no knowledge of your history or land, why I'm here or what I'm doing for that matter. And I keep asking myself, 'why me?'" I began, darting Draythian a stern look with just as harsh of a glare returned. "Some of you wish I never came. I get it, it shakes things up, makes it complicated. And then there's the rest of you, delighted and believing this is your time, your chance for survival," I went on, laying hold of Kaylaira's pleading gaze. "I know a man from my world, a fighter. A good man forced into an identical situation, and I was fortunate to seek his advice."

"And his guidance?" the mystery guy pursued.

It was the guy from before whose face I couldn't grasp, except now I could see him, and just a nudge of inspiration would explode his ambition my way. He wanted in. He wanted me there to fight.

"In few words, I'd be a fool not to help when knowing I was meant to," I went on.

An ember of determination ignited his chest as he listened to the passionate words of his future ally. My words, though simple, were like a battle cry, urging him forward with unwavering courage and conviction. Why so eager, and where did he rank amongst the others? Either way he spurred me on, with a contagion that ignited mine.

"*Those who deny freedom to others, deserve it not for themselves,*" I uttered.

"What does it mean?" he stood from across the flames.

"It's from a time in my world when things could've been better," I answered. "In short, how can I say no? How can one run for shelter, knowing his lack of action will be the downfall of another, when all that's needed is to stand and try? Even though I have no inkling how to proceed, I don't want to be that person. I'm willing to learn. I'm willing to fight, to stand and try, *if* you're willing to guide me."

Kaylaira smiled as wide as a rainbow. Her only contender? The mystery guy who stood opposite me with just as large of a resplendent grin.

"Some of you don't want me here, and prefer I return from where I came. Problem is, I don't know how. As far as I'm concerned it's no longer my choice. My decision is made, so you decide if you're willing to accept it," I told them.

Again I abandoned the circle, dumping my thoughts at the mercy of their feet before continuing to where the children waited. They clung to the perimeter, but Naymelia again boldly crossed the line.

"Will you not help us?" she asked, again embracing me as if I were some comforting figure.

"What do you need me to do?" I welcomed her small arms.

"Stop the bad guys from taking daddy."

"I want to. I want to stop the bad guys and hope I can. But that's for him to decide."

I welcomed the children's distraction, a playful stress outlet while the circle deliberated. Minutes became an eternity. Voices lowered then rose while stubborn hands flailed in anger. Emotions intensified then softened, and before long, they'd reached a decision.

"Jordan!" the mystery guy called.

I suspected he'd be the one, and the contentment on his face announced the outcome long before I reached the circle. That, and Kaylaira biting her lip while trying to conceal her smile, another cue that I'd won their favor. I tried resisting the urge to peer at Draythian's dissatisfied sulk, but no amount of willpower kept me from his evil glare. He was the one they rallied behind and who I assumed would inform me of their answer.

"After *much* division, we've voted in favor of your presence," he started. "You made it by one vote. So now you see how torn this makes us. I was against it, if you must know."

No shocker there.

"None of that matters now," Kaylaira interjected, freeing her smile from its prison.

Then Draythian gestured I resume my seat. "Per our timekeeper, we have no more than three days."

"What's normal procedure?" I asked.

"Normally, we bury deep in the caves," Kaylaira answered, "our second home."

"We store as much grain, water and supplies as possible, which we have nearly completed," a lone voice added. "The journey is all that's left before shutting ourselves in."

"How long do the visitors normally remain?" I asked.

"No more than several burns," Draythian answered. "But the transference of power is done in much less. So, what's your plan for us?"

I nearly choked on their silence. My plan? Had I missed something? Had no one heard the part where I emphatically stressed not having a clue what I was doing? They stared and expected leadership, awaiting an answer as I emptily returned to the flames, baffled and scrambling for what to say. Nervous, I twirled my finger through a blade of grass when a slow dragging thought finally leapt in my head, the children!

"The children," I gasped, happy to say anything. "Why not take them to the mountains as you normally would?"

"As assurance they survive?" someone asked.

"Exactly," I responded. "There's no reason to leave them vulnerable in this fight."

They quickly agreed, too quick, and again my mind raced in circles, drawing from the plethora of sci-fi flicks on what happens during an invasion.

"Kaylaira," I started. "You mentioned they seek out your planet for its unique energy source. How?"

"The deep," she answered, "just a small journey from here."

The deep? My apparent blank expression prompted another to explain.

"Imagine an open, endless pit," they said, "where no one has lived to speak of what resides in its belly."

"And from what legend tells us, only a wind driver can descend," Draythian affirmed.

An open endless pit? The deep sounded like a nightmare, or better yet where I'd die!

"Okay," I bravely contended, clearing nerves from my tone. "How deep? Fifty, one hundred feet or paces? More?"

Their uncomfortable expressions made it clear that I was the idiot among them, the most uninformed individual to ever exist.

"We are unaware of its end," Kaylaira spoke up. "But answers are said to reside in its extremities. It's their focal point when they come to thieve our planet's vitality."

"So getting to the bottom is the only way to find what's happening," I whispered. "Rope? Vines? We tie an endless link of vines until we reach the bottom. Descend that way?"

Why couldn't I have just shut my mouth? For a second time, their uncomfortable glances conveyed that I was the most ignorant person alive, wondering whom they'd just appointed as leader. I had to stop blurting nonsense and was again saved by Kaylaira who touched my hand, issuing lighter terms for me to grasp. "No amount of lacing will get you there. It must be you, from within, using the wind."

My gut sunk as their intense stares bore into me. I finally grasped what they were asking. They were silently urging I jump.

"We can practice," Kaylaira hurried to comfort me.

It was the first sign of pleasure on Draythian's face as the fear across mine brought utter joy to his. Guess I asked for it, but with no time to linger I brushed the thought for later, unwilling to further upset my grumbling intestines.

"Okay, okay. What else? Weapons? Guns, swords, bow and arrows? How do you defend or protect yourselves?" I asked.

"We have no such things. There's no need. We have no threats," Kaylaira answered. "Only wind drivers control the zephyr and they alone defended our world. Remember the will-benders? Any past attempt to retaliate resulted in near genocide."

Zephyr, still had no clue what it was. I wanted to ask, hating I'd look more foolish than I already did, but I needed to know. "And how exactly does this zephyr work?"

Buried in another unbearable lengthy silence, Kaylaira cut in. "Jordan, look at the fire," I looked. "Now look around it. What do you see?"

"Light? A glow?"

"Heat, air, energy!" another added to the lesson.

"Yes," Kaylaira continued, "A halo of energy beaming from its flames. On our world every gem, stone, lucent and mineral does the same, emitting a halo of matchless energy that lives in our air. We breathe it, use it daily for strength to heal to meditate just as you did in the forest."

"You see? The zephyr is much more than just the movement of air, but only wind drivers can tap into that energy, to control it, manipulate its power through the wind," a separate voice chimed in.

Beautifully explained I finally understood, but still doubted how I was to do it alone. How were they to join the fight? Me with a gust of wind was their idea of a winning strategy? I tried to refocus, but my suicidal plunge into a bottomless pit followed by battling an army by moving air unhinged me. I drew a blank, and not a word left my lips until the enthusiast who'd joined my side returned to my aid.

"Jordan, you're not meant to have all the answers, and perhaps that's something the rest of us should keep in mind," he scolded the group. "For now, learning how to use the zephyr through practice should be our first move. Know you're not alone. We all have our share of meditating and recalling to do. We meet every day, as often as we can until we come up with a viable plan. Anything remembered must be brought to the circle."

"This is your home now, Jordan. You belong here. Roam, search at your leisure, find your inspiration and answers from among us," Kaylaira added.

"For housing," Draythian started before Kaylaira cut him short.

"He is my guest he stays with me."

Guess that ruled out him being her boyfriend. My heart leapt with joy as he contested with a glare that cursed her decision with a thousand words, but no other seemed troubled by her request. Therefore, our meetup concluded, sending me straight to their timekeeper for an answer I needed alone.

"Time, how does it work with the stone in my possession?" I asked, explaining the repeating lapse that occurred each time I returned.

"The king's echo," she answered. "It is said that with the bijou, time and space between worlds is something we don't understand. However, the echo is believed to be a forewarning for the king, a safety that prevents him from returning to a place of harm. When away from his world, the echo would help the king know when and how to protect himself, from potential dangers to which he'd been previously exposed before the time he left."

Her back was towards me walking away before the last word left her mouth. Pretty sure she chose against me, but my mystery friend jumped in her place, stupefying me with a quick excited hug. My feet left the ground.

"I'm Jesriel," he bellowed while squeezing the life from me, and I don't believe he was trying.

"Jesriel, tough crowd. I owe you for the help." I sighed in relief. "Thank you."

"No, no, we should be indebted. Where most have reason to be afraid, this is a time many of us have longed to see. I am alone, with no family. The enemy took them many cycles ago, so every night I beg the skies for a long enough life to see the day we'd stand against them, success or failure," he proudly conveyed. "And you've granted me that wish."

With a smile and quick pat on the shoulder, he headed off ahead of Draythian, who spoke nothing as he ushered past. I didn't want him against me, I wanted him to know I was on their side. And as my eyes lowered to the fire and my hopeful spark diminished, it was Kaylaira who filled that gap of loneliness.

"Give him time," she advised. "They all need time. For now, that's enough. Rest your mind."

CHAPTER TWENTY-ONE

Rest my mind? If that didn't deserve a good laugh. Or that's at least what I believed before a glimpse of their village life caught me from beneath the canopy of trees. I quickened my pace and my worrisome thoughts vanished. I even forgot all we'd discussed as their nocturnal village sprung into a festival of alluring lights.

High in every tree, a lavish display of illuminated stones reminded me of the hanging lights in December. From pure whites to deep purples and vibrant blues, they twinkled and glowed, dancing in a symphony as they dangled from the limbs above, casting their glimmering reflections onto the river to repeat the enchanting scene twice. My attention hung in the air, lost in it all when she poked my side.

"Think you can manage?" she joked, placing my hand on the pulley of her tree.

That time I wasn't afraid, or perhaps too distracted to care with the luminous fantasy above. I nodded yes and stepped on while she cranked me toward the twinkling lights, feeling as if my head poked through the cosmos or as if every star had descended to their treetops.

Up I went, till the pulley bumped to a stop on her balcony ledge. No unwanted plunge that time, and the instant I stepped off I plopped on my butt with each leg dangled over the edge. Not once did my eyes retreat from the spectacle around. In no time, she was up the stairs and plopped beside me.

"I could look at this every night," I whispered, afraid my voice would shudder the peace.

"You and I both," she agreed as if it too were her first time.

"These glowing stones you carry, they're everywhere. What are they?" I asked.

"They're not just any stones, they're lucents," she answered. "And they're much more than just a glow! Each color you see serves a distinct purpose. When combined, they serve many. One day I hope to teach you, but for now, just let them be lights. By the way, it's time you chose your own."

Next to me lay the colorful heap of jewelry the children had gifted. Easy choice, a deep sky blue, my favorite color. I sifted the necklace from the bunch that matched the one around her neck.

"Cerulean," she beamed, "Great choice!"

With a white stone fastened to its side, she slipped the leather strap over my head, admiring the match of hers. Then her joy suddenly hardened.

"Cold?" I asked, as a chilling shudder trembled her shoulders. But it wasn't the weather. The air was impeccable and close to perfection. "Kaylaira? What is it?"

She stared into the distance, disordered and unsure of her fears.

"I'm not sure. It happens every so often, a flutter. The first time it happened I was a child. The same happens just moments before an arrival, and it's the same I felt just before finding you on the shore."

I tried deciphering her meaning, until a deathly cry from the distance pricked my ears, echoed through the wind as if it bellowed from a mountaintop. It came from the shore, with a second distressing plea belted right after. That time the cry was clear and I recognized the voice. I'd heard it a million times. Nijal! He'd fallen asleep too soon!

A third cry hurdled me to my feet, with Kaylaira giving no indication she'd heard the same. My mind blurred but my instincts kicked in, rushing me towards the source of the sound while barely registering my own actions. I didn't know it at the time, but I'd thoughtlessly leapt and risked my own safety. All I remember was a whoosh of air cooling my face, then the gritty soil scraping my elbows clean. My eyes were doused with sand. My mouth choked with its filth as my shoulders burned from skidding across the shore. I couldn't understand how I'd gotten there when the terror of Nijal's cries rumbled in.

"Jordan!" he screamed, awakening me to his scurrying silhouette.

His face was hidden in the shadows but I knew my friend. And the worst part? He wasn't alone. Adrenaline steeped my senses as he bolted toward me, his cries masked by thumping footsteps. Something hunted him.

"Jordan!" he cried again.

Nijal was husky, but shriveled beneath the mass of his stalker in the dark. I stiffened like a fish out of water. Only spatters of moonlight aided my eyes to a flash of teeth the length of my fingers, and a glint of razor white claws ready to split Nijal in half. What was I to do? Its arm lifted.

"Wind repulsion!" Nijal screamed. "Wind repulsion!"

Wind repulsion? Really? His branded term for 'knocking junk over?'

"Jordan, hurry!"

With no time to think, wind repulsion it was if it meant saving my friend. I cupped my hand like a fool and seized the open air. Up till then, I'd barely thrown enough to move a few grains of sand. That wouldn't do! I needed more!

My hands trembled with an overwhelming surge of power, crackling and swirling the air around my forearms as I summoned every ounce of strength within me. With a mighty heave, I launched myself forward like a bullet from a cannon as the towering fiend reached out to strike Nijal's head. I fell to my knees, unleashing a blast of energy that reverberated through the ground and sent a cloud of dirt flying into the air. The repulse hit and Nijal collapsed onto my shoulder, saved against our monstrous foe.

"My gosh it worked!" I yelled.

"Dude. What the hell?" he gulped. "I thought this place was warm and fuzzy."

"So did I," I countered. "I don't know what that is."

But it wasn't over. The creature reared, still shrouded in darkness as it belted a shrill that scared the death from our bones. And then it stormed us through the sand.

"Jordan, again!" Nijal hollered. "Hit it again!"

I heard him loud and clear but froze and became empty-headed. Weren't we in a dream? Shouldn't I have been able to just squeeze my eyes and wake up on the other side? I tried. I squeezed tight believing I'd find myself back in Nijal's room, buried in the comfort of his futon. But I wasn't, and the creature still stormed when Nijal screamed my name.

We cuddled, involuntarily, a memory I hoped would die with us as its shrill shredded my ears. The beast was upon us. I sensed the drawback of its hand ready to slit us in half when suddenly, it stopped. The air became silent and its grueling breaths eased. We should've been dead. We should've been nothing but scattered Jordan and Nijal fragments all over the shore. But we weren't, so I ventured to pry an eye open and found its pant-filling gaze just a finger's width from my head.

However, it never moved against us and its eyes settled on something behind. Slowly, we eased back, imprisoned in its horrifying glare as our spongy footsteps barely weighed the sand. I wanted to turn about. I wanted to learn what had seized its will, but the fear of breaking its hypnotic stare kept me from turning around.

Nijal was no help. His eyes were sealed, reverse dreaming of home while I put the space between us and the beast. All along it never moved, and with a little distance, I softly cranked my neck behind to find none other than Kaylaira. She stared back equally dumbfounded, but either way it was her doing, her presence that forced the creature to lower its hand and cower back to the trees.

Nijal dropped like a sack of stones. Tension exploded from our lungs from having suppressed the minutest exhale, from fear we'd spur its reaction. How hadn't we puked or pissed our pants?

"Kaylaira?" I finally wheezed, hunched on my knees. "What was that? Was that them? Was that a visitor, a MonTu?"

"No it wasn't. But I'm unsure what it was," she gasped, still as stupefied as us.

Or at least she pretended. There was something she knew, something that rang familiar before Nijal consumed her focus. His presence alarmed her as much as the beast.

"And this?" she asked, condemning his presence.

"A friend from home," I assured, resting my hands on her trembling arms. "Please, you can trust him. I asked him to be here. I need his help," I argued, though her suspicion remained.

Up till then, I hadn't realized he'd been mumbling a prayer.

"Nijal! We're safe now you can snap out of it. Besides, do you even know how to pray?" I questioned.

"Dude! I do now! I thought you said this place was warm and fuzzy. Since when did being chased by a childhood monster fit that description?" he freaked. "And how did you get that glowing necklace?"

So easily distracted. However, I hadn't noticed the cerulean lucent glowing around my neck.

"We don't know what that was," I ignored him.

"And your sand!" he diverted. "It's... twinkling?"

I peered the ground beneath my feet. He was right, the sand's iridescence bounced from the moon, glinting in the dark like a thousand tiny diamonds scattered across its surface. The entire shore illuminated with its ethereal glow and bristled with energy.

"We should go. Others may not take his arrival lightly. For now, we conceal him," Kaylaira suggested.

From the shore we crept back to her tree where she slackened thick fabric to conceal us inside.

"Nijal? What happened?" I asked, dying to know what he'd done. He answered my suspicion of having fallen asleep.

"Bro! I am so sorry I doubted you, this is real?!" he giggled, back to being a five-year-old. "And I thought you'd been tripping this whole time."

Nijal was no threat and she could clearly see. While he pinched his arms and face, it was his joyous demeanor that began to loosen her. I explained how much I needed him, mostly his big mouth to cover my tracks back home.

"He told me you were beautiful, but wow! Spot on. He was right. You're another level of stunning. I wasn't sure cuz sometimes his taste is a little off," he rambled.

My jealousy roused a little, and there's no telling what he'd have said next if I hadn't stopped him. To say he had a big mouth was an understatement, but under the circumstances, I didn't think he'd go from screaming death to flirting in the same breath. She didn't mind. In fact, her smile lingered on me longer than before, giving her subtle approval of what he'd divulged. In the end, I guess I had him to thank! I was just taken she managed to understand his verbiage. Nijal had a different way of speaking, but he'd consume all the love in the room. That was just the way he was.

"Kaylaira, the creature? You've seen it before I can tell. What was it?" I asked, breaking her daunting, flirtatious stare from Nijal's remarks.

She shook her head, aware of the answer yet still felt unsure.

"It's familiar to me, but I'm not sure why or how, and it's only happened a handful of times," she paused. "Each time it reacts the same—protective—then rushes off as if spooked whenever I'm near."

"Is it a threat?" Nijal continued.

"It's not," she confirmed, "I can assure you."

In perfect sync with her response, Wonder popped through the shades and lent me the pleasure of watching Nijal freak out across the floor.

"Is this one a threat?" he panted.

How I needed to see that! I fell on my back with joyous tears before he realized its harmless plight.

"Between now and you running on the beach I'd say you're getting pretty fast," I teased.

Wonder dallied to Kaylaira of course, cuddling beneath her arm when both her and Nijal prompted me to something of which I was unaware.

"Yeah, speaking of fast, how did you get from here all the way to the beach in seconds?" Nijal asked.

Good question, but I truthfully had no answer. I recalled the wind, the sand, but everything between was a fuzzy haze.

"It was bizarre. I heard your scream in the wind," I told him, trying to piece it together. "And then, I came running, I guess?"

"That far?" he objected. I woke up on the beach with that thing already chasing me, and you were there, in seconds. No way you ran, that's a full five-minute hike at full speed."

What he said made sense, but at the same time it didn't. How else could I have reached him?

"You don't remember, do you?" Kaylaira asked.

I shook my head, still sifting the foggy memory.

"You soared," she continued, as if I'd known. "You leapt from the balcony, through the air and vanished."

I tried remembering when Nijal startled me with what I knew would come. "Dude! I knew it! You can fly!"

For the life of me I couldn't recall! Ironically, it was like trying to remember a dream, leaving me skeptical even as Kaylaira confirmed its truth.

"So, now what?" Nijal asked.

"If I did it once, I guess it's time I do it again," I answered.

CHAPTER TWENTY-TWO

At 7 am the next morning I would've sworn I'd been run over by a train. Kaylaira squeezed every drop from the clock that evening, and the most I accomplished? A migraine and screaming bones that followed me back to Nijal's futon. We dressed to give his mom the appearance we were headed to school, but we weren't.

"Just give it time bro," Nijal cheered me as I fumbled to stand.

Though I'd choked under pressure and felt the night was a failure, his spirits soared. Being able to put on clothes while sitting, that was my success.

"Three days! I don't have time Nijal!" I snapped. "Just three days with an entire civilization of children and younger children counting on me! Me?"

I stood from his futon but instantly dropped to my butt.

"Yo, you good?" he scrounged to break my fall.

My head swirled. My mouth was as dry as tree bark. I could barely swallow, instantly rejuvenated by a bottle of water.

"I'm good," I insisted, shoving him from my arm. "Just needed a drink. Come to think of it, haven't been doing much of that or eating. I just wish there were a way I could practice from here."

"Not sure that's possible, but at least we know you can bring something back," he said with a glare at my chest.

As I followed his eyes below my chin to the cerulean lucent dangling around my neck, everything became *real* in ways it hadn't before! It wasn't a dream and that necklace was proof, something I pondered the entire drive to my home. How did it work? How was I here and there at the same time, able to travel with the necklace but the bijou could not? They were forces I doubted I'd ever understand as I obsessively rubbed the lucent between my fingers. Why the sudden nervous tick? Perhaps because it was tangible, and something I could hold from their world on ours that conveyed a sense of sanity.

"Listen," Nijal said. "I don't know what triggered you when you thought I was in danger. And no, I'm not asking you to get all sappy and tell me how much you love me. But whatever you felt that moment triggered something. Find more of that place, wherever and whatever it was. Use it."

"Yes coach," I sarcastically answered.

His words forced me back to his cry for help. What happened at that moment? Honestly, a flurry of thoughts took hold of me at once, but mostly fear, fear I'd lose him, fear I'd driven him into that life-altering mess. There was helplessness too, witnessing someone close battle an ocean I'd pushed them in, knowing I lacked the ability to swim them to safety. I'd drowned in fear and helplessness, but at the same time, an unknown confidence birthed something I knew I had.

He watched me ponder and waited for me to share. Instead, our overly compassionate moment ended with a burst of laughter.

"I overdid it, didn't I? Too sappy, right?" he joked.

"Yeah, we're not ready to share that level of comfort," I sneered.

"Good, cuz I was a little curious, but also a little nervous you were actually going to say it. Then I got a little nervous that I actually felt a little curious," he reversed, still cackling. "Know what I mean? So now, quickly getting that out of the way, sure Mom is gone before we pull up at your house and blow our cover?"

"Yeah she's gone. The place is ours all day, or night," I said.

"Awesome! This is so freaky!" he grunted, bouncing in his chair like an athlete before a game. "Still can't believe you were telling the truth! How much longer will it be dark there?"

"If we stay asleep till Mom gets home? That should roughly take us to four in the morning there?" I guessed.

"Only four? That's it?" he whined.

I agreed. The time difference was a drag, but in some ways it stretched my three day deadline. My problem was forcing myself asleep. It became a chore and tiring believe it or not. After finally being awake, I was in no hurry to close my eyes again.

We slopped down bowls of cereal then broke the monotony by snooping in Dad's office. Monotony replaced monotony as we scathed the boring material in one binder after another, though it did help having a second pair of eyes.

"Not sure why you thought I'd be any good at this. You're the one rocking an 'A' in geology while I flaunt a solid 'F'," he reminded me. "Wait, your old man saw a psychiatrist?"

Dad? A psychiatrist? Wrong person. But Nijal disproved it with a business card from the pages of a well-used, gray fabric book. Its outer threads were tattered like worn-out jeans, and its ample yellowed pages were sandy to touch. He chucked the card like a Frisbee, jarring my recollection the instant it landed my lap.

"A psychiatrist? Wait. I remember Mom repeating, *love people not rocks*. She wanted him to have more of a relationship with human beings than the stones in his office," I recalled.

Nothing more on the card or book rang a bell, so I shoved it down my pocket along with a sleeping pill down the hatch.

"Bottoms up," Nijal declared and downed his.

With a quick snooze we were back on the shore. Wonder insisted joining the team, and with a small fire and our lucents aglow, we lit the dark where Kaylaira wasted no time. The pressure mounted. Progress was slow and lethargic, hindering my first hour as I struggled to keep pace with her energy. She tried suppressing her disappointment, but I could see it wiggle its way between her brows.

"I can't do this!" I barked in frustration.

I swung my hand in agitation, hammering a chunk of rock with an unintentional gust of air that narrowly missed their heads. The two stumbled back, and even Wonder cowered behind Kaylaira's legs, unsure of who I'd become.

"Whoa! Hey man, find that calm and tranquil place. Remember?" Nijal coerced me.

"Sorry, I didn't mean that," I assured, lowering my hands with a calmer tone. "But hearing that over and over is not helping!"

"Remember the forest," Kaylaira exclaimed. "The serenity of your aria? There lies your answer. That is your tranquil place. Close your eyes and find the peace waiting for you in the air."

The zephyr's melody! The thought of it bounced me on my toes as I closed my eyes and took a deep breath in. The evening shrills and whistles conjured in the distance. They weren't as pronounced as the day, but in the cover of night they were there, shushing my pesky thoughts.

"Listen. Sift the air and carry those sounds toward you. It's quiet, but they can be stronger at night if you allow yourself to find them," she whispered.

It was her hand that unlocked a symphony of nature, each sound becoming a brushstroke in a masterpiece of calm. The waves whispered secrets, the fire crackled with warmth, and the creatures of the night sang in harmony, weaving a tapestry of serenity that enveloped me whole. And then, from within that cocoon of peace, my own melody emerged, soaring on the zephyr's wings by nature's whispers.

"Bro!" Nijal yelled.

Peculiarly, his voice reverberated from below, and what opened my eyes to search out his sound when I glared into the cliff top instead. My feet were thirty feet off the ground! And that dread and disbelief was all it took before the air rushed up my pants and I fell like a rock. Twenty feet, fifteen, ten. I clawed the open air as if scratching down a wall, dragging the current through my fingers. But it wasn't enough to stop me. Then wham!

My body became a puppet at the mercy of pain's invisible strings. Air ejected from my lungs. My neck collapsed in agony. The shock of a thousand volts jolted my spine as my back slapped ground. Nijal and Kaylaira ran to my side, but their touch was like a gentle breeze against my ravaged body, unable to break through the numbness that enveloped me.

"My back!" I gasped as the air forsook me, once my ally, now my enemy.

"His neck! Something snapped in his neck I heard it!!" Nijal cried.

She shoved him aside and centered herself in front of me. Her eyes were as wide as two moons, and her hands trembled like the strings of a plucked guitar.

"Breathe Jordan! Believe me, you need your mind more than ever now, I promise! We can push through it, just breathe," Kaylaira insisted. "Look in my eyes. Jordan, look at me."

I defied her glare, unable to lie still as pain overwhelmed my desire to live and breathe. For a moment I even gave in, before Kaylaira clamped the sides of my head and prodded me into her eyes to grasp life as she did.

"Jordan, breathe. You have to trust me, please. Remember, the zephyr is more than just air," she said, terrified, yet never losing control. "Inhale deep, here," she tapped my chest. "Force out the hurt. Drive it through the soil for it to bury your pain."

Nijal gushed fear, but his face also told me he was my friend as a dark sleep dragged me beneath its wing.

"No!" Kaylaira yelled, forcing my sight back into hers. Her tears swelled. Her voice quivered, but her composure kept. "Breathe, Jordan. I promise your mind is stronger. The pain will leave you with each breath you expel. Now breathe!"

Life rose in her eyes like the morning sun. It was infectious, overpowering the misery I wished would hurry and take me under.

But I believed in her and held to her command, embracing the air as I imagined the sand sopping up my agony. And then it moved, like a subtle shift of wind. It tormented me still, but it moved.

"Yes! Again!" she slapped my chest, her voice as sturdy as the ground that nearly took me.

She stroked the sides of my head, daring I pull from her will as I grappled air through my collapsing lungs, pleading the universe for the strength to exhale. The air left me and so did a mountain of pain, flowing beneath my skin like lava pulled from my limbs. I swore my back was afire, but it wasn't.

"It moved. I felt the pain move," I gasped.

"I know. Now again, breathe," she smiled, with a hope filled tear splatting on my chest.

The air rushed into my lungs, burning like hot coals as I exhaled a cry of agony. The pain clung like a leech, then slowly transformed into a sharp stab before an all-consuming itch threatened to drive me mad. But as I gasped for air the agony subsided, replaced by a wave of relief that washed over me like a lifeline. My toes and fingers tingled with renewed sensation, pulsating with the warmth of life once again. As I looked to Nijal's ghostly face, his hand clasped mine as he realized I'd triumphed over death.

"Dude, are you holding my hand?" I wheezed.

"Whoa!" he panicked, snatching his hand as if I hadn't noticed while his free hand wiped the tears from his eyes. "Look, um… that was a possible life and death situation, right? I got caught up. Thought you were gone, man. Promise to never speak of this again? Pinky swear?"

They eased me up with a sigh of laughter, then welcomed me back with a doting embrace. I could barely lift my arms around them. My muscles were as tight as knotted rope and my joints as stiff as a corpse. A lingering impression kept beneath my skin, like an imprint of pain though pain itself had left me.

"You'll feel some discomfort. It takes some getting used to," Kaylaira explained. "Just focus and embrace your aria till it flows second nature. It'll help you grow stronger."

Nijal glared the two of us like a lost child ditched in a parking lot by his mother. "Are one of you planning to explain what just happened?"

Words couldn't explain, but Kaylaira did her best to define the zephyr's flow and how they share its energy. "It only works after you've learned to mend with its properties."

That night on my deathbed I learned a crucial lesson. The zephyr, its energy, the melody… it all played a vital role in their survival, and I then understood why outlanders risked it all to harness their planet's strength. It healed my fractured neck and mended my bones! Who wouldn't want that power? If our people ever learned of this, I couldn't help but wonder if they'd behave the same.

"So if you're hurt, you just listen to the air for a song, breathe and then push it away?" Nijal asked as if we were high on drugs.

"Something to that effect. There are obviously things too demanding to overcome, but the deeper your connection, the quicker and stronger you defeat the harm," she told him, then her attention abruptly returned to me. "Now let us continue."

Continue? I'd fallen from a cliff and she wanted to shove me back on? Fortunately, after what I'd seen, I was game. The start was slow and shaky, but the deeper I connected the better my grasp. I'd soar for mere moments then reacquaint myself with the ground. But I never stopped trying and she never slowed for air. She couldn't afford to, there wasn't time. So, why would I?

"You got this man," Nijal clapped as I stood on a twenty-foot ledge.

Had he already forgotten I'd nearly died? My back cleaved the wall as stiff as a brick while my sweaty palms dissolved the clinched stone in my hand. Air spouts, or wind repulsion per Nijal, I could launch all day, but to walk on air was another matter. My first attempt rippled out a sea of dirt, clouding the air white before raining back down.

"You guys, okay?" I hawked.

They coughed out their lungs. I'd smothered them in a sand plume that kept them from my sight but was back at the wall when Nijal stopped me.

"Hey wait," Nijal coughed and waved the air clear, with an alternate plan in his head. "Let's think this through before you douse us with another dirt bath. Remember teaching me to swim?" he asked, something I'd never forget. "Didn't you say the air kinda feels like moving through water?"

"Sort of. Like a mesh between," I answered.

"There you go. So instead of leaping dead frog in the air, imagine diving into something buoyant that'll catch you, like water?" he suggested.

In so many words, he told me to trust, something I hadn't done before I was back on the ledge staring down. Trust the zephyr, know it was there and that it breathed through my every pore.

I strapped to that notion and freed myself of fear, shackled to my aria as I committed and let go. The air returned as my ally. The wind graced my face, and though it took a moment to realize, I never met ground.

"Yes! That's what I'm talking about!" Nijal celebrated.

He, Kaylaira and Wonder filled the air with sand in celebration.

"That's why I keep you around Nijal," I grumbled, juggling to keep balance.

A stroke from my hands sent me higher, all the way to the cliff's summit some fifty feet high. I was confident. It was time.

"Sure you ready?" Nijal yelled as I stepped from the ledge, but at that point it was mindless.

"Like you said," I told him, "It's just like water."

Then off the cliff I went.

CHAPTER TWENTY-THREE

Early evening back home, Nijal was a blabbering chatterbox with an endless battery, rehashing every detail with more enthusiasm than I could muster.

"Dude, do you realize where we just were? What you just did?" he blurted with a vigorous slap to my back. Ouch. It was still somewhat tender.

"For the tenth time Nijal, yes," I answered.

Finally, he'd seen it for himself. So why my lack of enthusiasm? Maybe it was the fall, or the dizzying twirl that spun my head as his image suddenly blurred. Then down I went.

"Whoa!" he uttered, catching me mid-fall for the second time in 24 hours.

But that time was worse. I barely scored the trash can as my head and gut teamed up and hurled out misery. Nijal spun his head away as far as it turned, dry heaving as my cereal and sour milk bubbled into the basket.

"Sorry man, but I can't help you," he gagged over to the kitchen sink.

I crashed my bed with no sense of direction. Up blended with left, left with down by the time Nijal returned with his shirt over his nose. He flung a damp towel at my face, instantly soothing the heat beading off my forehead.

"Man this sucks," I whined, feeling somewhat relieved as I sat up without my gut wrenching for round two.

"Why does this keep happening?" he asked.

"I'm not sure. Too much jumping back and forth maybe?" I said. "Who knows what toll it takes on my physical mind and body?"

He pleaded I take care and get an actual night's rest, something I was far from rejecting as I kissed Mom goodnight at six that evening. I assured her everything was okay, though she sensed it wasn't, then immediately knocked out with the stone hidden in Dad's office. Thankfully it worked and I slept like a baby, realizing how little rest I'd had. But the next morning I was back at it, waking to sleep, then sleeping to wake.

The routine dug a hole in all sense of normalcy as reality slipped from my grip. I was tired, confused as the dizzying spells became crueler. Blurred vision trailed each awakening, along with a loss of balance and the occasional vomit. In short, each time I awoke back home was pure misery and I only felt alive during my time on Elatia. I searched for ways to remain asleep and extend my time with Kaylaira, emptying Dad's bottle of scotch, upping the dosage on Nijal's pills to stave off disrupting sleep.

Real time became slothful but there it moved fast, and the next day or so with Kaylaira lagged a business week our time. I constantly hid at home and school, cramming handfuls of minutes to rest or to search hidden clues in Dad's office. And I wasn't alone. The candle burned at both ends, me back home and Kaylaira on Elatia. I objected, but she kept her promise and kept by my side, spurring me on during every waking hour. And it showed. My wind-driving had never been stronger.

The give-and-take circle occasionally met with not much to give or take. Jesriel, my enthusiast, remained an avid supporter, helping me explore my power while Draythian continued to shun me. He'd show his face on occasion, to scrutinize what little progress we'd made. I struggled not letting him slither beneath my skin and wished we were friends instead. At least Naymelia enjoyed my company. She still called me like a big brother or a beloved uncle, irksome to him I was sure. Nevertheless, it was the tender moments I'd catch between he and his daughter that reminded me of what they'd soon face.

That was enough to help me find the zephyr's rhythm. Unveiling it took more patience than I thought I had, but once unlocked, it flowed through me like a wild heartbeat. An early yoga class at the gym was intuitive, minus the tights. There I learned to breathe, to slow down and still myself in the moment, another nod I owed to Nijal. He'd cross to Elatia with me now and again, but I accomplished more without his frequent distractions. Or perhaps it was the quality time I spent with Kaylaira alone.

"Let's break the routine!" she exclaimed to Jesriel and I.

It was day two on their world and I'd finally made it to the big day of my jump. The village had yet awakened, and though we'd barely started, the tediousness had already set in. We were engaged in a simple task of catch and toss. Jesriel tossed stones and I was expected to catch them with no hands. That was the goal at least, but the bruises on my face and arms spelled the true story.

"I am *definitely* all for it," I agreed, pelted in the shoulder by another stone.

"Kaylaira, you really think now is the best time to go searching for thrills? We travel midday for his jump and have the children's farewell festival at moon rise. Besides, can't you see he and I are having way too much fun? Right, Jordan?" he sarcastically laughed as another stone whacked my elbow.

"Way too much fun," I shrieked.

"Yes, I can see and hate to spoil it," she insisted. "However, we've spent all this time practicing, and Jordan still remains unacquainted with who we are. He doesn't feel the spirit of our people nor knows what he fights for. His essence is half full. So how can he possibly face the MonTu with only a partial temper?"

I tried to understand her meaning but didn't. Her depth of feeling simply went beyond what I knew. Jesriel however, understood every word.

"Kaylaira is right. You're learning to bound under fear and anger when the core of our strength comes from happiness. Those are the moments you should experience with us," he agreed. "Perhaps that's what's missing to complete you."

"Happiness? How can you guys be happy at a time like this?" I questioned.

"My friend," he added, warmly placing his hand on my shoulder. "Finding happiness in moments such as these takes an astonishing, different kind of strength. That's what Kaylaira needs you to discover."

"Fun day! Whoo hoo!" Kaylaira howled as if I'd agreed. Mischief mashed to her face like a toddler's spaghetti meal. "Time to wake the children."

Wake the children? We carried nets to a field not far from the village, where they introduced me to a fruit they referred to as squishmelons. They were no bigger than grapefruits, plucked from trees but wrapped and filled like the skin and juice of a grape.

"So how does this help us wake the children?" I naively asked.

"Here, let me show you," she anxiously obliged.

That mischievous smile from before exploded across her face as she snagged a squishmelon and whipped off its outer skin. Then her grin widened, just as she buried my face in its sweet, cool pulp. Thus the designation, squishmelon.

"So, squishmelon," I coughed, saturated with the sticky juice that dripped from every orifice.

"Some things are best explained through action. Don't you agree?" Jesriel hysterically laughed. "So which little one should we target first?"

"Oh, Naymelia," I assured, still licking the sweet pulp from my lips. "Definitely Naymelia."

"Hmm, go right for the daughter of the guy that dislikes you most? I love it," Jesriel agreed. "Let's rile him up."

Armed with an armada of drippy weaponry, we stashed it on the platform of the center tree, typically used to address the village.

"Slosh a few kids in the face? Meet back shortly after?" Kaylaira cunningly planned.

Jesriel nodded with several juice bombs in his net. He headed one way, while Kaylaira and I marched on Draythian's landing. The thought of angering him both scared and excited me as we rode up the pulley of a neighboring tree. We crossed an upper branch that extended onto his balcony, finding him and Naymelia peacefully asleep behind their shades.

Kaylaira nodded to carry out the attack. She tossed the fruit, and I carried it with the wind, carefully hovering it above their heads. It was charming to see her playful side, watching as she gleefully signaled the countdown with her hands. Three, two, one, then it was bombs away.

Her laughter gave us away before the squishmelon had even dropped, but what a thrill to watch it burst on their heads. Naymelia leapt up gasping, followed by her choking father who leapt from his sheets. It wasn't the first time that game had been played I gathered, not with the way Naymelia immediately giggled from the juice glossing her lips. As for Draythian? Well, he spotted us peaking from the balcony and lunged.

I hurried to evade his raging path, but Kaylaira was unfazed. Her next squishmelon already hurled through the air, burying his face a second time as she'd daringly done to mine. It worked. Stopped him dead in his tracks, panting from the handfuls of goo jammed up his nose and mouth.

"Run!" Kaylaira laughed.

Traitor. She darted across the branch, already abandoning me to face him alone as he cleared the sweet sludge from his eyes. Then he lunged, the perfect chance to flex my talent he'd neglected as I leapt from the ledge through the air. Kaylaira however was relentless, launching a third at his feet to send him smack on his derriere. Even my butt tingled from his slap in the slippery goo.

"Whoo hoo!" she howled, undaunted as she fled across the branch.

Naymelia hopped over her father as if he didn't exist, bouncing on her tippy toes to watch my aerial descent.

"Come on," Kaylaira taunted her, so wound up she was out of breath.

Slowly, the children's sporadic screams blared across the village as Jesriel played Tarzan and swung through their tree homes. One tree after the next he squishmeloned every dry clothed child as if holding a grudge before joining us on the center platform.

"How many homes has he bombed?" I asked.

"Guessing? I'd say, five?" she supposed, not as impressed as I as the masses began to unfold.

We watched every family emerge, scurrying to their decks in search of their perpetrators. "Perfect targets," Kaylaira called them, then the squishmelon war began. Jesriel guarded the stairs and blasted anyone who neared. Kaylaira pursued a different strategy, tossing her fruit towards me as I released a strong gust behind.

"This game is much more fun when you're not getting hit by stones."

"And on the giving end," Jesriel laughed, leveling children like pesky brats.

"Keep going. Hurry!" Kaylaira laughed, tossing squishmelons like a fiend. "Trust me, this is not going to last forever!"

Truth be told, we looked to Draythian's tree where he, Naymelia and a revenge seeking battalion readied a payload of gushing fruit.

"Told you," she smirked.

"Get ready Jordan," Jesriel warned, barely holding off the bottom perimeter. "You're our defense."

Draythian was fired up, but redirected his aggression in hopes of teaching me a lesson. "Ready. Aim. Fire!" he yelled to his minions.

No less than twenty globs of flying pulp hurled our way.

"Wind. We need a strong wind!" Jesriel shouted, without realizing Nijal had coined the term as 'wind repulsion.'

I pulled the zephyr through the air and a rush of wind followed my hand. From left to right, every drop of sweetness was swept from the sky. The children above cheered. Those below mourned defeat, drenched by the hail of sweet rain. "No fair!" they gleefully shouted as it dumped on their heads, writhing Draythian even more so with vengeance in his eyes.

"Again!" he ordered, as their little fingers prepped a second wave, this time with two in each hand.

"Wait," Kaylaira told me, "Challenge yourself."

"How?"

"Catch them. All of them."

"Then throw them back," Jesriel grinned.

Could I? Did I have what it would take? I closed my eyes and accepted the challenge, seizing the zephyr as Draythian readied his troops.

"Ready, aim, fire," he yelled.

I stared into the back of my eyelids with both hands stretched ahead when a sixth sense prickled my pores. I hadn't felt it before, but knew it lingered beneath my skin since the day I'd arrived. I felt every melon barreling toward me as if they were extensions of my hands, their trajectory and speed, weight and density. And just before they drowned us in mush, I halted every last one of them, suspended in a moment frozen in time.

"Boy this is going to be good," Jesriel excitedly whispered.

The crowd gasped then grew silent, coercing my eyes open to see what I'd done. At first it startled me, seeing the effervescent aura dance from my hands like heatwaves shimmying off hot pavement.

"Wow. It's so beautiful," Kaylaira whispered, mesmerized by the shimmering ripples of color before her smile emptied into an unending pit. "Now, show them no mercy."

Glad we fought on the same squishmelon side. Draythian's giggly troops cowered as I drifted the melons toward them, but he stepped forward, enlightened by the mass of motion I could wield and control. At first, I taunted them with the dangling fruit, then squeezed my hands and exploded them like fireworks, burying him and his troops.

"Yes! Chew on that Draythian!" Jesriel yelled behind Kaylaira's victory laugh.

She howled as the village conceded and lifted their hands to surrender. But all was fair in love and war, and I still had a bone to pick with the one who started it all. She celebrated her victory, oblivious to the heap of squishmelons I'd floated above her head.

"Sorry Kaylaira," Jesriel grinned.

She looked up in time to catch sight of them, but it was too late. I squeezed and the children erupted in cheer, gladdened to watch their 'squishmelon queen' sop beneath a waterfall of sugar.

"Yes! All hail queen Kaylaira!" Jesriel laughed, slipping on the glazed floor from being unable to keep upright. In good sport, Kaylaira conceded, but what came thereafter couldn't have been more surreal.

"Wind driver!" an elated child screamed, before another caught his jubilant flow. "Wind driver!" Suddenly, their two voices sparked a chant that lit the others like a forest fire. "Wind driver! Wind driver!"

Their cheers both exhilarated and petrified me. What if I wasn't enough? What if I let them down and wasn't strong enough to save their precious lives against whatever foe was to come?

"Come on," Kaylaira jumped in, lifting my hand to burst the thought in my head. "Fun day hasn't ended. On to your next challenge."

Next up, lily pad rides. One pad had the strength to float two adults or three to four children. Jesriel and Draythian slashed the stems below and mounted each group atop their floating ride. I got the fun part, steering. There were fifteen to twenty floats, all maneuvered from my hands by wind gusts down a winding river.

Guiding the horde was beyond challenging, but Kaylaira and Jesriel's words proved to be true. I did connect with the village in ways I hadn't before, nourishing a new strength I'd never have found just catching rocks. The jubilant buzz carved on their young faces, even when crashing a group or two against the riverbank. It awakened an indescribable joy. Merrily and carefree, they whooshed downstream without a worry in the world, not one of them plagued by the imminent catastrophe that lurked in their skies. I was ready to fight.

After searing my brain for an hour of hyper focus, I collapsed, too exhausted to budge from the lily pad as we rested by a shore. The children used their lilies to slide down slopes while others frolicked in the river. The pain was worth it.

"Looks like you could use one of these," I heard. The voice disarmed me. It was Draythian's. Surprisingly, he'd swam up and jokingly handed me of all things, a squishmelon. "I promise, it's with good intention," he joked.

He didn't linger, but I felt relief to see he'd opened his heart as he continued to a group of children. Kaylaira poked a hole in its side and down the hatch it went. A burst of sweet, tangy juice flooded my mouth, instantly electrifying my senses as gobs of pulp released the fruit's essence.

"Wow!" I nearly choked, hurrying to take a bite of its flesh.

A vibrant symphony of sunshine and citrus followed, succulent and juicy, reminding me of the power of nature's candy. I couldn't help but laugh as it dribbled down my chin, lost in the exhilarating pleasure of the best fruit I'd ever had.

"If he brought you that, he's warming up to you," she smiled as we shared the treat.

"And for that I'm grateful," I replied.

"How are you feeling?"

"Like there's nothing left in me," I answered, still fending off exhaustion. "I think that's the most I've ever exerted myself."

"It's okay, you're still learning," she assured, bathing my hair with the river's cool water. "We as a people may not share your skill, but together we can master revitalizing your mind and strength. For now, just enjoy fun day. No need to stress over your midday voyage. Clear your mind and rest your thoughts."

My next voyage? The jump! The fun made me forget. How could I not worry about the biggest thing I'd ever do in life? I began to feel anxious, then remembered the same words she'd uttered all along, '*to embrace healing and avoid needlessly preoccupying myself with daunting tasks*.' Tougher to do than imagined, but her words and the inspiring sounds of nature as she bathed my hair, softened my tension onto the lily pad.

Our fingers found each other, fitting together perfectly like two pieces of a puzzle as every part of me felt it belonged. A sense of belonging washed over me, amplified by the gentle whispering breeze, the river's soothing trickle and the children's backsplash of laughter. Finding serenity became easier with every second, especially when she was near. However, as I closed my eyes, my mind drifted to an unknown place.

CHAPTER TWENTY-FOUR

Something was wrong! Very wrong! My eyes remained closed as I struggled to open them, trapping me in a haze within the prisons of my head. Where was Kaylaira's laugh? Why had the river's whoosh and the children's laughter abandoned me?

Sounds became muffled and sight became faint, as if Earth and Elatia were one and the same. I heard both sides in both places at once but couldn't look about to decipher the difference. I was as dead as a severed tree limb, along with my arms, legs and even the slightest wiggle of my lips. Where was I? Nijal called me from one place and Kaylaira from another, pleading I abandon wherever I'd gone. Problem was, I didn't know how.

Fear turned to worry and worry to panic as I lied unsure of which world I belonged to. A silent plea for 'help' rang loud in my head, but no one else could hear, no one knew where I was or how to reach me. So there I lay for a countless span of time, trapped in hopeless desperation as my real eyes shed a tear. That I felt. It trickled down my cheek as my only means of consolation.

With no escape, I could only retrace my aria. I hummed it, whistled it, played its tune in my head, in every form and variation with no concept of time. It settled me the same it always had, purging my worries and whooshing away my fears as I floated in a motionless state without a clue to what I'd begun. For how long? Who knows, until Nijal and Kaylaira's voice shouted as one from the same side.

"Jordan, you have to wake up!" he shouted.

His voice pierced that bubble and echoed in my ear, strengthened by Kaylaira's touch as she gently tapped my cheek. Both were prodding me to return from wherever I'd gone.

"Come back to me!" she whispered.

It was the last sound I heard before a chill crawled my spine, pulling me back to the lily pad where its waters awoke my senses. Slowly, my eyes blinked in light, finding Nijal and Kaylaira both staring as if the life in me had somewhat disappeared.

"Nijal?" I grumbled as I came to. "How did you get here? When did you arrive?"

"Jordan, we've got a problem," he ignored. "You're stuck in some kind of comma-like limbo. Come on, wake up man."

My head was on fire, and Kaylaira speckled me with water as I came to terms with what he'd said. Wasn't I back already?

"Coma? No no. It was weird. I was trapped in my head, dazed for a bit, but it's alright, I'm back now," I comforted him.

"Trust me, you're so not back, you're currently lying in the emergency room in a hospital bed," he informed.

CHAPTER TWENTY-FIVE

Hospital bed?! I thought back to our fruit fight and our stroll down the river. Kaylaira and I rested on a lily pad, then after that, everything went blank. Nijal hadn't seen me and figured to check in after school.

"You weren't just asleep like normal. This is different," he exclaimed.

"Different? How?" I asked.

"Sick," he dawdled, "And then… your mom found you."

"Mom?" I leapt from the leaf.

"Yes! She couldn't wake you and called 911. I tried covering, but there was nothing I could do. I'm telling you, you look like mud!" he stressed. "While she called, I did the only thing I could think of."

"What?" I asked.

"I took the stone and hid it when they picked you up. Man, you owe me! I had to fake the biggest acting career of my life—sobbing and crying, telling them I missed you and couldn't go the night without my friend until they let me in the room. That's where I am now after 'forcing' myself asleep, which they also know about by the way. We are in so much trouble, but first things first, you gotta wake up," he said.

"How did you find us?" I asked, what should've been my last concern.

Then Wonder leapt on his head as if they'd suddenly become besties, sending Nijal into a heart spasm. "Somehow, little dude remembered me and knew where to find you. Then I ran, *forever* and now I'm here."

"How did this happen?" Kaylaira asked.

"Long story," I regretted to say. "Let's just say falling asleep on my world hasn't been easy as of late, and I required a little help. Besides, when I fall asleep there, I come here; when I fall asleep here, who knows what happens."

"Not just sleep, coma," Nijal barked. "Courtesy of the scotch and pills?"

He was angry, but more concerned.

"What now?" Kaylaira worried.

"I guess I just wake up?"

"That's the problem, all those pills you've been popping like skittles have you seriously sedated. Maybe, now that you're conscious we can jumpstart you back home," he guessed.

By then a small audience had gathered, including Draythian.

"I have to go and fix this," I jumped up, woozy to stand.

But the sight of me abandoning them reverted Draythian to his old self. "Wait, go? What happens with later? The jump? Only one day remains for us to decide the best way to act, today being the most important. We were meant to find answers in the deep Jordan. You can't leave, we need to know."

"Look, I don't have time to explain but I have the king's echo, and I know it's something you can't understand, but right now this is more important for both of us," I answered.

"How?" he barked.

He was puffed up and agitated, his fist clenched and ready to brawl before Jesriel jumped between us.

"Against my will and the will of others we believed in you Jordan!" Draythian burned. "And now you have something more important? More important than our lives, than my daughter's?"

His every word spat like dragon fire, recounting how the children depended on me and how he'd placed his daughter's life in my hands. Others tried to calm him as he stormed past Jesriel, but I was in no condition to fight. There's no denying he could've taken me down, but the longer he rambled, the more his offensive words ground away the little control I had. Groggy and agitated from the sedation it was too much to bear, and the reason I reacted so senselessly. I tried holding back. I tried subduing my temper, but the urge to silence him became strong and ripped from my hand, like a wild dog pulling from its leash.

"Jordan, wait!" Kaylaira screamed.

She saw it before I knew what I'd done, the darkness in me, the shockwave that boomed from my hand. Everyone within ten feet flew like sheets on a clothesline. The children, Draythian, Nijal and Kaylaira, all whisked through the air before I clasped my fist.

"No! I'm sorry!" I cried. "I couldn't hold it in! I didn't mean it! I'm sorry."

I rushed to help the nearest one from the ground when they backed away with unease, leaving me discarded like a betraying enemy.

How had such a harsh response slipped so effortlessly? Instead of the friendship I once witnessed, fear now held their gaze and nothing I was capable of would make it right. I needed to leave, quick. So overwhelmed I dashed from the group, hoping I'd awaken and cross back home. But it was slow to come, and all I could do was run before Nijal and Kaylaira caught up to me.

"Jordan!" she yelled with Nijal trailing behind, "Jordan, please!"

I'd have rather kept running, but her plea weighed my footsteps still. She grabbed my arm and spun me into her eyes. I was quivering and flinched for a slap in the face when she smothered me with the warmth of her arms instead.

"It's okay," she whispered in my ear. "You didn't mean it, and I'll make them understand."

Nijal caught up out of breath. "Whatever that was we can talk about later. But now, we've gotta get you awake."

"You have to go," she acknowledged. "But first, be here, with me."

"Why?" I asked.

"The king's echo. When you return, I don't want you to relive any part of that moment. This is where I want you to be, *here* with me."

Her forehead pressed to mine to absorb my pain, letting the tension of our encounter wash clear from time. She understood my return would land me back in that moment and did everything she could to keep it from happening again.

"Now go," she pushed off. "I'll be waiting and we will mend this. Do not let it distract you from what you need to fulfill."

And off she sent me with a farewell kiss.

CHAPTER TWENTY-SIX

Nijal was right. My mind had awakened, but my real eyes were as stubborn as coffee stains. I knew I was back home, alerted by the beeping hospital monitors and that worn down feeling I'd felt from each crossover back home. That alone made it hard to wake up, but that day it weighed even harder, as if that bubble that encased me refused to give in, stretching and pulling to outmatch my strength.

"Come on man, you're almost there," Nijal coached me.

Then Mom's voice added to his plea. "Just a little further sweetheart, open your eyes."

Hearing her voice was the tug that brought me back, pulling me from a world of confusion into one of embarrassment! However, ignoring the soon to be repercussions, I wiggled my eyes and jostled through, slitting into the reality of medical tubes filling my arms. Mom's gentle squeeze gripped my left hand and Nijal's firmly gripped my right.

"Bingo, bruh!" Nijal yelled.

His sudden voice startled the staff. They patiently waited as Mom's head found my chest, soaking my gown with her tears. But I was obsessed and only thought to return to Elatia despite my current ailing health. However, I knew better than to ask to leave, ecstatic to hear the only word I listened for… 'discharged.'

After a consultation and an extensive flush to wash the poison from my veins, I was let go, leaving Nijal and I alone to face Mom's fury. Well, me that was, he'd already charred in the furnace.

"You haven't been yourself since the cave," Mom started. "I thought maybe you needed a little time and I chose to give you space to let you handle whatever you were going through, but I never imagined it mounting to this! Drinking? Sleeping pills, Jordan? Why? What were you thinking? And Nijal, if you were as good a friend as I hoped, how could you sit by and let it happen?"

The words nearly left my lips. I wanted to say it, I wanted to tell her what I was going through, but how? And then of all times? I even looked for Nijal's go-ahead to divulge or hold back, opening my mouth to let it fly when her hand slapped across my mouth.

"I couldn't wait any longer for you to tell me what's going on, so I took the liberty of scheduling you a counseling visit," she said. "You're going to see a psychiatrist."

"What? A psychiatrist? Mom!" I whined when Nijal nudged my seat.

"Hey. I love you, man, but maybe your mom's right," he reasoned. "Since your traumatic experience, maybe seeing a psychiatrist isn't a bad thing?"

Was he trying to gain her good side and steer clear of another lashing? So I thought, but it wasn't that. We knew each other well enough to blink words through a glare. But I'd been through a lot, and it slowed me from catching his gist before I finally caught on. *A psychiatrist!*

"Fine! When?" I abruptly agreed, forgetting not to make too drastic a change. Acting was Nijal's arena.

"We're headed there now," she shocked me.

Right then? The car ride was dead silent from that point on, with Nijal darting me glances in the rear-view mirror to not be so awkward. I attempted small talk, but nothing came to mind beyond, 'Mom I've been traveling to a distant world every night.'

"Never been to a psychiatrist. What exactly am I supposed to say?" I asked.

She *strongly* encouraged me to not hold back, with the added *I know you're hiding something* glare.

"Tell her the truth. Tell her everything, no matter how absurd," she slowly enunciated. "It's the only way your nightmares will get any better."

Nightmares? Had Nijal told her that much? I gave him a glance, but his shifting eyebrows told me he was as lost as I.

"Trust her. She's known our family for years," Mom went on.

"Can Nijal come along?" I asked.

Mom was acting strange. She wasn't behaving like, Mom. After a brief stare at him in the same mirror she nodded okay.

"Maybe she'll talk sense into him as well," she threw in.

Nijal and I thought we'd come up with a plan but were blindsided the moment we pulled up. Mom accompanied us to the front door, down the halls and straight to the doctor's office where she patiently waited. Dr. Tamera! Her name stretched on the door, the same name on the card Nijal whipped at me in Dad's office. He and I shared a stare, already getting *the told you so* eye.

Even weirder? Mom monitored the door as if I'd run before giving the doc a smile and nod, then the door abruptly closed behind. It was unsettling, triggering the doc to probe us the instant the door closed. She moved with quiet strength, and beneath her kindness laid an unbreakable resolve. Not only were our secrets safe with her, but her resilience also showed she wouldn't bend to whims or pressures. Firmly, she asked Nijal to sit quietly on the side and placed me on a sofa across from her view.

"I see why people confess in here," Nijal nervously joked. "Any way I can take one of these chairs for my room?"

Doc and I glanced him at the same time, prompting an immediate apology for having broken her first rule in record time. Truth be told, the same thought occurred as I sunk in the fabric. The chair swallowed me in comfort, and after a brief courteous intro, the words ripped from my mouth.

"There's no coincidence I'm here. We found your card hidden in an old book in my dad's office, and now you're the first-person Mom brings me to see. You knew him, didn't you? He came to see you? And for what? Why did he come? What did he say?" I asked in one jumbled sentence.

She pumped her hands like a foot tapping brakes, dropping her pen and notepad while urging me to breathe.

"I see you'd rather jump in the deep end, but I'm not convinced you're ready," she said. "So to give me an idea of whether you'll sink or float, let's start a little slower. If I see you're ready, I'll toss you right in."

"Fair enough," I nodded, nervously twiddling my fingers.

How was I to begin? Was I to trust her, completely? Was I to trust Mom's conviction, even though she had no idea what I was going through? Doc patiently waited as if she'd heard it all, the grandest, most ludicrous stories no matter how wild or contrived. Nothing would make her blink, so I dove right in.

"It's a recurring dream, so I thought," I started. "I close my eyes, and when they open I'm on another world, picking back up just moments before the time I left off."

"Why doubt it's just a dream?" she questioned me.

"Because dreams don't send you back with the gifts you've dreamt of," I said, poking my thumb against my leather necklace with the lucent tied at its end.

And then came the reaction I'd hoped for, her eyes exploding like a bag of heated popcorn kernels. She leaned close with her bottom jaw dropped as if it had been too long since she'd seen one last. Gently, she placed it in her palm, analyzing each angle with its reflective blue facets vaulting in her eyes.

"Guess you're ready for the deep end," she sat back and smiled.

"You've seen one?" I asked.

"More times than I can remember. Courtesy of your father," she said.

Having seen all she needed, she dove into the details of his visits, and his obsession with a so-called dream that Mom claimed swept him from reality. When asked to bring something back from his alternate world, he chose a lucent, wrapped around his neck on a similar scrap of thread.

"Just like you he was obsessed with sleep, constantly looking for new ways to sleep deeper, longer," she said.

She rushed to draw the window shades and anxiously flicked off the lights, imagining what would come next.

"I assume there's another marvel you possess?" she suggested.

I nodded for Nijal to pull the bijou from his pocket, initially as dead as a clump of dirt. But as he moved my direction her attention gained, ripping her from the window shades as its amber came aglow.

"How did you find this?" she gasped.

"Lying beneath a heap of rocks, in a caving exploration where this all began. Did Father show you one of these as well?" I asked.

Curiously, she didn't answer but flipped on the lights as she rummaged for what to say. Personally, I still pondered her connection with Dad. Why her? What made her so special?

"Of all people, my father comes to you describing his dreams and a stone from another world. And you believed him? You didn't think he was crazy? Why not?" I asked.

"Your father came to me because of my research on dreams, anomalous dreams at that," she explained. "And remember, he needed to sleep or focus at least. What do you know of hypnosis?" she asked.

"Oh boy. Here we go," Nijal uncomfortably interjected. No way he'd keep that quiet.

"Let me guess. Still under the assumption it's some form of hocus pocus?" she asked.

"You could say that. And of course the swinging watch," Nijal continued.

"Well let me disappoint you. It's not, and is in fact founded on *very* basic science," she said.

"How so?" I asked.

"Wait, are you actually going to listen to this?" Nijal discouraged.

Before I could answer she popped him a question. "You enjoy fishing?"

Which he answered with a resounding, "Hell no." "It's boring, for old dudes just sitting there staring at a rod in water."

"My sentiments exactly," she agreed, throwing him for a loop. "It was my father's favorite pastime, and just like you, I never understood why anyone would waste hours sitting in a boat staring at water. And even when he did finally catch something, he'd throw it back."

"So why do it?" Nijal asked, now engrossed.

"Simply put, it wasn't about catching a fish, it was the life he found staring in the water. That bobbing float that mesmerized him for hours was a form of hypnosis, or in terms you'd prefer, a stage of heightened focus, the fine line between being asleep and awake," she added. "Ever watch a child staring at his favorite cartoon, oblivious to his mother's persistent calls?"

Nijal scratched his head, guilty of having been that child.

"There you have it again, an intense focal point," she continued, "Another form of deep concentration or the word you don't like to hear. Some people view the day-to-day robotic routine of getting up, going to work, eating and sleeping as a form of hypnosis."

"Did my father learn how? Did he get to sleep, or focus whenever he needed?" I asked.

"Easily. All he needed was the sound of a special tune," she concluded.

CHAPTER TWENTY-SEVEN

I wasn't sure how to take the turn of events! Dad on Elatia, experiencing the same as I? How was I to explain my visit to Mom? She waited by the car, giving Nijal and I no time to rehearse our dialogue as she watched the door the instant we headed out. Worst yet, I'd gone to a psychiatrist and came out crazier than when I'd gone in?

With no more than a twenty-minute stroll home, I pleaded she let us meet her there instead. She threw a fit of course, claiming I was in no physical condition when Nijal vowed to call should an emergency arise. We were off the hook, for the moment, leaving Nijal and I to rehash every crumb during our walk back to the house.

Was Dad's bijou the same I possessed? Did he ever tell Mom? Was that the reason behind her sudden strange behavior? Were his 'geological expeditions' in fact moments he'd spent on Elatia, a different world perhaps? Who else knew of his discovery? Dr. Tamera needed time to think and agreed to reconvene another time, leaving Nijal and I to decipher it alone.

"Wait. I know how to do it. Just walk up to her and say, 'Mom, look, I sleep by day and fight crime in other worlds by night,'" Nijal laughed.

The funny part was no matter what I said or how I'd put it, that's exactly what she'd hear. He dropped me at the door as promised, leaving me to face the remaining fire on my own.

"Oh, wait," he added. "That tune in your head, the one she mentioned, why not whistle or hum it on a recorder?"

"Why?"

"I was thinking. Like doc said, if that sound is so 'special' and plays as your focal point, why not play it aloud instead of just in your head? Drown out everything else around."

"Is this another one of your sly attempts to recruit me in your band?" I laughed.

He was a musical prodigy, his fingers naturally born to glide across piano keys. To look at him and think classical music one would laugh. You'd think football instead. As for me? I struggled with the guitar. Okay, maybe I sucked, but his idea wasn't the worst.

"I'll get some of the others to play it as well. Could be a lot easier for you to zombie out," he added.

We high-fived and agreed to meet up later, with me heading in to face Mom alone. Surprisingly, she wasn't there, hopefully soothing her temper and clearing her head on her evening stroll. I saw what upset her as I passed a hallway mirror, catching the first glimpse of myself in a while. And wow, Nijal was right. I did look like mud. The pills, scotch and lack of true sleep had corroded away the good of me. My face wilted. My skin was pale and sockets sunken in my head, with a gloss of yellow replacing the white of my eyes.

I couldn't bear to face the mirror and continued to my room instead, finding a book propped on my freshly made bed. It was the old gray book from Dad's office where Nijal discovered Dr. Tamera's card. My heart leapt. What was it doing there? We'd clearly placed it back on Father's shelf. I tiptoed towards it as if it were a trap, then flipped through its pages to see what we'd missed. However, it was all the same, old yellow pages that defined Earth's crust.

"That was your father's favorite book," Mom startled me. "There's something special in those pages."

My heart thudded. Anxious to know her affiliation I set it aside.

"Mom. I need to know where you fit in?" I presumptuously asked.

She was calm, spooky calm, and it wouldn't have shocked me if she heard my thumping heart as she plopped next to me on my bed. She kissed the top of my head, then uttered the last response I'd expect to hear. "I don't."

She didn't? Clearly I was confused as she narrated Dad's work story, how special it was but what it eventually became. "He *loved* geology. When asked why, you know what he said? He'd say studying rock layers was the closest thing to a time machine we could ever have, and how he could travel thousands, millions, even billions of years in the past all from the knowledge of a single rock."

He was the best at what he did, a pioneer, but that level of genius came at a cost. It landed him a government contract, researching unidentifiable stones and their potential use when one caught his attention above the rest. A bijou! That's where the trouble began.

"It's like they kept him hostage. He could never sleep, his body began to change," she said, acknowledging the similarities with an eye sweep across my pale skin.

"Did he ever say what he worked on?" I asked.

"No," she said. "Instead, your father told me how much he loved us, which he never left room for doubt. And because of that love, he could never share what he'd learned. But somehow, he knew you'd end up finding it, and in case you did, he left this book."

She told me how the 'men in black' ravaged our home after his death, then questioned her hour after hour. But all the same, they came up dry.

"That's why he didn't tell me," she said. "And that's why I fought my entire life to keep you from following geology, hoping this day would never come. But somehow you came right back to it every time, even crawling through a cave to get a true sense of it."

"Mom. In the cave—" I began, but she stopped me.

"If your father loved me as much as he did and still chose to keep silent, then I trust it's not for me to know. But you're different. If you believe as he did in your heart that it's that important to follow, then finish it. Finish what he started, but be smart and do it the right way, without wasting away your mind and body. You'll have my support, but this is for you to discover alone."

With another kiss on the forehead and a promise I'd take better care, she left me, awestruck that Dad never uttered a word. Still, her having some sense of what I was going through lifted a load.

"Anything you need?" she asked before heading out.

Actually there was. Having wasted so much time walking, running or riding my bike, I knew my motorcycle would come in handy. Normally, I'd never burden her by asking a favor, but that felt different and I knew she'd understand.

"Well," I started, scratching my head and not wanting to ask. "My—"

"Motorcycle?" she finished with a smile. "You're right, I believe that's something we should look into."

I leapt in that book the instant she left my door, unsure what Dad expected me to find. Was I to read the whole thing? I flipped the pages in the vicinity where we'd found Dr. Tamera's card, scrutinizing the material with a hypnotic bore. Then came a sudden change.

Chapter eighteen, the same as my birthday, a highlighted letter marked in yellow on each page. In total there were nine, H-R-E-S-Y-U-I-M-A, it spelled. No word I recognized and it made no sense, but no other pages contained highlighted letters. It had to be a clue, and that book was the perfect disguise, old, raggedy and barely held to its stitching, the one book no one guessed to pull from the shelf. But what did it mean? A code? Another language?

Immediately, I typed the jumbled letters in my computer, rushing between languages to find a meaning. Nothing! I read them back to front, nada. I even rearranged them and scrambled their order, still nothing.

With the book aside, I rested my stinging eyes and reimagined the melody from the forest. Eventually it led to a hum, almost too despicable to verbalize when out came an old tape recorder from Dad's office. With a repeat of fast forward and rewind, my voice landed my aria when Nijal knocked on my door. He immediately understood what the letters meant.

"Dude, it's a cipher," he said without hesitation.

"What?"

"A word cipher," he continued, "it's probably a keyword to decipher a text."

My dumbfounded look prompted his explanation. After lining every letter of the alphabet side by side, directly beneath you'd do the same. Only difference with the second row, was to start with the first letter of your keyword under the letter A, followed by the keyword's remaining letters behind. Lastly, you'd finish that second row by scribbling every alphabet in order, next to your keyword, minus the letters used in the keyword itself.

"Every letter is coded, so now all you do is match up the corresponding letters," he explained. "Something that looks to you like JMTOR becomes a real word, like PIZZA, which I'm seriously lacking by the way."

"Yeah, I'm sure dad's scribbling secret codes about pizza," I responded, still grappling to understand.

"You know what I mean. Look, first you arrange these nine letters to form the keyword or it's pointless. Not to mention the fact that after figuring that out, you have to find the text it belongs to," he said.

"Mission impossible," I exclaimed.

"Yeah, it's kind of the whole purpose," he chuckled.

What keyword would Father use? We re-scribbled those nine letters a million times, Nijal with one notepad and me another, jotting every meaningful phrase we could find. YES MIRE, HER SAY, and my favorite being the two letters UM, describing my current sentiment. One scrunched paper after another flew against the wall, eventually covering the floor like a children's toy ball pit.

"Okay, okay, okay," Nijal said with growing frustration. "Enough of this, we can give it time, you should be focused on your jump anyway. Doesn't that go down the moment you get back?"

Tangled in my latest drama I'd completely forgotten the jump, or the burst of wind I'd sent through the group prior to my abrupt departure. Yeah Nijal, thanks! It was the exact opposite of what I needed to calm me but was quickly sidetracked the instant he hit play on my recorder. I couldn't stop him in time and out went his laughs at the crackles in my nonmusical tone.

"Why on Earth use a tape recorder?" he asked.

"I don't know, I guess it felt more personable with it being Dad's," I answered. "Besides, maybe it'll leave less of a trail."

He caught the vibe of my crackling tone in his head, staring down the ceiling with his eyes closed and his fingers playing a pretend piano as the composition clicked. He'd already pieced how he and his classical music buddies would harmonize the tune. Who was I kidding not to listen? When it came to music, the boy was a mastermind.

Pizza somehow made its way in from Mom. Collaborated? Not sure. But after a hot shower with her insistent lavender oil and a follow up with warm milk and cookies, my worries faded. It was time to face the others and make the jump. Would I return during Kaylaira's warm embrace, or the cold moment I hurled those children through the air like balls of lint?

Nijal snored long before I fell asleep, and I imagined he'd wake up on Elatia the moment I arrived. So with the sum of Mom's sleep concoctions, I left the bones of my bedroom and was back on Elatia, planted in a soft bed of grass. The air, the feel of their grass, it enlivened me. But as much as I wanted to relish that first touch, I couldn't. The sound of a strangled gasp filled the air, cutting through the soothing whispers of the wind and rustling grass. It was a sound of panic and fear, someone fighting for each breath, pleading for someone to save him from his own body's betrayal. It was Nijal!

CHAPTER TWENTY-EIGHT

I scrambled from the bed of grass. Nijal was on his back, battling the ground as if he'd been dropped in a sea of hungry waters, gasping for air like a drowning man's desperate cries.

"Nijal!" I grabbed him.

He instantly snapped from his nightmare, wheezing as if he'd swallowed an ocean.

"What happened? You're okay. Chill. I got you," I assured.

"No it's not all right," he yelled, yanking his arm away to catch his breath.

"What happened?" I asked, giving him space and time to adjust.

"What happened? You know what it's like to drown?" he yelled. "Well, imagine that feeling but it never ends. That's what I've felt the last twenty minutes waiting for you to get here. Trapped and drowning."

He couldn't crossover without me? I was stunned, and had assumed all along that any sleepyhead with the stone could make the voyage. But that wasn't the case. What had I unknowingly done each time I'd fallen asleep?

"Anyway, what happened to popping up where you were making out with your girl? Or better yet, the moment you know, you blasted me through air, which I haven't forgotten by the way," he blabbered.

He was right, I hadn't noticed. Where were we? Kaylaira and the others were nowhere to be found.

"Kaylaira!" I called, racing to where she'd left me with a kiss.

How long had we been gone? We'd returned to the point we'd left, but her absence quickly gave the sense that something was off, until Nijal spotted a trail of scattered petals leading into the distance.

"Okay. At least we know we're in the right place," I assumed.

"You know, this is really starting to get screwed up," Nijal ranted as we followed her trail of crumbs. "I sure hope you appreciate me as a friend."

"Of course I do, Nijal. Remember? Last night we got you JMTOR," I sarcastically added.

He whispered it again and again, bellowing a fake laugh when remembering his code for pizza as we embarked on our journey into the unknown. I could run forever with their air empowering my lungs, and even Nijal hung on a lot better than he would've back home. In less than a ten-minute sprint we'd covered a couple miles. Her petals became sporadic, but eventually led us to find her pacing alone.

"Kaylaira," I yelled ahead.

She doubled back flaring a smile with joy rushing into her eyes. My worries melted, freeing me from fear of being met with defiance as she embraced me like the first summer rain. Inner peace flooded me as I welcomed her arms.

"Felt like I'd never see you again," I whispered.

"I should've waited longer, but became afraid I'd miss you or you'd somehow made it to the deep without me," she uttered.

That was a first. She'd waited? How long and what of the king's echo? Why hadn't I returned before the point I'd left off?

"Kaylaira, something's changed. The echo, how long did you wait?" I asked.

"You left early in the second burn," she answered. "We're entering the fourth."

"Daylight?" Nijal guessed.

"Yeah. Four burns a day," I told him. "So if we left at let's say, elevenish this morning, that should put us around four in the afternoon?"

"Five hours lapsed?" Nijal claimed. "No delay? No repeat?"

"Kaylaira, what happened to the echo? Until now I always returned prior to the moment I departed. This is the first time I've missed more than an entire burn of your day," I explained.

A haunting reality glossed her face as she directed us up to what we hadn't noticed. Barely visible to the naked eye, high above the uppermost clouds, something peculiar hovered in their sky.

"The MonTu. They've arrived," she revealed.

CHAPTER TWENTY-NINE

My brain mushed into jelly. The MonTu were near and I was far from accomplishing what I needed to do. I became hesitant, uncertain I was capable of even handling the jump, and now them? The arrival, the jump, the scuffle I'd left behind; I couldn't process them all, yet there we were at the mystery hole they deemed 'the deep,' where Draythian and the others waited without a glimpse of contentment.

With the king's echo, I'd hoped to evade that moment all together, yet there I was forced to face them in the absence of its presence. Per Kaylaira, it was the arrival that induced changes. The planet sensed the MonTu's presence the same as they had, like a fully charged battery subtly losing power.

"More changes will come. The echo is only the beginning," she expounded as we neared the aggressive bunch.

To no surprise, Draythian's eyes were the first to prey on our approach, festering like a bowl of simmering stew. And he wasn't alone. Others from the circle mirrored his rage, a disheartening sight before Jesriel broke their rhythm with an infectious smile. It felt good to at least know he was onboard. As for Kaylaira, she approached like a swinging ax, daring anyone to speak against me as she boldly took my hand. With her firm grip and Jesriel's backing, the words made their way to my tongue.

"I owe each of you my deepest apology. That wasn't me from before. It's not what defines me or who I am. Sometimes, there's just more than I can handle happening on two worlds," I began. "The zephyr is new to me. My mind and body behave differently with each jump I make, and as a result, at times I'm finding I'm not… the same person I'm accustomed to being. Just ask the one who knows me best."

I looked to Nijal, whom they'd grown accustomed to having around. Amazingly enough, he said nothing, but gave a thumbs up as a testament to what I'd said.

"What counts is I'm here now," I fortified.

They kept silent for a beat, leaving me to wade alone in their current of hate before Jesriel erupted with an enthusiastic spark. "You're right! You're here, and that does count more than anything else I'd say. Anyone crazy and brave enough to do what you're about to, is okay by me."

He was first to approach and welcomed me with an embrace, followed by a tepid acknowledgment from a handful of others. But Draythian's interest were more set on our timeline.

"The arrival has begun and there's much to do. Let's see if we can find some answers," he ushered us along.

We emerged from the forest into a ninety-degree rock wall jutting twenty to thirty-feet high. Narrow steps carved into the rock created a steep, nearly perpendicular stairway to its surface.

"Okay, that doesn't look fun," Nijal remarked.

I had to agree, and while the others eagerly dashed up top, I strapped my father's watch to Kaylaira's wrist.

"I want you to have this. It belonged to my father," I told her. "I guess it's a little something I want you to remember me by, in case—"

Her finger pressed my sentence closed while her face happily beamed from the relic on her arm. I tasked Nijal with explaining its purpose. They'd no doubt have time during my death-defying plunge into the bottomless pit. With most already up top, it was our turn to climb.

Cautiously, we went up. One wrong step and we'd tumble back down like unwanted crumbs being brushed from a lap. For me it was an adventure. I'd grown accustomed to unfamiliar heights, but Nijal was a different story. He took each step with exaggerated precision, drenched with sweat and saliva dribbling from his mouth. He made it up before I did but had no words to describe what he gazed on the other side. And it wasn't till I was beside him that I gathered an understanding. We'd without a doubt made it to 'the deep.'

"Now who's pissing his pants?" Nijal shivered.

The sight was surreal, shattering my concept of what could exist as I glared into the illusion of a neurotic dream. As I peered into its vastness and felt its range, I realized how absurd of me to suggest a rope! The opening ventured beyond the span of my eyes. A mile? Two miles from one side to the other? It wasn't a hole; it was a missing chunk of planet.

The others traipsed to the lip of the ledge as if they strolled upon their lawns. Nijal slinked his way behind them, shuffling his feet to avoid any abrupt change when life left his face.

"Oh, God!" he heaved.

Vertigo nudged him forward against his will as his eyes absorbed what his brain couldn't handle. The hole summoned to pull him in.

"Nijal!" I yelled as his weight teetered forward.

Jesriel grabbed him and yanked him back to his butt. He hit hard, but the jolt never fazed him as he scooted back, all the way to the opposing edge from which we'd just climbed. His head slung over the side, and every morsel of fear ejected from his mouth. What had he seen? I'd never seen him so petrified and decided it was my turn to face the music.

Kaylaira took my hand and guided me over. Carefully, I shifted my foot till my shoe hung on the edge, then with a deep breath, I glanced down. My head suddenly weighed a thousand pounds, as if gravity had increased tenfold. The wind howled, amplifying the dizzying height that swirled my head as panic blurred my vision. My heart pounded as the ground seemed to slip away from me, paralyzing me with fear from the endless, black void waiting to swallow me whole. I struggled to keep balance as my weight titled forward, instantly struck by the faintness Nijal had felt.

As the darkness beckoned me, I too nearly fell in before breaking from its hold, then plopped on my butt right next to Nijal. It was the first time since I'd known him that he wasn't exaggerating, and in sympathy and remorse I crawled to his side, puking the warm bile of my stomach next to his.

"Oh god! What am I doing Nijal?" I gasped, when a hand landed each shoulder.

Jesriel's fell on one and Draythian's on the other.

"We understand if you feel it's impossible," Draythian said, while Jesriel added that no other had the courage to attempt what was to be done.

"Give me a moment. I just need a moment," I panted as they let me be.

I wiped the sludge from my mouth and caught my breath, turning to Nijal who fixated on the solid ground below us.

"I'm sorry man. I'm no help, I can't even look the other way."

I never intended to put him in such a compromising position.

"It's okay," I comforted him. "You've come this far with me, a lot further than I'd expect of anyone."

I lugged my body upright and crossed my legs, buttressing my will to stand on two legs. Finding calm wasn't as easy as before, not with their doubting whispers circling like vultures.

"What else can we do? Is there another way? How can we ask this of him, alone?" they asked, so easily losing faith in me.

It took an unknown strength to defy my fears, to stand on two shaky legs as I wobbled to the ledge. Vertigo reprised, but I clenched my teeth and bit it back in its place. My first glance hadn't deceived me. It was still there with no end, with no unit of measure that accurately gauged the depths below. Simply put, I stood at the edge of a seemingly endless abyss that dictated all I could ever fear. Its own cloud coverage hovered midrange. Distant waterfalls spilled from shelves, dropping till their waters fizzled to nothing.

The sight of it drowned the negative whispers around my ears before Kaylaira hushed their blaring insecurities. "He's strong enough. He can do it," she stated with utmost confidence.

Why such ironclad faith in me? I couldn't guess, but it was contagious and spread to the others, filling me with optimism as well. She inspired me and steadied my nerves, compelling me to believe I was ready for the task.

"How do you know this of him Kaylaira?" Draythian asked skeptically.

"I can't explain. I've never felt this before. But I tell you, believe in him, and he will be there for us in ways you could never imagine," she affirmed. Then suddenly, she stepped uncomfortably close to the edge as she turned to the group with her back toward the opening. "But what we ask also remains true. This is our world, not his. So how can we stand idle and ask this of him alone?"

Her foot dangled precariously over the gaping breach as her arms spread like an eagle's wings. Her gaze bore into mine, piercing through my soul with an intense connection, before a twisted smile spread across her face. Without hesitation, she let the full weight of her body carry her over the edge, down into the unknown depths below.

CHAPTER THIRTY

My hands were too slow, grasping nothing but air as my heart plummeted a million times over. The world seemed to slow down as she tumbled, each second stretching into an eternity as I helplessly watched her fall.

As the sound of my screams echoed in the empty void where she'd been, the rest of me thoughtlessly followed. No reasoning. No hesitance, just a numbing plunge into the beast's mouth with fear left on the ledge. I cared for nothing more than having the strength to save her.

I was seconds behind as the chilling winds scathed me when our eyes intermittently locked. She tumbled helplessly, but each glance acknowledged confidence in the person she believed I was. I dropped my head and burrowed through the air. My arms gripped to my side, nudging me closer when the cloud mist suddenly swallowed her down. I was blinded to where she'd gone, thickening each heart throb as unnerving thoughts gobbled me whole. Had the bottom taken her so quickly? Had I failed her act of confidence along with everyone above?

A burst of thin droplets showered me as I plunged through the mist, with panic threatening to take over. Easier said than done when dropping like a brick, unsure when the ground would suddenly slap you in the face. But it was now or never for me to give in to my fears or rise above them and take charge.

I closed my eyes and summoned the zephyr as the chilled air licked my skin. It spoke to my hands as if it had a voice, whispering secrets into the palms of my hands. I'd found her, still falling, and swiped the mist clear to set eyes on her descent. The zephyr flamed from my hands then it all came blaring in. Her speed and weight. The ground and our rate of fall, just as it had during the squishmelon fight. Then all the air I'd summoned thrusted from my hands.

The gales matched her descent then caught her weight, swirling around her body like a protective embrace. Inch by inch I nudged closer, till the air beneath heaved her into my arms. Our bodies met with a gentle collision, then her arms flung around me as we clung as one. She was afraid, excited, yet confident in my touch, but the cavern floor rose quickly.

"Hold tight!" I yelled.

Like a foot mashing brakes I fought our descent, thrusting my hand to buffer the air. The wind jarred my palm. I pressed harder, tempering our descent as the ground rushed to our face. Fifty feet, twenty, then ten. We each let out blood-curdling screams as our bodies jarred to a sudden stop. Our hearts raced. Our breaths came in ragged gasps as we hung in the air, just inches from the ground before we sloshed in a puddle. Her weight pressed the ground and mine into hers, pinning her quivering body beneath me.

"Are you out of your mind?" I chuckled, half-shocked, half-horrified as we trembled something fierce.

"Must be," her voice shook. "Still, I was right. And you followed, didn't you?"

Succumbing to the rush of adrenaline, she struggled to steady her trembling hand as she gently brushed my cheek.

"We all need a push," she continued.

"And you were mine," I grinned.

My mouth lowered and hers rose, colliding our lips with the past forgotten while our hearts pummeled like two bashing drums. It was our first kiss, a long-awaited moment that took an eternity to arrive. Our lips moved in sync, dancing together in a passionate rhythm before the rush of adrenaline left us snickering with joy. Neither of us wanted the moment to end, but the pit we lied in whispered otherwise.

It was as if the very planet was alive, every rock throbbing with energy and color. Light waves pulsated from cracks beneath the ground and ran up the cavernous walls. Vibrant greens and yellows danced together, gradually transitioning into fiery reds as if their color were blowing in the wind. Small basins of water held the same whooshing colors, gurgling like pools of hot lava but were frigid to touch.

"How are we ever going to find anything in this?" I asked, while my eyes adjusted to the near and far darkness.

"With an illuming lucent," she answered.

She was ready from the onset, leaving me to wonder if leaping was her plan all along. The white lucent around her neck beamed its brilliant light, bolstered by the smaller stones around her neck and hair. But the design of her bracelet intrigued me most.

Two metal bands locked together to form an inner and outer ring. The inner held a white lucent the size of a quarter, while the outer was laced with an array of others, each no bigger than a nickel. A twist rotated the outer loop and lined the white with another white, swelling our light across the wispy water droplets that gusted the air, barely wetting our heads from the hanging cloud above.

Beyond that cloud nothing was visible from the world above, no sun of day, no light to retrace our path of descent. Yet again, we caught the amazing, a bounding glow in its haze that mesmerized us with eerie energy.

We kept on our backs and inhaled the view, dazed by the unchartered world as her head pressed to my shoulder. The colors were so intense, almost as if they were reaching out to touch us as they flared up the mountain walls and into the cloud mist. The cloud glow gifted an aurora borealis before the colors dripped back down in the cascading waters. Hues of electric purples and blues fell down the walls, then seeped into pools and small resonant streams below. We were spellbound beneath its display, but with time against us we had to find answers, answers that were buried like a needle in a haystack.

I sat up and gazed our minuscule presence, dwarfed by the world we'd fallen in. There was no funnel that dropped us at a definitive point. It was a rutted valley with highs and lows. Jutting stone climbed as high as buildings and stretched endlessly into the distance. It was chaos. A rock maze we could trek for the rest of our lives with no inkling how to start or end... until I felt an itch.

"What?" she noticed, giving her exhausted eyes a rest.

"I don't know. Something further below?" I guessed. "This place is a rock jungle. We could spend years searching and still find nothing."

"Not here, but below? Something you sense?"

"Yeah, it's strange," I told her. "The same undying curiosity struck me before I entered the cave back home. It's the same feeling telling me that's where we head."

"Trust it. Follow it," she encouraged.

I headed to the nearest clearing, glancing below to the vague area that whispered for me to near. A glow pierced through the haze.

"There! Below!" she pointed.

We hustled downhill towards the point of her finger, battling broken terrain to a drop-off requiring a mountain-climber's descent. I hesitated. She didn't and dropped without a word, gripping tiny lips of stone with the edge of her fingers as she hustled her way down the slope. I, the 'wind driver,' reluctantly followed, shaky and unsteady till we touched flat ground! That's where all the glowing water descended.

Every pool and thin stream that coursed from all sides carried their water to that central space, a pool at center floor. The water was impossibly clear, like liquid crystal poured from the earth itself. It was the source of the glow's origin, and the closer we got the more intense its light.

"The all-lucent," Kaylaira gasped with her hand over her mouth.

"All-lucent?" I inquired.

"Yes, the water's glow, the origin of our power and the basis of our planet's vitality," she explained. "Something to remember, Jordan. Without the all-lucent, everything becomes as nothing."

I took those words and followed her hand into the pool, awaiting its jab of wintry cold on my finger. On the contrary, it was as tepid as bathwater, tempting our hands to play with its surface as we painted designs in its swirling colors. Pearl was the most prominent and the most brilliant to gaze and seemed to hold all the colors at once. But just before each shift in the water's shade, its bottom was rendered visible, with an undistinguishable object held in its depths.

"Hey, you see that? There, at the base?" I pointed through the dancing color of water.

"Yea, what is it?" she asked.

She tried to lift her weight for a better view when suddenly realizing she couldn't.

"Jordan! Our feet!" she alarmed me.

I looked to where we stood, baffled by the solid terrain that had suddenly devoured our feet.

"It's solid rock. How's this possible?" I asked, tussling to break loose.

"The deep!" she concluded. "I shouldn't be here. Only wind drivers were meant to descend. It's going to fight me. We need to get out, fast."

We were past our ankles when she clinched my shoulders and yanked herself free.

"Crawl to the pool!" I yelled, supporting her weight as she broke from the stone.

She could retrieve the object below while I hovered midair. That was our plan at least, but the deep had another. The instant her hand stretched to touch its waters, the pool hardened like a block of ice.

"The water, it's denying me!" she screamed.

She pounded her fist to break through while I continued to sink. So I thought to outsmart it, heaving her onto its surface with a gust of wind. But the deep denied us again, swatting her like a bug back next to me on the ground.

"Jordan!" she screamed.

Her palms sank beneath the rock and I was up to my knees, struggling to understand why the pool welcomed her before. What had we done differently? Then it dawned. Before, we'd submerged our hands together.

"Again! Together!" I hurried her as my knees dipped below.

A wind burst churned in each hand, one shattering the rock to free my imprisoned legs, the other hauling Kaylaira towards me like tumbleweed. Our hands collided and went for the water, instantly plunging through.

"That's it!" she gasped.

Hand in hand with a deep breath, we leapt in, swimming to that mysterious object in those deceiving waters. Twenty feet down! Worst yet, the deep wasn't done with us. Perched in the pool's belly awaited another surprise, an empty illusion that had deceived us again. Kaylaira was right. The deep was a death trap for those who didn't belong!

Empty-handed, she directed me up to a tunnel we'd missed halfway down. Except, we hadn't missed it. The tunnel's reflection never revealed itself until we'd reach the bottom, luring us into its depths for some inexplicable reason. I had no clue why, not until we made our ascent.

We pushed our way up, stoked to head through the hidden passageway when Kaylaira signaled to refresh her lungs. It was bizarre, but I realized I had no need to follow. Though I'd always struggled to hold my breath beyond a minute, there I had the lungs of a fish. The air I'd inhaled nurtured my lungs, expanding its gift within the walls of my chest. Who would've known? It was another perk of being a wind driver.

For the first time ever I smiled without choking, relishing my newfound ability when the thump of Kaylaira's fist demanded I look up. She was up top, frantic and once again fighting the surface. To our reckoning, it had solidified a second time. Her arms flailed wild. Her eyes screamed 'help' as her final breaths slipped, bashing with all she had to emerge on the other side. We were entombed and the tunnel was our only way out, but first, I had to calm her.

I barely felt dread as I rose to meet her. For once I was in my element, with an ocean of air bounding in my lungs as I swam to her and grasped the sides of her head. My hands were steady and lent her my peace, settling every bit of her anguish as her arms ceased to thrash. For the second time that day my lips pressed to hers, breathing into her lungs as she inhaled my offering. Her panic waned and her tremors ceased, blessing me with a half-granted smile to proceed through the tunnel.

Down we went into its spacious opening, with every gap of air in its channel filled to the brim. Her jewels lit our path, aided by the glowing cracks in the wall. I had no concern. I was poised and as calm as a sunset, with enough air strapped in my lungs to sustain us both. Our lips happily met, breathing life into her lungs as we pushed through the narrowing spillway.

I thought of the cave as the walls closed in, snugged and uniquely cozy, as if the earth embraced us like two strong arms. It became more of a forward crawl than a swim. Still, there was no need to panic, and I admired Kaylaira that much more as she blindly followed my lead, solely dependent on the air I'd provide. Could I have ever known such trust? I don't believe I could.

We travelled no more than a couple hundred feet when a rush of cool air breezed the top of our heads. We'd made it! Wherever that was, where our channel birthed a wide-open cavern. Our eyes slowly adjusted to the hint of light, to a stairwell of carved rock that fell beneath the water. We swam towards it and made the climb where Kaylaira lunged into the open and tasted a world of air.

"Nothing like air, is there? No matter what planet you're on, nothing will ever match a fresh breath," I said.

"Thank you. I wouldn't have made it out without you," she heaved as she crumpled on the stairs.

I left her to catch her breath to survey where we'd been dumped. The stairs emerging from below stretched wall to wall, fifty-five feet along our sides with only a few ascending above the water. A domed rock ceiling loomed nowhere within reach with stalactites of dangling lucents hanging twenty feet down. It was the top of the stairs, however, that piqued my interest, a lone structure protruding from the center floor.

"Ready to have a look?" I asked, curious what it held inside.

She nodded and pulled to her feet, just as excited for answers as we slinked up the steps. They were short, no longer than the length of my hand and barely welcomed the tip of my shoe, but not enough to sway us from the stone canopy perched at the top of our ascent.

"A dome snatcher?" she uttered surprised. "They exist in tales I never thought to be real. Yet here lies one before me? This is unreal."

The dome snatcher, a relic she only believed to exist in tales. She hurried beneath its umbrella shaped canopy that stood just above her head. It perched on four pillars and was barely wider than the span of my arms, with three sides blocked by a four-foot wall which left the side facing us as the only entrance.

However, something greater struck my eyes. The sight of it nearly tumbled me back down the stairs before my legs stiffened and held me in place. Kaylaira was oblivious, still babbling about the relic before seeing my blanket of confusion. She quickly rushed out and nudged my arm, wondering why all life in me had suddenly died.

"Jordan? What is it?" she asked, too afraid to move without my consent.

The cavern walls were littered with inscriptions, rows of jumbled letters in every direction that strung together with no significant meaning.

"Is it the lettering? Can you understand it?" she asked.

"No," my voice cracked. "I was hoping you did."

But it wasn't the inscriptions alone that rattled me, it was what lied at the heart of the canopy floor as well… the same fake rock from Dad's office. She watched it consume me and pled I explain.

"That rock. It isn't real," I told her, "It's fake."

"How do you know this?" she asked.

"I know, because my father kept one just like it on his table back home."

I wanted to move forward but was stuck in place, with greater fear mounting the longer I stared. How did it get there? It was a replica of course, yet still enough reason to be alarmed.

"What else is it?" she asked, watching my eyes bounce from the canopy floor back to the inscriptions on the wall.

"I don't understand what the inscriptions mean," I answered, "but without a doubt, these are my father's writings."

CHAPTER THIRTY-ONE

It was all true. Father had been in those caves, bolstering Dr. Tamera's words of his work on Elatia. But for what purpose? My thoughts crumbled like a sandcastle socked by a wave, and if it not for Kaylaira's pull on my arm, I may have hardened there forever.

"Come. Let's find out together," she urged, slapping away my reluctance.

I was afraid of what it would reveal, and it was her that coerced me to the wall to make sense of his writings. They had no clear-cut meaning, just row after row of scribbled letters across its stone. Drawn arrows speared off from the main texts as if further enlightenment came at later times. As I analyzed the texts, she retrieved the mock stone from the canopy floor.

"These letters, I believe they belong to a cipher," I said, detailing what Nijal explained from the alphabets highlighted in Father's gray book.

"Do you have the key word to open it?" she asked.

"No, working on it and its nothing I understand, but there's so much here."

I needed a pen and paper! There was no way of recalling all the lettering before me and how was I to ever find that place again? Another plunge? Into that black hole?

"You require a mimic lucent," she said.

A mimic lucent? The light from her bracelet had already dimmed as she rotated the outer band to a lemon-colored stone. The inner band she rotated as well, from the white illuming lucent to another with a distinct function.

"Remember the all-lucent?" she asked.

"Yes. Without the all-lucent everything becomes as nothing," I repeated.

The all-lucent sat at the center of her armband, like a pearl, with soft glimmers of every color reflecting from its crevices. It was reminiscent of the pool water above, and once aligned with the lemon-colored stone, a yellow hue burst from its edges. She aimed at the wall and swept over its surface, left to right, top to bottom, covering each inscription with its yellow light. Faint images of each letter lifted with each pass, drifting through the air to land in her jewel. In seconds, the wall was scanned.

"We reverse the process when you're ready to examine its detail," she said, winding the all-lucent back to white.

"You can duplicate them later?" I asked, bewildered, searching her bracelet as if the letters would slip out.

"Yes. And when there's time, I promise I'll teach you each mineral's function," she swore. "But for now, answers."

Minerals? That was the simplicity they'd given lucents?

"Now your turn," she said, handing me the replica stone from Dad's office.

What a mood killer. I plunged from exhilarated to overwhelmed, part of me wanting to pretend her hand was empty. But I took it, reluctantly, relieved of her prod in my ribs to the clatter of something inside. What would I find? It was no heavier than a soda can, the same as the rock back home with the same crevice in its center where both halves met. So, with a deep inhale and the assurance of Kaylaira's hand, I twisted each half and popped it open.

"By the mountain of Elatia!" her eyes swelled, gasping with her hands to her mouth.

My heart bulged and my breath seized. There, lighting the crevices of my eyes was the jade green hue of a second bijou. I'd found another?! I nearly dropped it from disbelief. What was I to do with it and where would it lead? Why had I of all people discovered a second?

"Another one?" I exclaimed distressed.

I wanted to close the lid and pretend it wasn't there. But answers I wanted and answers I'd found, all piling in a never-ending line of questions.

"This is no coincidence," she sighed, afraid and as puzzled as I. "A bijou hasn't been found in lifetimes and within burns you discover a pair?"

I buttoned it beneath my pocket, no longer wanting to acknowledge what I'd found as Kaylaira wandered back in the canopy.

"Anymore bijous to add to the collection?" I sarcastically asked, before wandering in behind her between the pillars.

The atmosphere shifted the moment I stepped in. Her eyes jutted to mine; sensing something was different before a surge of air whipped around our legs. Up and around us it flowed, tightening its current like a boa constrictor as its vortex inhaled our feet from the ground. Then suddenly I felt emptied inside, hollowed-out like a rotten tree trunk with no way of knowing where she ended and where I began.

"Jordan?" she screamed, hoping for an explanation I couldn't give.

It wasn't my doing and was out of my control. However, I never sensed the need to worry as the dome snatcher's winds churned within those pillars, with not as much as a breeze stirred beyond where we stood. We simply soared as it began to erase us from existence, like a pile of leaves met by a ferocious wind.

In seconds, we were no longer there, and the last image I recalled were her beautiful, downtrodden eyes as we drifted in a phase of time that didn't exist. The circling air halted. Neither of us were visible to the other nor ourselves as all touch with the physical world vanished. But she was with me, I could tell. I knew her conscience clung to that barren space she knew to be me, before the swirl shifted the other direction. Then, within a blink, we slowly transitioned back.

Bit by bit we molded back to our forms like a lump of clay shaped by two artistic hands. Our mass gained substance. The hollow inside fattened with flesh. Then the touch of her skin warmed my hand as those same beautiful eyes took form. We were whole again, before the swirling ceased and dumped us to our feet.

We both fumbled over the filthy stone, finding ourselves within the four pillars of yet another domed canopy. However, we were no longer buried in the slums of a cavern. We'd emerged like two butterflies above the skies as if someone removed the ceiling from that darkened world.

"Where are we?" she asked.

Without the slightest inkling, I vaulted to my feet and found the planet's curve below. It was Elatia! Its blue, green and white puffy clouds all lay just beneath our feet. Even the deep was visible from that height, a large dark hole in the heart of all that beauty.

"Is that—" I started, unable to finish from sheer terror.

"Yes," she panted.

Oblivious as to how we'd risen above their planet, we simply stood there in awe and stared down on her world.

"Mount Elatia!" she cried with cheer. "We've journeyed to Mount Elatia?"

"Mountain? We're on top of a mountain?" I asked beyond my wits.

A floating mountain orbiting space was the small object she'd pointed to in the sky. It was simply too far for Nijal or I to decipher at the time.

"Wait. Then the MonTu are here, on this mountain?" I asked, more frightened than dumbfounded.

The MonTu weren't arriving on some vessel as I'd assumed, they were arriving on that hunk of floating rock in the sky. That's when the puzzle fit in my tiny brain. The mountain. The deep. They were connected, and that floating mass was the missing piece, dredged from their land to leave that abysmal crater on its surface.

"We have to get off this thing!" I hurried.

But as we stepped from the canopy the view debilitated my urge. Spellbound in a soundless void, we took care not to disturb its peace as we looked upon it with silent eyes. Miles of emerald-green carpeted their land. The dynamic blues of their seas and rivers danced in the sunlight, contrasting the dark black hole plucked like a tree from a garden. From that height, the deep's vastness became real, and to wrestle our eyes away was even more torturous.

However, that day we learned that all that beauty had its limits, kept within the boundaries of an otherwise lifeless planet. The Elatia she knew was simply an oasis in a desert, and their remaining globe was as dead as a lump of gray mud, no different than the surface of our moon.

"Our world never fully healed?! Only a portion of it?!" she angrily exclaimed. "And it gets smaller with each arrival."

Their planet ran on life support, its pulse barely kept alive solely for the MonTu's selfish purposes. Still, there were questions as to where we stood, and the dome snatcher's long, descending steps became impossible for Kaylaira to ignore. Wherever it ended fell beyond our view, covered by the eerie lingering mist at the half mark of its stairs. To me it screamed 'time to leave,' breaking that warm comforting delight I'd felt till then as I searched the pillars for a key or loose stone to revert us back. But Kaylaira exited the canopy and moved down the steps.

"Wait, it's quiet. No one is here," she insisted.

I stretched my ears into the open with my eyes glued to those unnerving stairs. Not a breath. Not a whisper. It was barren and devoid of life.

"What are you thinking?" I asked, already hearing the premeditated whispers shout in her head.

"If no one's here, shouldn't we at least take a closer look and see what we find?"

CHAPTER THIRTY-TWO

Bingo. I knew it. She couldn't let the thought slide, not with what she felt was the perfect chance to snoop. In my opinion, if there were a worst idea in the history of worst ideas reconfigured to be any worse, that was it. Little had I planned to plunge thousands of feet just to emerge atop a glorious floating mountain. And now? She wanted to stick our nose in the fire, to smell the flames without getting burnt?

I combed for any reason to object but came up short as my inner coward cursed me useless. Then Kaylaira made the move, furthering her way down before I reluctantly followed into the lion's den. I was antsy, and the dreaded silence pestered my every step. Where was our enemy and what kept them entertained? Were they watching and knew we were there, waiting to pounce and gouge out my eyes?

We sunk into the layer of fog like a thick blanket of snow, treading each footstep as if we trotted on ice. Somehow, I made it up front with Kaylaira behind, steadying her pace with her hands on my shoulders as we staggered blindfolded into the fog. I couldn't see beyond two steps ahead. So with a gentle breeze I dispersed the mist, just enough to remain shrouded till my shoe landed ground.

I expected the plush grasses of Elatia, yet no cushioned blades greeted my step. Just the sharp crunch of dried twigs and crumbling leaves that had long returned to the earth. Gently, I poofed away another band of fog, glimpsing what we couldn't make out from above… a courtyard.

Its landing was siphoned of all green as if the moisture had been sapped from its bones. Small trees were brittle and barely stood, with twigs and bushes that snapped like crackers. A sprawling fountain that once loomed at its center sat idle, overrun with parched vines in a dried pool of gunk.

"What happened here?" I asked, stumped by what we'd found.

"Without the all-lucent, all becomes as nothing. It enlivens everything else and in turn feeds the zephyr. Without it, their life force vanishes, the same as our planet, the same as it will with us," she replied. "The MonTu have grown weak; that's the reason they return."

Weak is how we'd find them, crippled and debilitated? Was that why they spared showing their face? For me, that spelled an advantage. The unstoppable force I believed would drop from the sky was now as lifeless as those courtyard trees.

"Kaylaira," I excitedly jumped.

But a heavy swoop drubbed the air, drowning my words from a rock's throw ahead. We kept as still as the mountain while dissecting the haze, greeted by an assertive shadow whisking by on our sides.

"Aware of any freakish sized flyers up here?" I asked, slowly back stepping her up the stairs.

"No?" her voice shook.

The mist stirred with vibrations, drumming off the might of two ungodly wings and the wake of a feathery tail that snaked far behind. A twenty-foot shadow breached the shroud of mist, stumbling us up faster as it made its second sweep.

"This isn't one of ours," she finally answered. "And I wouldn't object to a little more clearance?"

My thoughts exactly. A strong gust abolished the haze, unveiling more of the same deadened courtyard with a stone wall no higher than my ankles marking its edge.

"Any tasty little morsels hidden in your pouch?" I asked as we quickened our retreat.

"Not for this."

A whistle speared the air, then a pair of wings sprung open like two parachutes. Our light became dark. My heart sped faster beneath my dwindled image, beneath the gloom and shadow of a thirty-foot flyer. A falcon? Its wingspan was impossible to measure, and each feather alone was the length of a palm branch. Its aura stained the air like flickering flames, each move painting the open with shades of vivid blue as its colors saturated the sky.

We'd tumbled halfway back up when it dove above our heads, roaring an ear-piercing squawk that shoved us on our face. It was more than a squawk; it was power, barely missing us by an inch before it spun back for a second round.

"See what's on its head?" Kaylaira pointed.

It was a lavishing work of art, a headpiece sculpted of metal, lined with lucents the size of bricks. Each flickered in intervals and seemed to maneuver its turns. It was less of a bird helmet, and more of a crown for an Egyptian god. But had it commanded it where to turn? An otherworld technology that fed his every move?

"Are those lucents?" I asked.

"Yes!" Kaylaira shouted back, still on the run.

It circled back for its second dive with ivory talons large enough to snatch up a horse. Missed again by an inch, but that time it hovered above. Kaylaira scurried up and I was right behind when its beak fell like a sledgehammer on the edge of my feet. The stone crumbled like Styrofoam. I pushed off as its beak lodged in stone, shoving Kaylaira by her butt with just a few steps to the dome. Its beak tore free, gushing wind from its wings as it smothered us with a flood of air. We could barely move, when I remembered my forgotten ally… air.

"Hey!" Kaylaira yelled with her face mashed to the stairs.

"I'm on it," I beat back.

I gripped the air and tore it like an old stuffed animal, as if ripping its head from its cotton filled body. The air vanished. The bird slammed to its breast as we reached the last step then vaulted from its talons in the heat of anger. I clenched Kaylaira's waist and shoved her in, praying a wind repulsion would keep it at bay as our shelter triggered to life. It worked!

A swirl of air encircled our feet and took us from the floor as my wind repulsion staggered the bird. The dome's winds reversed. I clenched Kaylaira, waiting for a gouge to pierce me through as the force I'd held it with gave way. It lunged, and its blade for a beak scathed my neck. But it didn't matter. We were no longer there, snorting out nervous laughter instead as we landed back in the depths of the cave. Again, we collapsed in disbelief.

"Can we please, not do that again?" she panted, both of us checking to see if we'd made it in one piece. "A portal, delivering us to the top of Mount Elatia? What range does this have? I can't wait to inform the others," she exclaimed.

That's where our enthusiasm split down two separate roads. Was all we'd experienced safe to share, alerting them to *all* we'd uncovered? I knew they withheld secrets in the give and take circle, and if Father left hidden clues for me to find, did I not bear the responsibility to learn what they were? To protect them till I disclosed what they meant?

"Kaylaira," I grumbled, "the second bijou. Is it something we need to tell the others?"

My question shriveled her back as if I'd presumptuously stepped on her toes.

"Why wouldn't we?" she asked with caution.

I had to choose my words to keep her on my side. Her, I knew I could trust. But what of the others?

"Just the second bijou," I said. "Let me first find what the inscriptions mean. Just, give me a chance to figure out what my father's telling me before we spread the news to others. I guess, let's be sure it's safe. You're the first to know when I find something, I promise, then you determine if it's worth sharing."

For a moment I felt her trust in me crack. Hesitance besieged her for what seemed forever before she looked me in the eyes and gave her answer.

"Okay," she agreed to my relief. "I understand. But you must hurry Jordan. You must decipher the code! We're nearly out of time, and you may discover something paramount before they arrive."

Those words put a weight on my chest that made it hard to breathe. Still, I had to be sure.

"Agreed," I said.

As a show of faith I handed her the second bijou, knowing she'd guard it with her life as she returned that trust with the inscriptions in her bracelet.

CHAPTER THIRTY-THREE

Only one day left. That's all that remained before I expended myself on our climb from the deep. I felt I'd never recover from it, and for the record, no I couldn't fly.

Our return up top eviscerated my mind and body with the head splitting effects carried with me back home. My nerves were shattered, the bulge of my eyes chaffed numb from constantly staring at a rock wall. I carried our combined weight for exhausting stretches at a time, past a few ledges then needing to stop before continuing the grueling climb. My fingernails bled empty from clinging to the shallow wall. There were moments when I forgot my name and nearly fell from exhaustion, or where I'd stop to reason who I was or why I was there. In short, we barely made it, and I couldn't have done it without Kaylaira's aid.

By dusk we'd neared the peak where all of me gave in, leaving the others to haul us up the remaining distance. Nijal coached me to life with sips of squishmelon water while Kaylaira shared our findings minus the second bijou. Per Nijal, they lauded our emergence and hailed me a hero as they inhaled Kaylaira's words right there on the ledge. They were eager to match what we'd found with their history. I remembered none of their merriments but at least had them back on my team.

Time, to say the least, misbehaved. Kaylaira and I explored no longer than an hour. But that, combined with our climb and hike back to the village, put Nijal and I on Elatia for a whopping four hours. That normally interpreted to half a day back home. Since I'd dozed off before nine the evening prior, I should've awakened twelve hours later around nine that next morning. Not a chance. My eyes struck the clock the moment it struck 4:18am, five hours ahead of where we'd normally be. Our timelines were running closer the same!

"Nijal!" I woke him, steering his eyes towards the clock.

"What? We hardly lost time? Our realities are nearly running the same?" he snapped awake.

"Yeah, so let's not waste it." I uttered, fumbling my pockets to find the mimic stone in Kaylaira's bracelet.

"Really? So early? On a weekend morning at that?" he protested.

But he followed my lead and ripped the posters from my walls of all the famed rock locations I'd hoped to visit one day. The Stone Forest in China, the Wave Rock in Australia, the Chocolate Hills in the Philippines to name a few. Nijal had the pencil and paper and I Kaylaira's bracelet, then it was lights out, turning my wall into a blank canvas.

"Everything becomes as nothing without the all-lucent," I whispered, then positioned the two stones as Kaylaira had.

The two gems aligned. The all-lucent struck the mimic stone and refracted the embedded text, splashing thousands of lemon-colored alphabets across my wall.

"That is sick!" Nijal muttered, with the two of us marveling the writing as if the sun had spelled out its words.

Line after line we took turns holding her bracelet, while the other scribbled the letters projected on the wall. Our arms cramped from holding still, our hands from writing, but our spirits had never soared higher as our journey took shape. The cave, the canopy and the other bijou, *finally* we felt progress. But after two hours and still writing, it was Mom's tone from down the hall that cautioned us with appeal.

"Jordan?" she called ahead.

So early? I knew Mom and that wasn't her tone. It held a warning and a heads up, much too fluffed and airy from her normal call.

"Quick! Hide everything," I told Nijal.

He stashed the notebook; I abrasively shoved the bracelet down the waistband in the back of my pants. Stupid move.

"Remind me not to touch that again, ever," Nijal whispered as he shoved the notebook in my pillowcase.

With the bijou shoved in an old pair of sneakers, blocked with the dirtiest socks I could find, the door swung open… and she wasn't alone. Two casually dressed men, in black slacks and gray polos, playacted on a friendly level as they stood behind.

"Jordan," she repeated with the same fluffed happiness, now gilded with a role-playing smile.

She was caught off guard, surprised to find the large sheets of poster paper ripped from my walls. But Mom was no novice and countered before I said a word.

"Didn't think you guys were painting till this afternoon," she threw in.

"Couldn't sleep," Nijal played along. He was so freaking natural I thought they'd rehearsed while I fought to erase my dumbfounded expression. "Why not get it out of the way so he doesn't ruin the rest of my weekend, right?" Nijal continued.

The two men fake chuckled while I recovered from the fact that a week had gone by.

"Jordan, these two gentlemen with the government had the privilege of working with your father. News of your recent cave burial concerned them, so they came all this way to assure there was nothing you might need?" she said.

Their eyes had roamed the room from the moment my door opened. Were they looking for the bijou? Before they stepped any further, I kindly escorted them outdoors away from the company of Mom and Nijal. I answered questions I assumed they'd ask, while more concerned with the bracelet scraping my butt cheeks, jostling it to keep it from slipping down my pants. 'How long was I trapped? What made me go? What did I do during my time there?' I obliged with nonchalant juvenile answers, careful not to say too much.

"Working with your father was always a pleasure. A man of remarkable talent who had a knack for some amazing discoveries," one remarked. "Your mother informed us you're anxious to follow his footsteps? Getting started can be costly, so we wanted you to know we'll gladly assist with any academic funding to accomplish that goal."

Funding? Didn't see that coming.

"Of course," the other abruptly added, "if you remember anything or run across whatever strikes you as unique, perhaps in your old man's office?"

"Or just care to one day swing by and see some of your father's work, be sure to let us know," the other finished.

Tempting, but they were baiting me. For what exactly, I didn't know at the time. But as I squashed the idea of their funding to fix my motor bike, I suddenly realized the hunk of junk wasn't even there. Did Mom have it taken? The thought of it was cut short as he handed me a card, with a fine print number inked across its face. I thanked them for their time and "promised" I'd call, but just before hopping in their ride, one paused and turned back.

"Just a side note, if you're painting, you may want to get some paint," he winked.

They were on to us, and I couldn't figure for the life of me if I'd somehow given away what we were up to. Did they know I had the bijou, or that I'd spent my days dreaming while traveling to another world? Baffled, I headed indoors as they pulled away, with Nijal jumping in my face the instant they were gone. What confused me most was Mom prepping pancakes as if it were an average weekend morning.

"Mom?" I cut Nijal short. "Not at all curious why two grown men wished to speak with your son!"

"No," she calmly answered as she stirred more batter.

Her behavior spooked Nijal and I.

"Okay. Well, have you noticed anything strange or bizarre in the last day or so?" I went on.

"You mean outside of my son trapping himself in a cave, then becoming an alcoholic and drug addict with his best friend within a week's time?" she threw in one breath.

"Oof," Nijal remarked, then snuck back into the bedroom out of harm's way.

It was a fair enough response, but not what I was looking for.

"No, not that," I replied. "Not anything pertaining to me, per say. Anything with, I don't know, time, the weather?" I asked, drawing her blank. "Anything that just felt off? Like maybe in your sleep that you couldn't explain?"

She gave the 'Jordan spit it out' glare and flipped another pancake.

"No," she sighed.

I knew she wondered when and how her son became so weird, but how was she being so nonchalant?! I couldn't figure!

"Mom! You're not interested in knowing why two government guys came looking for your son?" I asked, wondering how we started chatting in third person.

"Was it about your new drug addiction?" she joked.

She wouldn't stop taking it lightly and I couldn't figure why, shoving a plateful of pancakes in my chest when I tried mentioning more. She reminded me she didn't care to know, topping it off with an eye-piercing glower to leave her out of whatever it was. Gosh, I wished I could've told her, but I got it. Her value of obliviousness outweighed her danger of being aware.

Again, she begged I be careful, at least acknowledging with a sigh that her son was in over his head. If she only knew of the colossal bird, or my plunge into oblivion.

Nijal barely chewed breakfast and still had a mouthful of pancakes with syrup staining his lips when he closed the door back in my room. "What did they want?" he burst.

"I don't know, but they know I found something. I can't figure how," I told him.

"Sure we can trust the doc? She's the only person that knows any of this," he figured.

Right he was, and it was time I paid a second visit. If Mom assured Dad trusted her with his work, then there was no reason for me to not do the same.

Nijal had chores and left me scribbling alone, seconds from ripping out my hair from the never-ending cycle. Without him it was a mess! Propping the rolling bracelet on a set of books, finding where I'd left off, then remembering to jot down as many letters possible before squinting and losing my place again. Two pages took as long as six with Nijal, stinging my eyes like a splash of seawater the longer I glared those yellow glowing letters. My nerves were burnt and my muscles cramped. But how could I slow down, I still needed the keyword to make sense of it all.

I wiped the sting from my eyes from looking at those same nine letters, H-R-E-S-Y-U-I-M-A, and that was all it took to realize I needed fresh air. Atop my bike with the wind in my face, I rid myself of headaches and erased the burdens from my head. The deep and bijou, the government polo dudes and the MonTu's arrival; I left all of it and embraced the breeze.

Oh the joy from cycling, pumping my veins with freedom as I weaved through our local streets… until a blaring car horn stripped that peace. It wasn't the simple toot of an impatient driver. It wouldn't end and went on without a gasp.

If I knew then what I know now I never would've turned down that traffic-filled street. I would've avoided it and gone the other way, realizing the cars were being diverted from that god-awful blare for more than a special reason. But inquisitiveness got the best of me, hooking my pedaling feet across lawns and parking lots to the small crowd gathered around. At first, I didn't understand why all the fuss over two cars in a minor head-on collision. But as I continued over the broken glass, I just couldn't ignore that blatant horn.

It wouldn't stop. It kept blowing and no one from that gathered swarm dared approach the vehicle, not even the officer who'd arrived at the scene. The closer I came the louder a female's cries. It was unbearable to hear and the only sound that outmatched the horn. Others tried to comfort her, but she was inconsolable, with fresh blood painting her palms marking her as culprit. Curiosity inched me forward, but the smashed windshield on the opposing vehicle hampered a clear look in.

As the shattered glass became too thick to cross, I jumped from my bike and took the weight from my tires, crackling across asphalt to the second car. At first glance, I had no clue what I saw, believing my eyes deceived me. But the longer I stared, the more *horrid* it became and the less capable I was of pulling away. I tried, but my feet adhered to the ground, frozen in that abhorrent moment with my eyes glued to the driver.

It was a female, hunched over the steering wheel with a trickle of blood from a red dot in the middle of her forehead. I'll never forget the moment her face morphed into one of recognition. It haunted me all my days, along with the sound of that blaring horn. Still, for some reason, I couldn't move my eyes from that red dot that consumed me. That's when I realized what I stared at was real, and the longer I stared the more apparent it became. It wasn't just a dot; it was the entry point of a bullet. It wasn't just a female; it was Dr. Tamera.

Chapter Thirty-Four

My breath gave out, and the bike slipped from my grip as the warmth in my fingers plummeted cold. The clash of metal against the pavement jerked the officer's head my way.

"Hey! Keep moving, kid!" he yelled, but locked in place I couldn't move, prompting his second rebuke. "I said move along!"

He stormed toward me as if to throw me in jail when his steps slowed the closer he came. Then one hand clasped my shoulder and the other lifted my bike. But I just stood there, frozen in time.

"What happened?" I gasped. No voice, just air.

"What you see is all we know. Can you give me her name?" he solemnly asked.

I couldn't speak, couldn't breathe as I pulled from his grip, grabbing my bike as I tumbled back. Somehow, I never fell, but eventually found the nerve to turn the other direction. From there, it was one step at a time with no destination, just away before my walk jumpstarted a jog, my jog a sprint before I finally jumped on and pedaled like hell. I tried to out-pedal the image, the red dot and insistent horn, but no matter how fast or how far I went, it continued to churn in my head.

Who'd murdered the only person who knew what I was going through, the only person outside of Nijal? Were the two men who showed up at my home responsible? There had to be a correlation, but was I to run to them for help, the very ones who were possibly the cause? Who was next? Me? Mom? Nijal?

The weight of guilt nearly brought me to the ground but love of friend and family forced strength in my legs. Mom, I reasoned was safe. If anyone were to harm her for what she knew, it would've happened long before then. But Nijal was new to the game, tossed among wolves by the whims of my vulnerability and my lack of being able to handle it all alone.

I couldn't pedal to him fast enough. I slowed to catch a breath, instantly feeling I'd crack apart before it threw me back in an all-out race against time. I had to get to my friend, pedaling till nothing was left in my legs before I collapsed at his bedroom window.

"Nijal!" I yelled, crawling in before tumbling to the floor.

He was provoked and excited, constantly interrupting and not letting me speak. It didn't make a difference; I couldn't speak anyway. Without hesitation, he handed me a paper bag to calm my rapid breathing, and amid his rant about "music" and "the greatest piece ever," I blurted what he needed to hear.

"Nijal! Dr. Tamera's dead," I hurled, unintentionally shoving his enthusiasm out the window I'd crawled through.

He stopped mid-sentence with his mouth gaped wide, intent on uttering that last word as he plopped on his bed. His eyes stapled to the floor. His jaw hung low with the same look I imagined having when

I'd seen her first. It was as if he'd hijacked that horrid visual from my head as he stared into the fibers of his carpet, speechless, motionless, unable to reciprocate.

"Yeah, so the music piece we were doing," he continued in denial.

"Nijal!" I stopped him, watery-eyed, with my voice excelling to a yell. "I'm serious. Dr. Tamera is dead, and no, it wasn't an accident. I saw her myself, with a precision-placed bullet between her eyes, and I will never be able to forget or erase that image! What have we done?"

The horn. The red dot. Tears muscled through the restraints of my eyes with no way to stop them. I let them fall uninhibited, without the slightest bit of embarrassment. I let them soak his bedsheets as I plopped by his side and allowed emotion to run its course. I was done holding back.

"She was murdered, Nijal. Because of me," I wailed. "Is this what it feels like to fail? Me watching all those innocent children die, because of me? Because I wasn't strong enough? Because I stirred the pot and couldn't handle what came out of it? I don't want this. That level of guilt on my hand? I don't want any of it."

I tried educing Coach Johnson's inspiring words, 'how could I turn my back on them?' But Dr. Tamera's bloody diversions obstructed my admonition.

"H-How?" Nijal stuttered. "Why her? Because she spoke to us?"

"I don't know Nijal!" I yelled, suddenly repulsed at being so close to him. I jumped from his bed in a defensive stance. I didn't want to be close; to him or anyone else. "You need to watch your back. So from now on, stay away and keep to yourself! I don't want you near me again."

My words were far from true. He was my best friend, and had taken me further than I would've ever made it alone. But what was I to do? What if something were to happen to him because of me? The sudden thought of his life slashed from mine cut deeper than the need to keep him in it. So there I stood, firm and resolved.

"I mean it!" I confirmed, conjuring hate and the darkest sentiment I'd ever forced in my voice. "From now on, keep out of this and stay the hell away from me."

I flipped out the window, shuttering the sound of him screaming my name.

"Jordan!" he yelled, clamoring how the repercussion of her loss wasn't the end of our friendship.

Maybe he was right, maybe not, but unwilling to lose anything more, I wiped our lifetime of memories clean. His words fell on deaf ears as I stripped myself away, numbed, prying his voice from my newly calloused heart while I did the only thing that made sense anymore… I pedaled. I pedaled without restraint with each stride liberating me from guilt. Sleep, and I was tangled in a nightmare. Stay awake, and I was tormented by reality. With nowhere safe between, all I did was pedal, until I found myself outside of the cave.

Without hesitance I made the climb and spearheaded through its lacerating edges. A frigid jab to the fingers or gash to the elbow offered a release from the built-up tension. The pain was borderline rewarding, and the only evidence I currently existed in that world.

I bent, crawled and blindly fumbled through before stopping at the first void of light. Curled up on the damp floor, a flat rock became my pillow, and the wet stone welcomed me like a long-lost bed. Darkness shielded me from the outside world. On Elatia, it was the still of the forest or being perched by Kaylaira's side that detached me from the chaos around. But on Earth it was the cave, buried in silence as my serenade and the only place I felt I belonged.

I held the bijou as my beacon and refused to turn away, bathing in its honey glow as the hum of my aria echoed from my lips. The stone's endless specks eventually glistened, as if a galaxy had shattered and scattered its stardust within the rock. And the more I stared, the deeper I peered into the tiny portal, into the vibrant life of another world. Then one of those specks flickered like a heartbeat, catching my attention and holding it in place.

Somewhere in that floating moment, the subtlest whisper welcomed me in. I no longer hummed my aria but heard it instead. The cave's darkness softened, and the grip of its barricading walls opened wide. It took a beat to realize I was there, dwelling within that speckle of light on Elatia in the village. And of all places, I'd settled before the most vital tree home of all… Kaylaira's.

The village itself was still, but the faint strains of joyful melodies and laughter carried in from the distance from the children's farewell festival. A chorus of young voices sang in unison, accompanied by the rhythmic beating of drums and the tinkling of bells. The sounds echoed through the still village, a reminder of happier times before chaos would take over.

Even in their absence, their music brought a sense of light and hope to the lingering darkness. I thought to sit there, listen and absorb their cheer, but by some freak anticipation Kaylaira was there alone, perched on her balcony, resting her chin on her knuckles with her elbows propped on the ledge. She smiled down at me acknowledging I was there, almost anticipating my arrival.

I went for the stairs when a primal instinct to reach her faster pulled me back to the ground. With a flick of my wrist and a gentle twist of my fingertips, I summoned the wind to lift me instead. It responded to my every gesture, swirling and gusting around me, soaring me onto her balcony and straight into her embrace.

In her arms, a place of solace, my courage shattered like a wrecking ball through glass. She wept her anguish as well, consoling me with gentle strokes to my hair as if she'd felt what I'd been through. We'd fought hard to be strong, for the village, for each other, finally weakened by the culmination of it all.

"Why aren't you at the festival?" I asked.

"Because I hoped you'd come. I needed time with you alone, away from the others for a change," she cried in my ear.

"And I hoped you'd be waiting," I cried back. "I don't know if I can do it."

"I know," she confessed.

"Too much is happening here and back home. We've only begun and already I've lost a friend who had my father's trust. I hardly knew her, but never imagined this level of pain when the reason fell on me. And to know it could happen again, to you, to the children? It's not something I can bear," I grieved.

"I'm sorry," she consoled me with her hand. "Maybe we pushed too hard. Perhaps we hoped for a fancied dream we should have erased at the start. Why did we expect you to come here with only days to change a lifetime of history? To accomplish something no one ever has? It was selfish of us to have placed you in that position, and on myself and on behalf of my people, I sincerely apologize."

She buried my head in her mound of hair, prodding me to dump our affliction in one heaping pile on the floor, to empty myself of worry and provocation till we both were free of pain. In that moment, I let go of it all, completely enamoring us both in the most perfect way possible.

"You have such a meaningful attachment to others. You feel it makes you weak, but it doesn't. It makes you strong. In time, the universe will know just how strong you are, Jordan of Earth," she said, pulling me from her damp hair to look me in the eyes. "But this doesn't have to be that moment, and in no way forces you to battle our war. The rest of us can leave and head to the mountains for safekeeping, the same as we always have. We can live to fight another day, when we're ready."

My heart soared and plummeted, leaving a mixed swell in my chest as her words liberated me from the countless lives I'd possibly fail. But the guilt of failure burdened me too. Failure to act. Failure to step forward instead of shriveling out of fear. What hope could they have? And in the end, how many would succumb to death during the re-creation? That guilt would eat me alive for just as long.

I closed my eyes to choose a side, promptly reminded of that unrelenting image flaring through my head. The horn. The red dot. Dr. Tamera slouched in her vehicle. Instantly, I cowered. Instantly I opened my eyes with the answer already on my tongue.

"I can't, I'm sorry." I finally confessed.

CHAPTER THIRTY-FIVE

Nothing more was uttered on the matter. I wanted to forget and so did she, something we both thought impossible until we draped across her bed. We laughed, teased each other for the first time in days, enthralled in stories of each other's mischief as both worlds passed us by. We became who we were meant to be, two gabbing teens instead of saviors on pedestals expected to liberate their worlds.

"How's life on your world?" she asked, a question I never thought much of till then.

"Compared to here?" I started, "Chaotic, self-absorbed, busy, overwhelming. Like a song with too many sounds. It's crammed with things we don't need, things that take away from the true meaning of life."

"Which are?" she asked, clung to my words.

It was her bounteous intrigue, her glare that seduced words from my mouth that I never imagined being able to speak.

"Family. Loved ones. Each other," I answered.

Our family story inspired her, from Dad's occupation to me striving to mimic his footsteps which landed me on their shores. She grazed his watch on her wrist as I explained, with its value becoming priceless the longer I spoke of him.

"How about you? Any memories of your mother? Memories you can vividly relive?" I asked.

"Yes," she answered, eagerly rummaging a bowl next to her bed before revealing a mimic lucent.

She lay next to me and graced it with a tender kiss, then slipped it into an empty slot on her bracelet. A soft image billowed from the stone, illuminating the white fabric draping the top of her bed. We lay in silence, watching the young girl no older than Naymelia dance in a bed of endless flowers. It was her mother.

"I wish I had more, but it's the only image I have. Her name was Yasmeiruh," she barely whispered, with her eyes longing for the image above.

"Another ear-grabbing name," I told her.

Then lost in memory, she burrowed beneath my arm and pulled me close, placing the bracelet on my chest. The image played like a soundless movie.

"How long do we have?" she asked.

"Not long at all. I sort of hid myself back in a cave to be here," I laughed.

"What is it with you and dark, enclosed places?" she tittered. "I guess that's the explorer in you, the part of you that makes you unique."

"I guess so. Unlike here it's the only place quiet enough to hear myself think. I'm safe there for a little while, but should leave before our nightfall," I explained.

"Then I'm glad you're here. Come daylight, I'll inform the others that we'll continue our ways as before and hide in *our* caves," she laughed.

I objected to her facing the group alone and needlessly taking the brunt of my obligation. But she quieted me with a finger to my lips, forbidding I spoil the moment or her decision.

"Please, just hold me," she pleaded.

Never had empty time felt more meaningful. We lay for a pair of hours without words, me watching her peacefully drift asleep beneath the comfort of my arm. So innocent, yet so courageous. It wasn't fair. No matter how much I longed to fight I felt she'd be safer in the caves, free of my intervention. For the moment, I just wanted to slow time, but it's tiny specks of sand sped through the hourglass until our time finally ended.

"Promise you'll return," she whispered, merging her lips with mine as if I needed further reason to come back.

"I promise," I claimed, the last words I swore before I closed my eyes with her touch turning into a cold stone.

Back in the cave, the damp and unforgiving rock replaced the warmth of her body. My joints ached. My head pulsated behind my ear, reminding me a rock was never meant to be a pillow. But none of it mattered. My spirit was never-ending as I headed home through the fading day with a smile etched on my face. What a night to remember! Though fate decided I wasn't as strong as I'd hoped, I was determined to continue Father's legacy and help them in a way that truly mattered.

Mom greeted me at the door with a grievous hug, a hug acknowledging she'd discovered Dr. Tamera's plight. And though limited in what we said, she affirmed she was there for me though the itch to tell her everything drove me insane.

"Don't let it discourage you," she started. "For so many years, Dr. Tamera willingly protected whatever this was. She knew the risks. She knew the cost and still chose to guard it. Don't let that perish in vain by shrinking back and throwing your hands in the air. Now's not the time. She did it for a reason, and whatever that reason, by now I hope you understand its worth and value."

I kissed her cheek and gave her the most cherished hug I'd given since birth.

"What about you? Are you okay?" I asked, still holding her as if it were my last chance. "Or will this whole thing cause me to lose you as well?"

"Don't worry about me. I'm safe. I know nothing, remember? And they know that," she answered with a warming smile.

Her words restored my faith, and her embrace diminished my weakness.

"Now don't forget to eat," she ordered as she returned to Mother mode.

I slurped down her bowl of homemade chicken soup before heading to my room, immediately spotting a yellow sticky note on a package on my bed. 'Best friends don't die' it read, slapped in the middle of my iPod. Couldn't help but laugh. Perhaps Nijal had given me the benefit of doubt after knowing all I'd been through. He knew no part of me wanted to push him away, and how what I'd done was believed to be in his favor. I was blessed to have a friend like him, and he needed to know it.

Slouched in bed with my headphones on, I hit play. My heart goose-bumped with the first keystrokes of a piano as I grabbed my pillow like a long-lost puppy. The composition was pure genius. He'd captured my aria, ripped it from that dreadful hum I'd produced in my head to recreate something of pure elegance and beauty. It was euphoric and could only be truly felt from behind closed eyes where the zephyr filled the entire sky of my imagination.

It was thick like a never-ending rainbow with soft hued colors, swaying and moving with each tune played as if the melody stoked its graceful breeze. Piano strokes whisked me through its air, like a thousand exotic birds taking flight at once while a flute captured the children's laughter. Like two gentle hands seizing a butterfly, he grasped their playful innocence then released it to my ear. Harmony enveloped me as a bow crossed the thread of a violin, unearthing that perfect balance they'd found between their lives and nature.

I lay there as time withered, listening, curled in my blanket as the melody looped. My eager thoughts calmed just as they had in the forest and chaos somehow fell in place. My mom and best friend still backed my insanity, no matter how big a jerk I'd been. And the girl of my dreams—literally—understood my plea, and how that undertaking surpassed anything I could face alone.

Dr. Tamera's death, though unfortunate, opened so many questions, spurring me to find justice for her and Father's mysterious deaths. That evening, with the bijou locked away, I huddled beneath my headphones and slept like a corpse while the hours of peaceful rest cleared my head. And with the morning sun barely over the horizon, the simplest thought flipped me awake… Kaylaira's mother!

I tousled from my sheets to the notes Nijal and I had scribbled, opening them to the nine letters from Dad's book. H-R-E-S-Y-U-I-M-A. I'd rearranged them a thousand times, but that time my hand quivered as I grabbed a pen, writing the first letter crossing my mind. It was a 'Y,' matching the first sounds of her name before I proceeded with the remaining letters. I saw the end before I'd written it to completion.

Y-A-S-M-E-I-R-U-H! My father's keyword to the cipher, was her mother's name!

CHAPTER THIRTY-SIX

My grip wilted like a ninety-year-old's fingers and the pen cartwheeled from my hand. Yasmeiruh? Her mother's name was the keyword!

I grabbed a blank paper with my hand so unsteady that I pressed it against the desk to keep it from shaking. On one line, I rewrote her name just as Nijal instructed, followed with each letter of the alphabet minus her letters I'd written. On line two, A to Z, with each alphabet directly beneath a letter above to see what letters corresponded with each.

Next, the test. With the first line of Father's jumbled inscription, I used the cipher to match each letter above. 'Ancient civilization' were the first words to appear, and the pen cartwheeled from my hand a second time before I sprung from the table and paced the room. I'd found the key, but confusion soiled my zeal.

Why would the keyword be her mother's name and how did Father know her? Was it a random person he chose? A relationship? Did Mom know her? How old would the two have been? Teenagers? At first, the timeline seemed improbable, but then again, not with the way their time flowed.

Struggling not to speculate was impossible. My mind flooded with doubt. My excitement was divided from having found the keyword, but it was past my promised time to meet Kaylaira. I should've been there already to notify the others of the decision I'd made. Problem was, I couldn't sleep; then I remembered my headphones.

"Thank you, Nijal!" I uttered, with a kiss to the air for his remarkable gesture.

Where would I have been without him? I couldn't fathom it and rushed to plug in my tunes when a knock hit my door.

"Jordan? You have a visitor," Mom said.

Yes, Nijal! I swung the door open ready to make amends but found an eye-striking girl in front of me instead. Who was she? Her face was a mosaic of fear and pain. Shards of emotion spliced her features like broken glass. Her body was tense, her eyes filled with a wild, wounded fear as if trauma had left its mark.

I stuttered at the sight of her, then slammed my door behind, praying she hadn't caught sight of the filth in my room. Me, I couldn't hide. I'd skipped a change of clothes since I'd been in the cave, and it showed.

"Hi," I managed to utter, but she kept silent.

"Jordan, I'd like you to meet Dr. Tamera's daughter," Mom introduced her.

Daughter?! Oh the fright that ensued! I was the last to visit her mother. Why hadn't I thought of the possibility, a family member who'd knowingly visit me after her peculiar death?

"May I have a minute of your time?" she gloomily asked, with a hint of anger beneath.

"Sure," I humbly replied.

We both made our way to the porch with our senses heightened and on guard, curious of the secrets the other possessed. She was hesitant and looked at the ground at first, just as nervous as I, grasping for those first words to begin.

"I'm really sorry about your mother," I initiated.

She kept silent, but her eyes rose to a yellow envelope folded in her hand.

"If there's anything Mom or I can do to help, please let us know how," I went on.

"How did you know her?" she belted.

Her question teetered on an all-out wail, or a sudden slash to my face. My stomach knotted like a pretzel, then the little I knew of her left my lips, how I too remained clueless on her and Father's work. I mentioned our visit just days before, and her help with a certain "episode" I faced.

"Honestly, I don't know what's happening. I'm struggling to follow," I admitted.

"I hope you understand how hard it is to trust you, the guy who saw my mom before she was taken," she said.

I couldn't deny what she felt. Her reasoning defined the guilt that plagued me since I'd discovered her mother draped across the steering wheel.

"I know," I readily admitted. "I've been thinking the same. But I swear to you, I'd do anything to find her killer, and I'd do just as much for you to earn my trust."

The cracks in her broken heart slowly etched away at mine, and I would've done anything in my power for her that moment. As she looked at me with tears in her eyes, she saw my sorrow mirrored in her own. She knew I wanted to help but was as lost as she was.

"Please, what can I do?" I asked, extending my hand in trust.

She simply responded by handing the envelope she held. I feared grabbing it, feared accepting another puzzle piece I couldn't explain. My plate was toppling beyond my control. However, to accept it was the first step in gaining trust, and so I took it.

"What is it?" I asked.

She hadn't a clue. It was something her mother left behind with explicit instructions to deliver should something happen. My hands trembled fiercely as I tore the seam, before homing in on my lack of manners. Who knew what I was about to open, for myself or the person I was seconds from discovering it with? So, I stuck out my hand.

"I'm Jordan."

"Wendi," she smiled for a first as she accepted my greeting, before we anxiously tore the envelope apart.

Out fell a keycard and a green laminated slit of paper, with 'remember before opening' written in black on its outer sleeve. Typed in between? An address, '2116 Lakeview Dr.' with another scribble of letters typed below... 'Rhemiani.'

"Rhemiani? That's it, that's all there is," I uttered surprised, trying to fathom what I held.

With that word and address committed to memory, I divided the opposing plastics as if freeing a slice of cheese. The paper disintegrated, leaving us in an uncomfortable silence as its fragments drifted like ashes in a breeze.

"Okay?" I mumbled, stumped by the physics I'd witnessed. Where would that address take me, and was she to come along? I couldn't keep her from her mother's mission, and before realizing what I'd said, I'd already invited her. "Care to accompany me on your mother's final journey?"

Those words fell on her ears like a magic potion, instantly shifting doubt into a mountain of gratitude. Her head tottered yes as if I'd never ask, relieving her that I had no intention of hoarding the secret alone.

"I'll drive," she hurried to her car.

She was in, already strapped before I'd closed the car door with the address nearly in her phone. But a mysterious vehicle popped up a few streets behind.

"Wait, stop!" I blocked her, moving her attention to her rear-view mirror. "I had a couple of curious visitors yesterday and I'm not sure who they were. No phones, no trails, especially with the effort your mom went through to seal the evidence."

"What do we do?" she frantically asked.

I had an idea. Why not head to the one place I'd completely neglected the week before, school? She was close to my age and easily passed as a student, so to school it was. It gave me time to fill in the needed gaps; Nijal's assistance and her mother's attempt to help me as she had with Father. Shockingly, nothing I said fazed her one bit. Perhaps she didn't believe a story that bizarre, or perhaps she knew more than she'd let on.

The mystery vehicle kept its distance but also pulled into the student lot. Its dark tinted windows kept them obscure, so we jumped out and made a beeline for the music room, Nijal's first class. Fortunately, they hadn't started, and Nijal caught sight of me from a mile away.

"Really?" he said, eyeballing my lack of clean apparel. "You look like mud and now you're wearing it too?"

But I knew Nijal. I knew his interests would bypass our conflict the instant he saw who traveled with me. Leave it to an attractive girl to infect his selective amnesia.

"Well, hellooo! I'm Nijal," he charmed her, smothering her with attention as he cleared the nerves from his throat. "Jordan, first off, let me assure you all from the past can be buried, my friend. Pretend it never happened, though it did. My treat, I'll drop in a coin of forgiveness on this one."

"Great. That's what I was hoping," I quickly accepted, checking the hallways to assure our tails were clear. "As a matter a fact, how would you like to up the value on that coin and get to know Wendi a little better?"

At first, she was baffled at my use of her, then gathered my scheme to reel him in.

"I'd say, I'm game?" he assured, an answer I knew I had in the bag.

With Nijal on board all we needed was a car. His was no good. I was certain he was being probed as covertly as us, so a mutual friend became our answer. We turned his absolute "no" into a "he shouldn't", after the scrunched twenty-dollar bill left my pocket. Nijal wrapped it with a one, turning his "I shouldn't" into a "probably not" before Wendi joined the bid with a second twenty added to our naked stash.

"Well, just for a bit!" he agreed then relinquished his keys.

Nijal grabbed the car, I ran directions through a library computer while Wendi stashed our phones behind a set of books. We were on our way, and Nijal blabbered the entire thirty-minute drive! As usual, he was smitten and rambled one endless sentence the entire way. At least he kept Wendi entertained. She latched to his animated sarcasm I'd grown accustomed to while my thoughts leaned on everything else.

With time behaving the way it had, I completely missed my rendezvous with Kaylaira, forcing her to share my cowardly decision alone. What a lack of a man I was with another broken promise! How many more would I fail? How many more before she'd lose faith in me and join the others? At the same time, how could I have abandoned Wendi? With the dread of her loss weighing my shoulders, I couldn't win. I could never win.

We turned down a street filled with green hovering oaks, enough to snap me back to the present. That, and the lake that owned the horizon. Its sapphire waters poked between the tall brawny trees, reminiscent of the river village of Elatia. Homes were few and far between, and from one you could barely spot the next. No one walked the neighborly street. No cars sat along the picturesque road. We were alone, in a place intentionally kept from the rest, with the last of any community far from that road.

"And, we're here," Nijal slowed.

We each sat up anxious to find where her mother had led us, a place even more breathtaking than the street on which we'd arrived. A wall of impassable evergreens fenced the property, lending no way to glimpse inside. If not the evergreens, the warning signs and impressive "stay the hell away" gate were enough to cause concern. Who'd dare be so bold to enter? We were nervous enough, and the console with the slot for our keycard made it no less daunting.

"Sure we're not about to get shot?" Nijal jested with a hint of concern.

He'd read my mind, but over the reader the keycard went. The light lit green. The shielded gate tugged open to a long-necked driveway, then slammed closed the instant our bumper cleared. Nijal drove like a granny over the stone laid path, through a manicured lawn as green as lawns get. At the end of the pathway? A sleek one-level design. Large windows and a pristine exterior exuded luxury and sophistication, and the finery aroused Nijal a little more than it should've. He was out of the car before he'd even parked.

"Bro!" he yelled, calling our every detail.

Wendi and I proceeded with caution, wondering who watched the cameras that documented every angle of the property. No cars were present. No sound beyond the birds in the trees. We were alone, the only ones to rival the ambient sounds of the lake and forest.

We each propped our oily foreheads against a window on a glass wall surrounding the front entrance. From there we had an open view indoors, where the lake's sapphire water consumed me from the other side. Dare we enter? I pretended to be bold and waved the card across the second console. The light flicked green and the weighted door that could stop a car popped open. Again, Wendi and I stalled.

"Too dramatic. I can't take it," Nijal cracked. "We're doing this way too slow. We need to just bust up in there and let 'em know we're here."

Having forewarned us of his plan, Nijal flung the door open and rushed in.

"Yo!" he yelled.

His voice echoed over tile, granite and marble while Wendi and I followed with a more subtle debut. As impressive as the exterior was, the interior decor was equally stunning. I cut to the rear glass facing the water, bypassing a fireplace and looping sofa on my right with enough cushions to seat a small nation. To the left, a stunning marble topped bar stood as the centerpiece of the high-grade kitchen, the focal point of both rooms. The intricate veining in the white marble added a touch of elegance, glimmering under the soft glow of hanging pendant lights.

"This place is sick! And I think we're alone so we can totally snoop in their house," Nijal said.

To that, I agreed. It wasn't every day that kids like us could poke around in homes like those. So out the exterior glass doors I went, to a walkway insisting I visit the lake. But another surprise awaited; a reflection pool on my left, and a half-enclosed lounge to my right where I could slouch and do nothing for my remaining days.

"I say house party before the owners know we're here," Nijal jumped.

"Does he ever stop?" Wendi asked.

"No, but let me know if you ever find the off switch," I teased.

As we stepped down into the lounge area, a painting with no rights belonging where it hung latched my eyes. Its origin was unmistakable, a place that didn't exist on earth. Dumbstruck, I stared at the depiction, children swimming in a water hole encircled by tree roots. How had that image come to be on the wall?

"Us being here isn't a coincidence," I uttered.

"Why not? What is it?" Wendi dashed over to see for herself.

"This painting is a picture of their village. Which means, whoever lives here has been there," I explained.

A brash thump of metal on the concrete floor snagged our attention.

"Long live King Nijal!" Nijal yelled from behind.

He pompously held a four-foot staff in the doorway, standing erect as if he were royalty. But he alone hadn't startled me, it was the crown resting on his head, a small replica of the one the large falcon wore from atop the mountain.

"Nijal, take off the crown!" I yelled. He swiped it off as if his head would be set on fire. "Where'd you find that?" I asked!

"Over the mantle back inside," he mumbled.

Taken by the breathtaking lake, I'd completely bypassed it. Was it a replica? Did it have the same effects? How had something from their world made it to ours? I explained where I'd seen it and the danger it posed as we gently placed both pieces back above the fireplace. They'd been mounted there like two pieces of art.

The remaining house was of no interest, a couple bedrooms and baths, leaving the open kitchen as the bulk of the living space. After parading the property, we couldn't figure why we of all people were entrusted with its key. What were we to do with it? And the word below the address, "Rhemiani" what did it mean?

"There's something we're missing. Why be sent to an isolated home? There's something else here, something we haven't found," I told them.

I questioned Wendi for what she knew, but she was just as much in the dark. That envelope and a promise to deliver its contents was the extent of her knowledge. We put our heads together and derived we'd simply found an oasis, a place to relax and meditate on Earth. It made sense if that's what Father and Dr. Tamera used it for, that was undeniably clear.

"So, what's our next move?" Wendi asked.

She was invested, a lost soul anxious to belong on a team to find answers. It was nice having her around. It kept Nijal occupied and gave me moments to think. However, what was next? Time ticked away, fast, and I'd already foregone Kaylaira and the give and take circle. Were we where we were meant to be, a place to work and decode Father's journal?

"I need to get back to Elatia, but I have no clue how to focus here," I said.

A clink from the kitchen drew my attention to Nijal removing a glass and a bottle of scotch. Ironically, it was the same scotch we'd found in Dad's office.

"Well, the way I see it," he started, plopping on the sofa with his feet on the table. "I'm already in trouble for skipping school, so no need to rush back. Besides, Wendi's enjoying my company so much I'd hate to rob her of it. And you need a secret hideout where you can get back to saving the universe. Look outdoors; what better place?"

Wendi agreed.

"Did you bring it?" he asked.

I pulled the bijou from my pocket, fascinating Wendi as she took her first glimpse. Nijal was right, what better place to give it a go? Outdoors was simply sublime.

"We've got a few hours before we need to return that car. Plenty of time," Nijal said.

"And I can help you relax," Wendi added. "I wouldn't be Dr. Tamera's daughter if I hadn't learned a thing or two from my mother."

With the stage set, we settled in the shade beneath the lounging space next to the reflection pool. Those chairs were meant to nestle in for hours, and the soft hush of a fan cooled the outdoor space where my ears inhaled the reflection pool's hypnotic trickles.

"Okay, Nijal. Surprise," I said, handing him the notebook with Father's inscriptions. "No excuse of getting bored; there's plenty of work to do."

"You found the keyword?!" he jumped.

"Written up top, and yes I'll explain later," I told him.

He glanced Kaylaira's mother's name, scrunching his eyebrows with confusion, but I was unwilling to dive into who, what and where.

"I'll be out for a while. Sure you want to be stuck with this guy?" I clowned Wendi, sparking her true laughter for the first time. It was endearing and bashful, the first sound of our beginnings of trust.

"I can manage," she affirmed. "Now sit back, close your eyes and drift."

Her timid smile was the last I saw before the world hushed to silence. Melting into the plush fabric was effortless, tugging me in for a slumber while the bijou rested like a newborn atop my chest. Wendi unexpectedly nestled behind me and placed my head in her lap. I pretended it was no biggie, blindsided by her candor as her fingers gently caressed my skin. Her mother's work? At first, more erotic than relaxing.

"Take deep breaths," she whispered, gliding her fingers from my neck to my shoulders.

How could I possibly relax? Did she realize the effect of her touch? Her graze plumped arm chills I prayed she couldn't see.

"Umm, anyway I can get in on that action?" Nijal interrupted. "He needs backup, I kind of need to go with him too."

Wendi shushed him and made him promise to remain soundless if he was to stay. Remarkably, her bluntness tamed him. That alone was an impressive feat!

"Now, focus on the pool's ripples. It's why it's there, to help you focus," she returned to me.

Her fingers returned to the back of my neck, melting tension to mush as the weight of my head dropped in her palms. I eventually pushed past the elicited excitement and forced myself back to the ripples. My ears landed on its swirling rumples as daintily as a butterfly on a flower. Her indulgent whispers blended the soothing atmosphere. How long did I listen? I couldn't say. Before long I was standing in the heart of Elatia, adoring the river's gurgling ripples as both sounds became one and the same. But calm quickly escaped me. The once peaceful village had been thrown into an uproar.

CHAPTER THIRTY-SEVEN

The crossover held me in a lethargic web while I rummaged for Kaylaira like an inebriated fool. I stumbled upon Naymelia instead. She was on her knees, crying, holding her father who gripped the back of his head.

"What happened?" I asked.

"Jordan!" Draythian sat up irate.

I scrounged to help him to his feet, greeted by his fist like a bat. My teeth munched flesh, gushing blood like a burst ketchup packet in my cheek. I lost my balance and slapped the ground, but he wasn't finished. His eyes burned with hatred as he stumbled towards me, bent on pounding the life from my bones when Naymelia stifled his craving for vengeance.

"Nooo!" she yelled.

Her body flung across mine, screaming to protect me from her father's onslaught.

"Where have you been?" he yelled through her with anger shifting to pain.

My mouth was soaked with blood, and before I could speak, my eyes swung past him in the distance. The mountain loomed closer than ever; a behemoth seemingly suspended by some unseen magic.

To be honest, it was breathtaking, with its jagged peaks and rugged edges reaching towards the heavens. A thick layer of clouds surrounded it, almost as if it was resting upon them like a throne. Its shadow gradually covered the village as it descended, casting an eerie darkness over the once peaceful town.

It was obvious time had escaped me, and as I shuffled the numbers, I realized I'd been gone for nearly fourteen hours. Our timelines were running adjacent, and for that I felt his anger. I understood why every part of him hated me to the core. However, I needed him as a friend, not an enemy. Retaliation was far from my goal as I scooted Naymelia aside and spat the mouthful of blood, taking in the zephyr to mend my wounded cheek.

"Draythian, where's Kaylaira?" I stood and mumbled through the mending flesh.

"She told us, Jordan. She told us all we needed to hear. We unwillingly put faith and trust in you, for you to turn your back and leave us to die?!" he shouted. "And what of the remaining children? If we hadn't listened to you, they'd have had more time to get to safety."

"Draythian. There is more happening than you realize," I tried calming him, but he refused to listen.

"Oh yeah? And you're the only one this is happening to?" he threw back.

Those words sent a chill that left me fearing Kaylaira's absence. The way he uttered them struck a chord in my ear, sewn with the warning of a hidden message. Something more had taken place during my time away, something I'd missed or knew nothing of. I embraced Naymelia, thankful for her protection, then faced off with Draythian to grasp what he'd said.

"What is it?" I asked.

"Something Kaylaira didn't explain, and refused to let us tell you. She didn't want it to be the root of your decision," he continued. "So the only way we could stop this from getting worse was to let it happen. We sent the chosen to serve their purpose for the arrival."

He lingered with an eerie look that seeped in my eyes, hoping I'd derive my own conclusion. But I didn't. I couldn't. Trapped somewhere in the rearmost part of my brain, the answer hid and refused to evolve.

"Jordan," he glared, knowing I refused to complete the equation. "Jordan, you know what I'm about to tell you, but I guess you prefer hearing it aloud, don't you? Kaylaira's gone; she's one of the chosen."

Even as he uttered the words, my mind blocked me from hearing the truth.

"Jordan!" he yelled, fed up with my dead stare and cold silence.

I turned away, unsteady while my eyes searched for an anchor to keep the rest of me from spinning wild. I found a boulder and locked to it, refusing to pull away to anything else as it sat at the focus of my writhing anger. Kaylaira, the one confiding in me most shielded me from knowing the greatest sacrifice of all… the doom she'd soon suffer.

I was such a fool and had never felt so helpless. My palms tightened into a fist. The forest spun my head and that boulder lost its weight. Rage and sadness spumed in equal measures, stiffening the docile breeze into an aggressive wind. Then suddenly, with all that energy anchored in one spot, the boulder split in half. The rupture startled me. I'd never conjured that height of power until the softest touch gripped my hand. It was Naymelia's, shooing off that place of hopelessness like a pesky dog frightened by a stomping foot.

"Jordan, we need you," she pleaded, clueless to how drastic it had all become and the extent it affected her life.

The subtle grasp of her hand pulled me from the boulder, directing me to Draythian who'd concerned himself more with the wind. I didn't hate him, not even for the bloody cheek that had nearly healed. None of it was his fault. He merely defended his daughter and people and needed to know the best way how. Rightfully so, I applauded his effort.

"Okay. Okay," I thought in circles trying not to panic. "I need your help."

"Why should we trust you? You were a coward before and abandoned us. Why the difference now?" he contested.

Naymelia again cradled my fingers. Her timing was priceless, erasing that last creeping chance of doubt and fear.

"Because now it's personal," I answered. "And me 'abandoning you' isn't as painless as you think, nor was it cowardice. So we can stand and bicker, or you can point me in the right direction to get our friends back. Together or alone makes no difference, but I'd rather have you by my side."

The remaining members of the circle approached as my words settled in his heart, anxious and ready for a sense of direction.

"Continue with the evacuation," he addressed them. "Either best of hopes surviving the transference, or preferably, we come and get you before it takes place. Make sure every child is accounted for before abandoning the village. As for the rest of us, it's time we fight."

He knelt by Naymelia who still gripped my fingers and implored her with a beckoning tone. "My love, I need you to go with the others as planned."

His words struck her fragile emotions like a sledgehammer, bursting a tearful scream of condemnation loose. She grabbed my shirt and clinched his leg as her cries swelled from mellow to an ear-piercing shriek. Her sorrows plucked the strings in my heart. What would I have done as a father? Did I even have the strength to save him for her to see him again?

"Jordan, please! No!" she screamed.

Her eyes blurred the same as mine but there was nothing I could do, not the way she hoped for. Unable to tame her broken spirit, I pulled from her hand, knowing her lesser mind formed the wrong notion that I was abandoning her.

"Please!" Draythian yelled, grief-stricken as he summoned an older one to haul her away. "Take care of my daughter."

She kicked and screamed as they pried her unbreakable grip, pleading we do not leave her, promising she'd be a better child. My heart lobbed a knot in my throat, and because of me, I was forced to swallow the possibility that they may never reunite again.

"I hope this is worth it," he said with a stalling voice, before he disarmed his emotions from his daughter's cries and hardened himself for battle. "To the shore!" he yelled, rallying a group of us through the forest. He was the Draythian I knew again, his focus driven like a spear to our enemy's heart. "Oh yeah, remind me to thank you for that hit on the back of my head."

"Hit? What hit? You're blaming me for something I don't even know?" I asked as we scurried along the path.

"Well it was you who lit the fire in Jesriel's heart and now he's determined to fight, a little more than he should. He's also one of the chosen, but will probably end up jeopardizing the whole thing," he said.

If the four-chosen entered peacefully as planned, the transference would continue without interruption. However, Jesriel thanks to me, wielded an alternative other than peace and knocked Draythian cold the moment he objected. I couldn't let them die, especially not Kaylaira. For me that was never a viable plan. So, to the MonTu we marched without a shred of me backing down. Jesriel would have what he wished for, he'd have his fight.

Elatia's redemption had begun!

"Just a warning. There's no negotiating with them, and Jesriel's opposition *will* start a bigger war," Draythian warned. "That's why he knocked me blank the moment I tried to warn the others. So we have to reach them first or all else is lost."

I struggled holding back, knowing I could reach her a lot faster alone, but it wasn't the moment to abandon their march. Their greatest fight against their enemy was under way, and the spirited friction of companionship kept them ablaze. None of us knew what we were headed for. Lores revealed their enemies were ruthless, but would we find them the same? Regardless, we tore down the forest path with nothing held back, around the hole that constantly greeted me on arrival, and finally, not soon enough, the shore.

"There," Draythian spotted them from behind the trees where Kaylaira, Jesriel and two other chosen knelt in the sand.

I wanted to run to her with no reservations but paused from afar to observe our odds. Like ancient treasures, five golden, oval shaped pods jutted ten-feet high up from the shallows, their gleaming surfaces catching the sunlight with dazzling reflections. Four were already open. Each was large enough to accommodate a single body inside, ready with upright positions to whisk their occupants above. But the fifth pod at the center remained closed and, on its side, towering the other four nearly three times over. I saw no immediate threat, but knew an enigmatic mystery waited to be unraveled. But it wasn't enough to stop me from ensuring Kaylaira's safety.

Beyond the pods, no fighters nor army surrounded them. They appeared alone, other than a lone well-aged man beyond in his years. A large-knobbed cane held in his hand, steadying his feeble weight as he stood before them while engaged in some MonTu ceremonial ritual. He too wore a headpiece like the crown Nijal toyed with from above the mantle, and its stones illuminated in intervals, just as the falcon's had upon its head. What did it whisper? What command did it give?

I became antsy, unsure which one was Kaylaira. With the cloaks covering their heads, it was impossible to decipher who was who. But while three of the chosen kept in the sand, the fourth stood, accepting the old man's hand as he guided them to the first pod. Who was it?

I studied every flail as an ocean breeze flapped their fabrics, every flutter till the sleeve of that cloak rose in the wind. Kaylaira! The sun caught her metal, gleaming her bracelet's reflection straight across my eyes. My heart drummed. My insides gurgled with nervous energy. She was the first to be taken.

"Jordan? If you plan to keep her here better make it quick!" Draythian hurried me.

Adrenaline warped the flow of my fingers as I tapped into the air's fury. One hand hailed a down draft where I stood, and the other severed the gap between her and the capsule. But both gusts were unbalanced and too strong. The first hit Kaylaira and wrenched her through the air, ten feet back into the gritty water as the second blast erupted from the trees. It exploded with a temper across the sand, pounding the pod that awaited her and skittered it atop the ocean.

"I'd definitely say you made your intentions clear," Draythian sarcastically jabbed. "And in retaliation for Jesriel's strike to my head, I'll tell her you intentionally slammed her body back on the shore for not telling you," he threw in.

He darted a smile only archenemies give. And in Nijal's absence, Draythian declared himself as my sarcastic, sidekick commentator.

"Now let's go save them. For Elatia!" he roared.

We dove from the trees and rushed the shore like a storm as the three-chosen leapt from the sand. Jesriel yelled for reprisal, targeting the old man's face with a staff slung from beneath his fabric. We couldn't yield him in time, and away his staff wildly flew. Draythian was right, the fighter in him begged to tear from his leash.

He and the others subdued the old man while I hurried to Kaylaira. Her eyes enlarged at the sight of me as I pulled her from the sand. Then her body followed, striking me like a bolt of lightning as she wrapped me with cheer. She'd forgotten her strength compared to mine, knocking the breath from my lungs, but in that embrace an assuring thought dawned that would linger through time. No extreme would ever be too extreme when vying for her safety. Her being one of the chosen shouldn't have mattered, though it had, something I'd never allow again.

"I'm so sorry," I uttered, cradling her head to my chest. "I didn't know you were chosen, and I never meant to leave you, please believe me."

Her body shivered. Her teeth chattered as she tried voicing her fears. But despite her quiet words, her arms conveyed everything to me, reeling me in like tentacles as she ignored my belated arrival. To her, it only mattered that I came.

"What is the purpose of this?" the old man shouted. "I am the Pledgemaker, and you defiantly break a truce held for an eternity between us!"

The Pledgemaker? A closer look at the crown on his head revealed similar colored lucents from Kaylaira's bracelet. The sky-blue was ablaze, and I instantly wondered if his actions were a lack of choice.

"Truce?" Jesriel rebelled. "You call what you've done to us for ages a truce? Endless lifetimes of oppression? Slow deaths for our families once you've abandoned us?"

"Why not end this here, now?" I threw in. "Leave in peace and never return; there's no need to take this further."

The old man chuckled hard enough to crack a rib, by no means threatened at our storming advance as he jabbed his crinkled finger my direction. "Leave these people in peace? Have you lost your sense of reason young one? I am the Pledgemaker, tasked to assure the chosen's allegiance to their new leader, and I will fulfill my task. As for you, *land sweeper*, something greater is in store, but for the rest, you know the repercussions you've created."

Land sweeper? He'd already nicknamed me? Why not air or wind sweeper, and what was that "something greater in store?" I thought of the rebellion Kaylaira spoke of, the one her people attempted eons ago. Were those the repercussions he spoke of? Or something greater they'd refrained to reveal?

The knob of his cane flickered as he tapped it in water, and the gems in his crown synced in a rhythmic flow. Kaylaira gripped my hand and nudged me back as the old man's laughter sprung wild. Then the door on the center pod cranked open with a slow, painful drag. Jesriel and the others back stepped with us, leaving me foolish to believe that an aged man, struggling to keep balance was all they'd throw at us. But it was too late, and the deep breathed growls that grumbled from the pod proved it so. Whatever it was had been caged too long.

A ray of sunlight flickered inside, casting a spotlight on the three-foot whiskers and snarling snout in its path. We back stepped faster as that glimmer widened to reveal a pair of canines that were longer than my arm. Finally, the door was ajar, with the head of a feline stooping to press its way through.

"What on Earth?" I gasped.

"What on Elatia?" Kaylaira gasped the same.

We stood in disarray, daunted by the old man's cackles as a beast concocted from some drugged hallucination made its way out. Its hair glimmered like liquid gold with orange, yellows and red. Its mane swayed and danced like flames, ushering waves as if they had minds of their own, just as the falcon's feathers from atop the mountain. It looked down on the lot of us like a grown child above a litter of puppies. But what I feared most adorned its head, the same godlike crown entwined in its locks.

"Hope you brought a bigger stick!" Draythian yelled at Jesriel.

The Pledgemaker cackled as if he'd heard a joke that would endure his remaining days when his shaky voice was suddenly swallowed, eaten beneath a thundering roar that smothered all sound. But it wasn't just a roar. Its breath carried power and smacked us like a wave, tumbling us through sand and prying Kaylaira and I apart.

"Great!" I shouted. "An elephant lion wasn't enough? It had to have a windstorm for breath as well?"

Jesriel was first to stand indomitable, stampeding towards the beast with his wooden stick as if poised to face a litter of kittens. His rage vented with a hell-raising grunt as his staff anchored for a blow to the feline's kisser. But the feline detonated a second roar and Jesriel flailed like a feather in the wind, nailing the cliff wall where he knocked out cold. Then the beast bolted towards him like a limp piece of meat.

"Jordan?" Kaylaira freaked.

Panic ruffled my spine out to my fingertips, jolting a reflex from my hand. The feline pounced, but Jesriel spouted like a geyser, thirty feet high before I shoved his dead weight atop the cliff. The beast slammed the wall like a mallet, claiming nothing more than confusion and a mouth full of stone. The others cheered its fluster, but its aggression rebounded with the shake of its head before its dark golden eyes found Kaylaira and I.

He knew what I'd done, making us his new obsession as we tiptoed back from its pant wetting glare. That's when I knew my time had come. All those hours and evenings of practice at that very cliff. I'd thrived there a thousand times, and it was time I thrived once more!

"Ready?" Kaylaira panted, knowing what was ahead of us.

The feline fired like a bullet, clawing through shore in a sand flinging rage. Only then did I know terror, and in one word, it *suffocated* me. All thought, movement and action smothered beneath the one emotion claiming them all… fear. But I wasn't alone. Kaylaira's hand drove firm against my back, steadying me like the jab of a needle to ignite my pulse. Adrenaline bulldozed fear. Cowardice burned like paper in flames, and then an idea sparked, risky with no time to explain, but the distance between us left no choice.

"Yes, I'm ready. Are you?!" I threw back. "Make sure and grab the ledge."

"What?" she asked.

She had no clue that I'd toss her like a helpless infant, flying high on the wall and out of harm's reach. I prayed I gave enough warning and that she'd latch on in time. Or had I salvaged her from one death and plunged her into another? I had no way of knowing. The beast hounded me within the same breath. But with Kaylaira out of range, I unleashed the wind's fury.

A windstorm brewed behind one of the pods, hauling it towards my hand like a torpedo. I closed my eyes and felt its oncoming rage, treasuring the thought of my beloved as the beast lunged. My world went dark as I was swallowed in its shadow, but my zephyr sense spoke like the wind, joggling my eyes open from a clash above my head. The metal struck fiercely. The beast rolled and waddled, swatted like a snowflake from the air.

"Kaylaira!" I shouted, searching the wall the instant its shadow set me free.

My heart pounded then soothed when I found her on the ledge. Thankfully, she'd latched the top of the wall and had already ascended to Jesriel. That was my girl. But as for myself…

"Jordan look out!" Draythian hollered.

By the time I turned the feline was already in flight. Impulse jolted my arms, and the serried winds swirled to my defense with a bubble of protection slapped between us. It was an untested move I'd never practiced, but necessity fueled its power as the beast rammed head on, snarling and clawing at the invisible barrier. Its force heaved me back on my toes, swelling the nodes in my crackling ankles. I was weak and unstable, but the bubble remained intact. But how long could I manage?

It plowed me across sand like skates on ice before my frail heels hit the wall. Then my back. Then my head as I was completely sandwiched between. Lodged against rock, my muscles trembled weary with nowhere to go, and my shield slowly deflated from the press of its canines. It couldn't have been clearer, either its teeth would tear me apart or I'd suffocate and be crushed in my own protective bubble.

The air upheaved from my lungs with each breath harder to regain. Sharp stones punctured like daggers from behind, easing their flanks into the meat of my shoulders. There was no way of conjuring a stronger wind, not with those rocks wedged in my spine. But the beast shoved harder, sapping the little strength that remained as the stone wedged in my skull. Finally, my breath gave out with a final gasp, and the creature's jaws closed in like a dungeon.

CHAPTER THIRTY-EIGHT

I stared into that pit of gloom with its steamed breath fogging the glass of my eyes. Its fangs scathed my forehead like a slowly dragged fingernail. My resolve quit. I'd never seen my end so clear and chose to welcome its slaughter. My head bowed and my arms gave in when the unsettling roar of an unlikely ally secured my release.

The feline lunged to its rear, dumping me to my knees as my flesh pried from stone like a peeled off band-aid. As my airway opened, I sucked in all the air on Elatia when my eyes drifted to a dispiriting sight... a second feline.

My breaths shallowed once more as it too sized me up with its pretty, deadly gaze. Like a bull it readied its charge, dusting sand with paws larger than my torso as it challenged the first for dominion. Fortunately for me I was forgotten, bathed in the face with lumps of soil as the first contested with a lunge. But their battle was a ruse, and to my surprise the other scurried from the chase, buying me moments where I flattened over sand. I believed the ground quaked beneath me, only to realize it was my arms that shook the earth. What happened? I was safe, relieved, but it didn't add up.

I pushed up my weight on quivering palms to crawl for safe passage and find out why. What I found was an incredible disbelief. Kaylaira, Draythian and the others stood with outstretched arms with their bracelets aimed at a defining point. It took a breath to piece together, but I eventually realized what they'd done. Collectively, they'd used their mimic lucents to stream a farce image of the second feline, all channeled through Kaylaira's bracelet. I would've bet my life I'd seen the real thing, and apparently the first feline had as well.

"I would've watched it feast on you, but Kaylaira wouldn't oblige," Draythian smiled and helped me to my shaky feet.

I never cleared if he were joking, but at that moment I more than welcomed his hand. Jesriel and Kaylaira leapt from up top where I caught their descent with a cushioned wave. Both embraced me for their lives the moment they touched sand, but I owed them as much the same.

"Um, glad to see the love and all, but this won't last forever. That thing will be back any moment now, so what's our strategy?" Draythian interrupted.

Together we eyed the old man in the water still clutching his cane, obviously more than just a balancing stick. Our sudden intense interest spooked his courage, rallying an exceedingly slow attempt to run before we forced him down. Jesriel, again more hotheaded than I'd presumed, ripped the cane from his grip, arcing to fling it in the ocean.

"No Jesriel, wait!" I yelled.

I thrust my hand and clinched its tip. The bottom snapped loose, but momentum flung the rest into the shallows. What had I detached?

Hidden within the base of the cane gleamed a key barely the length of my hand. Its engineering was beguiling, a labyrinthine masterpiece carved out of glistening gold, like a smaller version of the iconic Empire State building. Its base was wide and solid, tapering gradually with every inch towards its crown. I counted five or six levels, each adorned with intricate ridges and grooves, an endless maze of joints and cavities intertwining in a thousand minuscule crossroads. It was both mesmerizing and overwhelming to behold.

"I think it's a key," I showed them.

"To open what?" Draythian asked.

Round and round I twirled it in my hand trying to decipher what. But back and forth between it and the old man, the answer poked me in the eye.

"The knob of that cane commands the animal. We need it back!" I rushed them.

Draythian dispatched others to retrieve it from its plunge, while I headed to the key's answer staring me in the eye… the old man's crown. His aged eyes ballooned as Jesriel happily forced him to his knees. Panic shuddered him to the bone. He knew what was about to happen. Smack in the middle of his fancy headpiece lay a keyhole, perfectly matching the key tip in my hand.

"No!" he shouted and weaseled, his flimsy body flailing while he sat in place. "No! Let it be! Please, no!"

Kaylaira head locked him as a roar spewed from the forest, swelling his rants and raves as I inserted the first inch of the metal tip. Click. A perfect fit that went no further than the first notch of the key's spread.

Tilted to its right it clicked again. The flickering lights faded, the crown split in three and each piece tumbled to the ground.

"No!" the old man screamed and grabbed his head. "The sound! The sound!" he yelled, thrashing in wet sand as if convulsing from a seizure.

Jesriel went to strike him when Kaylaira seized his hand.

"No, wait!" she insisted. "This isn't a spectacle," she said, stooping to the old man's level while gently caressing his arm. Cautious, she nudged closer. "It's okay," she uttered.

Her whispers could calm the ocean, and his convulsing behavior softened with each stroke of her hand. But in came a second roar.

"Guys? Now what?" Draythian asked.

The others still shuffled for the cane. I insisted they scramble as the no-longer deceived beast reared its head through the trees. The sight of it jumpstarted the old man's fear. He crawled back, deeper in the shallows as if witnessing it for a first before Kaylaira held him at bay. But why? He hadn't before.

"You know something? That beast has the same fixed opening in the front of its crown," Jesriel realized.

He was right, and I again instantly knew it had to be me.

"Okay. Either I use the key the same, or preferably, you find the other end of that knob and figure how to control it," I ordered. "We can't afford to let it wash away."

"What about you?" Kaylaira asked.

"Me? Time to be a wind driver," I said. "Let's see if I keep it angry enough to chase me till you guys figure how to use that stick."

With the key secured in my pocket I strode to the forest edge. I couldn't explain my sudden boldness to face it alone, but it spumed heavy, herded me straight towards its growling smirk with the wind unleashed in my back. It lunged to meet my defiance, each of us swathed with repugnance for the other like two angry rams on a collision course. But I wasn't stupid. Clearly, I was no match for a head on clash, so I stirred a wind squall of sand right in its eyes then leapt as its charge slackened in force. I'd never leapt so far, so fast, on and off the top of its spine and back to the ground with minimal exertion. Yeah, I was a wind driver.

I drew its anger to follow me through the trees, wrapping through the forest in an all-out chase. I dove over and slid beneath fallen branches, blew past large, wet leaves that slapped my skin like angry damp hands. It liberated me, the same exhilaration when speeding the streets on my motorbike. The air whipped through my fabrics and cooled my skin, inciting a rush of heightened awareness as the beast kept pace. It decapitated every stalk of vegetation that poked in his path, and I imagined it pictured them as my head. Still, for the first time ever, I felt no alarm.

I pushed harder as the zephyr's aura burst around me, testing my limits gripping the air as if it were two free hands propelling me forward. My feet landed pockets of wind, and before knowing it, I no longer touched the earth beneath me. I was running on air.

Confidence and cockiness become my crown as I taunted it closer to see if I'd get away. I did, then sent a hail of side winds to jumble its feet, stumbling it into every hurdle I found along the way when my memory suddenly jarred me. The hole in the forest! The one that entertained me on each arrival. It was just ahead, and my only crack at opening its crown.

I exploded toward the opening with the key in hand, slowed before its edge, then turned and faced the feline with adrenaline in my legs. My hands quivered with a surge of nerves and excitement, and I couldn't control them as I tapped into the zephyr. Either way it was time, and the feline bounded in.

We locked eyes, from thirty feet away through the swaying leaves when the surge of air bit my fingertips. Its mouth gaped at twenty feet, as if it had already caught me as the biting winds mounted in my palms. Ten feet and the beast no longer held. It rocketed forward and I leapt back, clearing the pit's wide-open gap as my hands drank the empowering winds.

I summoned a draft strong enough to knock a house from its foundation. It slammed with no shame, ricocheting me through the air before a tree behind stopped me with no remorse. I was still learning, and that stump proved a valuable lesson, jolting my shoulder like a surge of fierce lightning. I lay there in pain and didn't move, but neither did the beast. That was enough to force me past my agony and emboldened me to make the first move.

I couldn't see down but all was so quiet, as if all the forest listened to the soft whimper below. I scattered the mess I'd made and clawed through dirt, anxious to see the work of my hands, but the sight of it squeezed guilt from my heart instead. What had I done? Seconds before it wanted to shred me to bits, but because of me, now it barely laid with breath in its lungs.

"Not the time to get warm and squishy Jordan," I toughened up, then lowered myself into the hole.

Maybe I'd gone completely insane, or perhaps the tree stump had obliterated my judgment. Why else would I drop in for a nice tight snuggle? I practically gave it a second chance to rip me apart, but its droopy eyes barely gave me recognition, and its whimper softened to an asthmatic wheeze. So I got closer, never pulling from its disheartened eyes while I searched for signs of deceit. However, I found none.

"It's okay, buddy. I'm not here to hurt you. Hard to believe I know," I whispered.

What bad timing for a bad choice of words! Having fully descended, its true size became unbelievably believable. It could swallow my head like a lollipop if desired. And its mane? It alone could warm a dozen men. But its beauty overtook me, and its colors roused brighter with each advance as I dangled the key like a fish to a seal. That did it.

For the first time its eyes slanted towards me by an inch. It made no roar nor growl of displeasure, and it was far from leaping to life. Instead, it just gazed me with its ice cream eyes, like a kid seeking his reward at the end of a chore. It knew the key. It was aware of what I held, what it did and made no opposition towards it. That drove me forward, cushioning each foot as I extended the key to its head.

"You're tired of wearing it, aren't you?" I comforted it with my trembling hand. "How about we get you free?"

With utmost care the metal touched, and the key's first tier slipped into its crown. But the keyhole was much larger than the old man's and the second tier entered, followed by the third, then all trust disappeared.

The once dormant gems on its headpiece ignited, and its eyes sprung from trust to the belief of betrayal. Crap!

I swiped the key just in time as the point of its claw drew blood from my hand. It sprung on all fours with a returning roar, stuffing me against the wall to render me useless. My fortune had run dry, and all I could do was clinch and brace for a slash to take my head. Then suddenly, it leapt out.

I vomited relief in the dirt, then leapt in pursuit as it tore back to shore. Running was torturous, and neither of us could barely move as I clasped my shattered shoulder and tore through the roughage, thumping past branches with an on-and-off glimpse of its evading tail. We neared the shore, and I only needed to push beyond the final bend. That's where I collapsed.

My shoulder no longer bore each jabbing footstep. Agony swelled my head. My vision blurred as I watched the feline enter its pod with the door closed behind. What made it so? Kaylaira and the old man still wading in the shallows with his fingers tracing hers along the cane's digital knob. To my relief, they'd recovered it from the shoal.

I watched their celebration with my face half in sand as the pod rose and fled to the mountain. I was so close! So close to swiping the crown and knowing what would've happened. Better everyone was safe however, or at least that's what I convinced myself while trying to stand. I hobbled to them with the little strength left in my legs when a faint voice whispered through my head.

"Jordan, come back," the whisper pled.

Come back? At that moment? I couldn't! I had to keep focus and shooed off the whispers. But then they returned.

"Urgent Jordan, come back," it called again.

It was Nijal, with Wendi pleading along with him. They knew where I was, the urgency of what I was doing. So why call then? What had they discovered more pressing?

I shook off their whispers and made myself stay, hoping my insistence to remain asleep would warn them to back off. Then Kaylaira caught sight of me just in time, with the call of her voice settling me back on the present. I limped to their diminished merriment as the Pledgemaker suffered another bipolar episode. He convulsed and belittled everyone he'd just helped, then suddenly forgot it all, shoving all those around except for Kaylaira. She alone had earned his trust.

"We should take him back and see what he knows," Draythian admonished, handing me the top half of the cane.

I already had the key, did I really want more?

"Agreed. But that half stays with you," I declined.

He wanted it no more than I did, overwhelmed and aware he'd stepped into a messy puddle before trying to shoulder the responsibility to Jesriel. I cut him off.

"Jesriel," I called, handing him the three pieces of the Pledgemaker's crown. "Here, keep these safe. No telling if we may need it again. I'll keep the key, Draythian the cane, and each of us will keep guard of our possessions. If one of us is caught, we can hopefully rely on what another has to use against them."

Each accepted their new burden, then to the village with the Pledgemaker we returned.

CHAPTER THIRTY-NINE

What had I started? I was jumpy and on edge, turning to every sound the forest made as we trekked to the village to determine if our enemy followed. Just when I thought things were finally calm, the old man would suddenly launch into a disturbing rant.

"The MonTu will not be pleased. The MonTu will abhor us," he'd shout.

Kaylaira calmed him but I wrested for answers.

"What is MonTu?" I asked.

But he wouldn't answer. Just a blank stare into space and an occasional gaze at the mountain as his thoughts faded in the wind.

"How many are there? How can we fight them?" I implored, but he faintly wept as if all was lost.

"MonTu cannot be beaten. It has no equal, their entirety is countless," he sobbed.

It or they? A thing or an army? I needed to know, and waiting for him to divulge anything usable was utterly painful. How could I get him to cooperate? An idea sprung to light from the time I'd spoken to Mom on our living room sofa, with words all the way from Elatia. Sleep talking. Wendi and Nijal waited with me at the house, so why not use them as my helping hands?

I ushered the group ahead, knowing the old man's outbursts would never lend a chance to focus. Kaylaira wished to stay, but she was better off shielding the old man from Jesriel's recurring rage. Then alone and at peace, I plopped onto the wild foliage and closed my eyes, digging my hands through soil to deepen my connection with their land.

My thoughts and worries quieted, but I had to use caution. Too absorbed in my aria and I'd fall into limbo. Not strong enough and I'd wake up on the sofa with Wendi and Nijal. I felt like a gymnast with a sudden cramp shooting up my leg, desperately trying to maintain my balance on a narrow one-inch beam without taking a step, getting stuck, or tumbling off onto the mat below.

However, with the swoosh and sway of the breeze, my mind washed clear and I found a place of balance. The breeze set in the background. The ripples in the reflection pool took their place, marred by the pale sounds of Wendi and Nijal's tones. And then I called out, unsure they'd heard my distant voice before Nijal jumped to my call.

"Wendi, Jordan's telling us something!" Nijal spewed.

It worked. They'd heard me and I could picture his emphatic gestures with his every word.

"The MonTu," I went on. "I need to know of the MonTu."

"MonTu?" they questioned, trying to unravel what I'd spoken.

But the more I listened, the more I drifted to their side. My eyelids fluttered. I was still on the sofa nestled in Wendi's lap, her soft touch lulling me into contentment. But I couldn't give in! I resisted the pull of sleep with all I had to defeat that comfort and keep my eyes closed!

Quickly I found the swoosh and sway of the breeze when the pendulum swung to the other side. The draft whooshing through the forest leaves. The soil scrunched in my palms. It deepened my serenity and sunk me into the land when the appeal of falling to my aria became twice as strong.

Who in their right mind would choose to end an elating dream? At times, to dream is the greatest highlight in our life and we push hard to keep them from fading. That's what I felt then, and to pull away felt like I'd rejected the perfect moment. I nearly failed, and the only way I succeeded was by shouting the last word from Nijal's mouth.

"MonTu!" I shouted into the forest, thrusting my eyes open and nearly leaping from the ground.

I panted like a race dog and wore a ring of moisture around my neck as I slumped into the blissful sward of grass. I'd resisted that peace, but the second I arrived in the village I was back in chaos at the give-and-take circle.

A large clay pot hanging over the fire simmered the most succulent stew I'd savored to date. While the group deliberated, I scrutinized the old man's munches and chews. He was a complete loss. His hands trembled with each rise and fall of his spoon before he'd cough and choke on nearly every mouthful. He'd forgotten who he was, how to think and even eat, and our greatest efforts to embellish him derived the slightest results.

Fingers were nearly bitten. There were jostles too close to the fire as we questioned him like a child. "Who led him? What was MonTu and what were they like? Why call me land sweeper?" However, each inquiry was met with a vacant expression as if we'd spoken to him in different tongues. Only Kaylaira never lost patience.

"He should rest," she insisted.

We acceded against our will, knowing we'd push till he dropped if it meant getting what we were after, but not Kaylaira. As she gently helped him to his feet, the word 'Rhemiani' from Dr. Tamera's paper suddenly rang my head. Why then at that moment, I hadn't a clue.

"Rhemiani? What does it mean?" I asked aloud, doubtful of my enunciation.

"It means remember," Draythian answered with a look of surprise.

"But it's more than just a word. It carries a profound psychological effect," Jesriel responded.

"What effect?" I hastened.

"When uttered in the correct form, it's said to grant the ability to recall something of immense significance," Jesriel continued. "It's an ancient custom we have no need to perform. From where did you learn that word?" he asked, almost as if I'd pushed the boundaries of what I'd learned of them.

Their curiosity spooked me as the circle stopped, anxiously awaiting my lazy response. What was I to tell them without detailing where I'd found it written? My hesitance grew awkward, before Kaylaira rushed to my rescue.

"I taught him. It was written in the deep," she blared, smiling and winking to play along. "In case he was ever to forget me, I wanted to assure he had a way to remember."

While they bought it and resumed their meal, Kaylaira prodded me to escort the old man to a lower tree to rest, where she too pondered how I'd learned the word. She didn't ask, but curiosity burned in her expression as she let it be and entrusted me with its protection. I knew exactly how I'd use it when the time was right.

I wondered what the circle discussed as we put the Pledgemaker to rest, partly wishing I could eavesdrop on what they spilled in my absence. However, as Kaylaira draped the old man in the warmth of a blanket, just five words lured me back to his side.

"It's good to be home," he mumbled.

Her and my eyes clashed with disbelief as we stooped to his mouth to hear his grumbled words. But he instantly snored like a disheveled drunk, even as the sun still held high.

"I can't believe it. He's one of us? He must've been one of the chosen from long before our time," Kaylaira assumed.

We crouched on the floor next to his bed, weighing what he'd spoken in silence. Minutes passed and neither of us uttered a word. We just stared as he slept like a log and left our thoughts burning in circles.

"Allowing him to rest is our only hope at letting nature mend him. But he's been away too long. His mind is nearly beyond repair, and I fear his sanity may never recover in time," she said.

"Time," I whispered. "Always time."

Time ticked away as I tried to fill that uncomfortable silence with only one thought in my head… the unsettling mystery of her mother. Nervously, I scooted closer unsure how to begin.

"You've become quite the fighter, Sir Jordan," she jested. "Tell me, how was it facing the beast alone?"

She yearned to hear the results of her efforts and how our hours of practice paid off. I bragged a little of my fearless encounter, with the disappointment of not having unlocked the crown. Then abruptly, my thoughts rushed out.

"Kaylaira there's something else," I quickly shifted.

My palms were sweaty. My heart thumped as I reminded her of the writings on the wall and how the cipher and keyword would decode its meaning.

"The word? You've discovered it?" she anxiously followed.

"I have," I answered.

"Yes? Then what is it?" she jumped.

"The word Kaylaira, is Yasmeiruh, your mother's name."

Shock wiped the grin from her face as she searched my expression for hidden meanings.

"How is that possible? Why would it be my mother's name?" she asked.

"I'm not sure," I told her. "I've gone over the possibilities a thousand times, but apparently, your mother and my father knew one another very well."

I assured her I had no clue as to why or how and gave my word that her name had unlocked the puzzle. Then the dreaded thought reared, what were she and I to each other? I studied her wandering gaze from the facts I'd presented, waiting for the same notion to blossom in her head, but it never did. Did Dad have a relationship on Elatia, outside of Mom that made Kaylaira and I kin?

"Did you know your father?" I asked.

"Yes," she confirmed, "A random villager. You must understand, the priority following a transference is procreation, not a family bond. The need to remain strong, preserve our kind, and survive till the next arrival becomes our utmost importance; not love."

Her mother hated the idea and rejected it as long as she could, but the circle eventually overruled, forcing her to succumb to the rules for their need to procreate.

"I was told my 'father's' existence ceased the very next transference. Due to a lack of male gender, he and others fathered several during those cycles, but the revelation to whom was never permitted. Like most children here, I didn't have the luxury of getting to know him. He was barely around, forced to focus on our people as a whole rather than each individually. That's why I admire Draythian's dedication to his daughter," she said.

The more we spoke, the more she realized my conflict, and her response couldn't have been better.

"Your father, was he a kind man?" she asked.

"Extremely," I gushed, raving how loving a provider he was to Mom and I.

"Then you shouldn't worry," she continued with a stroke to my face. "The kind man you speak of was by no means the man others spoke of here. So push whatever worry you have from your head, no good will come from preoccupying your mind, especially now."

My doubts vanished with her reassurance and the warmth of her hand took on new meaning. We had no proof, but her words were backed with meaning. Dad would've never abandoned us, nor distanced himself from his own.

Drugged by the touch of her hand, I thought nothing more of it as the tension flushed from my neck and shoulders. I'd have given years of my life to hold to that fleeting moment, but before the feeling could sink in, a blood-curdling scream threw me right back on edge.

CHAPTER FORTY

We stumbled out to everyone frantically searching for an unseen terror in the sky.

"What is it?" Kaylaira yelled, as we found nothing but empty air.

"Shiny talons. They came from the trees out of nowhere," a villager stressed.

Shiny talons? Before I could formulate his words into a picture, a six-foot mechanical claw sprung from the trees. It moved like a predator stalking its prey, gleamed with a cold metal sheen, and three sharp points that glinted in the sunlight like razor-sharp icicles. It was reminiscent of those from vending machines to drop and scoop up a prize. And as we watched in horror, it latched to Jesriel like an eagle's claw to a fish, hoisting his weight then carrying him away with the ease of a feather in the wind.

"What are they?" Kaylaira cried.

"Machines! Contraptions like the pods that obey a given command," I shouted.

But it was beyond any machine I'd known. Its stealth evaded our ears, unlike the creaks and cracks of our machinery back home. No exhaust leaked from propulsion. No lanky chains or gears dragged it back from where it hailed. Jesriel was simply gone, as if the forest had suddenly grown a secret hand that unknowingly lurked in the shadows.

"The talons are only taking the chosen!" Draythian yelled.

His warning submerged me in fear. Kaylaira was the only chosen left.

"Stay close," I pulled her behind.

Back-to-back we circled, combing the trees for movement or sound.

"Behind you!" Draythian blurted.

My instincts kicked in as I shoved Kaylaira aside and leapt in its path instead. It struck my chest and threw its claws around me, clamping my arms to my side as my feet left the ground. Straight up it took me with remarkable ease then primed to haul me away. But the zephyr whispered its pull of direction, and I countered with a forceful wind.

A tug of war ensued then a haze of smoke ascended. Sparks spat wild from its rear as its clamps strained to maintain their grip. But my zephyr held strong, and the longer it held me, the more the pain crushing my chest fueled me to break from its prison. A claw went limp. I fell to my feet bolstering the air as the source of its hold gave way. Then with a primal roar, I snapped the clamps from my chest and buried the claw through the ground. But a second current tugged to my left.

"Get down!" I yelled.

The moment she hit the ground a second claw burrowed down as silent as a breeze. But I was ready. The zephyr bound to my hand, unearthing the clunker I'd just buried and thrusted it in its path.

The impact shattered them both, then a third hailed from my right. I couldn't help but wonder if it were an endless battle, if I'd tire and never win. But one look at Kaylaira's despair and the fight blazed back in my hands.

I summoned the wind on its tail and wrenched it towards me. The claw lost its reins and slung with no control, shattering into a thousand pieces across a nearby tree. While the others kept belly flopped and braced for a fourth, I spun in rage in search for more. But the air kept peaceful and still, with no threat alarming my senses.

Kaylaira sighed relief and we both smiled victory, then a mysterious shadow blanketed us like the shades of a window. Fear grew the span of her eyes, then mine as a well-acquainted squawk spun me behind. An unmistakable flare of brilliant blue colors burned through the air. The falcon! It was all too pretty to forget, yet too terrifying to want to remember as its weight flamed down on us both.

Its swoop nearly took my head before I dropped and embraced the earth. My cheek scraped the forest floor with its mass pinning me under. However, it wasn't me it craved. I wished it were, but there I lay useless, squinting one eyed as its talons snatched Kaylaira instead.

Somehow in that moment I remembered a hawk Father and I stalked gliding over a river. Its unbroken motion seared in my head, its effortless dive to snatch a fish before soaring back to the trees. It marveled me once but terrified me then as it took her from my reach with painless effort. In all my power, there was nothing I could do.

Hearing her belt my name in horror unhinged my sanity. I shuffled through dirt as it plucked her from the grass, useless beneath its weight till it moved and sprung me to my feet. A wind blast stirred in my hand. They soared thirty feet, but I could catch her. As I reared to swipe its wings from the sky, my next breath was whiplashed from my lungs. The jolt twisted my neck. Shock bit across my ribs as I slung from my feet, blindsided by a force I knew nothing of. By what? The bird had long gone.

I was barely coherent, learning to breathe as her image faded but her screams kept in my ears. She was mine to protect, a vow that drove my hands to dig through the soil to get her back. Blood trickled down my throat as I stood, feeling it before tasting it as I listened for the power that took me down. The footsteps of a stalking feline? It wasn't there, baffling me as that distant blue speck carried my beloved away.

I scrambled to find our predator as my sight staggered back, startled as a villager lofted past me as if his body carried no weight. I rushed to help, still searching the trees when a second body lobbed by me just as fiercely.

"Draythian!" I yelled, hoping he'd gotten a sense as to what preyed upon us.

Then I saw him in the distance, something far from the mythical creatures I'd encountered before that greeted me from afar with his terror filling eyes. It was the semblance of a man, one who punished us abhorrently with swells of air from his hands. It was what Kaylaira warned me of; this was a will-bender.

Draythian and the others converged but of what use? They never came within a breath of him, leaving the creatures I'd fought to be feared as lesser foes. The same crown-like headpiece topped his head, latched to a breathing mask that concealed the rest of his face. His movement terrified me. His efforts were never taxed, as if each bout had been executed thousands of times as a choreograph of wind left his hands without labor. I was awed, beholden by his artful skill, knowing he could defeat us a hundred times over. And he wasn't alone.

An accomplice whirred between the trees slashing villager after villager, all from the cue of the will-bender's hand. Always a resounding boom, then a flailing body, but whatever it was hurled too fast to follow. Its whereabouts deceived my ears as its echo whistled from each edge of the forest. In front, then behind, then another boom, until the culprit of destruction ricocheted back in his hand… a gilded boomerang.

He'd plowed through us like a sickle through weeds with every villager trampled and defeated. Only two defenders remained, Draythian and I, but I froze and watched in horror as Draythian stormed with passion. It would be his end. I saw it, felt the immense conjuring power as the boomerang left our enemy's hand.

"Draythian, don't!" I yelled.

But he persisted, bold and ready, swelling my desperation as the boomerang cut the air. Naymelia! Was she to grow up fatherless due to my blunted edge, my lack of action? Despair ignited a pulse in my stubborn hand, rupturing the air like a crackle of lightning. The forest divided in two as my winds raged down, plowing stones and branches aside as the two forces met. It was the most awe-inspiring display of power I'd experienced.

Nothing of the surrounding forest was left to stand. Draythian repelled into the unknown. The will-bender was buried beneath heaps of debris, with his mighty weapon sunk through a boulder like a knife through cheese. It was my strongest demonstration of power. However, because of it, and having freed Draythian from his death sentence, I had nothing left to give while the will-bender thrived with plenty more.

He tore from his buried heap with his eyes sunk in mine, waiting to see where my challenge stood. There wasn't one. And for that, in my momentary delay, he plucked me through the air like a fallen leaf and yanked me straight into his grip. He clasped my throat and lifted me off the ground at the mercy of the wind that amplified his physical power. Clearly, they kept in his favor without a thought lent to mine.

His fingers wouldn't budge no matter how hard I tried. His grip even held strong as I tried to awaken back home. My head dizzied. My awareness waned before he pulled me to the tip of his mask within earshot of his warning.

"We know where you hide your young," he sneered.

His mask muffled his voice, sounding like a distorted message coming through a spinning fan as he issued his decree.

"You have one burn to deliver our Pledgemaker and surrender to your cause, or we attack them first," he threatened. "We will continue our rituals with your chosen, then extract every speck of life force this planet has to offer."

I barely caught the message, on the verge of losing consciousness when he tossed me next to Draythian and powered zephyr in his hand. The boomerang shook and trembled in the boulder's clasp, then burst it into pieces as the metal clawed back into his grip. Before the rock pebbles had even hit ground, a boom rattled the treetops and gusted the forest alive as the falcon returned with an air of defiance.

There was nothing more to be said. The threat had been issued and the will-bender leapt on the flyer's back. All the while, he branded me with a death marking glare I could never forget. The way his eyes pierced my soul and shredded my hopes before the bird's wings rose high.

One flap, and a resounding boom sent a tsunami of debris on our heads. In seconds the bird catapulted above the horizon and left us far below. There was no rebounding, no standing to fight for Kaylaira's honor. We drowned in pain with our heads buried in grass, broken as our purpose fleeted away. For me, it was the unbreakable vow I'd given Kaylaira. For Draythian, the potential loss of his daughter whom he'd just pushed from his hand.

I was in agony and could only watch as he stood long before me. Would he treat me harshly in my time of need? I believed he would, but to my surprise he came to my aid with a newly attached warmth that was absent before. I struggled to keep the pain at bay. He knew it, and firmly gripped my shoulders with his head pressed to mine.

"Come on, don't die on me yet. Breathe," he whispered as we both ushered zephyr through our broken bodies. "We have reason to be broken; we both just faced our first will-bender."

For them healing was second nature, but he acknowledged my limits and knew I'd struggle without his guiding hand. Guilt consumed me for having believed he'd abandon me, or that he'd leave me to suffer the doom I'd dragged him in. But he never did. He waited as long as I needed to inhale life in my lungs while he surveyed the damage of his peers. We were shattered, all of us in both body and spirit.

Wonder sprang out of nowhere in a frenzy through the trees, grieving as he leapt on my shoulder with his head tossed between me and the sky. He desperately awaited my response. He too wanted Kaylaira and knew she'd been taken.

"I'm sorry buddy, she's gone," I muttered.

My words sprung him up the nearest tree, onto its highest branch staring longingly into the sky.

"What now?" Draythian sighed as clueless as I.

I had no answer. But just then, the old man came forth and spoke instead.

"You will need the weapon of a king to defeat this one, land sweeper," he said.

His words gave hope but came too late as two voices juddered me from the other side of the universe. Wendi and Nijal, and this time they refused to back down. I convulsed and couldn't hold still. Draythian saw it, me forcibly being pulled away without me having a choice in the matter.

"No, Jordan! Please! Not now!" he begged.

Despite my attempts to resist, I was pried from his desperate grip and thrown back to the other side.

CHAPTER FORTY-ONE

I lingered in the crossover from Kaylaira's abduction, with only retribution staining my mind. Meanwhile, Wendi and Nijal hovered me with anguished eyes, just to watch me explode with anger from having stirred me awake.

"Why now?! Why wake me? It wasn't time to come back!" I stormed.

I barely had the breath to speak, but they endured my insulting tone as if they were speaking to a ghost. It was Nijal's gawking at my red-covered fingers that snapped my defense. I gasped from what I saw then coughed a handful of blood, dropping my eyes to Wendi holding ice to my ribs.

"What were we supposed to do?" Nijal asked, as if their care meant nothing in the world. "Sit here and watch you bleed till nothing was left of you? Stand by and watch my best friend die? You know what this means, Jordan. Don't you? You dying there is damn close to you dying here. They're one in the same. Are you ready for that? Are you ready to hold that against us?"

He was right. What were they to do? What was I to do? What more could I sacrifice or give without it exploding in my face? Wendi read my fragility like an open book, the weakened part of me bursting to cave in before she grabbed Nijal's hand and shook him to stop. In silence, my new and old friend enclosed me with their arms, and that's all it took to loosen my tears. Wendi's pain unhinged as well. She'd held strong till then, leaving Nijal to be the strong one as he quickly came through.

"Oh, you guys. If you want me to cry with you, I'm not," he joked with a sigh, cuddling and playfully rocking us like two distraught children. "But I gotta admit, I'm having a hard time holding back."

That I needed, a hand on my back to keep me steady and strong.

"Now as much as I'd love to stay in this mushy moment, I can't. Cuz if we don't get this car back in time, I'm a dead man," he insisted.

Wendi nursed my wounds in the back seat with every bump reminding me how much I hurt. Their progress decoding Dad's journal became my only distraction.

"MonTu, what does it mean?" I winced.

"Means mountain of joint knowledge," Wendi responded.

"It's the mountain? No reference to their people or army?" I asked puzzled.

"No. Apparently, your peeps on Elatia were once badass and that mountain was untouchable. It's where royalty resided before it all changed. Doesn't say why but looks like the mother of all wars took place, them against a seriously massive coalition of advanced civilizations. What we couldn't find was who came out victorious. My guess, by a very slim margin? The other civilizations," Nijal explained. "Wendi's guess?"

"Neither," Wendi answered.

"Why so?" I asked.

"Because their mountain was taken, and there's no mention of the other groups survival either, just their knowledge left behind on that floating rock. There's no mention of who controls it and for all we know it could simply be a self-operating hub that functions with technology we'll never understand. I mean, they are so beyond our pathetic math and science. We're talking civilizations that frequented different parts of the universe as easily as we shift through the rooms in our homes," she went on.

Wendi was right, apparently knowing more of her mother's work than she'd let on. But I needed her help and brought them to date, from the Pledgemaker calling me land sweeper, to my latest whooping from what appeared to be another wind driver. Our split conclusions? Either the MonTu won and made the remaining wind drivers slaves, forcing them to maneuver the transference against their own planet, *or* the remaining wind drivers selfishly hijacked the mountain for personal gain. Both seemed logical, but the latter made less sense.

"Just hear me out. Doesn't seem your people always had the best of reputations, Jordan. You don't think they used that mountain to rule and conquer when it was in their possession?" Nijal offended me. "Ever think that alliance from dozens of other civilizations teaming up to fight them was due to their wrongful abuse of power? Maybe unlawful oppression? Same thing we see today, just on an unfathomable scale."

"That's not it. That can't be," I denied, reflecting on their peaceful and passive manner.

"Any proof, or just feelings?" Wendi asked with ice pressed to my wounds.

I knew the circle had kept me in the dark, but still shuffled for a reason to free them of Nijal's accusation. Then it hit me!

"Wait! The headpiece! The crown you toyed with from the fireplace?" I jumped, wincing from a stab in the ribs.

I explained how it mocked a mind controlling device, the key to open it on the Pledgemaker's staff and his drastic behavior once we removed the crown from his head.

"So MonTu are using mind control? Nice work, Sherlock," Nijal barked.

"Yeah, talking with the old man is bananas; it's nearly impossible to get a clear word from him. They're hopeful he heals, but I doubt it'll be in time," I explained, then my thoughts abruptly jumped to Kaylaira. "Nijal, I've gotta get back!"

"Whoa, whoa, whoa," he objected. "Do you see yourself in the mirror?" he asked, angling it to my bruised reflection.

"Why? What happened? Why the sudden urge to return?" Wendi asked.

I gave my latest ultimatum, Kaylaira missing, the children's pending doom…

"This is getting too real," Nijal spazzed, huffing as if he'd accepted the task instead of me. "So what's our plan? You can't just waltz back in there, not like this."

What was my plan? I thought long and hard, then gave my shocking answer. "I plan on a good night's rest," I stated. Both stared at me as if they'd heard wrong. "Like you said, dying there is as good as dying here. I have no clue what will happen when I return, and for now there's nothing I can do. So why not rest, think through it with a clear mind and enjoy what may be my final evening with Mom?"

As morbid as it sounded, they couldn't argue my point before we'd returned to the school. We scooped our phones and dropped off the car with our stalkers still looming near Wendi's vehicle.

"Okay, so what's your plan for that?" Nijal asked.

"Same as the other, nothing. Let them watch. There's nothing to see," I said. My better interests were telling him he'd been a true friend, especially after my poor behavior. "Hey, I'm glad you were there today. It meant a lot. Yeah, I know it's sappy and something we don't discuss, but hear me out," I threw before he'd cut my sentiment. "It's very possible I may never have this chance again, so probably not a bad time to start," I said.

He nodded and high-fived me from the driver's seat, his way of saying, 'I care.' Though no one followed us home we knew they'd keep their eyes on us, and he too needed to tread with care. Either way, my ride with Wendi was complete silence as we chewed on how much we'd already experienced together.

Such little time we'd been acquainted yet so dear she'd become. Personally, through the heartache and possible rising dangers, her refusal to give in impressed me to no end. She was eager to learn where our story would end and deserved to know she had my gratitude.

Once we arrived, she never waited for me to limp over to express how I felt. She rushed me instead, pulling me into a tight embrace as her body shook with sobs. I bit my lip, holding back my own emotions as she hung onto that squeeze.

"I'm sorry," she apologized. "It came and I couldn't stop it."

A good laugh composed her as I assured she wasn't a burden.

"Be careful Wendi. I lost your mother; I can't handle losing you as well. Anything comes up, you know where I am," I pleaded.

I staggered away before realizing a moment prior, the moment her and Nijal tried to wake me on the couch.

"Wendi?" I paused. "Earlier when you and Nijal tried to wake me, what was it?"

She smiled and shook her head as if its importance had expired.

"No worries Jordan. Like you said, tonight we rest."

I was glad to hear. I'd had enough surprises and needed to practice hiding my injuries from Mom. But of all times, she whipped the front door open and welcomed me with a gargantuan smile. I pretended not to ache and fumbled for what to say, saved by her enthusiasm as she handed me a small, golden box with a bright red bow wrapped to its surface.

"Open it," she hurried and bounced on her feet.

I failed to match her hurriedness, surprised she didn't snatch it back to open it for me. She barely contained herself as I opened the lid to a shiny "J" on a keyring nestled on a bed of cotton. My motorcycle!

"Yes!" I shouted to the air, flinching from the jab of laughter in my ribs. "Thank you, thank you, Mom!"

"Sorry it took long enough," she apologized.

Still bouncing, she reached to embrace me, and what a game spoiler that nearly was! Her animated squeeze shuddered my body and instantly threw her back to Mother mode.

"Jordan? What happened?" she shifted, tugging my shirt to see for herself.

She was relentless and it ached to fight her off. The more I pushed, the harder she struggled. I didn't know how to explain what she'd find, and in no way wanted to rehash the memory. I just wanted to be!

"Mom!" I yelled, then softened my tone. "Please. This key, this moment, I need it. Please don't take it away from me."

What did she see in my eyes? Pain? Guilt? Remorse? Whatever she saw stopped her with regret.

"Okay. Okay," she agreed, forcing her concern to the back of her head as she mustered a fake smile. "Come on! Let's go out back!"

She led me out back to a sheet shrouding my baby, then whipped off the fabric to keep me from hurting myself. Wow! Words left me.

"Like it?" she hungrily asked, spurred from the drop of my jaw.

"Like it?" I repeated, then fought through the pain to embrace her before the bike. "Yes Mom! Yes! This, this I needed!"

"I know honey," she replied.

Emotion hung in her embrace like an overhanging cloud. She knew something big would soon happen, just not quite what.

"Go ahead, look at your bike," she insisted, distracting herself from her climbing tears.

I struggled pulling away from her not wanting to let go, but then again, that next moment had evaded me too long. The bike gleamed like a midnight jewel, its chrome finishes glinting in the sun as if they were stars in a dark sky. The black coating gave it a mysterious and alluring luster, like a velvet cloak ready to obscure me at night. But I couldn't ignore my favorite color, the painted blue streaks that seemed to glow against its surface. Sleek. Edgy. Instinct told me to take it for a spin, but I was reluctant, I was in pain. Besides, I'd rather spend that evening with Mom, and what an evening to cherish it was.

Her street noodles with chicken and shrimp were out of this world! She poured me a glass of wine and spoke of nothing weighty as we giggled like two pretend drunks. We reminisced clumsy memories of Dad, vacations and his obsession of every flavored ice cream under the moon.

I thanked her for all she'd been to me, wondering in the back of my mind if I'd ever see her beyond that night. I went to question her safety but clinched my teeth, fighting emotion while retracting her concern from my mouth. She left her chair and held me, her arms whispering she understood what I needed while at the same time imparting strength. And that was how our night ended, her whooshing me off with a kiss on the head insisting to let her weep over the dishes alone.

Showered, and with the bijou locked away, I enjoyed the crisp clean sheets she'd placed on my bed, safe in my home with the weight of comfort tugging my eyelids closed. It was the best sleep I ever had in that bed… until a crash outdoors shook me awake that morning.

CHAPTER FORTY-TWO

What a sweet euphoric dream it was, a memorable delusion of myself, Mom and Dad as a family again, leisurely basking in fun when the screeching tires woke me from sleep. That, and Growl finally serving his purpose with a series of barks.

Instinct tore me from the sheets. With my backpack, stone and ready clothes next to my bed, I fell into the hallway to find Mom comforting Wendi. She was shivering at the kitchen table.

"What is it?" I asked.

"She was attacked," Mom huffed.

She scrounged the drawers for pen and paper, then shoved them to my chest along with Wendi's phone. A jumble of letters in an unreadable text from Nijal flashed across her screen. I looked to Mom, prompting me with a nod to figure it out while she handled Wendi.

At first, Nijal's random letters made zero sense, until I recalled the cipher! '*Coming for you. Get out. Beans.*' The letters spelled.

"Wendi, they came for you? Nijal too, he thinks they're coming here next," I informed.

She nodded, still shaken when Growl alerted us a second time, something I didn't think him capable of.

"And now you must go. Now!" Mom shoved us to the back door.

Go? How could I leave her? Who was coming and with what intention? I thought of the address to the hidden house, ready to blurt it out when her hand slapped across my mouth. She'd never stared at me the way she did then, bold, intense and assertive as if she flipped a switch and became someone else. Slowly, she uncovered my lips but never broke from my eyes.

"It's time you go and take Wendi with you," she repeated, solemn yet stern.

In her open palm? The key to my motorcycle.

"But Mom," I tried again, when her insistence blunted me with a second glare.

"Go," she commanded.

Growl threw a barking tantrum warning us to leave. So I forewent my emotions and abandoned Mom, grabbed Wendi and a helmet and pushed out the back door as a car skidded onto our lot. Every inch of me ached as I hurdled down the steps with the will-bender's imprint still embedded in my bones. Instinct whispered to turn back, but I remembered her glare, cursing me to dare resist her command.

That alone kept me forward, and with my helmet on and Wendi buried skintight behind, I locked into my world… street racer mode. The second my crotch hit the leather seat it lit me like a match. The familiar scent of gasoline and motor oil filled my nostrils as I turned the key, igniting the engine with a powerful roar. My fingers eagerly gripped the throttle, unleashing a burst of rumbling energy through the pipes.

It had been too long, my antidote to survive and I couldn't figure how I'd endured not riding for so long. For me, it was as natural as walking, something I'd done since I was six. To cut through air and forge a path through its defiant wind, that was the thrill, as if I'd somehow managed to defy nature's laws. Probably my first sign at being a wind driver.

I revved the engine and sent up a shower of dirt, spraying the house like water from a garden hose. The car caught on, then spun through our lawn with a second vehicle in pursuit. Nijal's cafe wasn't an option, not until I'd lost them, so the chase from hell began.

"Oh my God!" Wendi screamed.

She clutched my waist with all the might in her arms, burying her head between my shoulders as we pushed from zero to ninety within a heartbeat or two. It was her first bike ride from hell, but if she burrowed in and held on for dear life, a buck twenty on an open stretch would be cake. We slashed through parking lots and back yards to grow the space between us. They struggled to close the gap, and after a mere two minutes the sound of twisted metal wrapped a pole behind. One down, one to go.

We had to get him off our tail, quick. The longer we stirred the streets, the more attention, so I gladly gave what I believed they'd come for… the bijou. We burned a U in the pavement for a face off to play a game Nijal and I had mastered for years, 'whose rock could bash a can from a ledge while speeding past? I was the usual victor, but that time the rock was the bijou. And the substitute for the can? The driver's head.

"Sure about this?" Wendi disagreed.

"Absolutely not! But hold tight!"

She clenched tighter as his car squealed around the corner. I opened the throttle and lunged from zero to sixty, with the bijou in my grip and my eyes fixed on the square of his head. Fifty feet, thirty, twenty. I launched at the driver's head as if Elatia's winds were carried with it. He swerved to block our exit when the stone punched his glass like a pen through paper.

I squeezed the brakes and clenched the seat with my thighs, scraping the tip of his bumper as we pierced through his ambush. His tires howled wild. His car snaked with no direction, then pow, his airbag popped like a bomb. He'd met the edge of an old brick building. All was quiet as we looped back to the heap of smoking metal where a perfect hole had breached his glass.

"There's no movement. Is he dead? Did we kill him?" Wendi freaked.

Her arms trembled as if she'd sat in an icebox while I rethought my stupid plan. Had we killed him? Or what if I'd missed? I would've given him exactly what I guessed they were after. Fortunately, I hadn't.

I dropped the kickstand and slid off, readying my helmet as a mallet. Beyond the hiss and rising smoke, all was still, until an untimely flashback of Wendi's mom struck fierce. Why then with Wendi so close? It unbalanced me before I pushed to the driver, bloodied and slumped to his side with a knot the size of a baseball against his head. Slacks and a polo shirt. The same as the guys who'd visited that day but not the guys themselves.

I crept across the crackling glass, opened his door and grabbed the bijou from the floor when the call of a local chase rambled across his radio.

"Gotta go!" I yelled to Wendi, yanking the radio from his belt.

"Who are these guys? Is he still alive?" she panted.

"I believe so, but not our place to find out," I hurried.

The closing sound of sirens unnerved me and again I thought of Mom. Was she safe? I wanted to head home, even edged my wheels that direction when the realization of her timing struck me. The bike wasn't a coincidence. She knew things would get dicey and intentionally set up my getaway. That, and her assertive demand I leave with Wendi, convinced me that going home would be the last thing she'd want.

"Jordan," Wendi tapped me as the sirens grew louder.

I hopped on and lit the engine, peeling back to the first collision where an agent crawled out on all fours. But my remorse had more than vanished, as numbed as the helmet I swung against his jaw. Wendi snatched his radio, then we were off to Beans to find Nijal for a predawn meetup. As if Wendi needed coffee. She couldn't stand still.

"I can't believe this is happening," she paced and melted. "And you, how can you remain so calm?"

Her body quivered, overcome with fear and adrenaline competing for the same veins before I stepped in to thwart her endless strides. I shuffled my hands up and down her skin. She was cold as ice, yielding to the heat of my palms to bring comfort.

"Honestly Wendi, besides Mom, there's little left I care about compared to what I'm running to face. Either I cower from a few cops or brush it off and keep pushing to save an entire world," I said.

Her laugh sparked mine when we thought of what I'd said.

"Not every day you hear that," she laughed. "What'll happen?"

"I don't know anymore," I answered. "A group of guiltless children hope I can save them, and I allowed a special someone to be taken who I'm unsure I'll win back. In all honesty, I don't believe I'm strong enough to stop the death of their world, especially while a man beyond anything I've known waits to bury me where I stand—a second time at that."

"When you put it that way, I guess a few cops chasing you isn't a big deal, is it?" she teased. "But there's a way to win if you believe. There's always a way to win Jordan if you want it bad enough."

Her confidence triggered the Pledgemaker's last words.

"Maybe you're right. Right before you guys woke me at the lake house I was warned I needed the weapon of a king. And no, I have no clue what it is or where to find it," I told her.

"Wish I could help," she replied. "Beyond the lake address and the word scribbled on paper, I'm afraid I'm no use. What does it mean anyway, Rhemiani?"

"It's a word that carries a psychological meaning, to remember," I stuttered, struck by the light of what I needed to do next. "And I know just how to use it."

Just then, Nijal pulled up out back in his grandmother's car?

"What on Earth?!" he yelled. "First, wow, your mom knows bikes." he confessed, admiring the labor of its striking elements. "And second, we are so screwed! These dudes came to my house for me, what the hell is going on?"

"Mine and Wendi's as well. Why your grandmother's car?" I asked.

"Because they're tracking mine. Is that really relevant right now?" he spazzed. "Look, they put something on my car when we left the parking lot. Do you have any idea how much trouble I'll be in tomorrow for stealing granny's car? And what about your mom?"

My mom was his second mother, and he was just as heartbroken I'd left her behind before he started to hyperventilate. I grabbed him to pull it together. We needed a plan, not a rush to find a paper bag. First, we ditched our phones and used their two-way radios. Second, I issued Wendi, more composed than before, to secure the keycard to our safe house.

"Have you seen the streets? You think we're getting out? Cops are blocking every main road and pouring in by the minute," he warned.

"Then we unblock them."

Not being there for Mom deadened me like drug. I had no emotions, but I did find a creative aggression that helped me rationalize in ways I hadn't before.

"Wendi, you're better off with Nijal. I'll get the cops from the road to follow me, and you drive like hell. I have a better chance of losing them alone," I told them. "I'll find a way to meet you at the house, but if anything changes, radio me."

I nodded farewell as they parked on a side street with grandma's engine revving, then drove within fifty feet of the two officers blocking the main road. Sure enough, the trap sprang loose and the two peeled after me. Wendi and Nijal were my greatest concern, and I'd never felt more at peace than watching the diminished image of his grandmother's vehicle pull away in the distance. But back in the pursuit my wild side awakened, and a third unit joined in.

I burned down a slim alley with the three in tow, knowing those crossways like the back of my hand. A fourth popped on my left and forced me right when another blocked that path as well. They were on to me and intended to box me in. I skidded left, cramming between a patrol car and the wall as he swerved to block me. Close, and a second scrape to my knee can attest to that. But as a sixth car gunned in, I settled on not meeting Wendi and Nijal. I couldn't jeopardize their quiet getaway, so plan B it was.

I slipped from the bottlenecked alleyways and hit the main road, leaving the sardined officers to squeeze their way out while I listened for their whereabouts through the hijacked radios. But I still needed a place to head? Home wasn't an option, nor Nijal's. I thought of the caves but believed they'd look there first. They weren't amateurs, they knew my father's work. And as the sun peaked over the horizon and swept my cover of dark, I thought up the one location where a cluster of cars would stream… school.

"I'm bailing Nijal, you stick with plan A," I alerted over the radio.

"Can't make it out?" he worried.

"Not without them following? Keep at it, I'll be alright. I'll meet you on the other end when all this is through," I told him.

I had no way to reach them safely and felt more at ease with them clear of harm's way.

"Jordan, just remember your dad's writings. A lot of their history looks shady. Don't be blinded by everything they say. Trust your gut if something feels leery. So where you gonna head?" he followed.

"A favorite hangout," I hinted.

CHAPTER FORTY-THREE

Nijal was the only person who'd grasp I'd parked inside the old-school barn. Sirens were scarce there, so I nestled behind my favorite corner of hay trying to deflate my adrenaline.

It took all I had to meld with my aria, waiting for the stone's core to possess me even with the headphones pressed tight to my head. Wendi's hands sure made it easier, and without them all I did was stare, stare and stared a little more, struggling to hold out for my greater reward.

I glowered that stone until my pupils strained, rapt in its honey glow until an orange haze warmed my eyes. Then Elatia finally welcomed me with a foot stopping sunrise before I was off to the circle where they'd already gathered. Draythian presided and wasted no time showing his displeasure.

"Wait! You disappear without warning then just—" he stood combative.

"Save it Draythian," I stormed. My interests latched to the old man sitting alone outside their circle. "Unless you've uncovered something that'll help save your daughter, Kaylaira and everyone else, I don't want to hear it."

I carried a breed of aggression that none of them had witnessed. They bowed with a timid obeisance and left Draythian to challenge me alone. But he kept silent and even moved aside as I marched to the old man, slowing my invasiveness to keep him at peace.

"How did you rest?" I asked, touching his shoulder as gently as Kaylaira would.

He gave no response, but a lesser strain sapped his eyes as he latched my hand in a grandfatherly fashion. After fondly acknowledging me with a nod, I returned to the others.

"Rhemiani. How does it work?" I insisted.

None spoke up, till I sifted their elusive faces and found a restless girl, bursting to divulge what I was looking for.

"In theory," she boldly blurted, before her eyes wandered to the others to see if they'd approve. They obviously remained divided and she needed a nudge.

"Go on," I spurred her.

A deep breath bolstered her nerves, then she proceeded. "Its value is said to thrive by means of the interface lucent."

"Interface lucent?" I asked, assuming I'd heard wrong.

"Yes, like the cerulean one you wear," Draythian added.

I glanced at the sky-blue crystal dangling around my neck, then settled among them and assumed the reins. For once, it was time I filled the shoes as leader, asserting a confiding gaze for the shaken girl to carry on.

"If two share a strong enough bond they naturally connect by means of it. When used with that expression, it opens a channel of remembrance through the one who's forgotten. But we're unsure of its truth, we've never had reason to try."

Another lucent that was more than just a beacon of light. A stone that hoisted the ability to communicate! The crowns! No wonder the MonTu commandeered the feline, falcon, and will-bender, manipulating them all through that very lucent. What more were they capable of? There, among the miracles in their soil lay a means of communication of which we could only dream.

But would it work? Would the old man respond favorably if I tried? Or would it flip him into an irreversible delirium, kill him worst yet? I'd hate if he constituted as my first death, the first we'd rescued from decades of bondage just to lose his life by my stupid hand. He and I shared no better connection than any other at that circle, but I couldn't fight wondering if we'd fashion a strong enough bond.

To not try, would've been the first shovel in our graves, so I seized their silence and rose from the circle, perched before the emboldened girl with an outstretched hand. The group squirmed like an angered swarm of bees, but I'd remembered Kaylaira's words, 'Without the all-lucent all becomes as nothing.' All-lucents were the only way the other lucents fulfilled their purpose.

Some objected and urged her not to give in, but I remained steadfast, instilling her with enough confidence to pluck the stone from her bracelet. With the gem from my necklace snapped into hers, both came to life.

"Jordan, this is an act we've never performed. We can't guarantee how it works or what happens after," Draythian objected, but I continued steadfast toward the old man. "He's already fragile, what if this kills him? There'd be things we'd never uncover. We must give him time."

"We have no time!" I exploded, halting his tracks.

A hole began to burn through my conscience. 'What if he's right?' whispered through my head a million times. I had no clue what I was doing, to him or myself—but what choice did I have? Unshaken, I clenched the ocean blue sparkler and pushed on, warmly taking his hand with the glowing gem mashed between our palms. I was nervous, and he had no inkling what was to happen as my lips dithered to pronounce the word. But I couldn't dawdle, not then. So with as clear a mind possible I inhaled the zephyr, glared his eyes and spoke the word, "Rhemiani."

A jolt prickled my brain like the tip of a needle. But not mine alone, his as well. I knew from the sudden constant blink of his baffled eyes. The circle was soundless. Their eyes glued to the lost old man who searched for a familiar face in their sea of strangers. His breath thickened, then panicked rushed over him like an unpleasant wave.

He wrenched from my grip with his wrinkly fingers, moaning and clasping his head as he grumbled sounds I only thought accompanied death. I tried to comfort him, but he swatted me away. Another attempted, slapped just as hard as he wrestled from the two of us.

"Give him time," the girl I'd emboldened urged, tugging us back from his protected space.

Reluctant, we returned to the fire and let him be, mumbling his gibberish in a scramble for sanity.

"Okay, that went well," Draythian sarcastically added. "This isn't going to work. We need a viable plan to defeat the will-bender and find the 'weapon of a king', whatever that means."

Silence overtook us. The flames and morning birds were louder than our thoughts when the old man suddenly broke the still air. "Your origin to this life was s-sparked ages ago," he chimed, standing from his place of concealment.

Every bit of him seemed changed. There was effort in his eyes that bounded to the flames, where before I'd found nothing there. The circle kept stagnant, anticipating their lost piece of history it appeared he'd share, but his words undoubtedly bound to me.

"To be a w-wind driver," he went on, shoving his way next to me with his eyes still hooked in the flames, "means to come from royalty of this world."

"But how?" I asked, knowing my birthplace, Father's and his father as well.

"When time is less u-urgent, always seek the c-crown," he said. "It will show all you need. Just be careful, land sweeper. You f-falling to their cause would be a tremendous defeat, and they will extend themselves through great measures to secure you by their side."

Use the crown? That brainwashing scrap of metal? It had to be a trap. The old man had to be playing both sides. The moment I placed it on my head I'd be instantly obliged to fulfill their cause. I shook the suspicion, hungering to hear more of my mysterious past, but then again he was right, it wasn't the time. Strategizing to save the others was priority, but not before I asked one dying question.

"Why call me land sweeper?" I sought out.

The old man simply chuckled and twirled a blade of grass around his finger.

"Jordan, we don't have long with him. The questions must count," Draythian insisted.

I wondered why Draythian seemed so devout to avoid the topic. Another time, again? And again I left empty handed, wondering what it was they weren't telling me.

"Okay, the man in the mask, the will-bender, before leaving he spoke of continuing a ceremony," I went on.

"Yes. The c-crowning," the old man answered.

"What is it? Is that how they control you?" Draythian asked.

"Indeed," he said, "but more importantly, a means of extraction. It s-sees what you've learned and what you've passed along, how you've lived and survived, then adopts it into their gain of knowledge."

"And after?" I blurted.

"Then, I'm afraid there's l-little use for your loved ones. If seen beneficial, possibly the strongest of them shall be preserved to fill my place. I'm well past my years and I don't believe they'd think t-twice to replace an old man as me. You however, are an extraordinary bunch. You've come much f-farther than any before you, but I fear it remains in vain."

"Not if we find that weapon," Draythian bit. "Do you remember what or where it is? Does anyone in this circle have knowledge of a king's weapon passed along through our cycles? Any chance it lies at the bottom of the deep? Or the top of Mount Elatia itself?"

Draythian became frantic and was losing patience, and in that moment he and I connected stronger than ever. I thought back to the deep and the hidden chamber, the dome snatcher and mountain's peak, flooding my brain with the endless possible whereabouts when the image struck my head. I felt so dumb! How hadn't I realized it before then? The image flooded in as clear as day, Nijal fooling with a crown and playfully wielding a scepter chanting, "Long live King Nijal." The weapon of a king sat in the lake house above the mantle.

"Nijal's scepter?" I mistakenly mumbled aloud.

While the others homed in on my lack of voice, I pondered how the weapon had made it to Earth. Was it Dad?

"Could the weapon be an object back on my world?" I asked.

"There are no shortage of possibilities," the old man added.

The circle grew impatient for answers, but what was I to tell them? How would I even think to get it? I summarized the challenge, its location, me being trapped and the likelihood I'd never return if I attempted to retrieve it.

"It doesn't matter. It's too late, anyway," the old man said.

His words seemed to jumpstart the mountain's tremble. We jumped from the circle to watch as it hovered just a short distance above the deep. Slowly, its lower half started to unfold like a blooming flower, with boulders and chunks of debris falling from its cone-shaped base.

"The transference! How do we stop it?" I asked.

"There is no s-stopping MonTu. MonTu is simply knowledge," he said.

What on Earth did that mean? Again, he grabbed the sides of his head, reverting to one of his brief manic episodes. He was lost and the rest had to come without him. Nonetheless, a solution did persist.

"Draythian, still have the Pledgemaker's cane?" I asked.

"Of course," he answered, unable to pull his eyes from the mountain as the rest of us.

"Then we summon the bird," I informed. That got their attention.

"And the old man? We use him to get us around?" he asked, forming a plot with me.

"We could take him," I answered. "But he still isn't well. Besides, when the time comes and he feels better, there's a wealth of knowledge you can learn from him and use to evolve. He should stay here where it's safe; we shouldn't risk losing him again to their cause."

For a first since we'd met, Draythian admired that I'd put their future interest ahead of my own. Then we squelched that admiration and moved to fight! The villagers grabbed whatever was of use, sticks and stones from my perspective, but at least their spirit was eager. The key from the cane was strapped in my pocket. We had the cane, and in some ways the old man. It was as good as it would get, and time we made the best of it.

The old man's fingers daubed the cane's handle. The display lit up, firing a streak of flaming blue from the mountain within the same breath of his touch. The bird burrowed for us as if destined for suicide. One by one, each of us staggered back in its growing shadow, abandoning the circle to cower in the trees when it dropped upon us like an iron weight.

Its wings flared open. A windstorm smothered the fire and blew its ashes about. We were mashed to the ground like peanuts before a swift flap down folded its wings, anchoring its body like a towering mountain. Crouched in dirt, I began to doubt my stupid idea, knowing it had to be me to make the first move.

Soil crumbled from my garments as I stood and caught the falcon's eye, searching for a sense of connection to that majestic bird. The glowing lucents dimmed on its crown and nothing whispered not to approach. It didn't find me harmful or dangerous. I was an insect in its path, a worm to be swallowed if it desired, so I made my move.

It stood as solid as stone as I stretched my fingers to touch its frame. Its plush and indulgent feathers tickled my fingertips, with a perfect marriage of silk and fluff. I'd never felt anything softer. And the more I stroked its bed of fur, the more its plumage ruffled with consent, the first notion I had its approval as it awaited a command.

There was nothing to fear, and once the others noticed it was simply a playful ball of fur, they quickly abandoned the safety of the trees to indulge in its gentle nature. But my ambition pushed on, and I went for the helm on its back.

"Easy," I coaxed it while moving to its crest.

I'd never ridden a horse, but imagined it's what they frequently say to calm it before saddling up. To my surprise, it stooped and allowed me to climb on, already knowing what I was after. That roused the others to follow, a giddy handful filing in behind with a handful of others needing to stay. They'd protect the old man and resolve whatever anomalies the transference would trigger in the village.

"The main palace stands above the rest," the Pledgemaker instructed us. "That is where you'll find your friends. Now hold tight, and remember land sweeper, you are the one they lust for most."

The Pledgemaker initiated the sequence on his cane when Wonder hailed from the trees, leaping up the bird's side to latch to my shoulder. What a smart cookie. He'd discerned what was happening, knew it was Kaylaira we were after and pleaded with puppy-eyes to tag along. I didn't want the hindrance and tried shaking him to leave, but he held on for dear life and refused to let go.

"Fine," I gave in. "But stay out of our way."

With no backing him down, I clinched the bird's velvet fibers with Wonder's claws buried in my skin. Unburdened, the bird stooped for takeoff, handling our weight like flies on its back. The crown's flashing lucents colored the trees, then up and wide its wings spread. With one strong beat of its wings, a shockwave propelled us up like a roller coaster on steroids, and in seconds we were dozens of feet above ground.

"Whoohoo!" a girl screamed behind, embracing her offbeat adventure.

The air tasted of freedom, and the view left me unsure whether to stare at the majestic mountain where Kaylaira awaited, or gawk at the flawless blue and green below, where the Pledgemaker's last words rang strong in my ear.

"Are we there yet?" Draythian yelled.

It would've taken a pry bar to wedge his eyes apart. His skin took on shades of green while Wonder's arms constricted my neck. But what a bird's eye view it lent us. The higher we climbed, the more the mountain came into sharper focus, leaving me to marvel at its sheer magnificence and size.

At the base, a complex root system anchored its weight. Thick stalks and vines larger than any tree I'd seen wove and twisted together like the snake dreads of Medusa's hair. They held together the mountain's inner workings, preventing it from crumbling apart. But slowly they unfurled, unwinding like shoelaces as if they knew the way to reveal a brilliant stone nestled in its core. The all-lucent! Like a diamond in the rough, it rivaled the tallest of skyscrapers and was nearly as massive as the mountain itself.

Smaller vines unraveled on the perimeter, undraping thirty-to-forty-foot lucents of every color known. They hung in the roots like fish caught in a net, one row spiraling the next. I was baffled, awe-struck and speechless, then the all-lucent came alive. Its blinding glow rivaled the sun, forcing us to shield our eyes until a burst of orange lucents joined its brilliance. It was as if morning graced us a second time.

"What's happening? Why are only the orange ones lit?" I yelled over the wind.

"It's starting," Draythian hollered. "Those lucents can horde infinite levels of power."

Lucents for batteries? That's how the MonTu would drain their planet clean.

We continued past the mountain's underbelly, spiraling up to its elevating terrain where levels upon levels of structures rose. Stone housing, monuments, courtyards and temples, all part of the grand ascent to the mountain's crown jewel… the palace. One would assume that's where their architecture would end, but it didn't. It went on with ambition and reached higher in the sky, a tower beyond where I eyes could see.

However, none of it breathed life. The palace, the courtyards, none of it echoed the lustrous history that place once assumed. Without facts, the cold, empty silence told the story of a once prosperous kingdom that somehow failed. If only I knew what happened?

The falcon leveled off at the base of the palace, on a patch of crumbled grass at the edge of a stone stairway. As gracefully as it landed below it did so again, patiently lowering for us to disembark before it returned to the air. Draythian stumbled on wobbly feet, gasping with his head between his knees as he embraced land.

"Had enough?" I joked.

He returned my sarcasm with a shaky thumbs up before my eyes gobbled where we stood like candy. The stairway led up just a short distance, but each step stretched wide as if they went on forever. I leaned back as far possible without tilting over, tracing the palace's spire as far as I could. The beams were like massive redwood trees, reaching towards the sky with an imposing strength. They stood tall and proud, supporting a circular platform that seemed to defy gravity. I recognized the area. It's where Kaylaira and I were whisked to from the deep where I first encountered a fierce and less friendly falcon.

"Let's go," I ordered the group.

With Wonder impatiently trampling my shoulders and the others disposed for battle, we climbed the weathered and aged granite stairs that were rough like the skin of an ancient dragon. No doors or doorways welcomed us in, only a string of pillars that stretched the length of the palace. Each towered us ten times over, and it would've taken twice our number with conjoined arms just to stretch around the thick of one.

We tiptoed between their gargantuan legs, beneath their grand arches onto the main landing. It too was vast and grimy, an open floor that stretched like a vast and barren desert, begging to be filled with something, anything. The air was musty and stale, as if no one had entered its space in centuries while it waited for a breeze to come and stir up the silence. The absence of sound haunted me, and even the slightest sniffle could spark a panic attack.

"Where should we start?!" Draythian roared over my shoulder.

My nerves cracked like skates on a burdened lake of ice.

"Forgotten already?" I bit back in a whisper, while calming my heart. "My first time here, remember?"

Well, kind of in the palace at least. But I knew he was just as anxious. He too wondered where the will-bender lurked, the man who so easily made a mockery of our fight. I had no clue how to face him again, and that creeping thought unknowingly halted my step before Draythian nudged my back to keep on the move. From where did such boldness derive? I took some for myself and continued ahead.

The outdoor light streamed in between the columns, brightening the bare surface of the archaic walls. Opposite our side were equally sized pillars, leading to enclosed pass ways beyond. It was my glimpse into that unknown that stirred Wonder frantic. His eyes spread wide, driving him to fidget and tap my shoulder as he pointed to the only demarcation in that room, a three-foot, circular stone wall that rose from the center floor. I was curious, until an all too familiar roar reminded us to hurry. Our backs huddled together, each of us frantically searching for the feline's grumbling tone.

"It's somewhere outside the palace," a girl rattled and hunched tight.

Wonder leapt so fiercely he became too much to bear, heightening his aggression before I shoved him to the floor. But he didn't give in. He grabbed my arm, yanking me on a path from the others to one of the pass ways that lied beyond.

"What about the center?" I asked.

But he rejected me even more, demanding I pursue his course following a second roar. That one rumbled closer, as if it came from within the walls, and was the only reason I gave in to his lead. I barely kept pace as he bee lined across the open, abandoning the others as they shouted my name.

"Wonder, wait," I yelled, but he didn't listen.

Where was he leading me? What devoured his interest with such aggression? I didn't know, but he rushed left and dragged me down the stairs, through an arched hallway into a separate room. I halted in the entrance with my mouth hanging low, dwarfed and stupefied by what stood before me.

The room was dominated by a medieval apparatus, consuming the room with the spread of its sprawling limbs. I nearly forgot my purpose there. Sunlight streamed in from the archways above, passing through stained glass to paint the room in splashing colors. What a canvas of natural art, with colors that danced across the walls! It was spellbinding and sublime, and I roamed from one burst of color to the next like a child watching fireworks.

A stout metal trunk ascended from the floor, with lenses that sprawled on its branches like leaves on a tree. Some lenses were empty, some had lucents loaded in their frames, each catching and reflecting light in a different way. Some were large enough to cook the flesh from my bones if set in a ray of light, while others were no larger than a pair of eyeglasses. I'd have gawked and wandered through those hidden treasures all day, but a third roar reminded me of my need to hurry.

"Wonder, the others need me, what is it?" I stormed.

His will was as firm and ironclad as the mountain. And as I turned to abandon him, he leapt on an endless table, stashed with a horde of lucents where his feet and four arms went to work. He snatched the loose shards of different shapes, color and size, compiling them like jigsaw puzzles through every range of the empty lenses. And to think I nearly left him.

"Jordan, not the time!" Draythian's yell echoed through the halls.

Desperate to leave I backed up to the doorway when Wonder stopped me with a frantic yelp. He sprang to another table lined with crowns before shoving one on and off his head. It was the same the Pledgemaker wore, and the will-bender. I tried to stop him from putting it on, but he refused to let me near, shaking his head no while steadfast with his demonstration. Then I saw it. Nothing happened.

"You've been here before, haven't you?" I realized. My answer drove him wild, kicking artifacts and flinging them from the table because I could finally understand. "Wait! The crown has no effect on you, does it?" I asked.

His arms swung ballistic before he dashed back to the table, positioning dozens of lucent shards faster than I blinked. It was then I remembered Kaylaira's words, his ability to remember no matter the volume or complexity. Whatever he was up to he knew what he was doing, dashing up and across the limbs to fill the empty lenses he'd composed. No wires, no electrical components nor connections lined the trunk, but when the last piece shoved into position, the tree came alive.

"Jordan!" the others clamored from the other side.

They needed me. The feline had made its way in. Or was I to trust Wonder's insistence to remain? He pounced atop the largest lens desperate to drop it, but it wouldn't budge. That's what he needed me for, to help align the pattern! I took a gamble and disregarded the others, springing up to hang my weight from its bottom. Notch by notch I tugged till it clicked in position, while he raced without letup maneuvering the smaller loupes. With the last set-in place, he shoved me toward the exit.

I turned to sprint from the room when a collage of color clashed my eyes. Top to bottom from one lens to the next, they streaked faster with each passing second while Wonder stood motionless at the center floor. I wanted to stay. I wanted to witness what he'd accomplished, but the screams from the open sprinted me back up the stairs where my eyes locked in horror.

"No!" I burst and fell to my knees.

My heart shattered like crystal then pieced itself with rage. The girl who'd been ecstatic to ride the falcon, lied helpless as the feline's fangs tore into her flesh. I could barely process the horror when its eyes locked onto me, tossing her lifeless body aside as if it were wasteful junk. It was personal. It knew how much that sight would tear me apart, and only then I realized it was the feline from the shore.

It lashed toward me with a score to settle, but I'd never known such rage to permeate inside. It crazed me, drove me to gather all the winds I could harness as the incoming gusts dried my tears. How much was too much I didn't care. I was reckless and out of control, unable to look away from the young girl's haunting gaze as the feline charged. In her memory, a thrust of heated rage left my hands.

I knew what I'd done before the winds left my fingers but hate kept me from holding back. The stone floor buckled as the winds gunned down, shattering every bone beneath the animal's flesh. The floor sunk in. The winds raged on, battering the stone columns that guarded our entrance. Still, I didn't care, but the drain of power took its toll.

The energy expelled bled my emotion empty, collapsing me next to the young girl as stone walls crumbled down. Had Wonder occupied me needlessly? Had I left sooner I could've saved her, and that deep stomach-churning guilt kept me from glaring the other's sobbing faces. Their spark of hope vanished as each knelt by her side. What was I to say? What comfort could I give?

It didn't matter. We had no time to mourn. Not with the string of felines that stomped onto the fortress floor.

CHAPTER FORTY-FOUR

The roars grew increasingly ferocious as three felines circled like sharks on the hunt. Still, amidst that circle of beauty and fear, the others forewent their own comfort and huddled the young girl's corpse, keeping the beasts from taking more of her than they already had.

I huffed exhaustion and eased to my feet, pulling myself together with zephyr gathering at my fingers. But the felines were on to me. One roared to knock me off balance and spilled the power from my hands. Back on the shore I barely handled one, now three? Not to mention the mystery light from the pass way where Wonder remained, flashing sporadically like an old photo booth. Simply put, we were alone, trapped in our huddle with no one rushing to our aid.

The felines triangulated, one on each side with the third in front of me rearing to lunge. They thought me weak and incapable, sapped from grief and unable to protect the bunch of us. But it hadn't figured on the second breath I'd drawn, and it lunged prematurely. I hammered its snout fiercely into a wall of force. The clash shocked and backed it off in a heat of anger, wobbling to shake the jolt before it circled back. Then all three charged at once.

I drew my hands in desperation and wrapped the winds around us, submerging us within an impenetrable bubble of air. They bit, slashed and roared but nothing punctured through. We were safe for the moment, but that containment wouldn't hold. The effort to keep it strong drained more than what I had, and slowly, the three squeezed in.

"What now Jordan?" Draythian asked.

My arms cramped as they muscled in, and with all of me forced to focus I could barely respond. "I don't know but think of it quick. I can't keep holding!" I strained.

"Get ready!" Draythian roused the others. They tinkered with the sticks and stones they'd brought to fight while I dreaded the disaster about to befall us. "Jordan, on my mark!"

"Hurry?!" I yelled.

My arms trembled like a lost cause, then gave out. One last thrust was all I had, bulldozing them out to catch my breath when their claws dug in stone and sprung back. They would finish us off.

"Draythian!" I yelled, failing to see what kept he and the others from jumping to action.

I heaved enough air to slow the two flanking our sides, but the third raged straight for my head. It was the end of me. I'd barely given a fight, bracing like a mouse before a train with my failure flashing in my head. I closed my eyes and kissed Kaylaira farewell in my thoughts when an agonizing yelp forced them back open.

The feline and I stood nose to snout, with the heat of its breath on my skin when its eyes bulged from its skull. A three-fingered hand sunk in its forehead then its body lifted off the floor, pulled by four grotesque hands that gripped onto its mane. That's what delayed Draythian and the others and what had taken them by surprise. It was Wonder, perched beneath the lion's body dangling above his head.

The cute, cuddly ball of fur no longer stood before me. He towered me by six feet, hurling the feline like unwanted table scraps. I couldn't remember a happier moment in my life, elated that I'd fallen in his good grace as an unearthly roar erupted from his mouth!

How I needed his strength! It was the edge that propelled me up in the air as I retracted my sidewinds and smashed the other felines together. They struck like a hammer and anvil. The thunderous clash shook the stone, sending a shock through my body that stumbled the others back. We stood like titans on the brink of battle, our souls lit with the energy from the four windstorms conjuring in Wonder's palms. Wonder was a wind driver!

"What exactly were you guys up to in there?" Draythian screeched with his manhood as shriveled as mine.

"Some metal tree? A sizing device he knew to operate in a room in the rear," I explained.

"Well… nice work," he muttered. "Guess it's our time now."

I'd never had more fight in me than the moment Draythian ignited the rod in his hand. My power surged to life, swirling energy in each hand as Wonder squelched a fourth feline sneaking on his rear. The others ignited their bracelets and short rods, what I'd assumed were merely sticks and stones with orange lucents at their tips.

"The henna lucent," Draythian cheered me. "My favorite, to heat things up."

With a flick of a small lever on the rod's handle, an all-lucent struck the orange henna stone, blazing its glow like pulsating lava. A flash of heat warmed my face, then emptied a fiery streak into a feline's flesh. The feline squealed and battled for retreat as the smell of its roasted meat burned into my nostrils. One flip of the lever and both gems disengaged, sealing the streaking fire shut. Finally, we had a fight!

"You couldn't have done that earlier?" I scolded.

"We fighting or arguing like two little girls?" he contested.

He hurdled away before I could respond, joining the others to create a blazing incendiary display of light. Wonder and I bounced around the room like wind gusts, launching the felines into every surface like a game of ping pong. While immersed in the heat of battle and primed to engage another, Wonder yielded my readied arm, prodding me once more to head to the three-foot wall. With a quick look around the room the fight no longer needed me, and it was time I trusted what else he knew.

I embraced my mission and left the fight in their hands, went over the stunted wall at center floor to a stone stairway spiraling below. Down into the shadowy chamber I ran where a faint glow homed me in. As I descended the last step, my heart fluttered at the sight of Kaylaira. Her presence was a balm for my soul, a reminder that love and hope still existed amid battle and chaos. I was again at peace.

She, Jesriel and the other two were propped on their knees in a circle, surrounding the mountain's all-lucent stone that protruded up from the floor.

"Kaylaira," I whispered, tiptoeing over, still leery of the will-bender's whereabouts.

A crown like the old man's graced each of their heads, robbing them of their true selves. She'd always greeted me with large beaming eyes, but as I delved closer I found her sight stolen, her pupils glazed over by the all-lucent's waving pearl colors. It's what the old man warned, the flashing crowns that siphoned their memories for themselves. But to our fortune, the Pledgemaker's key sat ready to free them.

I slipped it from my pocket and slid the first notch in. The key clicked right. The glowing lucents darkened and the headpiece fell to the floor, but so did Kaylaira. I tried to wake her and beckoned her ear, but her limp response hurried me to Jesriel instead. He was no different, an unlocked headpiece and a faint response, the same I found with the other two. In the end, it was the mountain that finally awakened them.

The walls and floors trembled as the all-lucent dimmed to a lesser glow. But not our room alone. It was the mountain, shaking from its core before jolting the all-lucent into a bright, searing light. We needed to go. The transference had begun!

"Kaylaira," I begged and shook her till she woke. "Come on, it's me, Jordan."

"Jordan?" she softly repeated, using my name as a beacon as the glaze faded from her eyes. "You came for me?" she grinned, pulling us together for a sluggish kiss.

"Eww. That's gross," Jesriel grumbled from across the light.

He was slow to think, yet conscious enough to wreck our moment.

"Thank you Jesriel, for ruining such a beautiful memory. Either way, we have to move, now! The transference has begun," I hurried, coaching the four of them up the rattling stairs where they toppled like teenage drunks.

Their minds were zonked, poisoned with the little left in their tanks to make the crawl. Fortunately for us, Draythian and his fighters rushed to our aid and hauled us to their victory in the upper palace. Their skin and garments wore the blood from battle, but the felines were a smoldering heap of singeing fur. Our only threat? The thunderous boom from the transference outdoors, and Wonder rushing Kaylaira the instant she fell in his sight.

"Wonder?" she asked as he snatched her like candy.

"Not quite the same, is he?" I jested.

"What happened?" she gasped, swallowed in his furry embrace.

I described the metal tree, and my belief that the MonTu used it to alter his size.

"A stone forger?" she asked.

"Sounds like it, but why alter his size?" Jesriel asked.

"Because the crown has no effect on him. Apparently, he's immune to its effect which they perceived as a danger. But he's too important to dispose of, so they used it to alter his size before dumping him here," I guessed. "It's you we met on the beach the night Nijal arrived, wasn't it?" I asked.

His thumbs up confirmed I'd solved the mystery, before the mention of Nijal's name rolled my next problem in.

"King J!" I heard shouted from the pillars.

The voice. The verbology. Who in their right mind on Elatia would refer to me as 'King J?' It was undeniably one person alone, whose origin wasn't of that world… Nijal. I turned to find him and Wendi with a handful of villagers racing across the floor. My heart nearly stopped.

"What on Earth are you guys doing here?" I asked baffled.

"Long story short," he panted, "There are so many cops, but Coach Johnson snuck us through in the back of his trunk."

"What?" I asked dumbfounded.

"Yeah. I just begged him not to ask questions and told him it was for you. Then, for some reason, he just told us to jump in," he explained. "So we made it to the barn, fell asleep next to you, crossed to the village, and hitched a ride on the old dude's insanely large bird."

"All because we thought you might need this," Wendi added.

As she unveiled the staff that decorated the fire mantle, a fierce sense of competition channeled between her and Kaylaira's gaze.

"Um, everyone? Wendi… Wendi? Everyone," I stumbled, trying to ease the tension. "She's a dear friend, and I probably wouldn't be here without her help. Wendi… how did you know?" I asked.

"The weapon of a king? It hit me as soon as we made it to the house. I remembered Nijal fooling around with it and figured it's the weapon you were missing", she said.

"See. Pays to act stupid every now and then, doesn't it?" Nijal joked.

For once, I guess it did.

I twirled the staff for a glance over, barely feeling its weight though its power held strong in my hand. The metal was far from polished, worn from ages of oxidation and misuse. The once-shiny surface was now tarnished and dull. Speckles of gem dust scattered across its length, barely giving off any glimmer.

Elaborate etchings lined the entire shaft, each line and curve telling a story of its own. However, at its center, the weapon held a twelve-inch strip of tiny holes for a hand grip, with a cylinder of barely visible all-lucent tucked inside. Its purpose and power remained a mystery, waiting to be unlocked by someone brave enough to wield it.

"This thing come with instructions?" I asked without a clue.

"Unlikely. This is our first time seeing it, remember?" Draythian jested. "But whatever we do, we need to stop the mountain. It only takes moments for the transference to drain our planet's life."

While Elatia's power was being leached, Draythian and the others clustered for a plan while I sidelined Wendi and Nijal.

"Okay Nijal, you've pulled through more times than I can count. No need to stop now. So any idea how this works?" I asked, fiddling the metal.

Together we brainstormed, with Nijal in full geek mode while scrutinizing its detail.

"We can't overthink it. You use air as a weapon, and this thing is mostly hollow. So, pull air through it?" he inferred then handed it back.

Made sense, so I tapped into the wind and dragged it through its pores. The metal hummed like a gentle choir as the air swirled like a dwarfed vortex within the staff's lever. The harder I pulled the more it surged, its hum stirring and awakening something deep within the metal.

"Keep going. Don't stop!" Nijal hollered above the hum.

I wanted to unleash whatever roved inside, and the more the metal drank the wind the further they backed away. Then the all-lucent suddenly beamed to life and the hum hit a crescendo. A warmth ushered through my limbs, intoxicating me with clarity yet blurring my connection with any world. The lucent grew brighter and the metal chimed sharp.

"Go, go, go," Nijal chanted.

But I'd had enough. I'd tapped into something ancient, untouchable and infinitely powerful, igniting the force of kings and legends long past. Desperate to discharge that weight from my essence, I pointed the staff and hurled its anger, juddering a blast that nearly broke the palace.

"Yes!" Nijal jumped excitedly. "Gosh, why can't I be you right now?"

However, the flow of air kept spiraling, priming its vortex in the scepter's ore.

"I'm not sure," I told him.

Whispers floated in my head, telling me I'd topple mountains if I wished. At that moment I realized that power held danger, and that mere thought alone sent a mistakable blast from my hand. We jumped as I obliterated a nearby structure in the room, before I siphoned the air unsure to what extent that power would lead.

"You know, this is kind of our home," Jesriel joked. "Can we maybe just keep a little of it?"

"Depends if you guys have come up with a solution," I teased.

"We have. The crown," Jesriel started. "The harder we struggled to keep our thoughts, the greater volume of knowledge that streamed from their side."

"We believe that's why they dispose of us after the ceremony. Once they take what they need, our being alive becomes their disadvantage," the other chosen explained.

The longer Jesriel explained, the closer his dialogue matched the Pledgemaker's, of how the MonTu were nothing more than accumulated knowledge. There was no person, no army nor embodiment. The crowns were their sole means of connection, and the chosen from years past their temporary puppets.

"Its knowledge, so it can't be destroyed; it must be convinced," Jesriel advised. "If our will is stronger than theirs, then we can reason with it to abandon its cause. That's how we stop the transference!"

"How?" I asked.

"Same as they do, by using the crown," he said.

The sound of his plan unknowingly turned my nose up against him. I was skeptical and didn't like it one bit. Intentionally use the crowns? Reason with it?

"And if you can't change or convince it or they convince you instead, then what? What happens to you? What happens to everyone else?" I asked. "What strong enough conviction do you have to sway them otherwise?"

"You. I have you," he startled me.

I never expected to hear I was the answer to their equation. Then he explained how the mountain feared me, terrified of how far I'd helped their village to that point. For the first time it feared losing, feared its reasoning was somehow flawed. I looked to Kaylaira for backing and help.

"I don't know. It's a great risk. But… what Jesriel says is true; I too felt its fear," she added before the other two chosen acknowledged as well.

"Yeah but they just had you and look what happened. You didn't convince them then," Nijal argued.

"This time will be different," Jesriel countered. "It's like plunging in a river for the first time without knowing how to swim. You gather a sense of awareness, you learn how it flows. The second plunge is different."

Nijal subtly shook his head, also believing the scheme was flawed. What if what he'd told me before proved true? What if the Elatians were dark by nature? A nature that had been suppressed for ages, dying to resurface at first light. Was I to trust them?

"What if we just destroy it? The entire mountain?" I asked.

But they objected fiercely.

"Destroy it?" Draythian asked.

"Yes, using the large henna lucents strung from the bottom," I persisted. "You guys have a better understanding of them than I do, but from what I've seen, we can set off a chain reaction. The same concept used in those rods and cause enough heat to bring the whole thing down."

"Jordan, before Mount Elatia was taken, it housed our history, *all* of our history. This place can tell us everything we need to know of our past, where we've been, our purpose and it still rightly belongs to us, not the MonTu. How could you suggest we destroy it?" Jesriel objected.

Before uttering another word the room calmed to a still, and the hush of an eerie breeze blew in. My unease alerted the others. I knew the feeling and had felt it before. We were about to face the will-bender.

"He's here! The will-bender. Everyone out," I whispered, searching for his direction of arrival. "Nijal, where's the falcon?"

"Outside with the old man," he answered.

"You and Wendi have done your part. Now wake up and get out of here," I begged.

"Everyone else get to the falcon, now!" I shoved them.

While a stream of villagers trickled outdoors, Wendi and Nijal grasped each other's trembling hands, closing their eyes to evade what was to come, but neither moved an inch.

"What are you guys doing? Leave," I pleaded, but both struggled and headed nowhere.

"You're afraid," I told them.

"You damn right we're afraid," Nijal countered with a sneer. "This just got super real!"

"Yeah but that's the problem. Your fear in this moment is stronger than your reality back home. As long as you don't focus and calm down, you'll go nowhere," I explained.

However, my words came too late, and to our dismay our threat stepped in.

CHAPTER FORTY-FIVE

The mountain continued to drink the life from their surface, the green from their trees and the color from their land as the fear I'd preached to evade lashed me like a whip. I too began to fear my enemy, but even more, I feared failure. I feared not saving Kaylaira and the children, or those who'd fought bravely by my side and had given meaning to my life.

And just as that fear crept up with its hand, Draythian signaled from outdoors, mouthing they were unable to leave. Not even they could escape and were no longer out of our adversary's reach.

"They're trapped," Kaylaira confirmed. "As long as the extraction continues, there's no place to go."

"Then we fight," Jesriel proclaimed.

He grabbed a rod without a drop of hesitance in his bones, flipped the lever and spun towards the will-bender.

"For Elatia!" he declared.

Having come that far to rightfully claim what was theirs drove his valor far beyond my own. The henna lucent ignited and threw its heated rage across the room, smacking into the will-bender's hand where a cushion of air halted its reach. Then out came the boomerang. Jesriel charged valiantly with no letup in his feet before the spinning metal knocked the strength from his legs. His body recoiled and socked us like a fist, plowing the group of us onto the floor. However, the backbone he'd shown quickly goaded the others.

"For Elatia!" they rallied.

A barrage of blasts and shockwaves ignited war. Those who'd fled rushed in to fight, my chance to free Wendi and Nijal. I shoved them outdoors and down the stairs where the transference's deafening roar swallowed all sound.

"Leave. You guys can't be here!" I yelled, seeing a stubborn notion pop open in Wendi's head.

"We can't! And we can't go below so what are we supposed to do?" Nijal asked.

"The other monuments. Go, hide until you figure how to get out of here," I replied.

"Wait. I got it," she finally shouted. "If the crowns are the link to the MonTu, what happens if we destroy them? Their link, that knowledge is dead in the water. You can't destroy knowledge, you just make sure there's no way of getting it out. Right?"

I paused and tried to wiggle her from the idea, but her logic resonated loud and clear. Destroy the crowns and we destroy the MonTu's ability to deliver. Just as it made sense, a boom hurled Draythian out past us on the stairs. He shook the jolt, grabbed his shoulder and jumped to his feet, ready to charge back in.

"Draythian!" I halted him.

I was nervous he'd reject our plan, but to my satisfaction he didn't refute. Wendi and Nijal took the key to the crowns, with Nijal insisting to have a rod for protection. Draythian tossed his without question, unwilling to sacrifice time.

"Careful not to burn a hole through your face," Draythian warned.

In all of history, never had eyes beamed brighter than his. A childhood fantasy had become Nijal's reality.

"Do you have any idea the havoc I'm about to wreak with this thing?" he bounced like a child with Wendi rolling her eyes.

"Just please don't get killed," I begged.

I was in no better position, but either way, it was time to be a wind driver.

I told them about the crowns near the stone forger, then girded my nerves and raced up the stairs with my lethal adversary in my line of sight. He was fierce and assertive. Each defense and assault somehow outmatched the last. Head on, I was no match to stop him. Remove his crown? As if I could, remembering I'd revoked ownership of the key. His boomerang however, was our greatest threat, singlehandedly dropping more of us than his hands alone. It bolted with the zephyr's backing, slogging body after body in all corners of the room. Then I felt it, the connection between the metal and his palm, in some ways the same as I'd connected with the staff. Weaken it, and I'd weaken his feat.

I eyed the twirling metal with the scepter in hand, churning my angering winds through its grip. Its hum sang loud as I stormed across the floor, with the power of the king's weapon to harness as my own. A surge of power left my hand as the boomerang gunned for Jesriel's head. Our forces met. Jesriel was jettisoned and the shockwave crinkled the floor, but his boomerang clomped down lifelessly with their connection broken.

"I owe you," Jesriel mumbled as he stumbled back up.

"Pay me by distracting him with a blast from that rod, now!" I yelled.

Jesriel cranked the rod's fury while Wonder joined my side. Neither of us could take the will-bender alone, but together we were a force to be reckoned with. Wonder and I synced as if he'd read my thoughts as the will-bender disposed of Jesriel's blast. He then spun towards us, aware of the danger as Wonder and I sent a force to level a building. The gales struck. He tumbled like garbage in the wind and slammed into a nearby wall. I went to engage as debris crumbled atop his head, but remembered the plan was to weaken him one piece at a time. I needed to rid him of the boomerang.

"Draythian, the crowns!" I yelled, then snatched the boomerang and ran like hell.

I hurdled the stairs in a single leap, whisked through a courtyard and on a roof without a sip of air. From that vantage point, I hurled the deadly metal with all the might in my arm, relieved as it left the mountain and crossed the horizon before watching it vanish from sight. Then I was back indoors girded for battle.

The rock pile remained atop our rival. I wanted to think he'd perished. I wanted to believe we'd ended his threat while knowing that slim chance didn't exist. Meanwhile, Nijal, Draythian and the two girls stockpiled every crown they'd mustered.

"This is all of them," Nijal gasped.

"Then destroy them while we have the chance," I huffed.

Three henna lucents poured out their fury, melting the gems and metal to a heap of crisp. I sighed a second relief, but the transference raged on.

"Gosh, can I keep it?" Nijal joked as he kissed the rod.

"Fulfilled enough to leave yet?" I heckled.

"I am," he conceded.

Then Wendi engulfed me with an embrace I'll never forget. "Good luck and see you home," she uttered with a kiss to my cheek.

"You too. And be careful, this isn't over. There's a mess waiting for us there as well," I uttered.

Swathed in my arms, the weight of her suddenly vanished like a fuzzy dream.

"Be right there!" Nijal teased, fading his voice as she disappeared.

I turned to shove him goodbye as well when a cold notion struck hard. Where was Jesriel?

"Where's Jesriel?" I asked.

We searched our surroundings, scrambled and called his name when a startling twist befell us... the transference suddenly ceased. Every stone quaked still and the mountain no longer trembled. It should've been a cause for celebration, but we all sensed something was very wrong. What had Jesriel done?

I looked to the pile of rubble that still buried our enemy when a sudden draft of air yanked my senses. The metal claws! Three hurled in between the columns faster than I could move. One latched Kaylaira, the other two Draythian and Nijal then lifted them high. Rage raised the scepter's strength in my hand when the will-bender tore from his heap. His zephyr was primed to engage but so was mine. We were seconds from leveling the room, when a hard-pressed voice clamored our ears.

"Wait," the voice hammered like a crack of thunder.

It echoed from every corner, reverberated through every stone. It was a voice of command and dominance, but from where did it hail? The will-bender submitted and so did the claws, hoisting my friends motionless with all three in their grips. But who'd ordered the action? Suspicion haunted me, before the answer emerged from beneath the three-foot wall at center floor. I'd known it all along, but still gasped when seeing it with my very eyes.

It was Jesriel who'd risen, dawned with the last illuminated crown upon his head.

CHAPTER FORTY-SIX

He glared with no distinction as to who I was as I shouted his name with all the air in my lungs. It wasn't him. It wasn't my fiery friend from the give and take circle, the one who'd kept by my side day in and day out. His demeanor was altered, his pride and gaze addressing us as lowly, meaningless beings. His body was present, but his mind was light years away while the MonTu used his airway as their puppet piece.

"What do you want?" I hurled.

I ramped the scepter to fight as he perched himself atop a mound of rubble, methodically turning his head my way.

"You don't belong in our history's equation, what is it *you* want, land sweeper?" the voice returned.

"For this age-old conflict you've started to end," I answered.

"We've started?" he smirked, as if I were an oblivious child. "For what purpose? To return your people to the ways of their heart and continue what you began eons ago? To continue desolating empires across the universe?"

Desolate? I was adrift, and his belittling laughter dwindled my childish comprehension.

"You boldly ask for something so drastic while oblivious to its cause? How little does that make you feel?" he bullied me.

My head spun towards the others like a merry-go-round, wondering if his mysterious words trapped me alone or if I'd find them too just as puzzled. But no one returned my silent plea, an instant warning they'd kept me in the dark. What hadn't they revealed in the circle? I'd come to terms they'd foregone insignificant details, but this? Each became fidgety and elusive, unsure how to counter my inquiring glare.

"Kaylaira?" I called, believing she'd be the first to pull me from the mud.

She opened her mouth to speak, but Jesriel's imposter interjected.

"This society you've sought so deeply to protect, shelters you in darkness? Why do you believe this to be? Elatians. It is their history, Jordan, their very blood and nature, a nature you've fueled with your sweat and perseverance. It is a nature that exists, even in you."

"I think not," I threw back.

"Is that so? And yet here you are ready to vanquish our knowledge, the only remaining source of truth of the massacre from your hands. Countless galactic societies. Your very name, land sweeper, is not a title of our doing. It stems from your repeated actions from one millennia to the next, touting your abilities across the stars, suppressing life from one civilization after another with the pass of your hand."

"I know them, why would they do that?" I asked.

"They?" he laughed. "Looking for ways to shift blame does not remove it from those accountable. But to enlighten you, we asked the same and came up empty, leaving us to deduce it was simply for sport and fun, to watch empires crumble beneath your feet while you continued to rise. You witnessed the expanse of our ingenuity, watched us construct objects that could traverse the stars, and you opposed. You kept anyone who prospered under your leash of oppression, an oppression with no real meaning." he said, stepping down within an arm span of where I stood. "Therefore, the remainder of us had to act. We converged every bit of our resources to stop you while you destroyed our worlds. Those who fought died, others perished on their home worlds from lack of survival. So, knowledge is all that's left of us. Simply put, we are the remaining cure, the only suppressant that keeps you from regaining power, from spreading wild like an untamed plague across the barren universe."

His words pounded my heart, and yet, the others never spoke up to defend against his accusations.

"Kaylaira? Draythian?" I patiently asked.

Their metal claws lowered at the gesture of Jesriel's hand, then released both Draythian and Kaylaira. But still, their eyes eluded me, till Kaylaira confirmed with a shameful nod.

"Why didn't you tell me? Why keep me in the dark, about this? This?" I cried out.

"Because believe it or not, you *are* unique Jordan, much different than the lore of wind drivers before you of whom we've been taught. There was no way of achieving this without you. You presented us with a highly uncustomary opportunity we couldn't pass and look how far you've taken us," Draythian answered.

My heart skipped a beat or two. My legs shook weakly. I grasped the scepter to lean on and dropped to my knees, spinning in a whirl of confusion. How was I to proceed? It never occurred to me the MonTu were the victims, the true slaves bound by the burden of a bijou. I struggled confining tears that insisted on being freed, massaging the stab of betrayal in the dull pain in my chest. What had I done?

"The people simply want back what is theirs," Kaylaira's voice quivered.

"Theirs? And what of you?" I pointedly asked. "What's your reason?"

"Me? I want nothing more than to end the pattern of death," she sobbed. "Is that so wrong? We were desperate for change and you were our only way. What he speaks of is who we once were, but that couldn't be farther from the truth today and you know it. You were with us. You've seen it with your own eyes, felt it in your own heart."

Her whimpers hindered her words and kept her from acknowledging my disappointment. Was I to fight on? Would Dad? I'd never felt more lost or purposeless, still unable to grasp where his role fell in it all.

"Why have the mountain? What do you want with it once you've regained its possession?" I tested them.

"Nothing more than learn of our past, see where we belong and who we are, how we fit into the stream of life," Draythian answered. He too carried a sorrowful anger. "Imagine us seeing the true beauty of our planet for the first time, as it was meant to be. Imagine Jordan, finally being able to pass our culture down to our young and see them with their own, growing old, together. To not have the mountain is to not have a piece of our being, and for once we're so close to knowing the feeling of being whole."

A beautiful answer, but was it for show? Had all I'd seen amongst them been for show? The community, the children and games. I questioned how much of it was real. Still, Draythian's argument was genuine, and his passion to learn their truth drove from the soul of who he'd become, not what his ancestors made him out to be. His eyes couldn't have cried louder. How critical life had become for his people. How deeply he craved this for them and not selfish gain. It was their progress he wanted as a whole.

"And yet, what a quandary we face," the imposter interjected, manipulating Jesriel's smile into a sinister smirk. "Destroy you now for eternity, in a final effort to preserve our survival? Or relinquish all we've gained and let you bring us to an end, hoping you've restored your value and consideration for other's lives."

The swarm of information your brain computes in the blink of an eye, is astonishing. In fractions of a second, Dad taught me a lesson in his absence. "Would it be fair to judge you now based on decisions made as a child?" I remembered him asking. The reason? His rules on a new curfew.

In my younger years, I'd snuck to a park with a friend, figuring I'd simply sneak back unnoticed. But I couldn't have been more wrong, and found how hard it was to tiptoe past two police officers filling out a missing child's report at my door. His lesson years later while granting me new freedom? If it would forever be reasonable to judge me on that mishap years prior. His point was sharp. With change and growth in our family, mistakes from the past, especially those out of ignorance fell under things forgiven and forgotten.

Were Elatians to be treated any differently while fighting for change, growth and renewed freedom? Having been deceived by them didn't feel the greatest. In fact, it downright sucked and pricked me to the bone. But could I judge against them? Against Kaylaira? Hadn't they paid their debt?

I thought of Father and his inexplicable bond with Kaylaira's mother. What were they I hadn't figured, but I knew they weren't enemies. I thought of Naymelia and the innocent young she'd one day have, generations constantly deprived of meaningful lives. I could still feel the serenity and calm that radiated from their soil, heard the joyful sounds of their playful games, and held to the constant happiness that illuminated their faces.

All those jumbled thoughts and memories flashed in the blink of an eye, and altogether, I knew their debt had been paid. Besides, why seek recompense from someone's life who was never involved?

The thought nauseated me, knowing every action hinged on my word. And if I said the wrong thing was there a peaceful solution? Or would there instantly be all out war? Both sides hung to their terms. The will-bender readied to blast me from existence, while the others prepared to fight for their land. Nonetheless, my mind was made, and the room dropped to a whisper as I leaned on the scepter to stand. The floor seemed endless, but as everyone stepped forward to hear my words, I couldn't help but feel claustrophobic.

"Everyone changes," I started. "Even if what has been spoken is true, everyone changes. I refuse to believe the brood of people you speak of from centuries past are the same here before me today. It's true, I have felt it in my heart, felt its stroke deep in my soul. Their debt has been paid countless times over."

The room stood taller. Elatians beheld their first ally in a lifetime perched by their side. But Jesriel hesitated and moved away, sensing the MonTu's disapproval as they pulled him back.

"Very well," he readily uttered.

Then with the flick of his hand the will-bender plowed towards me, while the claws clasped Kaylaira and Draythian, and snatched them along with Nijal from the palace. My friends! I lunged to save them when a sudden rush of air fell like a bomb. It suffocated me, ground my face in the unforgiving floor as it crushed me to its surface. But hearing Kaylaira's fading cries for a second time, beckoned me to stand beneath the oppressive weight.

CHAPTER FORTY-SEVEN

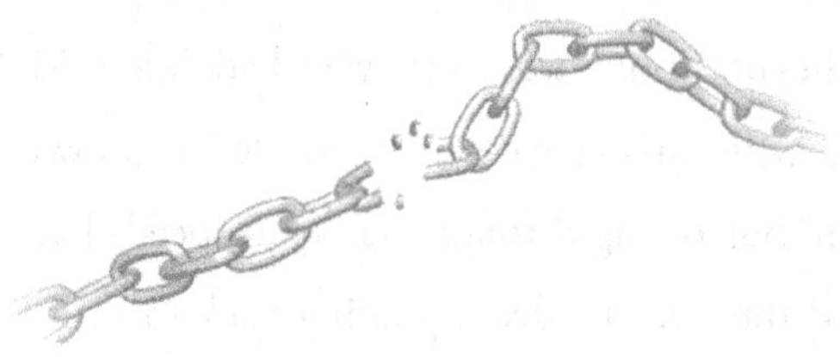

Funny thing about zephyr is it follows the path with the strongest attraction, and his connection held a lot stronger than mine… until I remembered the scepter in my hand. That tipped the scales, and the air became my ally as the scepter sopped in the weighing load. The greater the force he exerted, the more it absorbed, weakening their connection while strengthening mine.

The scepter thrummed my hands with a pulsing energy, gifting its power as we became one. In all his years he'd never faced an equal. It startled him and empowered me. The palace shook as if it feared our combined force, then with the power at bay, the wind repulsion left my hand. The will-bender resisted, but the rod and I were an unstoppable force, banishing him from sight before I could trace where I'd buried him. I didn't care to look for where he'd gone, I only thought to save my friends, starting with Jesriel.

I hurled a gust strong enough to knock the voice from his head, bowling him across the floor smack into the three-foot wall as I spun for the exit. Past the scaling pillars I was off the stairs, never touching ground as I traced the draft that pulled the others down, still lingering like a heavy perfume. In no time I was on their trail, then it all became a blur.

It was the same foggy haze as the evening Nijal arrived on Elatia. Adrenaline took my feet from the ground then a whisk of air brushed my face. Flashes of the physical world vanished, like a children's picture-flipping book with missing gaps between. Before knowing it, I was off the mountain, burrowing through gravity at speeds I couldn't explain. In seconds I'd traveled the deep, phasing back to reality as I emerged by my friends.

Together we plunged through the floor of misty air, them being dragged to their doom while the scepter writhed in my hand. I snapped their metal shackles and hoisted their weight, tugging like a jockey pulling back on his reins. Their speed waned and I took control, slowly descending till our feet touched the ground where the three of them collapsed on the rocky surface. Kaylaira gasped uncontrollably but was already in my arms while Draythian and Nijal splattered puke on the floor.

"I wanted to tell you," she babbled, with the little breath she had. "But the circle forbade it. They wouldn't let me tell you. I am so sorry, I wanted to tell you everything."

She caressed me without a pause, massaged her face through my skin as her lips nuzzled mine and begged I understand.

"It's true, Jordan," Draythian wheezed on all fours. "She wanted to tell you, but the circle refused. We had to believe you were on our side. Not all wind drivers have arrived with your moral compass."

Her pleading eyes told me she'd risk it all if it meant corroborating her virtue, even death. But there was no need. I felt every bead of truth rage from her hands and lips. She'd never hurt nor keep me in the shadows.

"I believe you," I quieted her with a smile.

The notion of us being wedged apart weighed heavier than that cursed fall.

"How much can I stress I did not want to do this?" Nijal grumbled still out of breath. "And yet you did it again? How? How did you catch us so fast? We dropped *forever*, and boom, you were there again."

I still had no explanation.

"I can't explain. It wasn't flying. I phased? Through space, through time? Like the night on the beach but I don't know how."

"Well, no need to explain because there is no time. We have to get back to the surface, now!" Draythian insisted. "If Jesriel failed and they restart the transference…"

"Then its crispy treats for us?" Nijal finished.

"I'm not sure what crispy treats means, but yes," Draythian jested. "It sounds exactly how our outcome will be!"

"Nijal, you have to get out of here," I beckoned.

But it was too late. A tunnel of plunging air drew my eyes above. The will-bender was there.

"Get ready. He's coming," I warned.

The reflection pool was just a short descent, a tranquil oasis amidst the rugged terrain. But the path down was littered with gouges and crevices, the perfect hiding spots to hide from danger.

"Kaylaira, get them to the bottom and find cover," I shoved them away.

They'd barely taken a few steps when the will-bender plunged like a torpedo. A shockwave jostled the earth. The ground trembled and buckled. Rocks that had stood firm for centuries tumbled like giant soccer balls raining from the sky. Draythian and I huddled together, shielding our heads from the crashing boulders that felt like bombs detonating overhead. The sound was deafening, like a thousand cannons firing at once that forced us to split ways.

The air was thick with dust and debris. Shattering pieces clawed my face and prickled my eyes while leaving no place to hide. I called the others but choked on the gritty air. They couldn't hear anyway, not with the debris lodged in our ears. Worst yet, with all the commotion, the scepter slipped from my hand, buried in a pile of destruction. Then suddenly, the bombardment stopped.

Where was Kaylaira? Where were Draythian and Nijal? Call for them and he'd have lunged the mountain on my head, much the same if I'd reached for the scepter only a few feet away. I stood motionless with the pool's reflection blinding me from seeing down. I needed patience. I needed to hone my skills and sense the zephyr, to feel the air and how it behaved.

I took a deep breath and forced myself still, immersing myself in the moment. The air was stagnant yet teemed with life, and the longer I kept motionless, the more vivid my surroundings became. The others kept impossibly quiet, holding their breaths in anticipation while the will-bender unknowingly revealed where he was. A slew of rocks hovered above his hand, waiting for one of us to make a move, but it was those minute vibrations that gave him away.

My only cue from the others came from a level below, an out-of-focus image, subtly signaling through the pool's aura that danced in the dust cloud. It was Nijal, holding up three fingers on one hand, and his blasting rod in the other. Then two fingers, warning me I had to protect him from whatever foolish move he was about to make. One finger, and he made his move.

With a flip of the rod's lever he leapt from his shelter, blasting a fury of fire at the wall above. But what the hell did he aim? He wasn't even close! The will-bender crouched with his face illuminated by fire, now lining up Nijal as his perfect strike. I waved my hand and cleared the air, in time to find a soccer sized stone speeding for Nijal's head. I clasped the zephyr and threw if from my hand, bursting it to pieces before it plowed his head. But another hurled right behind.

"Nijal!" I wheezed.

A paralyzing gasp overtook me as our lives together flickered by. All we'd done, the good, the bad, the stupid, especially the stupid. What had I dragged him into? Weak and powerless, I watched my friend take a hit he wouldn't survive when his body suddenly jostled forward. Draythian had tackled him and vaulted in his place.

The stone bludgeoned hard, flinging him like a wrecking ball as he sheltered Nijal's body. But amidst that confusion, my buddy's plan sparked alive. He never aimed for the will-bender, he just distracted him, flushed him out with a torrent of rocks. Sure enough, down they hailed.

The will-bender turned to repel the tumbling boulders. I forsook Draythian's body and grabbed the scepter, reviving its power before unleashing a vortex. But so did he, his striking like a runaway tank. All my weight sloped on the balls of my feet while I footed trenches to keep from blowing over.

"Jordan!" Kaylaira screamed.

Her plea cracked my focus and jostled my footing. I was barely upright when his winds overcame me, snapping my wrist and throwing spasms up my arm. Kaylaira fell in the corner of my eye, rattled as she stretched for Draythian's limp body.

"Jordan!" she begged.

But the will-bender's vortex pushed strong, skating me back, lashing my skin when the reason for her panic rang clear. It was the sinking stone that circled the pool, and Draythian was being sucked in. Only a wind driver was permitted on those grounds, and the more I thought to save him the more my focus shrank. My spine arched and crackled, unable to bear the force as I heaved all I had. Let up, and I'd have snapped like a cracker, and if it weren't for Nijal I probably would've.

He cupped his mouth only a few feet away, yelling from behind the safety of a crag. I heard nothing but the roaring air, blaring my ears like a freight train. But Nijal edged closer, one step from the shelter of his crag where he'd break like a toothpick if he inched any more. Even so he made the attempt, clinching the wall with one hand as his body left the ground, still throwing adamant gestures for me to act. Then, I felt the pointed edge of his finger like a sharp sword. The scepter! It was powered in my hand!

Its metal ushered a soft gleam. Its sharp hum of power breached my ears and permeated my lungs, flushing me with life and vigor. Better yet, it was primed to obey my command, infusing my battered arm with a rush of might. All I needed was to deliver.

His winds had lobbed me to a knee but that was the last of his time. Slowly, my wrist inched forward, pressing in defiance as I returned to a full stance. The scepter's surge was undying. I heard my aria within the metal's hum when the scepter suddenly became untamed. Its metal gleamed bright, and the all-lucent began to glow. Time became as sluggish as a slow drip of honey, slow enough for me to realize what was taking place… I was becoming the land sweeper.

I became frightened and empowered as the zephyr and I bound as one, then everything lost importance. The will-bender, the vortex he stirred, the depth we'd fallen or the once existing challenge of returning to the surface. The MonTu shriveled as a posing threat, and I began to transcend, rising above all fear and uncertainty.

The zephyr's aura flamed from my hands to the length of my arms, bestowing me with *absolute* tyrannical power. Everything and everyone around were weak and powerless, seeming to have no strength or purpose at all. If desired, all control was mine alone. Every whiff of air was my captive and the zephyr a vested slave, waiting for me to deliver its first command. I then understood the craving to wield it to completion, and I would've if I lingered a second more. But my friends needed me instead.

With the will-bender long forgotten, a modest push of my hand backed his winds to a pathetic draught. I could've finished him then and there. I knew it and so did he, evident for the first time in his dreading eyes. But wouldn't that have made me what I struggled not to become, the land sweeper? Or the very tyrants the MonTu described from our ancestor's past?

Despite all the will-bender had done, I resisted the urge to use my power to end his life, opting for a modest wind repulsion that sent him through a wall. He was down and I thought I was done. I believed I could control my actions, but the humming metal taunted me to achieve more and fulfill my purpose. And I obliged.

Eager, I lifted the scepter to do its bidding, to end the will-bender's existence when Kaylaira's scream jumped to desperation. With that height of power in my blood, she was the only force strong enough to snap me back to reality before realizing what I'd nearly done.

Immediately, I tossed the scepter in fear of its power, then lunged for my friends at the pool's ledge. Draythian had nearly submerged, and Kaylaira held tight as his only means to keep his head from drowning in stone. A blunt force of air left my hand and the stone obeyed, relinquishing its hold as Kaylaira pulled him to safe ground wearing a fat bruise on his head. However, life kept in his eyes.

"This is no doubt my least favorite place on the planet," he huffed on his back.

He was safe, but Nijal's gasp spun me to my rear. He clutched at his neck, constrained more than ten feet in the air as he held in the will-bender's grip. One startling move and he'd have squeezed Nijal like an empty juice box.

"Wait! What is it you want?" I desperately shouted.

"For you to embrace your purpose and the will of the MonTu," he contended.

I nearly risked it all. I nearly obeyed to save my friend's life when the lucents on his headpiece began to flicker. He staggered in thought, with no way of knowing what command he was being given. He became erratic and disheveled, then briefly recaptured his purpose as the blue jewel gleamed lukewarm. But the instant it faded he spun like a lost puppy, unsure how to proceed while Nijal held in his clasp. Without hurting Nijal I was useless, until a surprise rumble from the surface triggered time for a gamble.

"What's happening?" Kaylaira asked our foe, but he was just as delusional as we were.

"Is it the transference? Tell us or it kills us all, including you," Draythian warned him.

Their questions forced him to think, and while he struggled, I timed my strike.

"Get ready," I urged them under my breath.

I judged my aim with his flickering crown, but a boulder shaken from above lent my moment instead. His eyes looked up, and I drove forward.

"Now!" I yelled.

Kaylaira and Draythian opened fire. A scorching blast burned from Draythian's rod and a burst of icy cold from Kaylaira's bracelet. Draythian's blast he halted midair, but Kaylaira's sliced like a frozen knife while I tussled the winds from Nijal's neck. It felt like prying Growl's teeth from his favorite doll. But his grip eventually weakened and dropped Nijal to the floor, before the raining debris veiled him from our sight.

"It can't be the transference," Draythian yelled.

"Why not?" I hollered back.

"Because we'd be dead by now," Kaylaira screamed.

We couldn't see past the upper mist, just the beefed-up boulders that rained down to bury us alive. What was happening above? What more had Jesriel done? The will-bender reemerged and slewed us to the ground, recoiling the scepter with a gust to his hand. The others gasped with fear, but I did nothing. For them, to imagine that height of endless power in his hands, was a frightening thought and a reason to shudder. But there was no need for fear, for I'd discerned he knew no better.

The rod spat from his palm the instant he primed it with his winds, crippling his arm with a defiant burst. I knew because it marked me with its power, imprinted its will onto my skin the instant I'd laid my hand on it. And it was that failure that became our reprisal.

Nijal fired a blast without a second thought, with Kaylaira and Draythian flanking him in a show of united force. The sound of their combined blasts echoed through the air, but the will-bender held against them and contended their fight. It was I who had to deliver the final blow. My arms stretched high and amassed the turbulent winds, more than I knew to contain just as I'd done with the feline. The air crackled. The zephyr stirred wild then burned down like a shooting star.

"Jordan?" Nijal yelled as if I'd abandoned them, seeing the will-bender's strength reprise.

But I was with them, perched in the calm proceeding the storm. Even the will-bender felt the weight of its hailing, lifting a hand in desperation as the winds stormed down and crushed his attempt. The shockwave banished all sound. All was still as I looked to where I'd buried him with no motion crossing the floor. In time, he'd have used the zephyr to heal, and he was too much of a threat to let him continue to live. We needed to end him.

Draythian reached him first lying limp in the rubble, then primed his rod when Nijal jumped in his way.

"No!" he yelled, halting Draythian's wrath.

Violence wasn't the only way to end him, not when the Pledgemaker's key held in Nijal's hand. The instant I staggered over he handed it to me, and with my trembling arms I inserted it in. The notch turned. The crown unlocked and dropped to three pieces, unmasking the breather attached to his face. Zephyr spewed as it fell to the ground, then all balance left me. My chest tightened. Kaylaira caught my stumble as I stared in his confused beady eyes, trying to acknowledge why that grungy haired man stood before me.

"Dad?"

CHAPTER FORTY-EIGHT

My head whirl winded as I gazed the man who'd been absent for so many years. The longer I stared, the faster it spun and the louder his maddening scream rang my ears. Only the deep grumbled louder, as if the planet started to cave in on itself. I tried to speak. I tried to acknowledge who he was and tell the others, but shock stole my words.

"Dad?" I mumbled again.

My voice barely reached him as he clinched his head, mimicking the Pledgemaker as waves of insanity crashed in like an angry sea.

"No! D-don't say that. The MonTu forbid it," he mumbled, battling the notion I'd birthed in his head.

Then it slapped me. How had I not seen it? Ours was a lineage passed down through generations. The will-bender had to be my father, or his. I looked to Nijal, realizing it's what he and Wendi discovered at the lake house that day and decided it was best for me to learn on my own. Solemnly, he nodded and confirmed the suspicion.

"We agreed you needed to discover this for yourself," he said.

Wouldn't it have been better to tell me? Then again, perhaps he was right. Knowing would've further complicated what was already bizarre. How would I have responded? What would I have done differently that could've jeopardized both sides?

Dad needed to know it was me, so I reached to touch his face and let him know I was there. But he refused and slapped my hand, mumbling nonsense from being freed from their oppressive thoughts. Beneath his crazed shell he wasn't bitter nor angry. He simply tried to regain control and protect himself the only way he knew how.

"Jordan!" Kaylaira screamed.

I was in a trance, oblivious to the car sized boulder that split open above our heads. Where were we to go? How was I to save Dad? I couldn't leave him, but staying meant sacrificing my friends.

"Dad, get up, we can't stay!" I tried to reason. "There's a way to the surface. You know it, you've been there."

"The m-mountain descends," he uttered, painfully enunciating each syllable. "It will r-reconnect. When it does, b-be mindful, remember you are the l-land sweeper, you decide the f-fate of all worlds."

"What does that mean?" I frantically asked, but he said nothing further.

He'd used every ounce of strength to dictate those words before madness consumed him again. I tussled with his hands, again begging and pleading he get up. But I couldn't wait any longer, the crashing rocks fell too fast and the others had returned to the pool's edge. Without me, there was no escape.

"Jordan!" Nijal yelled.

Still, I implored one last time. "Dad please, get up! Hurry. Come with us. You can make it," I begged.

"Your f-friends," he answered, battling his craze while straining to speak. "They need you. Go. S-save them, and f-find me."

Find him? Father was alive. If he existed then and there, then somewhere he remained alive!

"Jordan!" the others desperately cried.

My first steps dragged, even as stones the size of dump trucks crashed down by my side. I'd deserted Mom, and now Dad? What kind of son I'd become I no longer knew, but with a better sense of urgency Dad lent a hand. Zephyr rushed his palms then struck me in the chest, heaving me back into the other's arms before the next stone claimed my head. They held me firm as we watched the power churn in his hands, repelling and blasting debris that would've hammered us to nothing. I'd just gotten him back and was already pressed to let go.

"I'll find you," I promised as the others pulled me away. "I promise I'll find you."

They hoped I'd follow as they shielded their heads, mucking over the sinking rock before it swallowed their feet. I was there. I stuck to them at my father's plea, latching their hands as we ran for the pool. We plunged in the instant I stepped on, me trailing the rear with Kaylaira guiding up front.

There was relief in her taking the lead. I was scatterbrained, my willpower compromised as I resisted the urge to swim back to Dad. How had he survived? Where had his original body been all those years and where would I find him? Earth? Elsewhere? He too called me land sweeper, but why? I knew the power it entailed, but did it enclose my fate?

Through the swimming hole the tunnel opened into the cavern. The deep's rumbling trembled its waters, with no danger present as we swam toward the steps. Kaylaira emerged first, then Nijal and Draythian. I was last, but the moment I came up for air, Nijal went missing.

"Where's Nijal?" I panicked.

The other two were oblivious and expected him there as well, pausing to catch their breath as they scanned the stairs.

"He was right behind me," Kaylaira huffed, frantically searching the water.

Had my eyes deceived me? The entire room fell within view, yet we scoured the confined dark like a dense forest. I saw him emerge, but he was no longer there.

"I saw him crawl up the steps out of the water. I promise he was right in front of me," Draythian assured.

"So did I," I answered baffled.

Where had he gone? Having just lost Dad I couldn't lose my best friend too. I plunged under and scoured the water, but he was nowhere to be found. Had he awakened and returned home? Was I to leave him in good faith? He could never emerge from the deep if I weren't with him. However, with no other option, I swam back and climbed the stairs, dreading the possibility of entombing my friend.

"Jordan, he must have awakened," Kaylaira assured. "He came from the water, clearly we'd see him if he were here."

She was right, and once again my greatest enemy reared its ugly head… time. No time to mourn Dad. No time to assure Nijal was safe. No time to wait below without needing to rise to the surface. I needed to know what Jesriel had done.

I raced into the dome snatcher with a sinking feeling in my gut. The brush of air took us from the floor as my arms encircled them, swirling our sides before emptying us of any substance defining who we were.

"I am so done with air rides," Draythian yelled as our bodies dissipated.

We phased through the void and absence of time before the opposing swirl regifted our mass. The mountain still shook. Our feet touched the trembling ground and our surroundings became tangible. While Draythian clung to the canopy's rails, Kaylaira wrapped me in consolation the moment her arms felt weight. She knew the double loss I was suffering.

"Jordan, he made it back. And your father is still alive. Somewhere. You just have to find him. I will help you find him," she comforted.

That was the first time I was numb to her touch. Regardless, Father was right, the mountain was sinking into its resting place, teetering the dome snatcher as it breached the deep's floor.

"Jesriel must have done it. He found a way to defeat the mountain," Kaylaira said, joyous, yet worried.

"Did he?" I asked in dismay.

"There's no transference. It's the only reason the mountain would fully descend," Draythian confirmed.

I was leery to trust and slow to believe. After centuries, had the MonTu suddenly given in? Was Jesriel really strong enough to defeat their will? And if so, at what cost?

Kaylaira stared into my suspicious eyes, conscious of the betraying thoughts that lied beneath. She saw my doubt and anger of loss, all meshed into one flustering emotion. It overwhelmed and clumped her with fear, dragging two lone tears from her eyes.

"I'm afraid," she admitted. "I'm afraid of what's to come. We've never been this far."

As Mount Elatia settled to a halt we dropped to our knees. For the first time in millennia, the mountain and deep were one again.

CHAPTER FORTY-NINE

We won. Everything we'd fought for was ours, a new reality none of us were sure how to handle. With the mountain stilled, we crept from the canopy down its never-ending stairs when an aftershock jangled our feet. We each held still.

"Any idea guys?" I asked before the mountain answered.

A pulse as bright as the all-lucent ruptured from the mountain's core. We quickened our descent and watched a wave disperse from all sides. Over the village and far beyond it went, disappearing from our sight before a boom trembled the far ends of the planet. Then the pulse returned the same as it left, over the trees and hills, ramming the mountain's feet before tumbling us into the courtyard.

It raged up the mountainside and through the palace walls, its power teeming through each blade of grass, teething its way up each stone that erected the mountain's fortresses till it made its way to us. It prickled my feet, surged energy like a trail of ants up my legs before crawling my arms and out my fingertips. We watched as it slithered the stairs, up to the stone canopy where it blasted into the skies from the dome snatcher's peak.

I looked to Draythian and Kaylaira, to see if they'd felt the same tingling beneath their skin. Draythian hadn't, but Kaylaira responded as I had, waving her hand through the air as if seeing it for the first time. It reminded me of the day I stepped on their shore.

"Kaylaira? What is it?" I asked.

Baffled, she couldn't answer, before the transformations around us stole our eyes. Stones that were grungy dark morphed into a glittering gray. The brown crunch of trees and grass refreshed to shades of vivid green, instantly gushing as if their blooms had been fast forwarded through time.

"Kaylaira, are you alright?" Draythian followed.

She giggled like a little girl in disbelief. And that's when I saw it, the zephyr's subtle motion from the gesture of her hand.

"Like you Jordan. A wind driver," she answered.

With each breath her life bar refilled. Her skin and flowing hair glossed more vibrantly, while her shimmering eyes mirrored the splendor around. But Draythian remained as he was, and that was the last thing I remembered before a dizzying spell shook my head. I became lightheaded and absent-minded, as if my body were on one world and my mind another when an absent stranger abruptly yelled in my head.

"No worries, we've almost got you," the voice said.

Suddenly, I fell to the grass, restricted as if some force detained me from moving about.

"Jordan, what's happening?" Kaylaira rushed to my side.

"I don't know. But it's getting stronger," I told her.

I grabbed my head as the deafening sound of a shovel scraping asphalt blared my ears. But I heard it alone. Neither Draythian nor Kaylaira responded to its clamor.

"What's wrong?" Kaylaira mouthed, with no sound from her lips.

I yelled back, unsure I'd even spoken her name as she reached to lift my head. I watched the unease swell her eyes with worry, then like a butterfly caught in a gust, her touch quickly fleeted, leaving me cold and longing for its return.

Where had it gone? Her, Draythian and the palace? They all forsook me, deserting me to the lone sound of that stranger's voice in my head.

"Man is someone looking out for you," the stranger chuckled. "But don't worry, you'll make it son."

I tried moving my head to find from where the voice came when a strap tightened to my forehead, fastening my eyes to water droplets lining a rock ceiling. It couldn't be! Quickly I shook that notion and stretched my eyes to a rugged man with "Franklin" stitched to his uniform. Just below his name? "First Response."

The harsh grating sound that tormented my head now reverberated through my entire body. It was me. My weight carried on a plastic board that scraped bedrock as they dragged me outdoors. Daylight smacked me in the eyes. Bold claps and cheerful whistles greeted me in the open air. Unsure how or for what reason, I was no longer on Elatia nor the barn. I was back in the cave.

CHAPTER FIFTY

I'd never felt more muddle-headed. My mind was a jumbled mess as I lay restless in a hospital bed, and I couldn't seem to untangle the events that had brought me there. With each passing moment, I grew anxious and more determined to unravel the mystery of what I'd gone through while fearing the answers that awaited me.

"Where's Wendi? Where's Nijal?" I raged, fighting the nurse pricking me with tubes and needles.

I was as weak as a wilted flower, but somehow managed the strength to keep them at bay.

"Sir," a doctor muttered, "We don't understand what happened to you, we're just trying to help. Continue fighting and you'll be restrained."

He was annoyed but I didn't care. I kept resisting, shoving anyone who neared while yanking loose whatever they dug in. My precedence rested with finding my friends.

"That's it, administer it," the doctor barked to the nurse.

A sting in the arm and all went heavy. My head sunk in my pillow. My sight spun into a black hole, and then there was nothing.

I kept that way for some time, till the solemn beep from a monitor eventually stirred my eyes. Whatever they'd administered knocked me unconscious, awarding them the victory of lining my arms with whatever they desired. I tried to yank them out, but my wrists were fastened with restraints! All I could do was study the room, believing I was alone till a rustling newspaper spun me to the corner.

Who'd placed themselves in my company when I'd been abandoned by everyone else? I couldn't see who hid behind, like a shadow of mystery and uncertainty. His black shoes were like mirrors, reflecting the sterile light of the hospital room back into itself. He sat cross legged, one shiny shoe pointed towards the floor while the other rested gracefully on top of the first, and his posture exuded confidence and authority. It was my bed creak that forced him to flip down a corner to unveil his face, one I was unfamiliar with.

"You know, you could be free of those if you weren't so hung up on fighting everyone trying to help you," he uttered.

"Who are you?" I threw. "Better yet, I don't care, just tell me where I can find Nijal."

"I tell you what, I help you, you help me?" he said, with a smirk I quickly adapted to hate.

"Sure, something like that," I lied.

"Good enough for me," he responded.

He quickly folded his paper and strutted to my side, loosening each strap before walking to the door. Did he actually trust me?

"You help me by staying in that bed," he highlighted, seeing I thought to make a run for it. "And I help you by letting you see your friend. Remember, that's how this works. It's how it will always work."

My friend? Did he mean Nijal? I instantly calmed, and the man I'd deemed Newspaper Guy opened the door and headed out as Nijal squeezed his way in.

"Nijal," I gasped.

I'd never felt so elated, such relief to gaze upon his familiar face and to know he'd made it back alive. He welcomed me with an embrace a friend gives once in a lifetime, a gesture that spoke volumes without a single word, and one that etched its way into my memory forever.

"Man, I'm so glad you're alive," I nearly cried. "I saw you in front of me, then looked down for a second and suddenly you weren't there."

But he pulled from me, shrouded in confusion. "What?" he asked.

"The deep," I went on, "In the water? I mean I know how much you hate swimming but after coming out, I wasn't sure where you'd—"

Something was wrong. His haunting expression stopped me from blabbering. Never had he beheld me with such judgmental eyes.

"Nijal?" I whispered, alerted to the possibility of an eavesdropper outdoors.

"Dude, what are you talking about?" he asked. "We didn't know you'd gone in. You do know you were alone, right? In the cave? For nearly a week? You went in the wrong tunnel."

"It's okay Nijal, at this point I don't care if they're listening or who knows, just, I'm glad you made it out alive. Okay?" I yammered.

But his expression remained unchanged. Sure he was glad to see me, but he scrutinized me as if I were nothing more than a hollow shell stuffed with a useless brain.

"Jordan. They figured I'd be the best to tell you," he stated, as his eyes began to mist. "I don't know why, but I guess, it is what it is. When Mom heard you'd gone missing, it was more than she could handle."

The sides of my throat turned to sawdust and a crippling ring pierced my ears. My heart fluttered then raced to a morbid pace.

"What? Mom knows where I was, in fact, I think she knows everything. I couldn't tell her specifics but I think she knows," I bit back.

"Jordan!" he abruptly intruded. "Your mom is dead. Either she burned the house down, or it caught fire while she was in it."

Nijal had always been a jokester, and though he'd gone too far I chose to ignore it, looking for any change or subtle gesture of deceit. But his gaze was steady and unbroken. Tears of rage blurred his vision until his eyes were nothing but pools of fiery red. Then his sorrow heightened to an unforgiving anger, slamming his fist into my bed. The rattling frame bounced across the room, but meanwhile, I felt nothing. I was dead from head to toe and in no way believed what he'd said.

"I don't get why you wouldn't call or text. We're thick and thin you and I, and you know if you'd called I would've foolishly gone in that cave right behind you. At least I would've been there and we could've safely gotten home, together," he regretted.

"Stop! Nijal, stop! What's the matter with you?" I stormed. "I don't care anymore, just stop traveling down whatever stupid road they have you on and tell me the truth. Where's Wendi?"

"Who the hell is Wendi?" he asked. "Jordan, listen to me! You went days without food and barely any water. You hallucinated, hypothermia set in. They caught you in the nick of time. In the real reality, this reality, your mother is dead! She's dead!"

It was those words that broke his tears as I watched him sob like a baby. Still, however solid his act, it couldn't be true. I stripped off the blankets and struggled to stand when he shoved me down by the shoulders. I had no strength to quarrel, and could only shout as he shushed me before the staff rushed in. The newspaper guy barged in behind.

"Okay, that's enough," he ordered. "He's getting anxious, let's keep him from harming himself."

The staff restrained me, hitting me with another sting in the arm of whatever sleep juice they'd administered before. My final dwindling image? Nijal abandoning me, traipsing backward till he disappeared out the door. I was alone!

"No! Nijal!" I cried, but he just kept going.

I fought my restraints as the staff followed him out. Only Paper Guy remained, and as the door closed my eyes grew heavy, leaving me to struggle to keep my reasoning alive. What happened to Nijal? What had they done to him? He was lying. It was a cover-up, and I held to that thought until the serum peaked. Then everything shifted the other direction. Was it a cover-up, a dream, or had I been in that cave the entire time? Was I so naive that I believed I'd traveled to a distant world, instead of some vivid hallucination?

I nearly laughed at the notion, forcing my eyes open one last time to find Paper Guy repositioned in his chair. He shot me a quick smile, then retreated behind the safety of his paper. But that sly grin. It was mischievous and meant trouble, a clear sign he had plans.

I looked at the vials trickling poison in my veins. What was it? A forget serum? The concoction clamped hard and shoved down my head, then my eyelids followed and began to close. They were confusing me and making me forget.

"Fight Jordan, fight. Don't forget," I shouted inside.

My outer voice faded like the rest of me and my thoughts began to drift. I couldn't forget! Not all I'd been through! The moment I'd awake, I'd break from that bed and learn of Mom's truth, then find whoever barred her in that cruel reality. Father was alive, somewhere, somehow. I'd seen him in the deep! And once freed, I'd scour the planet to find wherever he dwelt while bringing Wendi and Nijal to redemption.

I no longer had the bijou, but I'd dig those caves for an eternity to cross the universe to Kaylaira. She still lingered, deep in the recesses of my soul, a constant presence that I could never shake.

I still believed and my conviction would *never* falter. They'd been liberated, both Elatians and MonTu, each from the oppression of the other. None remained as slaves of the bijou! No one would deem my reality worthless, or as nothing more than a caverned dream. I was and would always be, a wind driver of Elatia!

The End